The yellowbacks... classics of popular fiction

The yellowjackets or yellowbacks were a great series of bestselling adventure and crime thrillers that had its origins in the mid to late 19th century following on from the 'penny dreadfuls'. They virtually began the mass market revolution of the early 20th century with a clear standard format and imprint/series livery (what would today be called branding). Hodder & Stoughton published the yellow jackets in two main series with series run dates of: 1923-1939 and later 1949-1957.

As the tagline ('where thrillers really began') on the back cover implies, the imprint and series focused on thrillers that were the bestsellers of their time. This current reissue or retro revival if you will, brings back many of these masterpieces, now classics in their own way and extends it further by including key titles from that period that were either great crime or thriller or even general commercial fiction (including sub-genres of noir, horror, gothic, romance, westerns etc) influences of their time. There are some perennial favourites and many rarities either lost or not easily available being revived in the current series. Writers and characters ranged from adventure heroes like Bulldog Drummond, Allan Quatermain, Richard Hannay or the Saint through thriller grandmasters Edgar Wallace and E. Phillips Oppenheim, crime and mystery maestros like Patricia Wentworth, GK Chesterton, Agatha Christie and the Detection club, to western and swashbucklers like Zane Grey, Max Brand, Captain Blood and even romance or general fiction classics like Hermina Black, Denise Robins, Marie Corelli or Stella Morton. These were books that had storytelling at their heart and always entertained.

The yellowbacks had both hardback (with varying design elements) and paperback (which built the series look) versions with the latter still carrying the imprint 'yellowjacket'. The current reissues pay tribute to both and use an amalgam of elements from both editions while retaining the complete yellow (or 'mustard-plaster') livery with the author's name in blue beveled type with a 'simulated emboss' effect and a white outer 'outline', and the book title in black. These reissues retain the distinctive size of the original mass market paperback and follow the three main category variations—the thrillers (crime, westerns, mystery, adventure) had blue lettering for the author's name, while Romance and 'softer general fiction had red; and other categories like humour had green.

For more detail and a full list of titles visit https://www.hachetteindia.com/home/yellowbacks

THE COMPLETE MARTIN HEWITT COLLECTION

VOLUME 2

THE COMPLETE MARTIN HEWITT COLLECTION

Arthur George Morrison (1863–1945) was an English author and journalist, known for his realistic novels about London's East End and for his detective stories. In 1890, he left his job as a clerk at the People's Palace and joined the editorial staff of the Evening Globe newspaper. The following year, he published a story titled 'A Street', which was subsequently published in book form in *Tales of Mean Streets* (1894). Around this time, Morrison was also producing detective short stories which emulated those of Conan Doyle about Sherlock Holmes. Three volumes of Martin Hewitt stories were published before the publication of the novel for which Morrison is most famous: *A Child of the Jago* (1896). Other less well-received novels and stories followed, until Morrison effectively retired from writing fiction around 1913. Between then and his death, he seems to have concentrated on building his collection of Japanese prints and paintings.

Amongst his other works are *Martin Hewitt: Investigator* (1894), *Zig-Zags at the Zoo* (1894), *Chronicles of Martin Hewitt* (1895), *Adventures of Martin Hewitt* (1896), and *The Hole in the Wall* (1902).

THE
COMPLETE MARTIN
HEWITT COLLECTION

Arthur Morrison

VOLUME 2

Adventures of Martin Hewitt
The Red Triangle: Further Chronicles of Martin Hewitt

The Complete Martin Hewitt
Adventures of Martin Hewitt Published by Ward Lock, London, 1896
The Red Triangle: Further Chronicles of Martin Hewitt First Published by
Eveleigh Nash, London, in 1903 and L. C. Page & Company, Boston also in 1903

This Hodder Yellowback edition © Hachette India 2023
(Registered Name: Hachette Book Publishing India Pvt. Ltd.)
An Hachette UK Company www.hachetteindia.com

1

All rights reserved. No part of the publication may be reproduced, stored in a retrieval system (including but not limited to computers, disks, external drives, electronic or digital devices, e-readers, websites), or transmitted in any form or by any means (including but not limited to cyclostyling, photocopying, docutech or other reprographic reproductions, mechanical, recording, electronic, digital versions) without the prior written permission of the publisher, nor be otherwise circulated in any form of binding or cover other than that in which it is published and without a similar condition being imposed on the subsequent purchaser.

The texts in these editions in most cases have been reprinted as is, with minimal editorial changes and by and large no bowdlerizing for political correctness; though in some editions, a few words and phrases considered archaic, or those considered offensive now, along with archaic punctuation may have been modified in places to make the text more accessible to today's readers. The narratives, language, beliefs, social mores and/or cultural depictions, in these volumes are a reflection of their times and must be viewed as such. They may also contain certain cultural, racial and gender prejudices and stereotypes that may be outdated or clearly wrong then and wrong today; but their removal would be tantamount to claiming these prejudices never existed. The Publisher does not endorse or support those depictions or stereotypes; and these books have been made available for a discerning audience that will read it for entertainment value and a chronicle/record of popular fiction of past times.

Cover design by Priya Singh adapted from the original classic yellowjacket by Hodder & Stoughton.

Cover illustration by Ishan Trivedi.

Series note: Some of the books in the series (unless otherwise credited) may have cover or inside illustrations from the original yellowbacks or early editions, and while full restoration has been attempted, some images may be grainy or faded due to the condition of the original material. The end notes or bonus material or blurb details may have been sourced from the public domain or free use publications such as Wikipedia and attribution is hereby made also allowing similar free use reproduction from here. Sources requiring further specific attribution may write in and further detailing and/or corrections shall be made in subsequent printings/editions.

Reprint specifications may be subject to change including but not limited to finishes, paper, colour sections.

ISBN: 978-93-5731-209-7

Hachette Book Publishing India Pvt. Ltd.
4th & 5th Floors, Corporate Centre,
Plot No. 94, Sector 44, Gurugram – 122 003, India

Typeset in Electra LT STD 10/12.5 pt by Manipal Technologies Limited, Manipal

Printed and bound in India by Manipal Technologies Limited, Manipal

CONTENTS

1. Adventures Of Martin Hewitt   1
2. The Red Triangle:
   Further Chronicles of Martin Hewitt   209

Adventures of Martin Hewitt
Third Series

"AN' WHICH IS THE HONOURABLE JINTLEMAN AS DO BE
BURRNIN' TO PRISINT ME WID A BIT O' GOOLD?"

CONTENTS

1.	The Case of the "Flitterbat Lancers"	5
2.	The Case of the Dead Skipper	38
3.	The Case of Mr Geldard's Elopement	71
4.	The Case of the late Mr Rewse	108
5.	The Affair of Mrs Seton's Child	144
6.	The Case of the Ward Lane Tabernacle	179

1

THE CASE OF THE "FLITTERBAT LANCERS"

I

In none of the cases of investigation by Martin Hewitt which I have as yet recorded had I any direct and substantial personal interest. In the case I am about to set forth, however, I had some such interest, though legally, I fear, it amounted to no more than the cost of a smashed pane of glass. But the case in some ways was one of the most curious which came under my notice, and completely justified Hewitt's oft repeated dictum that there was nothing, however romantic or apparently improbable, that had not happened at some time in London.

It was late on a summer evening, two or three years back, that I drowsed in my armchair over a particularly solid and ponderous volume of essays on social economy. I was doing a good deal of reviewing at the time, and I remember that this particular volume had a property of such exceeding toughness that I had already made three successive attacks on it, on as many successive evenings, each attack having been defeated in the end by sleep. The weather was hot, my chair was very comfortable, the days were tiring, and the book had somewhere about its strings of polysyllables an essence as of laudanum.

Still something had been done on each evening, and now on the fourth I strenuously endeavoured to finish the book. Late as it was, my lamp had been lighted but an hour or so, for there had been light enough to read by, near the window, till well past nine o'clock. I was just beginning to feel that the words before me were sliding about and losing their meanings, and that I was about to fall asleep after all, when a sudden crash and a jingle of broken glass behind me woke me with a start, and I threw the book down. A pane of glass in my window was smashed, and I hurried across and threw up the sash to see, if I could, whence the damage had come.

"A PANE OF GLASS IN MY WINDOW WAS SMASHED."

I think I have somewhere said (I believe it was in describing the circumstances of the extraordinary death of Mr Foggatt) that the building in which my chambers (and Hewitt's office) were situated was accessible—or rather visible, for there was no entrance—from the rear. There was, in fact, a small courtyard, reached by a passage from the street behind, and into this courtyard my sitting-room window looked.

"Hullo, there!" I shouted. But there came no reply. Nor could I distinguish anybody in the courtyard. It was at best a shadowy place at night, with no artificial light after the news agent—who had a permanent booth there—had shut up and gone home. Gone he was now, and to me the yard seemed deserted. Some men had been at work during the day on a drainpipe near the booth, and I reflected that probably their litter had provided the stone wherewith my window had been smashed. As I looked, however, two men came hurrying from the passage into the court, and going straight into the deep shadow of one corner, presently appeared again in a less obscure part, hauling forth a third man, who must have already been there in hiding. The man—who appeared, so far as I could see, to be smaller than either of his assailants—struggled fiercely, but without avail, and was dragged across toward the passage leading to the street beyond. But the most remarkable feature of the whole thing was the silence of all three men. No cry, no exclamation, or expostulation escaped any one of them. In perfect silence the two hauled the third across the courtyard, and in perfect silence he swung and struggled to resist and escape. The matter astonished me not a little, and the men were entering the passage before I found voice to shout at them. But they took no notice, and disappeared. Soon after I heard cab wheels in the street beyond, and had no doubt that the two men had carried off their prisoner.

"THE MAN... STRUGGLED FIERCELY."

I turned back into my room a little perplexed. It seemed probable that the man who had been borne off had broken my window. But why? I looked about on the floor, and presently found the missile. It was, as I had expected, a piece of broken concrete, but it was wrapped up in a worn piece of paper, which had partly opened out again as it lay on my carpet, thus indicating that it had only just been hastily crumpled round the stone. But again, why? It might be considered a trifle more polite to hand a gentleman a clinker decently wrapped up than to give it him in its raw state; but it came to much the same thing after all if it were passed through a shut window. And why a clinker at all? I disengaged the paper and spread it out. Then I saw it to be a rather hastily written piece of manuscript music, whereof I append a reduced facsimile:—

This gave me no help. I turned the paper this way and that, but could make nothing of it. There was not a mark on it that I could discover, except the music and the scrawled title, "Flitterbat Lancers," at the top. The paper was old, dirty, and cracked. What did it all mean? One might conceive of a person in certain circumstances sending a message—possibly an appeal for help—through a friend's window, wrapped round a stone, but this seemed to be nothing of that sort. It was not a message, but a hastily written piece of music, with no bars or time marked, just as might have been put down by somebody anxious to make an exact note of an air, the time of which he could remember. Moreover, it was years old, not a thing just written in a recent emergency. What lunatic could have chosen this violent way of presenting me with an air from some forgotten "Flitterbat Lancers"? That indeed was an idea. What more likely than that the man taken away *was* a lunatic and the others his keepers? A man under some curious delusion, which led him not only to fling his old music notes through my window, but to keep perfectly quiet while struggling for his freedom. I looked out of the window again, and then it seemed plain to me that the clinker and the paper could not have been intended for me personally, but had been flung at my window as being the only one that showed a light within a reasonable distance of the yard. Most of the windows about mine were those of offices, which had been deserted early in the evening.

Once more I picked up the paper, and with an idea to hear what the 'Flitterbat Lancers' sounded like, I turned to my little pianette and strummed over the notes, making my own time and changing it as seemed likely. But I make nothing of it, and could by no means extract from the notes anything resembling an air. I considered the thing a little more, and half thought of trying Martin Hewitt's office door, in case he might still be there and could offer a guess at the meaning of my smashed window and the scrap of paper. It was most probable, however, that he had gone home, and I was about resuming my social economy when Hewitt himself came in. He had stayed late to examine a bundle of papers in connection with a case just placed in his hands, and now, having finished, came to find if I were disposed for an evening stroll before turning in — a thing I was in the habit of. I handed him the paper and the piece of concrete, observing, "There's a little job for you, Hewitt, instead of the stroll. What do those things mean?" And I told him the complete history of my smashed window.

Hewitt listened attentively, and examined both the paper and the fragment of paving. "You say these people made absolutely no sound whatever?" he asked.

"None but that of scuffling, and even that they seemed to do quietly."

"Could you see whether or not the two men gagged the other, or placed their hands over his mouth?"

"No, they certainly didn't do that. It was dark, of course, but not so dark as to prevent my seeing generally what they were doing."

"And when you first looked out of the window after the smash, you called out, but got no answer, although the man you suppose to have thrown these things must have been there at the time, and alone?"

"That was so."

Hewitt stood for half a minute in thought, and then said, "There's something in this; what, I can't guess at the moment, but something deep, I fancy. Are you sure you won't come out now?"

On this my mind was made up. That dreadful volume had vanquished me altogether three times already, and if I let it go again it would haunt me like a nightmare. There was indeed very little left to read, and I determined to master that and draft my review before I slept. So I told Hewitt that I *was* sure, and that I should stick to my work.

"Very well," he said; "then perhaps you will lend me these articles?" holding up the paper and the stone as he spoke.

"Delighted to lend 'em, I'm sure," I said. "If you get no more melody out of the clinker than I did out of the paper, you won't have a musical evening. Goodnight!"

Hewitt went away with the puzzle in his hand, and I turned once more to my social economy, and, thanks to the gentleman who smashed my window, conquered. I am sure I should have dropped fast asleep had it not been for that.

II

At this time my only regular daily work was on an evening paper, so that I left home at a quarter to eight on the morning following the adventure of my broken window, in order, as usual, to be at the office at eight; consequently it was not until lunchtime, when my work was over, that I had an opportunity of seeing Hewitt. I went to my own rooms first, however, and on the landing by my door I found the housekeeper in conversation with a shortish, sun-browned man with a goatee beard, whose accent at once convinced me that he hailed from across the Atlantic. He had called, it appeared, three or four times during the morning to see me, getting more impatient each time. As he did not seem even to know my name, the housekeeper had not considered it expedient to say when I was expected, nor indeed to give him any information about me, and he was growing irascible under the treatment. When I at last appeared, however, he left her and approached me eagerly.

"See here, sir," he said, "I've been stumpin' these here durn stairs o' yours half through the mornin'. I'm anxious to *a*pologise, I reckon, and fix up some damage."

He had followed me into my sitting-room, and was now standing with his back to the fireplace, a dripping umbrella in one hand, and the forefinger of the other held up shoulder-high and pointing, in the manner of a pistol, to my window, which, by the way, had been mended during the morning, in accordance with my instructions to the housekeeper.

"Sir," he continued, "last night I took the extreme liberty of smashin' your winder."

"Oh," I said, "that was you, was it?"

"It was, sir—me. For that I hev come humbly to apologise. I trust the draft has not discommoded you, sir. I regret the acci*dent*, and I wish to pay for the fixin' up and the general inconvenience." He placed a sovereign on the table. "I 'low you'll call that square now, sir, and fix things friendly and comfortable as between gentle*men*, an' no ill will. Shake."

And he formally extended his hand.

I took it at once. "Certainly," I said, "certainly. As a matter of fact, you haven't inconvenienced me at all; indeed, there were some circumstances about the affair that rather interested me. But as to the damage," I continued, "if you're really anxious to pay for it, do you mind my sending the glazier to you to settle? You see, it's only a matter of half a crown or so at most." And I pushed the sovereign toward him.

"But then," he said, looking a trifle disappointed, "there's general discommodedness, you know, to pay for, and the general *sass* of the liberty to a stranger's winder. I ain't no down-easter—not a Boston dude—but I reckon I know the gentlemanly thing, and I can afford to do it. Yes. Say now, didn't I startle your nerves?"

"Not a bit," I answered, laughing. "In fact, you did me a service by preventing me going to sleep just when I shouldn't; so we'll say no more of that."

"Well—there was one other little thing," he pursued, looking at me rather sharply as he slowly pocketed the sovereign. "There was a bit o' paper round that pebble that came in here. Didn't happen to notice that, did you?"

"Yes, I did. It was an old piece of manuscript music."

"That was it—just. Might you happen to have it handy now?"

"Well," I said, "as a matter of fact a friend of mine has it now. I tried playing it over once or twice, as a matter of curiosity, but I couldn't make anything of it, and so I handed it to him."

"Ah!" said my visitor, watching me narrowly, "that's a nailer, is that 'Flitterbat Lancers'—a real nailer. It whips 'em all. Nobody can't get ahead of that. Ha, ha!" He laughed suddenly—a laugh that seemed a little artificial. "There's music fellers as 'lows to set right down and play off anything right away that can't make anything of the 'Flitterbat Lancers.' That was two of 'em that was monkeyin' with me last night. They never could make anythin' of it at all, and I was tantalizing them with it all along till they got real mad, and reckoned to get it out o' my pocket and learn it off quiet at home, and stop all my chaff. Ha, ha! So I got away for a bit, and bein' a bit lively after a number of tooth-lotions (all three was much that way), just rolled it round a stone and heaved it through your winder before they could come up, your winder bein' the nearest one with a light in it. Ha, ha! I'll be considerable obliged if you'll get it from your friend right now. Is he stayin' hereabout?"

The story was so ridiculously lame that I determined to confront my visitor with Hewitt, and observe the result. If he had succeeded in making any sense of the "Flitterbat Lancers," the scene might be amusing. So I answered at once, "Yes; his office is only on the floor below; he will probably be in at about this time. Come down with me."

We went down, and found Hewitt in his outer office. "This gentleman," I told him with a solemn intonation, "has come to ask for his piece of manuscript music, the 'Flitterbat Lancers.' He is particularly proud of it, because nobody who tries to play it can make any sort of tune out of it, and it was entirely because two dear friends of his were anxious to drag it out of his pocket and practice it over on the quiet that he flung it through my window-pane last night, wrapped round a piece of concrete."

The stranger glanced sharply at me, and I could see that my manner and tone rather disconcerted him. But Hewitt came forward at once. "Oh, yes," he said. "Just so—quite a natural sort of thing. As a matter of fact, I quite expected you. Your umbrella's wet—do you mind putting it in the stand? Thank you. Come into my private office."

We entered the inner room, and Hewitt, turning to the stranger, went on: "Yes, that is a very extraordinary piece of music, that 'Flitterbat Lancers.' I have been having a little practice with it myself, though I'm really nothing of a musician. I don't wonder you are anxious to keep it to yourself. Sit down."

The stranger, with a distrustful look at Hewitt, complied. At this moment, Hewitt's clerk, Kerrett, entered from the outer office with a slip of paper. Hewitt glanced at it, and crumpled it in his hand. "I am engaged just now," was his remark, and Kerrett vanished.

"And now," Hewitt said, as he sat down and suddenly turned to the stranger with an intent gaze, "and now, Mr Hoker, we'll talk of this music."

The stranger started and frowned. "You've the advantage of me, sir," he said; "you seem to know my name, but I don't know yours."

Hewitt smiled pleasantly. "My name," he said, "is Hewitt— Martin Hewitt, and it is my business to know a great many things. For instance, I know that you are Mr Reuben B. Hoker, of Robertsville, Ohio."

"MR HOKER."

The visitor pushed his chair back, and stared. "Well—that gits me," he said. "You're a pretty smart chap, anyway. I've heard your name before, of course. And—and so you've been a-studyin' of the 'Flitterbat Lancers,' have you?" This with a keen glance in Hewitt's face. "Well, well, s'pose you have. What's your opinion?"

"Why," answered Hewitt, still keeping his steadfast gaze on Hoker's eyes, "I think it's pretty late in the century to be fishing about for the Wedlake jewels, that's all."

These words astonished me almost as much as they did Mr Hoker. The great Wedlake jewel robbery is, as many will remember, a traditional story of the sixties. I remembered no more of it at the time than probably most men do who have at some time or another read up the *causes célèbres* of the century. Sir Francis Wedlake's country house had been robbed, and the whole of Lady Wedlake's magnificent collection of jewels stolen. A man named Shiels, a strolling musician, had been arrested and had been sentenced to a long term of penal servitude. Another man named Legg—one of the comparatively wealthy scoundrels who finance promising thefts or swindles and pocket the greater part of the proceeds— had also been punished, but only a very few of the trinkets, and those quite unimportant items, had been recovered. The great bulk of the booty was never brought to light. So much I remembered, and Hewitt's sudden mention of the Wedlake jewels in connection with my broken window, Mr Reuben B. Hoker, and the "Flitterbat Lancers," astonished me not a little.

As for Hoker, he did his best to hide his perturbation, but with little success. "Wedlake jewels, eh?" he said; "and—and what's that to do with it, anyway?"

"To do with it?" responded Hewitt, with an air of carelessness. "Well, well, I had my idea, nothing more. If the Wedlake jewels have nothing to do with it, we'll say no more about it, that's all. Here's your paper, Mr Hoker—only a little crumpled. Here also is the piece of cement. If the Wedlake jewels have nothing to do with the affair you may possibly want that too—I can't tell." He rose and placed the articles in Mr Hoker's hand, with the manner of terminating the interview.

Hoker rose, with a bewildered look on his face, and turned toward the door. Then he stopped, looked at the floor, scratched his cheek, and finally, after a thoughtful look, first at me and then at Hewitt, sat down again emphatically in the chair he had just quitted, and put his hat on the ground. "Come," he said, "we'll play a square game. That paper has something to do with the Wedlake jewels, and, win or lose, I'll tell you all I know about it. You're a smart man—you've found out more than I know already—and whatever I tell you, I guess it won't do me no harm; it ain't done me no good yet, anyway."

"Say what you please, of course," Hewitt answered, "but think first. You might tell me something you'd be sorry for afterward. Mind, I don't invite your confidence."

"Confidence be durned! Say, will you listen to what I say, and tell me if you think I've been swindled or not? There ain't a creature in this country whose advice I can ask. My 250 dollars is gone now, and I guess I won't go skirmishing after it anymore if you think it's no good. Will you do so much?"

"As I said before," Hewitt replied, "tell me what you please, and if I can help you I will. But remember, I don't ask for your secrets."

"That's all right, I guess, Mr Hewitt. Well, now, it was all like this." And Mr Reuben B. Hoker plunged into a detailed account of his adventures since his arrival in London.

Relieved of repetitions, and put as directly as possible, it was as follows: Mr Hoker was a wagon-builder, had made a good business from very humble beginnings, and intended to go on and make it still a better. Meantime, he had come over to Europe for a short holiday—a thing he had promised himself for years. He was wandering about the London streets on the second night after his arrival in the city, when he managed to get into conversation with two men at a bar. They were not very prepossessing men altogether, though flashily dressed. Very soon they suggested a game of cards. But Reuben B. Hoker was not to be had in that way, and after a while they parted. The two were amusing fellows enough in their way, and when Hoker saw them again the next night in the same bar, he made no difficulty in talking with them freely. After a time, and after a succession of drinks, they told him that they had a speculation on hand—a speculation that meant thousands if it succeeded—and to carry out which they were only waiting for a paltry sum of £50. There was a house, they said, in which they were certain was hidden a great number of jewels of immense value, which had been deposited there by a man who was now dead. Exactly in what part of the house the jewels were to be found they did not know. There was a paper, they said, which was supposed to contain some information, but as yet they hadn't quite been able to make it out. But that would really matter very little if once they could get possession of the house. Then they would simply set to work and search from the topmost chimney to the lowermost brick if necessary. Anyhow, the jewels must be found sooner or later. The only present difficulty was that the house was occupied, and that the landlord wanted a large deposit of rent down before he would consent to turn out his present tenants and give them possession at a higher rental. This deposit and other expenses, would come to at least £50, and they hadn't the money. However, if any friend of theirs who meant business would put the necessary sum at their disposal, and keep his mouth shut, they would make him an equal partner in the proceeds with themselves; and as the value of the whole haul would probably be something not very far off £20,000, the speculation would bring a tremendous return to the man who was smart enough to see the advantage of putting down his £50.

Hoker, very distrustful, skeptically demanded more detailed particulars of the scheme. But these the two men (Luker and Birks were their names, he found, in course of talking) inflexibly refused to communicate.

"Is it likely," said Luker, "that we should give the 'ole thing away to anybody who might easily go with his £50 and clear out the bloomin' show? Not much. We've told you what the game is, and if you'd like to take a flutter with your £50, all right; you'll do as well as anybody, and we'll treat you square. If you don't—well, don't, that's all. We'll get the oof from somewhere—there's blokes as 'ud jump at the chance, I can tell you—only they're inconvenient blokes to deal with, as I'll explain if you come in with us. Anyway, we ain't going to give the show away before you've done somethin' to prove you're on the job, straight. Put your money in, and you shall know as much as we do."

Then there were more drinks, and more discussion. Hoker was still reluctant, though tempted by the prospect, and growing more venturesome with each drink.

"Don't you see," said Birks, "that if we was a-tryin' to 'ave you we should out with a tale as long as yer arm, all complete, with the address of the 'ouse and all. Then I s'pose you'd lug out the pieces on the nail, without askin' a bloomin' question. More fool you, that's all. As it is, the thing's so perfectly genuine that we'd rather lose the chance and wait for some other bloke to find the money than run a chance of givin' the thing away. It ain't you wot'll be doin' a favour, mind. If it's anybody, it's us. Not that we want to talk of favours at all, if you come to that. It's a matter o' business, simple and plain, that's all it is. If you're willin' to come in with the money that we can't do without—very well. If you ain't, very well too, only we ain't goin' to give the thing away to an outsider. It's a question of either us trustin' you with a chance of collarin' £20,000, or you trustin' us with a paltry £50. We don't lay out no 'igh moral sentiments, we only say the weight o' money is all on one side. Take it or leave it, that's all. 'Ave another Scotch?"

The talk went on and the drinks went on, and it all ended, at "chucking-out time," in Reuben B. Hoker handing over five ten-pound notes, with smiling, though slightly incoherent, assurances of his eternal friendship for Luker and Birks.

In the morning he awoke to the realization of a bad head, a bad tongue, and a bad opinion of his proceedings of the previous night. In his sober senses it seemed plain that he had been swindled. He had heard of the confidence trick, to which many Americans had unaccountably fallen victims (for to him the trick had always seemed very thin), and he had sworn that something better than the confidence trick would be required to get over *him*. But now there seemed no doubt that this was no more than the confidence trick over again, in a new and more impudent form. All day he cursed his fuddled foolishness, and at night he made for the bar that had been the scene if the transaction, with little hope of seeing either Luker or Birks, who had agreed to be there to meet him. There they were, however, and, rather to his surprise, they made no demand for more money. They asked him if he understood music, and showed him the worn old piece of paper containing the manuscript "Flitterbat Lancers." The exact spot, they said, where the jewels were hidden was supposed to be indicated somehow and somewhere on that piece of paper. Hoker did not understand music, and could find nothing on the paper that looked in the least like a direction to a hiding-place for jewels or anything else.

Luker and Birks then went into full particulars of their project. First, as to its history. First, as to its history. The jewels were the famous Wedlake jewels, which had been taken from Sir Francis Wedlake's house in 1866 and never heard of again. A certain Jerry Shiels had been arrested in connection with the robbery, had been given a long sentence of penal servitude, and had died in gaol. This Jerry Shiels was an extraordinarily clever criminal, and travelled about the country as a street musician. Although an expert burglar, he very rarely perpetrated robberies himself, but acted as a sort of travelling fence, receiving stolen property and transmitting it to London or out of the country. He also acted as the agent of a man named Legg, who had money, and who financed any likely-looking project of a criminal nature that Shiels might arrange or recommend. Luker and Birks explained that there were many men of this class, and that it was to them that they had referred on the previous evening, when they said that there were "blokes that would jump at the chance" of financing the present venture.

Jerry Shiels traveleld with a "pardner"—a man who played the harp and acted as his assistant and messenger in affairs wherein Jerry was reluctant to appear personally. When Shiels was arrested, he had in his possession a quantity of printed and manuscript music, and after his first remand his "pardner," Jimmy Snape, applied for the music to be given up to him, in order, as he explained, that he might earn his living. No objection was raised to this, and Shiels was quite willing that Snape should have it, and so it was handed over. Now among the music was a small slip, headed "Flitterbat Lancers," which Shiels had shown to Snape before the arrest. In case of Shiels being taken, Snape was to take this particular slip to Legg as fast as he could. The slip indeed carried about it, in some unexplained way, which Legg understood, an indication of the place in which Shiels had concealed the bulk of the Wedlake jewels, and the whole proceeding was an ingenious trick invented by Shiels (and used before, it was supposed) to communicate with Legg while under arrest.

Snape got the music, but, as chance would have it, on that very day Legg himself was arrested, and soon after was sentenced also to a term of years. Snape hung about in London for a little while, and then emigrated. Before leaving, however, he gave the slip of music to Luker's father, a rag-shop keeper, who was a friend of his, and to whom he owed money. He explained its history, and hoped that Luker senior would be able to recoup himself for the debt, and a good deal over. Then he went. Luker senior had made all sorts of fruitless efforts to get at the information concealed in the paper. He had held it to the fire to bring up concealed writing, had washed it, had held it to the light till his eyes ached, had gone over it with a magnifying glass—all in vain. He had got musicians to strum out the notes on all sorts of instruments—backwards, forwards, alternately, and in every other way he could think of. If at any time he fancied a resemblance in the resulting sound to some familiar song-tune, he got that song and studied all its words with loving care, upside-down, right-side up—every way. He took the words "Flitterbat Lancers" and transposed the letters in all directions, and did everything else he could think of. In the end he gave it up, and died. Now lately, Luker junior had been impelled with a desire to see into the matter. He had repeated all the parental experiments, and more, with chemicals, and with the same lack of success. He had taken his "pal" Birks into his confidence, and together they had tried other experiments still—usually very clumsy ones indeed—till at last they began to believe that the message had probably been written in some sort of invisible ink which the subsequent washings and experiments had erased altogether. But he had done one other thing: he had found the house which Shiels rented at the time of his arrest, and in which a good quantity of stolen property— not connected with the Wedlake case—was discovered. Here, he argued, if anywhere, Jerry Shiels had hidden the jewels. There was no other place where he could be found to have lived, or over which he had sufficient control to warrant his hiding valuables therein. Perhaps, once the house could be properly examined, something about it might give a clue as to what the message of the "Flitterbat Lancers" meant. At any rate, message or none, anybody in possession of the house, with a certain amount of patience, secrecy, and thoroughness, could in time make himself master of every possible hiding-place, and could completely excavate the backyard. The trouble was that the house was occupied, and that money was wanted to get possession. It was with the view of providing this that they had decided to broach the subject to Hoker.

Hoker, of course, was anxious to know where the house in question stood, but this Luker and Birks would on no account inform him. "You've done your part," they said, "and now you leave us to do ours. There's a bit of a job about gettin' the tenants out. They won't go, and it'll take a bit of time before the landlord can make them. So you just hold your jaw and wait. When we're safe in the 'ouse, and there's no chance of anybody else pokin' into the business, then you can come and help find the stuff if you like. But you ain't goin' to 'ave a chance of puttin' in first for yourself this journey, you bet."

Hoker went home that night sober, but in much perplexity. The thing might be genuine, after all; indeed, there were many little things that made him think it was. But then, if it were, what guarantee had he that he would get his share, supposing the search turned out successful? None at all. But then it struck him for the first time that these jewels, though they may have lain untouched so long, were stolen property after all. The moral aspect of the affair began to trouble him a little, but the legal aspect troubled him more. That consideration, however, he decided to leave over, for the present at any rate. He had no more than the word of Luker and Birks that the jewels (if they existed) *were* those of Lady Wedlake, and Luker and Birks themselves only professed to know from hearsay. At any rate, his £50 was gone where he felt pretty sure he would have a difficulty in getting it back from, and he determined to wait events. But at least he made up his mind to have some little guarantee for his money. In accordance with this resolve, he suggested, when he met the two men the next day, that he should take charge of the slip of music and make an independent study of it. This proposal, however, met with an instant veto. The whole thing was now in their hands, Luker and Birks laid it down, and they didn't intend letting any of it out. If Hoker wanted to study the "Flitterbat Lancers," he could do it in their presence, and if he were dissatisfied he could go to the next shop. Altogether it became clear to the unhappy Hoker that now he had parted with his money he was altogether at the mercy of these fellows, if he wished to get any share of the plunder, or even to see his money back again. And if he made any complaint, or if the matter became at all known, the affair would be "blown upon," as they expressed it, and his money would be gone. Mostly, though, he resented their bullying talk, and he determined to get even in the matter of the music. He resolved to make up a piece of paper, folded as like the slip as possible, and substitute one for the other at their next meeting. Then he would put the "Flitterbat Lancers" in some safe place, and face his fellow-conspirators with a hand of cards equal to their own. He carried out his plan the next evening with perfect success, thanks to a trick of "passing" cards which he had learned in his youth, and thanks also to the contemptuous indifference with which Luker and Birks had begun to regard him. He got the slip in his pocket, and left the bar. He had not gone far, however, before Luker discovered the trick, and soon he became conscious of being followed. He looked for a cab, but he was in a dark street, and no cab was near. Luker and Birks turned the corner and began to run. He saw they must catch him, and felt no doubt that it they did he would lose the slip of paper, the £50, and everything. They were big, active fellows, and could probably do as they liked with him—especially since he could not call for help without risking an exposure of their joint enterprise. Everything depended now on his putting the "Flitterbat Lancers" out of their reach, but where he could himself recover it. Then it would form a sort of security for his share of the venture. He ran till he saw a narrow passage-way on his right, and into this he darted. It led into a yard where stones were lying about, and in a large building before him he saw the window of a lighted room a couple of floors up. It was a desperate expedient, but there was no time for consideration. He wrapped a stone in the paper and flung it with all his force through the lighted window. Even as he did it he heard the feet of Luker and Birks as they hurried down the street. The rest of the adventure in the court I myself saw.

Luker and Birks kept Hoker in their lodgings all that night. They searched him unsuccessfully for the paper; they bullied, they swore, they cajoled, they entreated, they begged him to play the game square with his pals. Hoker merely replied that he had put the "Flitterbat Lancers" where they couldn't easily find it, and that he intended playing the game square so long as they did the same. In the end they released him, apparently with more respect for his cuteness than they had before entertained, advising him, at any rate, to get the paper into his possession as soon as he could. With this view he repaired again to the scene of his window-smashing exploit, and having ascertained the exact position of the window in the building, began his morning's attack on my outer door.

"And now," said Mr Hoker, in conclusion of his narrative, "perhaps you'll give me a bit of Christian advice. You're up to as many moves as most people over here. Am I playin' a fool-game running after these toughs, or ain't I? I wouldn't have told you what I have, of course, if it wasn't clear that you'd got hold of the hang of the scheme somehow. Say, now, is it all a swindle?"

Hewitt shrugged his shoulders. "It all depends," he said, "on your friends Luker and Birks, as you may easily see for yourself. They may want to swindle you of your money and of the proceeds of the speculation, as you call it, or they may not. I'm afraid they'd like to, at any rate. But perhaps you've got some little security in this piece of paper. One thing is plain: they certainly believe in the deposit of jewels themselves, else they wouldn't have taken so much trouble to get the paper back, on the chance of seeing some way of using it after they had got into the house they speak of."

"Then I guess I'll go on with the thing, if that's it."

"That depends, of course, on whether you care to take trouble to get possession of what, after all, is somebody else's lawful property."

Hoker looked a little uneasy. "Well," he said, "there's that, of course. I didn't know nothin' about that at first, and when I did I'd parted with my money and felt entitled to get something back for it. Anyway, the stuff ain't found yet. When it is, why then, you know, I might make a deal with the owner. But, say, how did you find out my name, and about this here affair being jined up with the Wedlake jewels?"

Hewitt smiled. "As to the name and address, you just think it over a little when you've gone away, and if you don't see how I did it, you're not so cute as I think you are. In regard to the jewels—well, I just read the message of the 'Flitterbat Lancers,' that's all."

"You read it? Whew! That beats! And what does it say, and where? How did you fix it?" Hoker turned the paper over eagerly in his hands as he spoke.

"See, now," said Hewitt, "I won't tell you all that, but I'll tell you something, and it may help you to test the real knowledge of Luker and Birks. Part of the message is in these words, which you had better write down: *'Over the coals the fifth dancer slides, says Jerry Shiels the horney.'*"

"What?" Hoker exclaimed, "fifth dancer slides over the coals? That's a mighty odd dance-figure, anyway, lancers or not. What's it all about?"

"About the Wedlake jewels, as I said. Now you can go and make a bargain with Luker and Birks. The only other part of the message is an address, and that they already know, if they have been telling the truth about the house they intend taking. You can offer to tell them what I have told you of the message, after they have told you where the house is, and proved to you that they are taking the steps they talk of. If they won't agree to that, I think you had best treat them as common rogues (which they are), and charge them with obtaining your money under false pretences. But in any case don't be disappointed if you see very little of the Wedlake jewels."

Nothing more would Hewitt say than that, despite Hoker's many questions; and when at last Hoker had gone, almost as troubled and perplexed as ever, my friend turned to me and said, "Now, Brett, if you haven't lunched, and would like to see the end of this business, hurry up!"

"The end of it?" I said. "Is it to end so soon? How?"

"Simply by a police raid on Jerry Shiels's old house with a search warrant. I communicated with the police this morning before I came here."

"Poor Hoker!" I said.

"Oh, I had told the police before I saw Hoker, or heard of him, of course. I just conveyed the message on the music slip — that was enough. But I'll tell you all about it when there's more time; I must be off now. With the information I have given him, Hoker and his friends may make an extra push and get into the house soon, but I couldn't resist the temptation to give the unfortunate Hoker some sort of a sporting chance — though it's a poor one, I fear. Get your lunch as quickly as you can, and go at once to Colt Row, Bankside — Southwark way, you know. Probably we shall be there before you. If not, wait."

Hewitt had assumed his hat and gloves as he spoke, and now hurried away. I took such lunch as I could in twenty minutes, and hurried in a cab towards Blackfriars Bridge. The cabman knew nothing of Colt Row, but had a notion of where to find Bankside. Once in the region I left him, and then Colt Row was not difficult to find. It was one of those places that decay with an access of respectability, like Drury Lane and Clare Market. Once, when Jacob's Island was still an island, a little farther down the river, Colt Row had evidently been an unsafe place for a person with valuables about him, and then it probably prospered, in its own way. Now it was quite respectable, but very dilapidated and dirty, and looked as unprosperous as a street well can. It was too near the river to be a frequented thoroughfare, and too far from it to be valuable for wharfage purposes. It was a stagnant backwater in the London tide, close though it stood to the full rush of the stream. Perhaps it was sixty yards long — perhaps a little more. It was certainly very few yards wide, and the houses at each side had a patient and forlorn look of waiting for a metropolitan improvement to come along and carry them away to their rest. Many seemed untenanted, and most threatened soon to be untenable. I could see no signs as yet of Hewitt, nor of the police, so I walked up and down the narrow pavement for a little while. As I did so, I became conscious of a face at a window of the least ruinous house in the row, a face that I fancied expressed particular interest in my movements. The house was an old gabled structure, faced with plaster. What had apparently once been a shop-window, or at any rate a wide one, on the ground floor, was now shuttered up, and the face that watched me—an old woman's—looked from a window next above. I had noted these particulars with some curiosity, when, arriving again at the street corner, I observed Hewitt approaching, in company with a police inspector, and followed by two unmistakable "plain-clothes" men.

"Well," Hewitt said, "you're first here after all. Have you seen any more of our friend Hoker?"

"No, nothing."

"Very well—probably he'll be here before long, though."

The party turned into Colt Row, and the inspector, walking up to the door of the house with the shuttered bottom window, knocked sharply. There was no response, so he knocked again; but equally in vain.

"All out," said the inspector.

"No," I said; "I saw a woman watching me from the window above not three minutes ago."

"Ho, ho!" the inspector replied. "That's so, eh? One of you—you, Johnson—step round to the back, will you? You know the courts behind."

One of the plain-clothes men started off, and after waiting another minute or two the inspector began a thundering cannonade of knocks that brought every available head out of the window of every inhabited room in the Row.

The woman's face appeared stealthily at the upper window again, but the inspector saw, and he shouted to her to open the door and save him the necessity of damaging it. At this the woman opened the window, and began abusing the inspector with a shrillness and fluency that added a street-corner audience to that already congregated at the windows.

"Go away, you blaggards!" the lady said, among other things; "you ought to be 'orse-w'ipped, every one of ye! A-comin' 'ere a-tryin' to turn decent people out o' 'ouse and 'ome! Wait till my 'usband comes 'ome—'e'll show yer, ye mutton-cadgin' scoundrels! Payin' our rent reg'lar, and good tenants as is always been—as you may ask Mrs Green next door this blessed minute—and I'm a respectable married woman, that's what I am, ye dirty great cow-ards!"—this last word with a low, tragic emphasis.

Hewitt remembered what Hoker had said about the present tenants refusing to quit the house on the landlord's notice. "She thinks we've come from the landlord to turn her out," he said to the inspector.

"We're not here from the landlord, you old fool!" the inspector said, in as low a voice as could be trusted to reach the woman's ears. "We don't want to turn you out. We're the police, with a search-warrant to look for something left here before you came; and you'd better let us in, I can tell you, or you'll get into trouble."

"'Ark at 'im!" the woman screamed, pointing at the inspector. "'Ark at 'im! Thinks I was born yesterday, that feller! Go 'ome, ye dirty pie-stealer, go 'ome! 'Oo sneaked the cook's watch, eh? Go 'ome!"

The audience showed signs of becoming a small crowd, and the inspector's patience gave out. "Here, Bradley," he said, addressing the remaining plain-clothes man, "give a hand with these shutters," and the two—both powerful men—seized the iron bar which held the shutters, and began to pull. But the garrison was undaunted, and, seizing a broom, the woman began to belabour the invaders about the shoulders and head from above. But just at this moment the woman, emitting a terrific shriek, was suddenly lifted from behind and vanished. Then the head of the plain-clothes man who had gone round the houses appeared, with the calm announcement, "There's a winder open behind, sir. But I'll open the front door if you like."

"THE WOMAN BEGAN TO BELABOUR THE INVADERS ABOUT THE SHOULDERS
AND HEAD FROM ABOVE."

Then there was a heavy thump, and *his* head was withdrawn; the broom was probably responsible. The inspector shouted impatiently for the front door to be opened, and in a minute or two the bolts were shot, and it swung back. The placid Johnson stood in the passage, and as we passed in he said, "I've locked 'er in the back room upstairs." As a matter of fact we might have guessed it. Volleys of screeches, punctuated by bangs from contact of broom and door, left no doubt.

"It's the bottom staircase, of course," the inspector said; and we tramped down into the basement. A little way from the stairfoot Hewitt opened a cupboard door, which enclosed a receptacle for coals. "They still keep the coals here, you see," he said, striking a match and passing it to and fro near the sloping roof of the cupboard. It was of plaster, and covered the underside of the stairs.

"And now for the fifth dancer," he said, throwing the match away and making for the staircase again. "One, two, three, four, five," and he tapped the fifth stair from the bottom. "Here it is."

The stairs were uncarpeted, and Hewitt and the inspector began a careful examination of the one he had indicated. They tapped it in different places, and Hewitt passed his hand over the surfaces of both tread and riser. Presently, with his hand at the outer edge of the riser, Hewitt spoke. "Here it is, I think," he said; "it is the riser that slides."

He took out his pocket-knife and scraped away the grease and paint from the edge of the old stair. Then a joint was plainly visible. For a long time the plank, grimed and set with age, refused to shift; but at last, by dint of patience and firm fingers, it moved, and in a few seconds was drawn clean out from the end, like the lid of a domino-box lying on its side.

Within, nothing was visible but grime, fluff, and small rubbish. The inspector passed his hand along the bottom angle. "Here's a hook or something, at any rate," he said. It was the gold hook of an old-fashioned earring, broken off short.

Hewitt slapped his thigh. "Somebody's been here before us," he said "and a good time back too, judging from the dust. That hook's a plain indication that jewellery was here once, and probably broken up for convenience of carriage and stowage.

There's plainly nothing more, except—except this piece of paper." Hewitt's eyes had detected—black with loose grime as it was—a small piece of paper lying at the bottom of the recess. He drew it out and shook off the dust. "Why, what's this?" he exclaimed. "More music! Why, look here!"

We went to the window, and there saw in Hewitt's hand a piece of written musical notation, thus:—

Hewitt pulled out from his pocket a few pieces of paper. "Here is a copy I made this morning of the 'Flitterbat Lancers,' and a note or two of my own as well," he said. He took a pencil, and, constantly referring to his own papers, marked a letter under each note on the last-found slip of music. When he had done this, the letters read:—

"*You are a clever cove whoever you are but there was a cleverer says Jim Snape the horney's mate.*"

"You see?" Hewitt said handing the inspector the paper. "Snape, the unconsidered messenger, finding Legg in prison, set to work and got the jewels for himself. He either had more gumption than the other people through whose hands the 'Flitterbat Lancers' has passed, or else he had got some clue to the cipher during his association with Shiels. The thing was a cryptogram, of course, of a very simple sort, though uncommon in design. Snape was a humorous soul, too, to leave this message here in the same cipher, on the chance of somebody else reading the 'Flitterbat Lancers.'"

"But," I asked, "why did he give that slip of music to Luker's father?"

"Well, he owed him money, and got out of it that way. Also he avoided the appearance of 'flushness' that paying the debt might have given him, and got quietly out of the country with his spoils. Also he may have paid off a grudge on old Luker—anyhow, the thing plagued him enough."

The shrieks upstairs had grown hoarser, but the broom continued vigorously. "Let that woman out," said the inspector, "and we'll go and report. Not much good looking for Snape now, I fancy. But there's some satisfaction in clearing up that old quarter-century mystery."

We left the place pursued by the execrations of the broom wielder, who bolted the door behind us, and from the window defied us to come back, and vowed she would have us all searched before a magistrate for what we had probably stolen. In the very next street we hove in sight of Reuben B. Hoker in the company of two swell-mob-looking fellows, who sheered off down a side turning at sight of our group. Hoker, too, looked rather shy at sight of the inspector. As we passed, Hewitt stopped for a moment and said, "I'm afraid you've lost those jewels, Mr Hoker; come to my office tomorrow, and I'll tell you all about it."

III

"The meaning of the thing was so very plain," Hewitt said to me afterwards, "that the duffers who had the 'Flitterbat Lancers' in hand for so long never saw it at all. If Shiels had made an ordinary clumsy cryptogram, all letters and figures, they would have seen what it was at once, and at least would have tried to read it; but because it was put in the form of music, they tried everything else but the right way. It was a clever dodge of Shiels's, without a doubt. Very few people, police officers or not, turning over a heap of old music, would notice or feel suspicious of that little slip among the rest. But once one sees it is a cryptogram (and the absence of bar-lines and of notes beyond the stave would suggest that) the reading is as easy as possible. For my part I tried it as a cryptogram at once. You know the plan—it has been described a hundred times. See here—look at this copy of the 'Flitterbat Lancers.' Its only difficulty—and that is a small one—is that the words are not divided. Since there are on the stave positions for less than a dozen notes, and there are twenty-six letters to be indicated, it follows that crotchets, quavers, and semiquavers on the same line or space must mean different letters. The first step is obvious. We count the notes to ascertain which sign occurs most frequently, and we find that the crotchet in the top space is the sign required—it occurs no less than eleven times. Now the letter most frequently occurring in an ordinary sentence of English is *e*. Let us then suppose that this represents *e*. At once a coincidence strikes us. In ordinary musical notation in the treble clef the note occupying the top space would be E. Let us remember that presently. Now the most common word in the English language is *the*. We know the sign for *e*, the last letter of this word, so let us see if in more than one place that sign is preceded by two others identical in each case. If so, the probability is that the other two signs will represent *t* and *h*, and the whole word will be *the*. Now it happens in no less than four places the sign *e* is preceded by the same two other signs—once in the first line, twice in the second, and once in the fourth. No word of three letters ending in *e* would be in the least likely to occur four times in a short sentence except *the*. Then we will call it *the*, and note the signs preceding the *e*. They are a quaver under the bottom line for the *t*, and a crotchet on the first space for the *h*. We travel along the stave, and wherever these signs occur we mark them with *t* or *h*, as the case may be. But now we remember that *e*, the crotchet in the top space, is in its right place as a musical note, while the crotchet in the bottom space means *h*, which is no musical note at all. Considering this for a minute, we remember that among the notes which are expressed in ordinary music on the treble stave, without the use of ledger lines, *d e* and *f* are repeated at the lower and at the upper part of the stave. Therefore, anybody making a cryptogram of musical notes would probably use one set of these duplicate positions to indicate other letters, and as *h* is in the lower part of the stave, that is where the variation comes in. Let us experiment by assuming that all the crotchets above *f* in ordinary musical notation have their usual values, and let us set the letters over their respective notes. Now things begin to shape. Look toward the end of the second line: there is the word *the* and the letters *f f t h*, with another note between the two *f*s. Now that word can only possibly be *fifth*, so that now we have the sign for *i*. It is the crotchet on the bottom line. Let us go through and mark the *i*s. And now observe. The first sign of the lot is *i*, and there is one other sign before the word *the*. The only words possible here beginning with *i*, and of two letters, are *it*, *if*, *is* and *in*. Now we have the signs for *t* and *f*, so we know that it isn't *it* or *if*. *Is* would be unlikely here, because there is a tendency, as you see, to regularity in these signs, and *t*, the next letter alphabetically to *s*, is at the bottom of the stave. Let us try *n*. At once we get the word *dance* at the beginning of line three. And now we have got enough to see the system of the thing. Make a stave and put G A B C and the higher D E F in their proper musical places. Then fill in the blank places with the next letters of the alphabet downward, *h i j*, and we find that *h* and *i* fall in the places we have already discovered for them as crotchets. Now take quavers, and go on with *k l m n o*, and so on as before, beginning on the A space. When you have filled the quavers, do the same with semiquavers—there are only six alphabetical letters left for this—*u v w x y z*. Now you will find that this exactly agrees with all we have ascertained already, and if you will use the other letters to fill up over the signs still unmarked you will get the whole message:—

> "'In the Colt Row ken over the coals the fifth dancer slides says Jerry Shiels the horney.'

"THE FIFTH DANCER SLIDES."

"'Dancer,' as perhaps you didn't know, is thieves' slang for a stair, and 'horney' is the strolling musician's name for a cornet player. Of course the thing took a little time to work out, chiefly because the sentence was short, and gave one few opportunities. But anybody with the key, using the cipher as a means of communication, would read it as easily as print.

Snape used the same cipher in his jocular little note to the next searcher in the Colt Row staircase.

"As soon as I had read it, of course I guessed the purport of the 'Flitterbat Lancers.' Jerry Shiels's name is well-known to anybody with half my knowledge of the criminal records of the century, and his connection with the missing Wedlake jewels, and his death in prison, came to my mind at once. (The police afterwards, by the way, soon identified his old house in Colt Row from their records.) Certainly here was something hidden, and as the Wedlake jewels seemed most likely, I made the shot in talking to Hoker."

"But you terribly astonished him by telling him his name and address. How was that?"

Hewitt laughed aloud. "That," he said; "why, that was the thinnest trick of all. Why, the man had it engraved at large all over the silver band of his umbrella handle. When he left his umbrella outside, Kerrett (I had indicated the umbrella to him by a sign) just copied the lettering on one of the ordinary visitors' forms, and brought it in. You will remember I treated it as an ordinary visitor's announcement. Kerrett has played that trick before, I fear." And he laughed again.

On the afternoon of the next day Reuben B. Hoker called on Hewitt and had half an hour's talk with him in his private room. After that he came up to me with half a crown in his hand. "Sir," he said, "everything has turned out a durned sell. I don't want to talk about it anymore. I'm goin' out o' this durn country. Night before last I broke your winder. You put the damage at half a crown. Here is the money. Good day to you, sir."

And Reuben B. Hoker went out into the tumultuous world.

2

THE CASE OF THE DEAD SKIPPER

I

It is a good few years ago now that a suicide was investigated by a coroner's jury before whom Martin Hewitt gave certain simple and direct evidence touching the manner of the death, and testifying to the fact of its being a matter of self-destruction. The public got certain suggestive information from the bare newspaper report, but they never learnt the full story of the tragedy that led up to the suicide that was so summarily disposed of.

The time I speak of was in Hewitt's early professional days, not long after he had left Messrs. Crellan's office, and a long time before I myself met him. At that time fewer of the police knew him and were aware of his abilities, and fewer still appreciated them at their true value. Inquiries in connection with a case had taken him early one morning to the district which is now called "London over the border," and which comprises West Ham and the parts there adjoining. At this time, however, the district was much unlike its present self, for none of the grimy streets that now characterize it had been built, and even in its nearest parts open land claimed more space than buildings.

Hewitt's business lay with the divisional surgeon of police, who had, he found, been called away from his breakfast to a patient. Hewitt followed him in the direction of the patient's house, and met him returning. They walked together, and presently, as they came in sight of a row of houses, a girl, having the appearance of a maid-of-all-work, came running from the side door of the end house—a house rather larger and more pretentious than the others in the row. Almost immediately a policeman appeared from the front door, and, seeing the girl running, shouted to Hewitt and his companion to stop her. This Hewitt did by a firm though gentle grasp of the arms; and, turning her about, marched her back again. "Come, come," he said, "you'll gain nothing by running away, whatever it is." But the girl shuddered and sobbed, and cried incoherently, "No, no—don't; I'm afraid. I don't like it, sir. It's awful. I can't stop there."

She was a strongly-built, sullen-looking girl, with prominent eyebrows and a rather brutal expression of face; consequently her extreme nervous agitation, her distorted face and her tears were the more noticeable.

"What is all this?" the surgeon asked as they reached the front door of the house. "Girl in trouble?"

The policeman touched his helmet. "It's murder, sir, this time," he said, "that's what it is. I've sent for the inspector, and I've sent for you too, sir; and of course I couldn't allow anyone to leave the house till I'd handed it over to the inspector. Come," he added to the girl, as he saw her indoors, "don't let's have anymore o' that. It looks bad, I can tell you."

"Where's the body?" asked the surgeon.

"First-floor front, sir—bed-sittin'-room. Ship's captain, I'm told. Throat cut awful."

"Come," said the surgeon, as he prepared to mount the stairs. "You'd better come up too, Mr Hewitt. You may spot something that will help if it's a difficult case."

Together they entered the room, and, indeed, the sight was of a sort that any maid-servant might be excused for running away from. Between the central table and the fireplace the body lay, fully clothed, and the whole room was in a great state of confusion, drawers lying about with the contents spilt, boxes open, and papers scattered about. On a table was a bottle and a glass.

"Robbery, evidently," the surgeon said as he bent to his task. "See, the pockets are all emptied, and partly protruding at the top. The watch and chain has been torn off, leaving the swivel in the buttonhole."

"Yes," Hewitt answered, "that is so." He had taken a rapid glance about the room, and was now examining the stove, a register, with close attention. He shut the trap above it and pushed to the room door. Then very carefully, by the aid of the feather end of a quill pen which lay on the table, he shifted the charred remains of a piece or two of paper from the top of the cold cinders into the fire shovel. He carried them to the sideboard, nearer the light from the window, and examined them minutely, making a few notes in his pocket-book, and then, removing the glass shade from an ornament on the mantelpiece, placed it over them.

"There's something that *may* be of some use to the police," he remarked, "or may not, as the case may be. At any rate, there it is, safe from draughts, if they want it. There's nothing distinguishable on one piece, but I think the other has been a cheque."

The surgeon had concluded his first rapid examination, and rose to his feet. "A very deep cut," he said, "and done from behind, I think, as he was sitting in his chair. Death at once, without a doubt, and has been dead seven or eight hours I should say. Bed not slept in, you see. Couldn't have done it himself, that's certain."

"The knife," Hewitt added, "is either gone or hidden. But here is the inspector."

The inspector was a stranger to Hewitt, and looked at him inquiringly till the surgeon introduced him and mentioned his profession. Then he said, with the air of one unwillingly relaxing a rule of conduct, "All right, doctor, if he's a friend of yours. A little practice for you, eh, Mr Hewitt?"

"Yes," Hewitt answered modestly. "I haven't had the advantage of any experience in the police force, and perhaps I may learn. Perhaps also I may help you."

This did not seem to strike the inspector as a very luminous probability, and he stepped to the landing and ordered up the constable to make his full report. He had brought another man with him, who took charge of the door. By this time, thinly populated as was the neighbourhood, boys had begun to collect outside.

The policeman's story was simple. As he passed on his beat he had been called by three women, who had a light ladder planted against the window-sill of the room. They feared something was wrong with the occupant of the room, they said, as they could not make him hear, and his door was locked; therefore they had brought the ladder to look in at the window, but now each feared to go and look. Would he, the policeman, do so? He mounted the ladder, looked in at the window, and saw — what was still visible. He had then, at the women's urgent request, entered the house, broken in the door, and found the body to be dead and cold. He had told the women at once, and warned them, in the customary manner, that any statement they might be disposed to volunteer would be noted and used as evidence. The landlady, who was a widow, and gave her name as Mrs Beckle, said that the dead man's name was Abel Pullin, and that he was a captain in the merchant service, who had occupied the room as a lodger since the end of last week only, when he had returned from a voyage. So far as she knew, no stranger had been in the house since she last saw Pullin alive on the previous evening, and the only person living in the house, who had since gone out, was Mr Foster, also a seafaring man, who had been a mate, but for some time had had no ship. He had gone out an hour or so before the discovery was made—earlier than usual, and without breakfast. That was all that Mrs Beckle knew, and the only other persons in the house were the servant and a Miss Walker, a school teacher. They knew nothing; but Miss Walker was very anxious to be allowed to go to her school, which, of course, he had not allowed till the inspector should arrive.

"HE MOUNTED THE LADDER AND LOOKED IN AT THE WINDOW."

"That's all right," the inspector said. "And you're sure the door was locked?"

"Yes, sir, fast."

"Key in the lock?"

"No, sir. I haven't seen any key."

"Window shut, just as it is now?"

"Yes, sir; nothing's been touched."

The inspector walked to the window and opened it. It was a wooden-framed casement window, fastened by the usual turning catch at the side, with a heavy bow handle. He just glanced out and then swung the window carelessly to on its hinges. The catch, however, worked so freely that the handle dropped and the catch banged against the window frame as he turned away. Hewitt saw this, and closed the casement properly, after a glance at the sill.

The inspector made a rapid examination of the clothing on the body, and then said, "It's a singular thing about the key. The door was locked fast, but there's no key to be seen inside the room. Seems it must have been locked from the outside."

"Perhaps," Hewitt suggested, "other keys on this landing fit the lock. It's commonly the case in this sort of house."

"That's so," the inspector admitted, with the air of encouraging a pupil. "We'll see."

They walked across the landing to the nearest door. It had a small round brass scutcheon, apparently recently placed there. "Yale lock," said the inspector. "That's no good." They went to the third door, which stood ajar.

"Seems to be Mr Foster's room," the inspector remarked; "here's the key inside."

They took it across the landing and tried it. It fitted Captain Pullin's lock exactly and easily. "Hullo!" said the inspector, "look at that!"

Hewitt nodded thoughtfully. Just then he became aware of somebody behind him, who had arrived noiselessly. He turned and saw a mincing little woman, with a pursed mouth and lofty expression, who took no notice of him, but addressed the inspector. "I shall be glad to know, if you please," she said, "when I may leave the house and attend to my duties. My school has already been open for three-quarters of an hour, and I cannot conceive why I am detained in this manner."

"Very sorry, ma'am," the inspector replied. "Matter of duty, of course. Perhaps we shall be able to let you go presently. Meanwhile perhaps you can help us. You're not obliged to say anything, of course, but if you do we shall make a note of it. You didn't hear any uncommon noise in the night, did you?"

"Nothing at all. I retired at ten, and I was asleep soon after. I know nothing whatever of the whole horrible affair, and I shall leave the house entirely as soon as I can arrange."

"Did you have any opportunity of observing Mr Pullin's manners or habits?" Hewitt asked.

"Indeed, no. I saw nothing of him. But I could hear him very often, and his language was not of the sort I could tolerate. He seemed to dominate the whole house with his boorish behaviour, and he was frequently intoxicated. I had already told Mrs Beckle that if his stay were to continue mine should cease. I avoided him, indeed, altogether, and I know nothing of him."

"Do you know how he came here? Did he know Mrs Beckle or anybody else in the house before?"

"That also I can't say. But Mrs Beckle, I believe, knew all about him. In fact I have sometimes thought there was some mysterious connection between them, though what I cannot say. Certainly I cannot understand a landlady keeping so troublesome a lodger."

"You have seen a little more of Mr Foster, of course?"

"Well, yes. He has been here so much longer. He was more endurable than was Captain Pullin, certainly, though *he* was not always sober. The two did not love one another, I believe."

There the inspector pricked his ears. "They didn't love one another, you say, ma'am. Why was that?"

"Oh, I don't really know. I fancy Mr Foster wanted to borrow money or something. He used to say Captain Pullin had plenty of money, and had once sunk a ship purposely. I don't know whether or not this was serious, of course."

Hewitt looked at her keenly. "Have you ever heard him called Captain Pullin of the *Egret*?" he asked.

"No, I never heard the name of any vessel."

"There's just one thing, Miss Walker," the inspector said, "that I'm afraid I must insist on before you go. It's only a matter of form, of course. But I must ask you to let me look round your room—I shan't disturb it."

Miss Walker tossed her head. "Very well then," she said, turning toward the door with the Yale lock, and producing the key; "there it is." And she flung the door open.

The inspector stepped within and took a perfunctory glance round. "That will do; thank you," he said; "I am sorry to have kept you. I think you may go now, Miss Walker. You won't be leaving here today altogether, I suppose?"

"No, I'm afraid I can't. Good morning."

As she disappeared by the foot of the stairs the inspector remarked in a jocular undertone, "Needn't bother about *her*. She isn't strong enough to cut a hen's throat."

Just then Miss Walker appeared again and attempted to take her umbrella from the stand—a heavy, tall oaken one. The ribs, however, had become jammed between the stand and the wall; so Miss Walker, with one hand, calmly lifted the stand and disengaged the umbrella with the other. "My eyes!" observed the inspector, "she's a bit stronger than she looks."

The surgeon came upon the landing. "I shall send to the mortuary now," he said. "I've seen all I want to see here. Have you seen the landlady?"

"No. I think she's downstairs."

They went downstairs and found Mrs Beckle in the back room, much agitated, though she was not the sort of woman one would expect to find greatly upset by anything. She was thin, hard, and rigid, with the rigidity and sharpness that women acquire who have a long and lonely struggle with poverty. She had at first very little to say. Captain Pullin had lodged with her before. Last night he had been in all the evening, and had gone to bed about half-past eleven, and a quarter of an hour later everybody else had done so, and the house was fastened up for the night. The front door was fully bolted and barred, and it was found so in the morning. No stranger had been in the house for some days. The only person who had left before the discovery was Mr Foster, and he went away when only the servant was up. This was unusual, as he usually took breakfast in the house. What had frightened the girl so much, she thought, was the fact that after the door had been burst open she peeped into the room, out of curiosity, and was so horrified at the sight that she ran out of the house. She had always been a hardworking girl, though of sullen habits.

The inspector made more particular inquiries as to Mr Foster, and after some little reluctance Mrs Beckle gave her opinion that he was very short of money indeed. He had lost his ship sometime back through a neglect of duty, and he was not of altogether sober habits; he had consequently been unable to get another berth as yet. It was a fact, she admitted, that he owed her a considerable sum for rent, but he had enough clothes and nautical implements in his boxes to cover that and more.

Hewitt had been watching Mrs Beckle's face very closely, and now suddenly asked, with pointed emphasis, "How long have you known Mr Pullin?"

Mrs Beckle faltered, and returned Hewitt's steadfast gaze with a quick glance of suspicion. "Oh," she said, "I have known him, on and off, for a long time."

"A connection by marriage, of course?" Hewitt's hard gaze was still upon her.

Mrs Beckle looked from him to the inspector and back again, and the corners of her mouth twitched. Then she sat down and rested her head on her hand. "Well, I suppose I must say it, though I've kept it to myself till now," she said resignedly. "He's my brother-in-law."

"Of course, as you have been told, you are not obliged to say anything now; but the more information you can give the better chance there may be of detecting your brother-in-law's murderer."

"Well, I don't mind, I'm sure. It was a bad day when he married my sister. He killed her—not at once, so that he might have been hung for it, but by a course of regular brutality and starvation. I hated the man!" she said, with a quick access of passion, which however she suppressed at once.

"And yet you let him stay in your house?"

"Oh, I don't know. I was afraid of him; and he used to come just when he pleased, and practically take possession of the house. I couldn't keep him away; and he drove away my other lodgers." She suddenly fired up again. "Wasn't that enough to make anybody desperate? Can you wonder at anything?"

She quieted again by a quick effort, and Hewitt and the inspector exchanged glances.

"Let me see, he was captain of the sailing ship *Egret*, wasn't he?" Hewitt asked. "Lost in the Pacific a year or more ago?"

"Yes."

"If I remember the story of the loss aright, he and one native hand—a Kanaka boy—were the only survivors?"

"Yes, they were the only two. He was the only one that came back to England."

"Just so. And there *were* rumours, I believe, that after all he wasn't altogether a loser by that wreck? Mind, I only say there were rumours; there may have been nothing in them."

"Yes," Mrs Beckle replied, "I know all about that. They said the ship had been cast away purposely, for the sake of the insurance. But there was no truth in that, else why did the underwriters pay? And besides, from what I know privately, it couldn't have been. Abel Pullin was a reckless scoundrel enough, I know, but he would have taken good care to be paid well for any villainy of that sort."

"Yes, of course. But it was suggested that he was."

"No, nothing of the sort. He came here, as usual, as soon as he got home, and until he got another ship he hadn't a penny. I had to keep him, so I know. And he was sober almost all the time from want of money. Do you mean to say, if the common talk were true, that he would have remained like that without getting money of the owners, his accomplices, and at least making them give him another ship? Not he. I know him too well."

"Yes, no doubt. He was just now back from his next voyage after that, I take it?"

"Yes, in the *Iolanthe* brig. A smaller ship than he has been used to, and belonging to different owners."

"Had he much money this time?"

"No. He had bought himself a gold watch and chain abroad, and he had a ring and a few pounds in money, and some instruments; that was all, I think, in addition to his clothes."

"Well, they've all been stolen now," the inspector said. "Have you missed anything yourself?"

"No."

"Nor the other lodgers, so far as you know?"

"No, neither of them."

"Very well, Mrs Beckle. We'll have a word or two with the servant now, and then I'll get you to come over the house with us."

Sarah Taffs was the servant's name. She seemed to have got over her agitation, and was now sullen and uncommunicative.

She would say nothing. "You said I needn't say nothin' if I didn't want to, and I won't." That was all she would say, and she repeated it again and again. Once, however, in reply to a question as to Foster, she flashed out angrily, "If it's Mr Foster you're after you won't find 'im. 'E's a gentleman, 'e is, and I ain't goin' to tell you nothin'." But that was all.

Then Mrs Beckle showed the inspector, the surgeon, and Hewitt over the house. Everything was in perfect order on the ground floor and on the stairs. The stairs, it appeared, had been swept before the discovery was made. Nevertheless, Hewitt and the inspector scrutinised them narrowly. The top floor consisted of two small rooms only, used as bedrooms by Mrs Beckle and Sarah Taffs respectively. Nothing was missing, and everything was in order there.

The one floor between contained the dead man's room, Miss Walker's, and Foster's. Miss Walker's room they had already seen, and now they turned into Foster's.

The place seemed to betray careless habits on the part of its tenant, and was everywhere in slovenly confusion. The bedclothes were flung anyhow on the floor, and a chair was overturned. Hewitt looked round the room, and remarked that there seemed to be no clothes hanging about, as might have been expected.

"No," Mrs Beckle replied; "he has taken to keeping them all in his boxes lately."

"How many boxes has he?" asked the inspector. "Only these two?"

"That is all."

The inspector stooped and tried the lids.

"Both locked," he said. "I think we'll take the liberty of a peep into these boxes."

He produced a bunch of keys and tried them all, but none fitted. Then Hewitt felt about inside the locks very carefully with a match, and then taking a button-hook from his pocket, after a little careful "humouring" work, turned both the locks, one after another, and lifted the lids.

Mrs Beckle uttered an exclamation of dismay, and the inspector looked at her rather quizzically. The boxes contained nothing but bricks.

"THE BOXES CONTAINED NOTHING BUT BRICKS."

"Ah," said the inspector, "I've seen that sort of suits o' clothes before. People have 'em who don't pay hotel bills and such like. You're a very good pick-lock, by the way, Mr Hewitt. I never saw anything quicker and neater."

"But I *know* he had a lot of clothes," Mrs Beckle protested. "I've seen them."

"Very likely—very likely indeed," the inspector answered. "But they're gone now, and Mr Foster's gone with 'em."

"But—but the girl didn't say he had any bundles with him when he went out?"

"No, she didn't; and she didn't say he hadn't, did she? She won't say anything about him, and she says she won't, plump. Even supposing he *hadn't* got them with him this morning, that signifies nothing. The clothes are gone, and anybody intending a job of *that* sort"—the inspector jerked his thumb significantly towards the skipper's room—"would get his things away quietly first, so as to have no difficulty about getting away himself afterwards. No; the thing's pretty plain now, I think; and I'm afraid Mr Foster's a pretty bad lot. Anyway, I shouldn't like to be in his shoes."

"Nor I," Hewitt assented. "Evidence of that sort isn't easy to get over."

"Come, Mrs Beckle," the inspector said, "do you mind coming into the front room with us? The body's covered over with a rug."

The landlady disliked going, it was plain to see, but presently she pulled herself together and followed the men. She peeped once distrustfully round the door to where the body lay, and then resolutely turned her back on it.

"His watch and chain are gone, and whatever else he had in his pockets," the inspector said. "I think you said he had a ring?"

"Yes, one—a thick gold one."

"Then that's gone too. Everything's turned upside down, and probably other things are stolen too. Do you miss any?"

"Yes," Mrs Beckle replied, looking round, but avoiding with her eyes the rug-covered heap near the fireplace. "There was a sextant on the mantelpiece: it was his; and he kept one or two other instruments in that drawer"—pointing to one which had been turned out—"but they seem to be gone now. And there was a small ship, carved in ivory, and worth money, I believe—that's gone. I don't know about his clothes; some of them may be stolen or they may not." She stepped to the bed and turned back the coverlet. "Oh," she added, "the sheets are gone from the bed too!"

"Usual thing," the inspector remarked; "wrap up the swag in a sheet, you know—makes a convenient bundle. Nothing else missing?"

The landlady took one more look round and said doubtfully, "No, no, I don't think so. Oh, but yes," she suddenly added, "uncle's hook."

"Oh," remarked the inspector with dismal jocularity, "he's took uncle's hook as well as his own, has he? What was uncle's hook like?"

"It wasn't of much value," Mrs Beckle explained; "but I kept it as a memorial. My great-uncle, who died many years ago, was a sea-captain too, and had lost his left hand by accident. He wore a hook in its place—a hook made for him on board his vessel. It was an iron hook screwed into a wooden stock. He had it taken off in his last illness, and gave it to me to mind against his recovery. But he never got well, so I've kept it over since. It used to hang on a nail at the side of the chimney-breast."

"No wounds about the body that might have been made with a hook like that, doctor, were there?" the inspector asked.

"No, no wounds at all but the one."

"Well, well," the inspector said, moving toward the door, "we've got to find Foster now, that's plain. I'll see about it. You've sent to the mortuary, you say, doctor? All right. You've no particular reason for sending the girl out of doors today, I suppose, Mrs Beckle?"

"I *can* keep her in, of course," the landlady answered. "It will be inconvenient, though."

"Ah, then keep her in, will you? We mustn't lose sight of her. I'll leave a couple of men here, of course, and I'll tell them she mustn't be allowed out."

Hewitt and the surgeon went downstairs and parted at the door. "I shall be over again tomorrow morning," Hewitt said, "about that other matter I was speaking of. Shall I find you in?"

"Well," the doctor answered, "at any rate they will tell you where I am. Goodmorning."

"Goodmorning," Hewitt answered, and then stopped. "I'm obliged for being allowed to look about upstairs here," he said. "I'm not sure what the inspector has in his mind, by the way; but I should think whatever I noticed would be pretty plain to him, though naturally he would be cautious about talking of it before others, as I was myself. That being the case, it might seem rather presumptuous in me to make suggestions, especially as he seems fairly confident. But if you have a chance presently of giving him a quiet hint, you might draw his special attention to two things—the charred paper that I took from the fireplace and the missing hook. There is a good deal in that, I fancy. I shall have an hour or two to myself, I expect, this afternoon, and I'll make a small inquiry or two on my own account in town. If anything comes of them I'll let you know tomorrow when I see you."

"Very well, I shall expect you. Goodbye."

Hewitt did not go straight away from the house to the railway station. He took a turn or two about the row of houses, and looked up each of the paths leading from them across the surrounding marshy fields. Then he took the path for the station. About a hundred yards along, the path reached a deep, muddy ditch with a high hedge behind it, and then lay by the side of the ditch for some little distance before crossing it. Hewitt stopped and looked thoughtfully at the ditch for a few moments before proceeding, and then went briskly on his way.

That evening's papers were all agog with the mysterious murder of a ship's captain at West Ham, and in next morning's papers it was announced that Henry Foster, a seafaring man, and lately mate of a trading ship, had been arrested in connection with the crime.

II

That morning Hewitt was at the surgeon's house early. The surgeon was in, and saw him at once. His own immediate business being transacted, Hewitt learned particulars of the arrest of Foster. "The man actually came back of his own accord in the afternoon," the surgeon said. "Certainly he was drunk, but that seems a very reckless sort of thing, even for a drunken man. One rather curious thing was that he asked for Pullin as soon as he arrived, and insisted on going to him to borrow half a sovereign. Of course he was taken into custody at once, and charged, and that seemed to sober him very quickly. He seemed dazed for a bit, and then, when he realised the position he was in, refused to say a word. I saw him at the station. He had certainly been drinking a good deal; but a curious thing was that he hadn't a cent of money on him. He'd soon got rid of it all, anyhow."

"Did you say anything to the inspector as to the things I mentioned to you?"

"Yes, but he didn't seem to think a great deal of them. He took a look at the charred paper, and saw that one piece had evidently been a cheque on the Eastern Consolidated Bank, but the other he couldn't see any sort of sign upon. As to the hook, he seemed to take it that that was used to fasten in the knot of the bundle, to carry it the more easily."

"Well," Hewitt said, "I think I told you yesterday that I should make an inquiry or two myself? Yes, I did. I've made those inquiries, and now I think I can give the inspector some help. What is his name, by the way?"

"Truscott. He's a very good sort of fellow, really."

"Very well. Shall I find him at the station?"

"Probably, unless he's off duty; that I don't know about. But I should call at the house first, I think, if I were you. That is much nearer than the station, and he might possibly be there. Even if he isn't, there will be a constable, and he can tell you where to find Truscott."

Hewitt accordingly made for the house, and had the good fortune to overtake Truscott on his way there. "Good morning, inspector," he called cheerily. "I've got some information for you, I think."

"Oh, goodmorning. What is it?"

"It's in regard to *that* business," Hewitt replied, indicating by a nod the row of houses a hundred yards ahead. "But it will be clearer if we go over the whole thing together and take what I have found out in its proper place. You're not altogether satisfied with your capture of Foster, are you?"

"Well, I mustn't say, of course. Perhaps not. We've traced his doings yesterday after he left the house, and *perhaps* it doesn't help us much. But what do you know?"

"I'll tell you. But first can you get hold of such a thing as a boat-hook? Any long pole with a hook on the end will do."

"I don't know that there's one handy. Perhaps they'll have a garden rake at the house, if that'll do?"

"Excellently, I should think, if it's fairly long. We will ask."

The garden rake was forthcoming at once, and with it Hewitt and the inspector made their way along the path that led towards the railway station and stopped where it came by the ditch.

"I've brought you here purely on a matter of conjecture," Hewitt said, "and there may be nothing in it; but if there is it will help us. This is a very muddy ditch, with a soft bottom many feet deep probably, judging from the wet nature of the soil hereabout."

He took the rake and plunged it deep into the ditch, dragging it slowly back up the side. It brought up a tangle of duckweed and rushes and slimy mud, with a stick or two among it.

"Do you think the knife's been thrown here?" asked the inspector.

"Possibly, and possibly something else. We'll see." And Hewitt made another dive. They went along thus very thoroughly and laboriously, dragging every part of the ditch as they went, it being frequently necessary for both to pull together to get the rake through the tangle of weed and rubbish. They had worked through seven or eight yards from the angle of the path where it approached the ditch, when Hewitt stopped, with the rake at the bottom.

"Here is something that feels a little different," he said. "I'll get as good a hold as I can, and then we'll drag it up slowly and steadily together."

He gave the rake a slight twist, and then the two pulled steadily. Presently the sunken object came away suddenly, as though mud-suction had kept it under, and rose easily to the surface. It was a muddy mass, and they had to swill it to and fro a few times in the clearer upper water before it was seen to be a linen bundle. They drew it ashore and untied the thick knot at the top. Inside was an Indian shawl, also knotted, and this they opened also. There within, wet and dirty, lay a sextant, a chronometer in a case, a gold watch and chain, a handful of coins, a thick gold ring, a ship carved in ivory, with much of the delicate work broken, a sealskin waistcoat, a door key, a seaman's knife, and an iron hook screwed into a wooden stock.

"THEY HAD TO SWILL IT BEFORE IT WAS SEEN TO BE A LINEN BUNDLE"

"Lord!" exclaimed Inspector Truscott, "what's this? It's a queer place to hide swag of this sort. Why, that watch and those instruments must be ruined."

"Yes, I'm afraid so," Hewitt answered. "You see, the things are wrapped in the sheets, just as you expected. But those sheets mean something more. There are *two*, you notice."

"Yes, of course; but I don't see what it points to. The whole thing's most odd. Foster certainly would have been a fool to hide the things here; he's a sailor himself, and knows better than to put away chronometers and sextants in a wet ditch — unless he got frightened, and put the things there out of sight because the murder was discovered."

"But you say you have traced his movements after he left. If he had come near here while the police were about, he would have been seen from the house. No, you've got the wrong prisoner. The person who put those things there didn't want them again."

"Then do you think robbery wasn't the motive, after all?"

"Yes, it was; but not *this* robbery. Come, we'll talk it over in the house. Let us take these things with us."

Arrived at the house, Hewitt immediately locked, bolted, and barred the front door. Then he very carefully and gently unfastened each lock, bolt, and bar in order, pressing the door with his hand and taking every precaution to avoid noise. Nevertheless the noise was considerable. There was a sad lack of oil everywhere, and all the bolts creaked; the lock in particular made a deal of noise, and when the key was half turned its bolt shot back with a loud thump.

"Anybody who had once heard that door fastened or unfastened," said Hewitt, "would hesitate about opening it in the dead of night after committing murder. He would remember the noise. Do you mind taking the things up to the room—*the* room—upstairs? I will go and ask Mrs Beckle a question."

Truscott went upstairs, and presently Hewitt followed. "I have just asked Mrs Beckle," he said, "whether or not the captain went to the front door for any purpose on the evening before his death. She says he stood there for some half an hour or so smoking his pipe before he went to bed. We shall see what that means presently, I think. Now we will go into the thing in the light of what I have found out."

"Yes, tell me that."

"Very well. I think it will make the thing plainer if I summarise separately all my conclusions from the evidence as a whole, from the beginning. Perhaps the same ideas struck you, but I'm sure you'll excuse my going over them. Now here was a man undoubtedly murdered, and the murderer was gone from the room. There were two ways by which he could have gone—the door and the window. If he went by the window, then he was somebody who did not live in the place, since nobody seemed to have been missing when the girl came down, though, mind you, it was necessary to avoid relying on all she said, in view of

"'HE STOOD THERE FOR SOME HALF AN HOUR OR SO SMOKING HIS PIPE BEFORE HE WENT TO BED.'"

her manner, and her almost acknowledged determination not to incriminate Foster. It seemed at first sight probable that the murderer had gone out by the door, because the key was gone entirely, and if he had left by the window he would probably have left the key in the lock to hinder anybody who attempted to get in with another key, or to peep. But then the blind was *up*, and was found so in the morning. It would probably be pulled down at dark, and the murderer would be unlikely to raise it except to go out that way. But then the casement was shut and fastened. Just so; but can't it be as easily shut and fastened from the outside as from the in? The catch is very loose, and swings by itself. True, this *prevents* the casement shutting when it is just carelessly banged to, but see here." He rose and went to the window. "Anybody from outside who cared to hold the catch back with his finger till the casement was shut as far as the frame could then shut the window completely, and the catch would simply swing into its appointed groove.

"'THE CATCH WOULD SIMPLY SWING INTO ITS APPOINTED GROOVE.'"

"And now see something more. You and I both looked at the sill outside. It is a smooth new sill—the house itself is almost new; but probably you saw in one place a sharply marked pit or depression. Look, it seems to have been drilled with a sharp steel point. It was absolutely new, for there was the powder of the stone about the mark. The wind has since blown the powder away. Now if a man had descended from that sill by means of a rope with a hook at the end, that was just the sort of mark I should expect him to leave behind. So that at any rate the balance of probability was that the murderer had left by the window. But there is another thing which confirms this. You will remember that when Mrs Beckle mentioned that the sheets were gone from the bed you concluded that they had been taken to carry the swag."

"Yes, and so they were, as we have seen here in the bundle."

"Just so; but why *both* sheets? One would be ample. And since you allude to the bundle, why both sheets as well as the Indian shawl? This last, by the way, is a thing Mrs Beckle seems not to have missed in the confusion, or perhaps she didn't know that Pullin possessed it. Why all these wrappings, and moreover, *why the hook?* The presumption is clear. The bundle was already made up in the Indian shawl, and required no more wrapping. The two sheets were wanted to tie together to enable the criminal to descend from the window, and the hook was the very thing to hold this rope with at the top. It was not necessary to tie it to anything, and it would not prevent the shutting of the window behind. Moreover, when the descent had been made, a mere shake of the rope of sheets would dislodge the hook and bring it down, thus leaving no evidence of the escape—except the mark on the sill, which was very small.

"Then again, there was no noise or struggle heard. Pullin, as you could see, was a powerful, hard-set man, not likely to allow his throat to be cut without a lot of trouble, therefore the murderer must either have entered the room unknown to him—an unlikely thing, for he had not gone to bed—or else must have been there with his permission, and must have taken him by sudden surprise. And now we come to the heart of the thing. Of the two papers burnt in the grate—you have kept them under the shade, I see—one bore no trace of the writing that had been on it (many inks and papers do not after having been burnt), but the other bore plain signs of having been a cheque. Now just let us look at it. The main body of the paper has burnt to a deep gray ash, nearly black, but the printed parts of the cheque—those printed in coloured inks, that is—are of a much paler gray, quite a light ash colour. That is the colour to which most of the *pink* ink used in printing cheques burns, as you may easily test for yourself with an old cheque of the sort that is printed from a fine plate with water-solution pink ink. The *black* ink, on the other hand, such as the number of the cheque is printed in, has charred black, and by sharp eyes is quite distinguishable against the general dark gray of the paper. The cinder is unfortunately broken rather badly, and the part containing the signature is missing altogether. But one can plainly see in large script letters part of the boldest line of print, the name of the bank. The letters are *e r n C o n s o*, and this must mean the Eastern Consolidated Bank. Of course you saw that for yourself."

"Yes, of course I did."

"Fortunately the whole of the cheque number is unbroken. It is B/K63777. Of course I took a note of that, as well as of the other particulars distinguishable. It is payable to Pullin, clearly, for here is the latter half of his Christian name, Abel, and the first few letters of Pullin. Then on the line where the amount is written at length there are the letters *u s a n d* and *p*. Plainly it was a large cheque, for thousands. At the bottom, where the amount is placed in figures, there is a bad break, but the first figure is a 2. The cheque, then, was one for £2000 at least. And there is one more thing. The cinder is perfect and unbroken nearly all along the top edge, and there is no sign of crossing, so that here is an open cheque which any thief might cash with a little care. That is all we can see; but it is enough, I think. Now would a thief, committing murder for the sake of plunder, *burn* this cheque? Would Pullin, to whom the money was to be paid, burn it? I think not. Then who in the whole world *would* have any interest in burning it? Not a soul, with one single exception—*the man who drew it.*"

"Yes, yes. What! do you mean that the man who drew that cheque must have murdered Pullin in order to get it back and destroy it?"

"That is my opinion. Now who would draw Pullin a cheque for £2,000? Anybody in this house? Is it at all likely? Of course not. Again, we are pointed to a stranger. And now remember Pullin's antecedents. On his last voyage but one his ship, the *Egret*, from Valparaiso for Wellington, New Zealand, was cast away on the Paumotu Islands, far out of her proper course. There was but a small crew, and, as it happened, all were lost except Pullin and one Kanaka boy. The *Egret* was heavily insured, and there were nasty rumours at Lloyd's that Captain Pullin had made sure of his whereabouts, taken care of himself, and destroyed the ship in collusion with the owners, and that the Kanaka boy had only escaped because he happened to be well acquainted with the islands. But there was nothing positive in the way of proof, and the underwriters paid, with no more than covert grumblings. And, as you remember, Mrs Heckle told us yesterday Pullin on his return had no money. Now suppose the story of the intentional wreck were true, and for some reason Pullin's payment was put off till after his next voyage, would the people who sent their men to death in the Pacific hesitate at a single murder to save £2,000? I think not.

"After I left you yesterday I made some particular inquiries at Lloyd's through a friend of mine, an underwriter himself. I find that the sole owner of the *Egret* was one Herbert Roofe, trading as Herbert Roofe & Co. The firm is a very small one, as shipping concerns go, and has had the reputation for a long time of being very 'rocky' financially; indeed, it was the common talk at Lloyd's that nothing but the wreck of the *Egret* saved Roofe from the bankruptcy court, and he is supposed now to be 'hanging on by his eyelashes,' as my friend expresses it, with very little margin to keep him going, and in a continual state of touch-and-go between his debit and credit sides. As to the rumours of the wilful casting away of the *Egret*, my friend assured me that the thing was as certain as anything could be, short of legal proof. There was something tricky about the cargo, and altogether it was a black sort of business. And to complete things he told me that the bankers of Herbert Roofe & Co. were the Eastern Consolidated."

"Phew! This is getting pretty warm, I must say, Mr Hewitt."

"Wait a minute; my friend aided me a little further still. I told him the whole story—in confidence, of course—and he agreed to help. At my suggestion he went to the manager of the Eastern Consolidated Bank, whom he knew personally, and represented that among a heap of cheques one had got torn, and the missing piece destroyed. This was true entirely, except in regard to the heap—a little fiction which I trust my friend may be forgiven. The cheque, he said, was on the Eastern Consolidated, and its number was B/K63777. Would the manager mind telling him which of his customers had the cheque book from which that had been taken? Trace of where the cheque had come from had been quite lost, and it would save a lot of trouble if the Bank could let him know. 'Certainly,' said the manager; 'I'll inquire.' He did, and presently a clerk entered the room with the information that cheque No. B/K63777 was from a book in the possession of Messrs. Herbert Roofe & Co."

The inspector rose excitedly from his chair. "Come," he said, "this must be followed up. We mustn't waste time; there's no knowing where Roofe may have got to by this."

"Just a little more patience," Hewitt said. "I don't think there will be much difficulty in finding him. He believes himself safe. As soon as my friend told me what the Bank manager had said, I went round to Roofe's office to ascertain his whereabouts, prepared with an excuse for the interview in case I should find him in. It was a small office rather, over a shop in Leadenhall Street. When I asked for Mr Roofe, the clerk informed me that he was at home confined to his room by a bad cold, and had not been at the office since Tuesday—the next day but one before the body was discovered. I appeared to be disappointed, and asked if I could send him a message. Yes, I could, the clerk told me. All letters were being sent to him, and he was sending business instructions daily to the office from Chadwell Heath. I saw that the address had slipped inadvertently from the clerk's mouth, for it is a general rule, I know, in city offices to keep the principals' addresses from casual callers. So I said no more, but contented myself with the information I had got. I took the first opportunity of looking at a suburban directory, and then I found the name of Mr Roofe's house at Chadwell Heath. It is Scarby Lodge."

"I must be off, then, at once," Truscott said, "and make careful inquiries as to his movements. And those cinders— bless my soul, they're as precious as diamonds now! How shall we keep them from damage?"

"Oh, the glass shade will do, I fancy. But wait a moment; let us review things thoroughly. I will run rapidly over what I suggest has happened between Roofe and Pullin, and you shall stop me if you see any flaw in the argument. It's best to make our impressions clear and definite. Now we will suppose that the *Egret* has been lost, and Pullin has come home to claim the reward of his infamy. We will suppose it is £2,000. He goes to Roofe and demands it. Roofe says he can't possibly pay just then; he is very hard up, and the insurance money of the *Egret* has only just saved him from bankruptcy. Pullin insists on having his money. But, says Roofe, that is impossible, because he hasn't got it. A cheque for the amount would be dishonoured. The plunder of the underwriters has all been used to keep things going. Roofe says plainly that Pullin must wait for the money. Pullin can't reveal the conspiracy without implicating himself, and Roofe knows it. He promises to pay in a certain time, and gives Pullin an acknowledgment of the debt, an I O U, perhaps, or something of that kind, and with that Pullin has to be contented, and, having no money, he has to go away on another voyage, this time in a ship belonging to somebody else, because it would look worse than ever if Roofe gave him another berth at once. He makes his voyage and he returns, and asks for his money again. But Roofe is as hard up as ever. He cannot pay, and he cannot refuse to pay. It is ruin either way. He knows that Pullin will stand no more delay, and may do something desperate, so Roofe does something desperate himself. He tells Pullin that he must not call at his office, nor must anybody see them together anywhere for fear of suspicion. He suggests that he, Roofe, should call at Pullin's lodgings late one night, and bring the money. Pullin is to let him in himself, so that nobody may see him. Pullin consents, and thus assists in the concealment of his own murder. He stands at the front door smoking his pipe (you remember that Mrs Beckle told me so), waiting for Roofe. When Roofe comes, Pullin takes him very quietly up to his room without attracting attention. Roofe, on his part, has prepared things by feigning a bad cold and going to bed early, going out—perhaps through the window—when all his household is quiet. There are plenty of late trains from Chadwell Heath that would bring him to Stratford.

"Well, when they are safely in Pullin's room, Roofe hears the front door shut and bolted, with all its squeaks and thumps, and decides that it won't be safe to go out that way after he has committed his crime. The men sit and talk, and Pullin drinks. Roofe doesn't. You will remember the bottle on the table, with only one glass. Roofe produces and writes a cheque for the £2,000, and Pullin hands back the I O U, which Roofe burns. *That* would be the lower of the two charred pieces of paper, which we have there with the other, but can't read.

"Then the crime takes place. Perhaps Pullin drinks a little too much, perhaps he dozes—we shall never know, unless Roofe confesses circumstantially. At any rate, Roofe gets behind him, uses the sharp seaman's knife he has brought for the purpose, and straightway the skipper is dead at his feet. Then Roofe gets back the cheque and burns *that*. After that he ransacks the whole room. He fears there may be some documentary evidence, unguarded letters or something of the sort, which, being examined, may throw some light on the *Egret* affair. There are none. Then he sets about his escape. He has the whole night before him, and to make the thing look like a murder for ordinary plunder, and at the same time account for the upset room, he takes away all the dead man's valuables, tied in that shawl. He sees the hook — just the thing he wants — and of course the sheets are an obvious substitute for a rope. He takes away the door-key, to make it seem likely that somebody inside the house had been the criminal, and then he simply goes away through the window, as I have already explained. At 5.45 there would be a train to Chadwell Heath, and that would land him home early enough to enable him to regain his bedroom unobserved. After that he wisely maintains the pretence of illness for a day or two.

"I guessed that the things carried off would be in that ditch, for very simple reasons. I looked about the house, and the ditch seemed the only available hiding-place near. More, it was on the way to the station, the direction Roofe would naturally take. He would seize the very first opportunity of getting rid of his burden, for every possible reason. It was a nuisance to carry; he could not account for it if he were asked; and the further he carried it before getting rid of it, the more distinct the clue to the direction he had taken, supposing it ever were found. As I quite expected, my guess was right. The behaviour of some of the people in the house might have been suspicious, if I hadn't had so strong a clue in my hand, leading in another direction. Foster, poor fellow, has probably pawned all his clothes, one after another, and put those bricks in his boxes to conceal the fact, so that Mrs Beckle might not turn him away. He owed her so much that at last he hadn't the face to go and eat her breakfast when he had no money to pay for it. He went out early, met friends, got 'stood' drinks and came back drunk. The girl Taffs very naturally ran from the horrible sight in this room, and probably Foster had been kind to her at some time or another, so that when she found he was suspected she refused to give any information."

"Yes," the inspector said, "it certainly seems to fit together to the smallest bit as you put it. There's a future before you, Mr Hewitt. You ought to be in the force. But now I must go to Chadwell Heath. Are you coming?"

III

At Chadwell Heath it was found that a first-class return ticket to Stratford had been taken just before the 10.54 train left on the last night Abel Pullin was seen alive, and that the return half had been given up by a passenger who arrived by the first train soon after six in the morning The porter who took the ticket remembered the circumstance, because first-class tickets were rare at that time in the morning, but he did not recognise the passenger, who was muffled up.

"But I think there's enough for an arrest without a warrant, at any rate," Truscott said. "We shall be able to walk round and pick up a little more evidence after that. I am off to Scarby Lodge. Can't afford to waste any more time. He was foolish to take a first-class ticket, anyway. That singles a man out, and he might easily have been recognised. He was smart enough not to use his season ticket, though. That would have done him clean."

Scarby Lodge was a rather pretentious house, standing in about three acres of ground. The path to the front door was well shaded, and it was arranged that Truscott should wait aside till Hewitt had sent in a message asking to see Mr Roofe on a matter of urgent business, and that then both should follow the servant to his room. This was done, and as the parlourmaid was knocking at the bedroom door she was astonished to find Hewitt and the police inspector behind her. Truscott at once pushed open the door, and the two walked in.

It was a large, well-lighted room, and at the far end a man sat in his dressing-gown near a table, on which stood several medicine bottles. He was a man apparently of about thirty-eight, well built, and with sharp features. He frowned as Truscott and Hewitt entered, but betrayed no sign of emotion, carelessly taking one of the small bottles from the table at his side. "What do you want here?" he said.

"Sorry to be so unceremonious, Mr Roofe," Truscott said, advancing up the long room, "but I am a police officer, and it is my duty to arrest you on a serious charge—a charge of murder on the person of—Stop, sir! Let me see that!"

"'STOP, SIR! LET ME SEE THAT!'"

But it was too late. Before Truscott could reach him, Roofe had swallowed the contents of the small bottle, and, swaying once, dropped to the floor as though shot. A faint smell as of bruised almonds rose in the air.

Hewitt stooped over the man. "Dead," he said; "dead as Abel Pullin. It is prussic acid. He had arranged for instant action if by any chance the game went against him."

But Inspector Truscott was troubled. "This is a nice thing," he said, "to have a prisoner commit suicide in front of my eyes. It'll be an unpleasant job for me, I'm afraid. But you can testify that I hadn't time to get near him, can't you? Indeed he *wasn't* a prisoner at the time, for I hadn't arrested him, in fact."

3

THE CASE OF MR GELDARD'S ELOPEMENT

I

Many people have been surprised at the information that, in all Martin Hewitt's wide and busy practice, the matrimonial cases whereon he has been engaged have been comparatively few. That he has had many important cases of the sort is true, but among the innumerable cases of different descriptions they make a small percentage. The reason is that so many of the persons wishing to consult him on such concerns were actuated by mere unreasoning or fanciful jealousy that Hewitt would do no more in their cases than urge reconciliation and mutual trust. The common "private inquiry" offices chiefly flourish on this class of case, and their proprietors present no particular reluctance to taking it up. In any event it means fees for consultation and "watching"; and recent newspaper reports have made it plain that among some of the less scrupulous agents a case may be manufactured from beginning to end according to order. Again, Hewitt had a distaste for the sort of work commonly involved in matrimonial troubles; and with the immense amount of business brought to him, rendering necessary his rejection of so many commissions, it was easy for him to avoid what went against his inclinations. Still, as I have said, matrimonial cases there were, and often of an interesting nature, taking rise in no fanciful nor unreasoning jealousy.

When, on its change of proprietorship, I accepted my appointment on the paper that now claims me, I had a week or two's holiday pending the final turning over of the property. I could not leave town, for I might have been wanted at any moment, but I made an absorbing and instructive use of my leisure as an amateur assistant to Hewitt. I sat in his office much of the time, and saw more of the daily routine of his work than I had ever done before; and I was present at one or two interviews that initiated cases that afterwards developed striking features. One of these—which indeed I saw entirely through before I resumed my more legitimate work—was the case of Mr and Mrs Geldard.

Hewitt had stepped out for a few minutes, and I was sitting alone in his private room, when I became conscious of some disturbance in the outer office. An excited female voice was audible making impatient inquiries. Presently Kerrett, Hewitt's clerk, came in with the message that a lady—Mrs Geldard was the name on the visitor's slip that she had filled up—was anxious to see Mr Hewitt, at once, and failing himself, had decided to see me, whom Kerrett had calmly taken it upon himself to describe as Hewitt's confidential assistant. He apologised for this, and explained that he thought, as the lady seemed excited, it would be as well to let her see me to begin with, if there was no objection, and perhaps she would begin to be coherent and intelligible by Hewitt's arrival, which might occur at any moment. So the lady was shown in. She was tall, bony, and severe of face, and she began as soon as she saw me: "I've come to get you to get a watch set on my husband. I've endured this sort of thing in silence long enough. I won't have it. I'll see if there's no protection to be had for a woman treated as I am— with his goings out all day 'on business' when his office is shut up tight all the time. I wanted to see Mr Hewitt himself, but I suppose you'll do, for the present at any rate though I'll have it sifted to the bottom and get the best advice to be had, no matter what it costs though I *am* only a woman with nobody to confide in or to speak a word for me and I'm not going to be crushed like a fly as I'll soon let him know."

Here I seized a short opportunity to offer Mrs Geldard a chair, and to say that I expected Mr Hewitt in a few minutes.

"Very well, I'll wait and see him. But you have to do with the watching business, no doubt, and you'll understand what it is I want done; and I'm sure I'm justified, and mean to sift it to the bottom, whatever happens. Am I to be kept in total ignorance of what my husband does all day when he is supposed to be at business? Is it likely I should submit to that?"

I said I didn't think it likely at all, which was a fact. Mrs Geldard appeared to be about the least submissive woman I ever saw.

"No, and I won't, that's more. Nice goings on somewhere, no doubt, with his office shut up all day and the business going to ruin. I want you to watch him. I want you to follow him tomorrow morning and find out all he does and let me know. I've followed him myself this morning and yesterday morning, but he gets away somehow from the back of his office, and I can't watch on two staircases at once, so I want you to come and do it, and I'll—"

Here fortunately Hewitt's arrival checked Mrs Geldard's flow of speech, and I rose and introduced him. I told him shortly that the lady desired a watch to be set on her husband at his office, and a report to be given her of his daily proceedings. Hewitt did not appear to accept the commission with any particular delight, but he sat down to hear his visitor's story. "Stay here, Brett," he said, as he saw my hands stretched towards the door. "We've an engagement presently, you know."

The engagement, I remembered, was merely to lunch, and Hewitt kept me with some notion of restricting the time which this alarming woman might be disposed to occupy. She repeated to Hewitt, in the same manner, what she had already said to me, and then Hewitt, seizing his first opportunity, said, "Will you please tell me, Mrs Geldard, definitely and concisely, what evidence, or even indication, you have of unbecoming conduct on your husband's part, and substantially what case you wish me to take up?"

"Case? Why, I've been telling you." And again Mrs Geldard repeated her vague catalogue of sufferings, assuring Hewitt that she was determined to have the best advice and assistance, and that therefore she had come to him. In the end Hewitt answered: "Put concisely, Mrs Geldard, I take it that your case is simply this. Mr Geldard is in business as, I think you told me, a general agent and broker, and keeps an office in the city. You have had various disagreements with him—not an uncommon thing, unfortunately, between married people—and you have entertained certain indefinite suspicions of his behaviour. Yesterday you went so far as to go to his office soon after he should have been there, and found him absent and the office shut up. You waited some time, and called again, but the door was still locked, and the caretaker of the building assured you that Mr Geldard usually kept his office thus shut. You knocked repeatedly, and called through the keyhole, but got no answer. This morning you even followed your husband and saw him enter his office; but when, a little later, you yourself attempted to enter it, you once more found it locked and apparently tenantless. From this you conclude that he must have left his rooms by some back way, and you say you are determined to find out where he goes and what he does during the day. For this purpose you, I gather, wish me to watch him and report his whole day's proceedings to you?"

"Yes, of course; as I said."

"I'm afraid the state of my other engagements just at present will scarcely admit of that. Indeed, to speak quite frankly, this mere watching, especially of husband or wife, is not a sort of business that I care to undertake, except as a necessary part of some definite, tangible case. But apart from that, will you allow me to advise you? Not professionally, I mean, but merely as a man of the world. Why come to third parties with these vague suspicions? Family divisions of this sort, with all sorts of covert mistrust and suspicion, are bad things at best, and once carried as far as you talk of carrying this, go beyond peaceable remedy. Why not deal frankly and openly with your husband? Why not ask him plainly what he has been doing during the days you were unable to get into his office? You will probably find it all capable of a very simple and innocent explanation."

"Am I to understand, then," Mrs Geldard said, bridling, "that you refuse to help me?"

"I have not refused to help you," Hewitt replied. "On the contrary, I am trying to help you now. Did your husband ever follow any other profession than the one he is now engaged in?"

"Once he was a mechanical engineer, but he got very few clients, and it didn't pay."

"There, now, is a suggestion. Would it be very unlikely that your husband, trained mechanician as he is, may have reverted so far to his old profession as to be conceiving some new invention? And in that case, what more probable than that he would lock himself securely in his office to work out his idea, and take no notice of visitors knocking, in order to admit nobody who might learn something of what he was doing? Does he keep a clerk or office boy?"

"No, he never has since he left the mechanical engineering."

"Well, Mrs Geldard, I'm sorry I have no more time now, but I must earnestly repeat my advice. Come to an understanding with your husband in a straightforward way as soon as you possibly can. There are plenty of private inquiry offices about where they will watch anybody, and do almost anything, without any inquiry into their clients' motives, and with a single eye to fees. I charge you no fee, and advise you to treat your husband with frankness."

Mrs Geldard did not seem particularly satisfied, though Hewitt's rejection of a consultation fee somewhat softened her. She left protesting that Hewitt didn't know the sort of man she had to deal with, and that, one way or another, she must have an explanation.

"Come, we'll get to lunch," said Hewitt. "I'm afraid my suggestion as to Mr Geldard's probable occupation in his office wasn't very brilliant, but it was the pleasantest I could think of for the moment, and the main thing was to pacify the lady. One does no good by aggravating a misunderstanding of that sort."

"Can you make any conjecture," I said, "at what the trouble really is?"

Hewitt raised his eyebrows and shook his head. "There's no telling," he said. "An angry, jealous, pragmatical woman, apparently, this Mrs Geldard, and it's impossible to judge at first sight how much she really knows and how much she imagines. I don't suppose she'll take my advice. She seems to have worked herself into a state of rancour that must burst out violently somewhere. But lunch is the present business. Come."

The next day I spent at a friend's house a little way out of town, so that it was not till the following morning, about the same time, that I learned from Hewitt that Mrs Geldard had called again.

"Yes," he said; "she seems to have taken my advice in her own way, which wasn't a judicious one. When I suggested that she should speak frankly to her husband, I meant her to do it in a reasonably amicable mood. Instead of that, she appears to have flown at his throat, so to speak, with all the bitterness at her tongue's disposal. The natural result was a row. The man slanged back, the woman threatened divorce, and the man threatened to leave the country altogether. And so yesterday Mrs Geldard was here again to get me to follow and watch him. I had to decline once more, and got something rather like a slanging myself for my pains. She seemed to think I was in league with her husband in some way. In the end I promised — more to get rid of her than anything else — to take the case in hand if ever there were anything really tangible to go upon; if her husband really did desert her, you know, or anything like that. If, in fact, there were anything more for me to consider than these spiteful suspicions."

"I suppose," I said, "she had nothing more to tell you than she had before?"

"Very little. She seems to have startled Geldard, however, by a chance shot. It seems that she once employed a maid, whom she subsequently dismissed, because, as she tells me, the young woman was a great deal too good-looking, and because she observed, or fancied she observed, signs of some secret understanding between her maid and her husband. Moreover, it was her husband who discovered this maid and introduced her into the house, and furthermore, he did all he could to induce Mrs Geldard not to dismiss her. He even hinted that her dismissal might cause serious trouble, and Mrs Geldard says it is chiefly since this maid has left the house that his movements have become so mysterious. Well it seems that in the heat of yesterday's quarrel Mrs Geldard, quite at random, asked tauntingly how many letters Geldard had received from Emma Trennatt lately — Emma Trennatt was the girl's name. This chance shot seemed to hit the target. Geldard (so his wife tells me, at any rate) winced visibly, paled a little, and dodged the question. But for the rest of the quarrel he appeared much less at ease, and made more than one attempt to find out how much his wife really knew of the correspondence she had spoken of. But as her reference to it was of course the wildest possible fluke, he got little guidance, while his better-half waxed savage in her triumph, and they parted on wild-cat terms. She came straight here, and evidently thought that after Geldard's reception of her allusion to correspondence with Emma

Trennatt—which she seemed to regard as final and conclusive confirmation of all her jealousies—I should take the case in hand at once. When she found me still disinclined, she gave me a trifling sample of her rhetoric, as no doubt commonly supplied to Mr Geldard. She said in effect that she had only come to me because she meant having the best assistance possible, but that she didn't think much of me after all, and one man was as bad as another, and so on. I think she was a trifle angrier because I remained calm and civil. And she went away this time without the least reference to a consultation fee one way or another."

"SIGNS OF SOME SECRET UNDERSTANDING."

I laughed. "Probably," I said, "she went off to some agent who'll watch as long as she likes to pay."

"Quite possibly." But we were quite wrong. Hewitt took his hat, and we made for the staircase. As we opened the landing-door there were hurried feet on the stairs below, and as it shut behind Mrs Geldard's bonnet-load of pink flowers hove up before us. She was in a state of fierce alarm and excitement that had oddly enough something of triumph in it, as of the woman who says, "I told you so." Hewitt gave a tragic groan under his breath.

"Here's a nice state of things I'm in for now, Mr Hewitt," she began abruptly, "through your refusing to do anything for me while there was time though I was ready to pay you well as I told your young man but no, you wouldn't listen to anything, and seemed to think you knew my business better than I could tell you and now you've caused this state of affairs by delay perhaps you'll take the case in hand now?"

"But you haven't told me what has happened—" Hewitt began, whereat the lady instantly rejoined, with a shrill pretence of a laugh, "Happened? Why, what do you suppose has happened after what I have told you over and over again? My precious husband's gone clean away, that's all. He's deserted me and gone nobody knows where. That's what's happened. You said that if he did anything of that sort you'd take the case up; so now I've come to see if you'll keep your promise. Not that it's likely to be of much use *now*."

We turned back into Hewitt's private office, and Mrs Geldard told her story. Disentangled from irrelevances, repetitions, opinions and incidental observations, it was this. After the quarrel Geldard had gone to business as usual, and had not been seen nor heard of since. After her yesterday's interview with Hewitt, Mrs Geldard had called at her husband's office and found it shut as before. She went home again, and waited, but he never returned home that evening, nor all night. In the morning she had gone to the office once more, and finding it still shut, had told the caretaker that her husband was missing, and insisted on his bringing his own key and opening it for her inspection. Nobody was there, and Mrs Geldard was astonished to find folded and laid on a cupboard shelf the entire suit of clothes that her husband had worn when he left home on the morning of the previous day. She also found in the waste-paper basket the fragments of two or three envelopes addressed to her husband, which she brought for Hewitt's inspection. They were in the handwriting of the girl Trennatt, and with them Mrs Geldard had discovered a small fragment of one of the letters, a mere scrap, but sufficient to show part of the signature "Emma," and two or three of a row of crosses running beneath, such as are employed to represent kisses. These things she had brought with her.

Hewitt examined them slightly, and then asked, "Can I have a photograph of your husband, Mrs Geldard?"

She immediately produced, not only a photograph of her husband, but also one of the girl Trennatt, which she said belonged to the cook. Hewitt complimented her on her foresight. "And now," he said, "I think we'll go and take a look at Mr Geldard's office, if we may. Of course I shall follow him up now." Hewitt made a sign to me, which I interpreted as asking whether I would care to accompany him. I assented with a nod, for the case seemed likely to be interesting.

I omit most of Mrs Geldard's talk by the way, which was almost ceaseless, mostly compounded of useless repetition, and very tiresome.

The office was on a third floor in a large building in Finsbury Pavement. The caretaker made no difficulty in admitting us. There were two rooms, neither very large, and one of them at the back very small indeed. In this was a small locked door.

"That leads on to the small staircase, sir," the caretaker said in response to Hewitt's inquiry. "The staircase leads down to the basement, and it ain't used much 'cept by the cleaners."

"If I went down this back staircase," Hewitt pursued, "I suppose I should have no difficulty in gaining the street?"

"Not a bit, sir. You'd have to go a little way round to get into Finsbury Pavement, but there's a passage leads straight from the bottom of the stairs out to Moorfields behind."

"Yes," remarked Mrs Geldard bitterly, when the caretaker had left the room, "that's the way he's been leaving the office every day, and in disguise, too." She pointed to the cupboard where her husband's clothes lay. "Pretty plain proof that he was ashamed of his doings, whatever they were."

"Come, come," Hewitt answered deprecatingly, "we'll hope there's nothing to be ashamed of—at any rate till there's proof of it. There's no proof as yet that your husband has been disguising. A great many men who rent offices, I believe, keep dress clothes at them—I do it myself—for convenience in case of an unexpected invitation, or such other eventuality. We may find that he returned here last night, put on his evening dress, and went somewhere dining. Illness, or fifty accidents, may have kept him from home."

But Mrs Geldard was not to be softened by any such suggestion, which I could see Hewitt had chiefly thrown out by way of pacifying the lady, and allaying her bitterness as far as he could, in view of a possible reconciliation when things were cleared up.

"*That* isn't very likely," she said. "If he kept a dress suit here openly, I should know of it; and if he kept it here unknown to me, what did he want it for? If he went out in dress clothes last night, who did he go with? Who do you suppose, after seeing those envelopes and that piece of the letter?"

"Well, well, we shall see," Hewitt replied. "May I turn out the pockets of these clothes?"

"Certainly; there's nothing in them of importance," Mrs Geldard said. "I looked before I came to you."

Nevertheless Hewitt turned them out. "Here is a cheque-book with a number of cheques remaining. No counterfoils filled in, which is awkward. Bankers, the London Amalgamated. We will call there presently. An ivory pocket paper-knife. A sovereign purse—empty." Hewitt placed the articles on the table as he named them. "Gold pencil case, ivory folding rule, russia-leather card-case." He turned to Mrs Geldard. "There is no pocketbook," he said, "no pocket-knife and no watch, and there are no keys. Did Mr Geldard usually carry any of these things?"

"Yes," Mrs Geldard replied, "he carried all four." Hewitt's simple, methodical calmness, and his plain disregard of her former volubility, appeared by this to have disciplined Mrs Geldard into a businesslike brevity and directness of utterance.

"As to the watch now. Can you describe it?"

"Oh, it was only a cheap one. He had a gold one stolen—or at any rate he told me so—and since then he has only carried a very common sort of silver one, without a chain."

"The keys?"

"I only know there *was* a bunch of keys. Some of them fitted drawers and bureaux at home, and others, I suppose, fitted locks in this office."

"What of the pocket-knife?"

"That was a very uncommon one. It was a present, as a matter of fact, from an engineering friend, who had had it made specially. It was large, with a tortoise-shell handle and a silver plate with his initials. There was only one ordinary knife-blade in it; all the other implements were small tools or things of that kind. There was a small pair of silver calipers, for instance."

"Like these?" Hewitt suggested, producing those he used for measuring drawers and cabinets in search of secret receptacles.

"Yes, like those. And there were folding steel compasses, a tiny flat spanner, a little spirit level, and a number of other small instruments of that sort. It was very well made indeed; he used to say that it could not have been made for five pounds."

"Indeed?" Hewitt cast his eyes about the two rooms. "I see no signs of books here, Mrs Geldard—account-books I mean, of course. Your husband must have kept account-books, I take it?"

"Yes, naturally, he must have done. I never saw them, of course, but every business man keeps books." Then after a pause Mrs Geldard continued: "And they're gone too. I never thought of *that*. But there, I might have known as much. Who can trust a man safely if his own wife can't? But *I* won't shield him. Whatever he's been doing with his clients' money he'll have to answer for himself. Thank Heaven I've enough to live on of my own without being dependent on a creature like him! But think of the disgrace! My husband nothing better than a common thief—swindling his clients and making away with his books when he can't go on any longer! But he shall be punished, oh yes; *I'll* see he's punished, if once I find him!"

Hewitt thought for a moment, and then asked, "Do you know any of your husband's clients, Mrs Geldard?"

"No," she answered, rather snappishly, "I don't. I've told you he never let me know anything of his business—never anything at all; and very good reason he had too, that's certain."

"Then probably you do not happen to know the contents of these drawers?" Hewitt pursued, tapping the writing-table as he spoke.

"Oh, there's nothing of importance in them—at any rate in the unlocked ones. I looked at all of them this morning when I first came."

The table was of the ordinary pedestal pattern with four drawers at each side and a ninth in the middle at the top, and of very ordinary quality. The only locked drawer was the third from the top on the left-hand side. Hewitt pulled out one drawer after another. In one was a tin half full of tobacco; in another a few cigars at the bottom of a box; in a third a pile of notepaper headed with the address of the office, and rather dusty; another was empty; still another contained a handful of string. The top middle drawer rather reminded me of a similar drawer of my own at my last newspaper office, for it contained several pipes; but my own were mostly briars, whereas these were all clays.

"There's nothing really so satisfactory," Hewitt said, as he lifted and examined each pipe by turn, "to a seasoned smoker as a well-used clay. Most such men keep one or more of them for strictly private use." There was nothing noticeable about these pipes except that they were uncommonly dirty, but Hewitt scrutinised each before returning it to the drawer. Then he turned to Mrs Geldard and said: "As to the bank now—the London Amalgamated, Mrs Geldard. Are you known there personally?"

"Oh, yes; my husband gave them authority to pay cheques signed by me up to a certain amount, and I often do it for household expenses, or when he happens to be away."

"Then perhaps it will be best for you to go alone," Hewitt responded. "Of course they will never, as a general thing, give any person information as to the account of a customer; but perhaps, as you are known to them, and hold your husband's authority to draw cheques, they may tell you something. What I want to find out is, of course, whether your husband drew from the bank all his remaining balance yesterday, or any large sum. You must go alone, ask for the manager, and tell him that you have seen nothing of Mr Geldard since he left for business yesterday morning. Mind, you are not to appear angry, or suspicious, or anything of that sort, and you mustn't say you are employing me to bring him back from an elopement. That will shut up the channel of information at once. Hostile inquiries they'll never answer, even by the smallest hint, except after legal injunction. You can be as distressed and as alarmed as you please. Your husband has disappeared since yesterday morning, and you've no notion what has become of him; that is your tale, and a perfectly true one. You would like to know whether or not he has withdrawn his balance, or a considerable sum, since that would indicate whether or not his absence was intentional and premeditated."

Mrs Geldard understood and undertook to make the inquiry with all discretion. The bank was not far, and it was arranged that she should return to the office with the result.

As soon as she had left, Hewitt turned to the pedestal table and probed the keyhole of the locked drawer with the small stiletto attached to his penknife. "This seems to be a common sort of lock," he said. "I could probably open it with a bent nail. But the whole table is a cheap sort of thing. Perhaps there is an easier way."

He drew the unlocked drawer above completely out, passed his hand into the opening and felt about. "Yes," he said, "it's just as I hoped — as it usually is in pedestal tables not of the best quality; the partition between the drawers doesn't go more than two-thirds of the way back, and I can drop my hand into the drawer below. But I can't feel anything there — it seems empty."

He withdrew his hand and we tilted the whole table backward, so as to cause whatever lay in the drawers to slide to the back. This dodge was successful. Hewitt reinserted his hand and withdrew it with two orderly heaps of papers, each held together by a metal clip.

The papers in each clip, on examination, proved to be all of an identical character, with the exception of dates. They were, in fact, rent receipts. Those for the office, which had been given quarterly, were put back in their place with scarcely a glance, and the others Hewitt placed on the table before him. Each ran, apart from dates, in this fashion: "Received from Mr J. Cookson 15s., one month's rent of stable at 3, Dragon Yard, Benton Street, to" — here followed the date. "Also rent, feed and care of horse in own stable as agreed, £2. — W. GASK." The receipts were ill-written, and here and there ill-spelt. Hewitt put the last of the receipts in his pocket, and returned the others to the drawer. "Either," he said, "Mr Cookson is a client who gets Mr Geldard to hire stables for him, which may not be likely, or Mr Geldard calls himself Mr Cookson when he goes driving — possibly with Miss Trennatt. We shall see."

The pedestal table put in order again, Hewitt took the poker and raked in the fireplace. It was summer, and behind the bars was a sort of screen of cartridge paper with a frilled edge, and behind this various odds and ends had been thrown — spent matches, trade circulars crumpled up, and torn paper. There were also the remains of several cigars, some only half smoked, and one almost whole. The torn paper Hewitt examined piece by piece, and finally sorted out a number of pieces, which he set to work to arrange on the blotting pad. They formed a complete note, written in the same hand as were the envelopes already found by Mrs Geldard — that of the girl Emma Trennatt. It corresponded also with the solitary fragment of another letter which had accompanied them, by way of having a number of crosses below the signature, and it ran thus: —

Tuesday Night.

Dear Sam, — Tomorrow, to carry. Not late because people are coming for flowers. What you did was no good. The smoke leaks worse than ever, and F. thinks you must light a new pipe or else stop smoking altogether for a bit. Uncle is anxious.

E<small>MMA</small>.

Then followed the crosses, filling one line and nearly half the next — seventeen in all.

Hewitt gazed at the fragments thoughtfully. "This is a find," he said — "most decidedly a find. It looks so much like nonsense that it must mean something of importance. The date, you see, is Tuesday night. It would be received here on Wednesday — yesterday — morning. So that it was immediately after the receipt of this note that Geldard left. It's pretty plain the crosses don't mean kisses. The note isn't quite of the sort that usually carries such symbols, and moreover, when a lady fills the end of a sheet of notepaper with kisses she doesn't stop less than half way across the last line—she fills it to the end. These crosses mean something very different. I should like, too, to know what 'smoke' means. Anyway this letter would probably astonish Mrs Geldard if she saw it. We'll say nothing about it for the present." He swept the fragments into an envelope, and put away the envelope in his breast pocket. There was nothing more to be found of the least value in the fireplace, and a careful examination of the office in other parts revealed nothing that I had not noticed before, so far as I could see, except Geldard's boots standing on the floor of the cupboard wherein his clothes lay. The whole place was singularly bare of what one commonly finds in an office in the way of papers, hand-books, and general business material.

Mrs Geldard was not long away. At the bank she found that the manager was absent, and his deputy had been very reluctant to say anything definite without his sanction. He gave Mrs Geldard to understand, however, that there was a balance still remaining to her husband's credit; also that Mr Geldard had drawn a cheque the previous morning, Wednesday, for an amount "rather larger than usual." And that was all.

"By the way, Mrs Geldard," Hewitt observed, with an air of recollecting something, "there *was* a Mr Cookson I believe, if I remember, who knew a Mr Geldard. You don't happen to know, do you, whether or not Mr Geldard had a client or an acquaintance of that name?"

"No, I know nobody of the name."

"Ah, it doesn't matter. I suppose it isn't necessary for your husband to keep horses or vehicles of any description in his business?"

"No, certainly not." Mrs Geldard looked surprised at the question.

"Of course—I should have known that. He does not drive to business, I suppose?"

"No; he goes by omnibus."

"But as to Emma Trennatt now. This photograph is most welcome, and will be of great assistance, I make no doubt. But is there anything individual by which I might identify her if I saw her—anything beyond what I see in the photograph? A peculiarity of step, for instance, or a scar, or what not."

"Yes, there is a large mole—more than a quarter of an inch across, I should think—on her left cheek, an inch below the outer corner of her eye. The photograph only shows the other side of the face."

"That will be useful to know. Now has she a relative living at Crouch End, or thereabout?"

"Yes, her uncle; she's living with him now—or she was at any rate till lately. But how did you know that?"

"The Crouch End postmark was on those envelopes you found. Do you know anything of her uncle?"

"Nothing, except that he's a nurseryman, I believe."

"Not his full address?"

"No."

"And Trennatt is his name?"

"Yes."

"Thank you. I think, Mrs Geldard," Hewitt said, taking his hat, "that I will set out after your husband at once. You, I think, can do no better than stay at home till I have news for you. I have your address. If anything comes to your knowledge, please telegraph it to my office at once."

The office door was locked, the keys were left with the caretaker, and we saw Mrs Geldard into a cab at the door. "Come," said Hewitt, "we'll go somewhere and look at a directory, and after that to Dragon Yard. I think I know a man in Moorgate Street who'll let me see his directory."

We started to walk down Finsbury Pavement. Suddenly Hewitt caught my arm and directed my eyes toward a woman who had passed hurriedly in the opposite direction. I had not seen her face, but Hewitt had. "If that isn't Miss Emma Trennatt," he said, "it's uncommonly like the notion I've formed of her. We'll see if she goes to Geldard's office."

We hurried after the woman, who, sure enough, turned into the large door of the building we had just left. As it was impossible that she should know us, we followed her boldly up the stairs, and saw her stop before the door of Geldard's office, and knock. We passed her as she stood there—a handsome young woman enough—and well back on her left cheek, in the place Mrs Geldard had indicated, there was plain to see a very large mole. We pursued our way to the landing above and there we stopped in a position that commanded a view of Geldard's door. The young woman knocked again and waited.

"This doesn't look like an elopement yesterday morning, does it?" Hewitt whispered. "Unless Geldard's left both this one and his wife in the lurch."

The young woman below knocked once or twice more, walked irresolutely across the corridor and back, and in the end, after a parting knock, started slowly back downstairs.

"Brett," Hewitt exclaimed with suddenness, "will you do me a favour? That woman understands Geldard's secret comings and goings, as is plain from the letter. But she would appear to know nothing of where he is now, since she seems to have come here to find him. Perhaps this last absence of his has nothing to do with the others. In any case, will you follow this woman? She must be watched; but I want to see to the matter in other places. Will you do it?"

Of course I assented at once. We had been descending the stairs as Hewitt spoke, keeping distance behind the girl we were following. "Thank you," Hewitt now said. "Do it. If you find anything urgent to communicate, wire to me in care of the inspector at Crouch End Police Station. He knows me, and I will call there in case you may have sent. But if it's after five this afternoon, wire also to my office. If you keep with her to Crouch End, where she lives, we shall probably meet."

We parted at the door of the office we were at first bound for, and I followed the girl southward.

This new turn of affairs increased the puzzlement I already laboured under. Here was the girl Trennatt—who by all evidence appeared to be well acquainted with Geldard's mysterious proceedings, and in consequence of whose letter, whatever it might mean, he would seem to have absented himself—herself apparently ignorant of his whereabouts, and even unconscious that he had left his office. I had at first begun to speculate on Geldard's probable secret employment; I had heard of men keeping good establishments who, unknown to even their own wives, procured the wherewithal by begging or crossing-sweeping in London streets; I had heard also—knew, in fact, from Hewitt's experience—of well-to-do suburban residents whose actual profession was burglary or coining. I had speculated on the possibility of Geldard's secret being one of that kind. My mind had even reverted to the case, which I have related elsewhere, in which Hewitt frustrated a dynamite explosion by his timely discovery of a baker's cart and a number of loaves, and I wondered whether or not Geldard was a member of some secret brotherhood of Anarchists or Fenians. But here, it would seem, were two distinct mysteries, one of Geldard's generally unaccountable movements, and another of his disappearance, each mystery complicating the other. Again, what did that extraordinary note mean, with its crosses and its odd references to smoking? Had the dirty clay pipes anything to do with it? Or the half-smoked cigars? Perhaps the whole thing was merely ridiculously trivial after all. I could make nothing of it, however, and applied myself to my pursuit of Emma Trennatt, who mounted an omnibus at the Bank, on the roof of which I myself secured a seat.

II

Here I must leave my own proceedings to put in their proper place those of Martin Hewitt as I subsequently learnt them.

Benton Street, he found by the directory, turned out of the City Road south of Old Street, so was quite near. He was there in less than ten minutes, and had discovered Dragon Yard. Dragon Yard was as small a stable-yard as one could easily find. Only the right-hand side was occupied by stables, and there were only three of these. On the left was a high dead wall bounding a great warehouse or some such building. Across the first and second of the stables stretched a long board with the legend, "W. Gask, Corn, Hay, and Straw Dealer," and underneath a shop address in Old Street. The third stable stood blank and uninscribed, and all three were shut fast. Nobody was in the yard, and Hewitt at once proceeded to examine the end stable. The doors were unusually well finished and close-fitting, and the lock was a good one, of the lever variety, and very difficult to pick. Hewitt examined the front of the building very carefully, and then, after a visit to the entrance of the yard, to guard against early interruption, returned and scrambled by projections and fastenings to the roof. This was a roof in contrast to those of the other stables. They were of tiles, seemed old, and carried nothing in the way of a skylight; evidently it was the habit of Mr Gask and his helpers to do their horse and van business with gates wide open to admit light. But the roof of this third stable was newer and better made, and carried a good-sized skylight of thick fluted glass. Hewitt took a good look at such few windows as happened to be in sight, and straightaway began, with the strongest blade of his pocket-knife, to cut away the putty from round one pane. It was a rather long job, for the putty had hardened thoroughly in the sun, but it was accomplished at length, and Hewitt, with a final glance at the windows in view, prised up the pane from the end and lifted it out.

The interior of the stable was apparently empty. Neither stall nor rack was to be seen, and the place was plainly used as a coach or van house simply. Hewitt took one more look about him, and dropped quietly through the hole in the skylight. The floor was thickly laid with straw. There were a few odd pieces of harness, a rope or two, a lantern, and a few sacks lying here and there, and at the darkest end there was an obscure heap covered with straw and sacking. This heap Hewitt proceeded to unmask, and having cleared away a few sacks, left revealed about half a dozen rolls of linoleum. One of these he dragged to the light, where it became evident that it had remained thus rolled and tied with cord in two places for a long period. There were cracks in the surface, and when the cords were loosened the linoleum showed no disposition to open out or to become unrolled. Others of the rolls on inspection exhibited the same peculiarities. Moreover, each roll appeared to consist of no more than a couple of yards of material at most, though all were of the same pattern. Every roll, in fact, was of the same length, thickness, and shape as the others, containing somewhere near two yards of linoleum in a roll of some half-dozen thicknesses, leaving an open diameter of some four inches in the centre. Hewitt looked at each in turn, and then replaced the heap as he had found it. After this, to regain the skylight was not difficult by the aid of a trestle. The pane was replaced as well as the absence of fresh putty permitted, and five minutes later Hewitt was in a hansom bound for Crouch End.

He dismissed his cab at the police station. Within he had no difficulty in procuring a direction to Trennatt, the nurseryman, and a short walk brought him to the place. A fairly high wall, topped with broken glass, bounded the nursery garden next the road, and in the wall were two gates, one a wide double one for the admission of vehicles, and the other a smaller one of open pales, for ordinary visitors. The garden stood sheltered by higher ground behind, whereon stood a good-sized house, just

"HALF A DOZEN ROLLS OF LINOLEUM"

visible among the trees that surrounded it. Hewitt walked along by the side of the wall. Soon he came to where the ground of the nursery garden appeared to be divided from that of the house by a most extraordinarily high hedge extending a couple of feet above the top of the wall itself. Stepping back, the better to note this hedge, Hewitt became conscious of two large boards, directly facing each other, with scarcely four feet space between them, one erected on a post in the ground of the house, and the other similarly elevated from that of the nursery, each being inscribed in large letters, "TRESPASSERS WILL BE PROSECUTED." Hewitt smiled and passed on; here plainly was a neighbour's quarrel of long standing, for neither board was by any means new. The wall continued, and keeping by it Hewitt made the entire circuit of the large house and its grounds, and arrived once more at that part of the wall that enclosed the nursery garden. Just here, and near the wider gate, the upper part of a cottage was visible, standing within the wall, and evidently the residence of the nurseryman. It carried a conspicuous board with the legend, "H. M. Trennatt, Nurseryman." The large house and the nursery stood entirely apart from other houses or enclosures, and it would seem that the nursery ground had at some time been cut off from the grounds attached to the house.

Hewitt stood for a moment thoughtfully, and then walked back to the outer gate of the house on the rise. It was a high iron gate, and as Hewitt perceived, it was bolted at the bottom. Within the garden showed a neglected and weed-choked appearance, such as one associates with the garden of a house that has stood long empty.

A little way off a policeman walked. Hewitt accosted him and spoke of the house. "I was wondering if it might happen to be to let," he said. "Do you know?"

"No, sir," the policeman replied, "it ain't; though anyone might almost think it, to look at the garden. That's a Mr Fuller as lives there — and a rum 'un too."

"Oh, he's a rum 'un, is he? Keeps himself shut up, perhaps?"

"Yes, sir. On'y 'as one old woman, deaf as a post, for servant, and never lets nobody into the place. It's a rare game sometimes with the milkman. The milkman, he comes and rings that there bell, but the old gal's so deaf she never 'ears it. Then the milkman, he just slips 'is 'and through the gate rails, lifts the bolt and goes and bangs at the door. Old Fuller runs out and swears a good 'un. The old gal comes out, and old Fuller swears at 'er, and she turns round and swears back like anything. She don't care for 'im — not a bit. Then when he ain't 'avin' a row with the milkman and the old gal he goes down the garden and rows with the old nurseryman there down the 'ill. He jores the nurseryman from 'is side o' the hedge, and the nurseryman he jores back at the top of 'is voice. I've stood out there ten minutes together and nearly bust myself a-laughin' at them gray-'eaded old fellers a-callin' each other everythink they can think of; you can 'ear 'em 'alf over the parish. Why, each of 'em's 'ad a board painted, 'Trespassers will be Prosecuted,' and stuck 'em up facin' each other, so as to keep up the row."

"Very funny, no doubt."

"Funny? I believe you, sir. Why, it's quite a treat sometimes on a dull beat like this. Why, what's that? Blowed if I don't think they're beginning again now. Yes, they are. Well, my beat's the other way."

There was a sound of angry voices in the direction of the nursery ground, and Hewitt made toward it. Just where the hedge peeped over the wall the altercation was plain to hear.

"You're an old vagabond, and I'll indict you for a nuisance."

"You're an old thief, and you'd like to turn me out of house and home, wouldn't you? Indict away, you greedy old scoundrel!"

These and similar endearments, punctuated by growls and snorts, came distinctly from over the wall, accompanied by a certain scraping, brushing sound, as though each neighbour were madly attempting to scale the hedge and personally bang the other.

Hewitt hastened round to the front of the nursery garden and quietly tried first the wide gate and next the small one. Both were fastened securely. But in the manner of the milkman at the gate of the house above, Hewitt slipped his hand between the open slats of the small gate and slid the night-latch that held it. Within the quarrel ran high as Hewitt stepped quietly into the garden. He trod on the narrow grass borders of the beds for quietness' sake, till presently only a line of shrubs divided him from the clamorous nurseryman. Stooping and looking through an opening which gave him a back view, Hewitt observed that the brushing and scraping noise proceeded, not from angry scramblings, but from the forcing through an inadequate opening in the hedge of some piece of machinery which the nurseryman was most amicably passing to his neighbour at the same time as he assailed him with savage abuse, and received a full return in kind. It appeared to consist of a number of coils of metal pipe, not unlike those sometimes used in heating apparatus, and was as yet only a very little way through. Something else, of bright copper, lay on the garden-bed at the foot of the hedge, but intervening plants concealed its shape.

"FORCING THROUGH THE HEDGE SOME PIECE OF MACHINERY."

Hewitt turned quickly away and made towards the greenhouses, keeping tall shrubs as much as possible between himself and the cottage, and looking sharply about him. Here and there about the garden were stand-pipes, each carrying a tap at its upper end and placed conveniently for irrigation. These in particular Hewitt scrutinised, and presently, as he neared a large wooden outhouse close by the large gate, turned his attention to one backed by a thick shrub. When the thick undergrowth of the shrub was pushed aside a small stone slab, black and dirty, was disclosed, and this Hewitt lifted, uncovering a square hole six or eight inches across, from the foreside of which the stand-pipe rose.

THE STAND-PIPE IN THE NURSERY GARDEN.

The row went cheerily on over by the hedge, and neither Trennatt nor his neighbour saw Hewitt, feeling with his hand, discover two stop-cocks and a branch pipe in the hole, nor saw him try them both. Hewitt, however, was satisfied, and saw his case plain. He rose and made his way back toward the small gate. He was scarce halfway there when the straining of the hedge ceased, and before he reached it the last insult had been hurled, the quarrel ceased, and Trennatt approached. Hewitt immediately turned his back to the gate, and looking about him inquiringly hemmed aloud as though to attract attention. The nurseryman promptly burst round a corner crying, "Who's that? who's that, eh? What d'ye want, eh?"

"Why," answered Hewitt in a tone of mild surprise, "is it so uncommon to have a customer drop in?"

"I'd ha' sworn that gate was fastened," the old man said, looking about him suspiciously.

"That would have been rash; I had no difficulty in opening it. Come, can't you sell me a buttonhole?"

The old man led the way to a greenhouse, but as he went he growled again, "I'd ha' sworn I shut that gate."

"Perhaps you forgot," Hewitt suggested. "You have had a little excitement with your neighbour, haven't you?"

Trennatt stopped and turned round, darting a keen glance into Hewitt's face. "Yes," he answered angrily, "I have. He's an old villain. He'd like to turn me out of here, after being here all my life-and a lot o' good the ground 'ud be to him if he kep' it like he keeps his own! And look there!" He dragged Hewitt toward the "Trespassers" boards. "Goes and sticks up a board like that looking over my hedge! As though I wanted to go over among his weeds! So I stuck up another in front of it, and now they can stare each other out o' countenance. Buttonhole, you said, sir, eh?"

The old man saw Hewitt off the premises with great care, and the latter, flower in coat, made straight for the nearest post-office and despatched a telegram. Then he stood for some little while outside the post-office deep in thought, and in the end returned to the gate of the house above the nursery.

With much circumspection he opened the gate and entered the grounds. But instead of approaching the house he turned immediately to the left, behind trees and shrubs, making for the side nearest the nursery. Soon he reached a long, low wooden shed. The door was only secured by a button, and turning this he gazed into the dark interior. Now he had not noticed that close after him a woman had entered the gate, and that that woman was Mrs Geldard. She would have made for the house, but catching sight of Hewitt, followed him swiftly and quietly over the long grass. Thus it came to pass that his first appraisal of the lady's presence was a sharp drive in the back, which pitched him down the step to the low floor of what he had just perceived to be merely a tool-house, after which the door was shut and buttoned behind him.

"HIS FIRST APPRISAL OF THE LADY'S PRESENCE WAS A SHARP DRIVE IN THE BACK."

"Perhaps you'll be more careful in future," came Mrs Geldard's angry voice from without, "how you go making mischief between husband and wife and poking your nose into people's affairs. Such fellows as you ought to be well punished."

Hewitt laughed softly. Mrs Geldard had evidently changed her mind. The door presented no difficulty; a fairly vigorous push dislodged the button entirely, and he walked back to the outer gate chuckling quietly. In the distance he heard Mrs Geldard in shrill altercation with the deaf old woman. "It's no good you a-talking," the old woman was saying. "I can't hear. Nobody ain't allowed in this here place, so you must get out. Out you go, now!" Outside the gate Hewitt met me.

III

My own adventures had been simple. I had secured a back seat on the roof of the omnibus whereon Emma Trennatt travelled south from the Bank, from which I could easily observe where she alighted. When she did so I followed, and found to my astonishment that her destination was no other than the Geldards' private house at Camberwell—as I remembered from the address on the visitor's slip which Mrs Geldard had handed in at Hewitt's office a couple of days before. She handed a letter to the maid who opened the door, and soon after, in response to a message by the same maid, entered the house. Presently the maid reappeared, bonneted, and hurried off, to return in a few minutes in a cab with another following behind. Almost immediately Mrs Geldard emerged in company with Emma Trennatt. She hurried the girl into one of the cabs, and I heard her repeat loudly twice the address of Hewitt's office, once to the girl and once to the cabman. Now it seemed plain to me that to follow Emma Trennatt farther would be waste of time, for she was off to Hewitt's office, where Kerrett would learn her message. And knowing where a message would find Hewitt sooner than at his office, I judged it well to tell Mrs Geldard of the fact. I approached, therefore, as she was entering the other cab, and began to explain, when she cut me short. "You go and tell your master to attend to his own business as soon as he pleases, for not a shilling does he get from me. He ought to be ashamed of himself, sowing dissension between man and wife for the sake of what he can make out of it, and so ought you."

I bowed with what grace I might, and retired. The other cab had gone, so I set forth to find one for myself at the nearest rank. I could think of nothing better to do than to make for Crouch End Police Station and endeavour to find Hewitt. Soon after my cab emerged north of the city I became conscious of another cab, whose driver I fancied I recognised, and which kept ahead all along the route. In fact it was Mrs Geldard's cab, and presently it dawned upon me that we must both be bound for the same place. When it became quite clear that Crouch End was the destination of the lady I instructed my driver to disregard the police-station and follow the cab in front. Thus I arrived at Mr Fuller's house just behind Mrs Geldard, and thus, waiting at the gate, I met Hewitt as he emerged.

"Hullo, Brett!" he said. "Condole with me. Mrs Geldard has changed her mind, and considers me a pernicious creature anxious to make mischief between her and her husband; I'm very much afraid I shan't get my fee."

"No," I answered, "she told me you wouldn't."

We compared notes, and Hewitt laughed heartily. "The appearance of Emma Trennatt at Geldard's office this morning is explained," he said. "She went first with a message from Geldard to Mrs Geldard at Camberwell, explaining his absence and imploring her not to talk of it or make a disturbance. Mrs Geldard had gone off to town, and Emma Trennatt was told that she had gone to Geldard's office. There she went, and then we first saw her. She found nobody at the office, and after a minute or two of irresolution returned to Camberwell, and then succeeded in delivering her message, as you saw.

Mrs Geldard is apparently satisfied with her husband's explanation. But I'm afraid the revenue officers won't approve of it."

"The revenue officers?"

"Yes. It's a case of illicit distilling—and a big case, I fancy. I've wired to Somerset House, and no doubt men are on their way here now. But Mrs Geldard's up at the house, so we'd better hurry up to the police station and have a few sent from there. Come along. The whole thing's very clever, and a most uncommonly big thing. If I know all about it—and I think I do—Geldard and his partners have been turning out untaxed spirit by the hundred gallons for a long time past. Geldard is the practical man, the engineer, and probably erected the whole apparatus himself in that house on the hill. The spirit is brought down by a pipe laid a very little way under the garden surface, and carried into one of the irrigation stand-pipes in the nursery ground. There's a quiet little hole behind the pipe with a couple of stopcocks—one to shut off the water when necessary, the other to do the same with the spirit. When the stopcocks are right you just turn the tap at the top of the pipe and you get water or whisky, as the case may be. Fuller, the man up at the house, attends to the still, with such assistance as the deaf old woman can give him. Trennatt, down below, draws off the liquor ready to be carried away. These two keep up an ostentatious appearance of being at unending feud to blind suspicion. Our as yet ungreeted friend Geldard, guiding spirit of the whole thing, comes disguised as a carter with an apparent cart-load of linoleum, and carries away the manufactured stuff. In the pleasing language of Geldard and Co., 'smoke,' as alluded to in the note you saw, means whisky. Something has been wrong with the apparatus lately, and it has been leaking badly. Geldard has been at work on it, patching, but ineffectually. 'What you did was no good' said the charming Emma in the note, as you will remember. 'Uncle was anxious.' And justifiably so, because not only does a leak of spirit mean a waste, but it means a smell, which some sharp revenue man might sniff. Moreover, if there is a leak, the liquid runs somewhere at random, and with any sudden increase in volume attention might easily be attracted. It was so bad that 'F.' (Fuller) thought Geldard must light another pipe (start another still) or give up smoking (distilling) for a bit. There is the explanation of the note. 'Tomorrow, to carry' probably means that he is to call with his cart—the cart in whose society Geldard becomes Cookson—to remove a quantity of spirit. He is not to come late because people are expected on floral business. The crosses, I *think*, will be found to indicate the amount of liquid to be moved. But that we shall see. Anyhow, Geldard got there yesterday and had a busy day loading up, and then set to repairing. The damage was worse than supposed, and an urgent thing. Result, Geldard works into early morning, has a sleep in the place, where he may be called at any moment, and starts again early this morning. New parts have to be ordered, and these are delivered at Trennatt's today and passed through the hedge. Meantime Geldard sends a message to his wife explaining things, and the result you've seen."

At the police station a telegram had already been received from Somerset House. That was enough for Hewitt, who had discharged his duty as a citizen and now dropped the case. We left the police and the revenue officers to deal with the matter and travelled back to town.

"Yes," said Hewitt on the way, after each had fully described his day's experiences, "it seemed pretty plain that Geldard left his office by the back way in disguise, and there were things that hinted what that disguise was. The pipes were noticeable. They were quite unnecessarily dirty, and partly from dirty fingers. Pipes smoked by a man in his office would never look like that. They had been smoked out of doors by a man with dirty hands, and hands and pipes would be in keeping with the rest of the man's appearance. It was noticeable that he had left not only his clothes and hat, but his boots behind him. They were quite plain though good boots, and would be quite in keeping with any dress but that of a labourer or some such man in his working clothes. Moreover, the partly-smoked cigars were probably thrown aside because they would appear inconsistent with Geldard's changed dress. The contents of the pockets in the clothes left behind, too, told the same tale. The cheap watch and the necessary keys, pocketbook and pocket-knife were taken, but the articles of luxury, the russia leather card-case, the sovereign purse and so on, were left. Then we came on the receipts for stable-rent. Suggestion—perhaps the disguise was that of a carter.

"Then there was the coach-house. Plainly, if Geldard took the trouble thus to disguise himself, and thus to hide his occupation even from his wife, he had some very good reason for secrecy. Now the goods which a man would be likely to carry secretly in a cart or van, as a regular piece of business, would probably be either stolen or smuggled. When I examined those pieces of linoleum, I became convinced that they were intended merely as receptacles for some other sort of article altogether. They were old, and had evidently been thus rolled for a very long period. They appeared to have been exposed to weather, but on the outside only. Moreover they were all of one size and shape, each forming a long, hollow cylinder, with plenty of interior room. Now from this it was plainly unlikely that they were intended to hold *stolen* goods. Stolen goods are not apt to be always of one size and shape, adaptable to a cylindrical recess. Perhaps they were smuggled. Now the only goods profitable to be smuggled nowadays are tobacco and spirits, and plainly these rolls of linoleum would be excellent receptacles for either. Tobacco could be packed inside the rolls and the ends stopped artistically with narrow rolls of linoleum. Spirits could be contained in metal cylinders exactly fitting the cavity, and the ends filled in the same way as for tobacco. But for tobacco a smart man would probably make his linoleum rolls of different sizes, for the sake of a more innocent appearance, while for spirits it would be a convenience to have vessels of uniform measure, to save trouble in quicker delivery and calculation of quantity. Bearing these things in mind, I went in search of the gentle nurseryman at Crouch End. My general survey of the nursery ground and the house behind it inspired me with the notion that the situation and arrangement were most admirably adapted for the working of a large illicit still—a form of misdemeanour, let me tell you, that is much more common nowadays than is generally supposed. I remembered Geldard's engineering experience, and I heard something of the odd manners of Mr Fuller; my theory of a traffic in untaxed spirits became strengthened. But why a nursery? Was this a mere accident of the design? There were commonly irrigation pipes about nurseries, and an extra one might easily be made to carry whisky. With this in mind I visited the nursery with the result you know of. The stand-pipe I tested (which was where I expected—handy to the vehicle-entrance) could produce simple New River water or raw whisky at command of one of two stopcocks. My duty was plain. As you know, I am a citizen first and an investigator after, and I find the advantage of it in my frequent intercourse with the police and other authorities. As soon as I could get away I telegraphed to Somerset House. But then I grew perplexed on a point of conduct. I was commissioned by Mrs Geldard. It scarcely seemed the loyal thing to put my client's husband in gaol because of what I had learnt in course of work on her behalf. I decided to give him, and nobody else, a sporting chance. If I could possibly get at him in the time at my disposal, by himself, so that no accomplice should get the benefit of my warning, I would give him a plain hint to run; then he could take his chance. I returned to the place and began to work round the grounds, examining the place as I went; but at the very first outhouse I put my head into I was surprised in the rear by Mrs Geldard coming in hot haste to stop me and rescue her husband. She most unmistakably gave me the sack, and so now the police may catch Geldard or not, as their luck may be."

They did catch him. In the next day's papers a report of a great capture of illicit distillers occupied a prominent place. The prisoners were James Fuller, Henry Matthew Trennatt, Sarah Blatten, a deaf woman, Samuel Geldard, and his wife Rebecca Geldard. The two women were found on the premises in violent altercation when the officers arrived, a few minutes after Hewitt and I had left the police station on our way home. It was considered by far the greatest haul for the revenue authorities since the seizure of the famous ship's boiler on a wagon in the East End stuffed full of tobacco, after that same ship's boiler had made about a dozen voyages to the Continent and back "for repair." Geldard was found dressed as a workman, carrying out extensive alterations and repairs to the still. And a light van was found in a shed belonging to the nursery loaded with seventeen rolls of linoleum, each enclosing a cylinder containing two gallons of spirits, and packed at each end with narrow linoleum rolls. It will be remembered that seventeen was the number of crosses at the foot of Emma Trennatt's note.

THE PRISONERS.

The subsequent raids on a number of obscure public-houses in different parts of London, in consequence of information gathered on the occasion of the Geldard capture, resulted in the seizure of a large quantity of secreted spirit for which no permit could be shown. It demonstrated also the extent of Geldard's connection, and indicated plainly what was done with the spirit when he had carted it away from Crouch End. Some of the public-houses in question must have acquired a notoriety among the neighbours for frequent purchases of linoleum.

4

THE CASE OF THE LATE MR REWSE

I

Of this case I personally saw nothing beyond the first advent in Hewitt's office of Mr Horace Bowyer, who put the case in his hands, and then I merely saw Mr Bowyer's back as I passed downstairs from my rooms. But I noted the case in full detail after Hewitt's return from Ireland, as it seemed to me one not entirely without interest, if only as an exemplar of the fatal ease with which a man may unwittingly dig a pit for his own feet—a pit from which there is no climbing out.

A few moments after I had seen the stranger disappear into Hewitt's office, Kerrett brought to Hewitt in his inner room a visitor's slip announcing the arrival on urgent business of Mr Horace Bowyer. That the visitor was in a hurry was plain from a hasty rattling of the closed wicket in the outer room where Mr Bowyer was evidently making impatient attempts to follow his announcement in person. Hewitt showed himself at the door and invited Mr Bowyer to enter, which he did, as soon as Kerrett had released the wicket, with much impetuosity. He was a stout, florid gentleman with a loud voice and a large stare.

"Mr Hewitt," he said, "I must claim your immediate attention to a business of the utmost gravity. Will you please consider yourself commissioned, wholly regardless of expense, to set aside whatever you may have in hand and devote yourself to the case I shall put in your hands?"

"Certainly not," Hewitt replied with a slight smile. "What I have in hand are matters which I have engaged to attend to, and no mere compensation for loss of fees could persuade me to leave my clients in the lurch, else what would prevent some other gentleman coming here tomorrow with a bigger fee than yours and bribing me away from you?"

"But this—this is a most serious thing, Mr Hewitt. A matter of life or death—it is indeed!"

"Quite so," Hewitt replied; "but there are a thousand such matters at this moment pending of which you and I know nothing, and there are also two or three more of which you know nothing, but on which I am at work. So that it becomes a question of practicability. If you will tell me your business I can judge whether or not I may be able to accept your commission concurrently with those I have in hand. Some operations take months of constant attention; some can be conducted intermittently; others still are a mere matter of a few days—many of hours simply."

"I will tell you then," Mr Bowyer replied. "In the first place, will you have the kindness to read that? It is a cutting from the *Standard's* column of news from the provinces of two days ago."

Hewitt took the cutting and read as follows:—

"The epidemic of smallpox in County Mayo, Ireland, shows few signs of abating. The spread of the disease has been very remarkable considering the widely-scattered nature of the population, though there can be no doubt that the market-towns are the centres of infection, and that it is from these that the germs of contagion are carried into the country by people from all parts who resort thither on market days. In many cases the disease has assumed a particularly malignant form, and deaths have been very rapid and numerous. The comparatively few medical men available are sadly overworked, owing largely to the distances separating their different patients. Among those who have succumbed within the last few days is Mr Algernon Rewse, a young English gentleman who has been staying with a friend at a cottage a few miles from Cullanin, on a fishing excursion."

ALGERNON REWSE.

Hewitt placed the cutting on the table at his side. "Yes?" he said inquiringly. "It is to Mr Algernon Rewse's death you wish to draw my attention?"

"It is," Mr Bowyer answered; "and the reason I come to you is that I very much suspect—more than suspect, indeed—that Mr Algernon Rewse has *not* died by smallpox, but has been murdered—murdered cold-bloodedly, and for the most sordid motives, by the friend who has been sharing his holiday."

"In what way do you suppose him to have been murdered?"

"That I cannot say—that, indeed, I want you to find out, among other things—chiefly, perhaps, the murderer himself, who has made off."

"And your own status in the matter," queried Hewitt, "is that of—?"

"I am trustee under a will by which Mr Rewse would have benefited considerably had he lived but a month or two longer. That circumstance indeed lies rather near the root of the matter. The thing stood thus. Under the will I speak of—that of young Rewse's uncle, a very old friend of mine in his lifetime—the money lay in trust till the young fellow should attain twenty-five years of age. His younger sister, Miss Mary Rewse, was also benefited, but to a much smaller extent. She was to come into her property also on attaining the age of twenty-five, or on her marriage, whichever event happened first. It was further provided that in case either of these young people died before coming into the inheritance, his or her share should go to the survivor. I want you particularly to remember this. You will observe that now, in consequence of young Algernon Rewse's death, barely two months before his twenty-fifth birthday, the whole of the very large property—all personalty, and free from any tie or restriction—which would otherwise have been his, will, in the regular course, pass, on her twenty-fifth birthday, *or on her marriage*, to Miss Mary Rewse, whose own legacy was comparatively trifling. You will understand the importance of this when I tell you that the man whom I suspect of causing Algernon Rewse's death, and who has been his companion on his otherwise lonely holiday, is engaged to be married to Miss Rewse."

Mr Bowyer paused at this, but Hewitt only raised his eyebrows and nodded.

"I have never particularly liked the man," Mr Bowyer went on. "He never seemed to have much to say for himself. I like a man who holds up his head and opens his mouth. I don't believe in the sort of modesty that he showed so much of—it isn't genuine. A man can't afford to be genuinely meek and retiring who has his way to make in the world—and he was clever enough to know *that*."

"He is poor, then?" Hewitt asked.

"Oh yes, poor enough. His name, by the by, is Main—Stanley Main—and he is a medical man. He hasn't been practising, except as assistant, since he became qualified, the reason being, I understand, that he couldn't afford to buy a good practice. He is the person who will profit by young Rewse's death—or at any rate who intended to; but we will see about that. As for Mary, poor girl, she wouldn't have lost her brother for fifty fortunes."

"As to the circumstances of the death, now?"

"Yes, yes, I am coming to that. Young Algernon Rewse, you must know, had rather run down in health, and Main persuaded him that he wanted a change. I don't know what it was altogether, but Rewse seemed to have been having his own little love troubles and that sort of thing, you know. He'd been engaged, I think, or very nearly so, and the young lady died, and so on. Well, as I said, he had run down and got into low health and spirits, and no doubt a change of some sort would have done him good. This Stanley Main always seemed to have a great influence over the poor boy—he was about four or five years older than Rewse—and somehow he persuaded him to go away, the two together, to some outlandish wilderness of a place in the West of Ireland for salmon-fishing. It seemed to me at the time rather a ridiculous sort of place to go to, but Main had his way, and they went. There was a cottage—rather a good sort of cottage, I believe, for the district—which some friend of Main's, once a landowner in the district, had put up as a convenient box for salmon-fishing, and they rented it. Not long after they got there this epidemic of small-pox got about in the district—though that, I believe, has had little to do with poor young Rewse's death. All appeared to go well until a day over a week ago, when Mrs Rewse received this letter from Main." Mr Bowyer handed Martin Hewitt a letter, written in an irregular and broken hand, as though of a person writing under stress of extreme agitation. It ran thus:—

"My dear Mrs Rewse,—
"You will probably have heard through the newspapers—indeed I think Algernon has told you in his letters—that a very bad epidemic of smallpox is abroad in this district. I am deeply grieved to have to tell you that Algernon himself has taken the disease in a rather bad form. He showed the first symptoms today (Tuesday), and he is now in bed in the cottage. It is fortunate that I, as a medical man, happen to be on the spot, as the nearest local doctor is five miles off at Cullanin, and he is working and travelling night and day as it is. I have my little medicine chest with me, and can get whatever else is necessary from Cullanin, so that everything is being done for Algernon that is possible, and I hope to bring him up to scratch in good health soon, though of course the disease is a dangerous one. Pray don't unnecessarily alarm yourself, and don't think about coming over here, or anything of that sort. You can do no good, and will only run risk yourself. I will take care to let you know

how things go on, so please don't attempt to come. The journey is long and would be very trying to you, and you would have no place to stay at nearer than Cullanin, which is quite a centre of infection. I will write again tomorrow.

> "Yours most sincerely,
> "STANLEY MAIN."

Not only did the handwriting of this letter show signs of agitation, but here and there words had been repeated, and sometimes a letter had been omitted. Hewitt placed the letter on the table by the newspaper cutting, and Mr Bowyer proceeded.

"Another letter followed on the next day," he said, handing it to Hewitt as he spoke; "a short one, as you see; not written with quite such signs of agitation. It merely says that Rewse is very bad, and repeats the former entreaties that his mother will not think of going to him." Hewitt glanced at the letter and placed it with the other, while Mr Bowyer continued: "Notwithstanding Main's persistent anxiety that she should stay at home, Mrs Rewse, who was of course terribly worried about her only son, had almost made up her mind, in spite of her very delicate health, to start for Ireland, when she received a third letter announcing Algernon's death. Here it is. It is certainly the sort of letter that one might expect to be written in such circumstances, and yet there seems to me at least a certain air of disingenuousness about the wording. There are, as you see, the usual condolences, and so forth. The disease was of the malignant type, it says, which is terribly rapid in its action, often carrying off the patient even before the eruption has time to form. Then—and this is a thing I wish you especially to note—there is once more a repetition of his desire that neither the young man's mother nor his sister shall come to Ireland. The funeral must take place immediately, he says, under arrangements made by the local authorities, and before they could reach the spot. Now doesn't this obtrusive anxiety of his that no connection of young Rewse's should be near him during his illness, nor even at the funeral, strike you as rather singular?"

"Well, possibly it is; though it may easily be nothing but zeal for the health of Mrs Rewse and her daughter. As a matter of fact, what Main says is very plausible. They could do no sort of good in the circumstances, and might easily run into danger themselves, to say nothing of the fatigue of the journey and general nervous upset. Mrs Rewse is in weak health, I think you said?"

"Yes, she's almost an invalid, in fact; she is subject to heart disease. But tell me now, as an entirely impartial observer, doesn't it seem to you that there is a very forced, unreal sort of tone in all these letters?"

"Perhaps one may notice something of the sort, but fifty things may cause that. The case from the beginning may have been worse than he made it out. What ensued on the receipt of this letter?"

"Mrs Rewse was prostrated, of course. Her daughter communicated with me as a friend of the family, and that is how I heard of the whole thing for the first time. I saw the letters, and it seemed to me, looking at all the circumstances of the case, that somebody at least ought to go over and make certain that everything was as it should be. Here was this poor young man, staying in a lonely cottage with the only man in the world who had any reason to desire his death, or any profit to gain by it, and he had a very great inducement indeed. Moreover he was a medical man, *carrying his medicine chest with him*, remember, as he says himself in his letter. In this situation Rewse suddenly dies, with nobody about him, so far as there is anything to show, but Main himself. As his medical attendant it would be Main who would certify and register the death, and no matter what foul play might have taken place he would be safe as long as nobody was on the spot to make searching inquiries—might easily escape even then, in fact. When one man is likely to profit much by the death of another a doctor's medicine chest is likely to supply but too easy a means to his end."

"Did you say anything of your suspicions to the ladies?"

"Well—well, I hinted perhaps—no more than hinted, you know. But they wouldn't hear of it—got indignant, and 'took on' as people call it, worse than ever, so that I had to smooth them over. But since it seemed somebody's duty to see into the matter a little more closely, and there seemed to be nobody to do it but myself, I started off that very evening by the night mail. I was in Dublin early the next morning, and spent that day getting across Ireland. The nearest station was ten miles from Cullanin, and that, as you remember, was five miles from the cottage, so that I drove over on the morning of the following day. I must say Main appeared very much taken aback at seeing me. His manner was nervous and apprehensive, and made me more suspicious than ever. The body had been buried, of course, a couple of days or more. I asked a few rather searching questions about the illness, and so forth, and his answers became positively confused. He had burned the clothes that Rewse was wearing at the time the disease first showed itself, he said, as well as all the bedclothes, since there was no really efficient means of disinfection at hand. His story in the main was that he had gone off to Cullanin one morning on foot to see about a top joint of a fishing-rod that was to be repaired. When he returned early in the afternoon he found Algernon Rewse sickening of smallpox, at once put him to bed, and there nursed him till he died. I wanted to know, of course, why no other medical man had been called in. He said that there was only one available, and it was doubtful if he could have been got at even a day's notice, so overworked was he; moreover he said this man, with his hurry and over-strain, could never have given the patient such efficient attention as he himself, who had nothing else to do. After a while I put it to him plainly that it would at any rate have been more prudent to have had the body at least inspected by some independent doctor, considering the fact that he was likely to profit so largely by young Rewse's death, and I suggested that with an exhumation order it might not be too late now, as a matter of justice to himself. The effect of that convinced me. The man gasped and turned blue with terror. It was a full minute, I should think, before he could collect himself sufficiently to attempt to dissuade me from doing what I had hinted at. He did so as soon as he could by every argument he could think of—entreated me, in fact, almost desperately. That decided me. I said that after what he had said, and particularly in view of his whole manner and bearing, I should insist, by every means in my power, on having the body properly examined, and I went off at once to Cullanin to set the telegraph going, and see whatever local authority might be proper. When I returned in the afternoon Stanley Main had packed his bag and vanished, and I have not heard nor seen anything of him since. I stayed in the neighbourhood that day and the next, and left for London in the evening. By the help of my solicitors proper representations were made at the Home Office, and, especially in view of Main's flight, a prompt order was made for exhumation and medical examination preliminary to an inquest. I am expecting to hear that the disinterment has been effected today. What I want you to do, of course, is chiefly to find Main. The Irish constabulary in that district are fine big men, and no doubt most excellent in quelling a faction fight or shutting up a shebeen, but I doubt their efficiency in anything requiring much more finesse. Perhaps also you may be able to find out something of the means by which the murder—it is plain it is one—was committed. It is quite possible that Main may have adopted some means to give the body the appearance, even to a medical man, of death from smallpox."

"That," Hewitt said, "is scarcely likely, else, indeed, why did he not take care that another doctor should see the body before the burial? That would have secured him. But that is not a thing one can deceive a doctor over. Of course in the circumstances exhumation is desirable, but if the case *is* one of smallpox, I don't envy the medical man who is to examine. At any rate the business is, I should imagine, not likely to be a very long one, and I can take it in hand at once. I will leave tonight for Ireland by the 6.30 train from Euston."

"Very good. I shall go over myself, of course. If anything comes to my knowledge in the meanwhile, of course I'll let you know."

An hour or two after this a cab stopped at the door, and a young lady dressed in black sent in her name and a minute later was shown into Hewitt's room. It was Miss Mary Rewse. She wore a heavy veil, and all she said she uttered in evidently deep distress of mind. Hewitt did what he could to calm her, and waited patiently.

At length she said: "I felt that I must come to you, Mr Hewitt, and yet now that I am here I don't know what to say. Is it the fact that Mr Bowyer has commissioned you to investigate the circumstances of my poor brother's death, and to discover the whereabouts of Mr Main?"

"Yes, Miss Rewse, that is the fact. Can you tell me anything that will help me?"

"No, no, Mr Hewitt, I fear not. But it is such a dreadful thing, and Mr Bowyer is—I'm afraid he is so much prejudiced against Mr Main that I felt I ought to do something—to say something at least to prevent you entering on the case with your mind made up that he has been guilty of such an awful thing. He is really quite incapable of it, I assure you."

"Pray, Miss Rewse," Hewitt replied, "don't allow that apprehension to disturb you. If Mr Main is, as you say, incapable of such an act as perhaps he is suspected of, you may rest assured no harm will come to him. So far as I am concerned, at any rate, I enter the case with a perfectly open mind. A man in my profession who accepted prejudices at the beginning of a case would have very poor results to show indeed. As yet I have no opinion, no theory, no prejudice—nothing indeed but a bare outline of facts. I shall derive no opinion and no theory from anything but a consideration of the actual circumstances and evidences on the spot. I quite understand the relation in which Mr Main stands in regard to yourself and your family. Have you heard from him lately?"

"Not since the letter informing us of my brother's death."

"Before then?"

Miss Rewse hesitated.

"Yes," she said, "we corresponded. But—but there was really nothing—the letters were of a personal and private sort—they were—"

"Yes, yes, of course," Hewitt answered, with his eyes fixed keenly on the veil which Miss Rewse still kept down. "Of course I understand that. Then there is nothing else you can tell me?"

"No, I fear not. I can only implore you to remember that no matter what you may see and hear, no matter what the evidence may be, I am sure, sure, *sure* that poor Stanley could never do such a thing." And Miss Rewse buried her face in her hands.

Hewitt kept his eyes on the lady, though he smiled slightly, and asked, "How long have you known Mr Main?"

"'HOW LONG HAVE YOU KNOWN MR MAIN?'"

"For some five or six years now. My poor brother knew him at school, though, of course, they were in different forms, Mr Main being the elder."

"Were they always on good terms?"

"They were always like brothers."

Little more was said. Hewitt condoled with Miss Rewse as well as he might, and she presently took her departure. Even as she descended the stairs a messenger came with a short note from Mr Bowyer enclosing a telegram just received from Cullanin. The telegram ran thus: —

Body exhumed. Death from shot-wound. No trace of smallpox. Nothing yet heard of Main. Have communicated with coroner. — O'Reilly.

II

Hewitt and Mr Bowyer travelled towards Mayo together, Mr Bowyer restless and loquacious on the subject of the business in hand, and Hewitt rather bored thereby. He resolutely declined to offer an opinion on any single detail of the case till he had examined the available evidence, and his occasional remarks on matters of general interest, the scenery and so forth, struck his companion, unused to business of the sort which had occasioned the journey, as strangely cold-blooded and indifferent. Telegrams had been sent ordering that no disarrangement of the contents of the cottage was to be allowed pending their arrival, and Hewitt well knew that nothing more was practicable till the site was reached. At Ballymaine, where the train was left at last, they stayed for the night, and left early the next morning for Cullanin, where a meeting with Dr O'Reilly at the mortuary had been appointed. There the body lay stripped of its shroud, calm and gray, and beginning to grow ugly, with a scarcely noticeable breach in the flesh of the left breast.

"The wound has been thoroughly cleansed, closed and stopped with a carbolic plug before interment," Dr O'Reilly said. He was a middle-aged, grizzled man, with a face whereon many recent sleepless nights had left their traces. "I have not thought it necessary to do anything in the way of dissection. The bullet is not present, it has passed clean through the body, between the ribs both back and front, piercing the heart on its way. The death must have been instantaneous."

Hewitt quickly examined the two wounds, back and front, as the doctor turned the body over, and then asked: "Perhaps, Dr O'Reilly, you have had some experience of a gunshot wound before this?"

The doctor smiled grimly. "I think so," he answered, with just enough of brogue in his words to hint his nationality and no more. "I was an army surgeon for a good many years before I came to Cullanin, and saw service in Ashanti and in India."

"Come then," Hewitt said, "you're an expert. Would it have been possible for the shot to have been fired from behind?"

"Oh, no. See! the bullet entering makes a wound of quite a different character from that of the bullet leaving."

"Have you any idea of the weapon used?"

"A large revolver, I should think; perhaps of the regulation size; that is, I should judge the bullet to have been a conical one of about the size fitted to such a weapon — smaller than that from a rifle."

"Can you form an idea of from what distance the shot was fired?"

Dr O'Reilly shook his head. "The clothes have all been burned," he said, "and the wound has been washed, otherwise one might have looked for powder blackening."

"Did you know either the dead man or Dr Main personally?"

"Only very slightly. I may say I saw just such a pistol as might cause that sort of wound in Main's hands the day before he gave out that Rewse had been attacked by smallpox. I drove past the cottage as he stood in the doorway with it in his hand. He had the breach opened, and seemed to be either loading or unloading it — which it was I couldn't say."

"Very good, doctor, that may be important. Now is there any single circumstance, incident or conjecture that you can tell me of in regard to this case that you have not already mentioned?"

Doctor O'Reilly thought for a moment, and replied in the negative. "I heard, of course," he said, "of the reported new case of small-pox, and that Main had taken the case in hand himself. I was indeed relieved to hear it, for I had already more on my hands than one man can safely be expected to attend to. The cottage was fairly isolated, and there could have been nothing gained by removal to an asylum—indeed there was practically no accommodation. So far as I can make out nobody seems to have seen young Rewse, alive or dead, after Main had announced that he had the smallpox. He seems to have done everything himself, laying out the body and all, and you may be pretty sure that none of the strangers about was particularly anxious to have anything to do with it. The undertaker (there is only one here, and he is down with the smallpox himself now) was as much overworked as I was myself, and was glad enough to send off a coffin by a market cart and leave the laying out and screwing down to Main, since he had got those orders. Main made out the death certificate himself, and, since he was trebly qualified, everything seemed in order."

"The certificate merely attributed the death to smallpox, I take it, with no qualifying remarks?"

"Smallpox simply."

Hewitt and Mr Bowyer bade Dr O'Reilly good morning, and their car was turned in the direction of the cottage where Algernon Rewse had met his death. At the Town Hall in the market-place, however, Hewitt stopped the car and set his watch by the public clock. "This is more than half an hour before London time," he said, "and we mustn't be at odds with the natives about the time."

As he spoke Dr O'Reilly came running up breathlessly. "I've just heard something," he said. "Three men heard a shot in the cottage as they were passing, last Tuesday week."

"Where are the men?"

"I don't know at the moment; but they can be found. Shall I set about it?"

"If you possibly can," Hewitt said, "you will help us enormously. Can you send them messages to be at the cottage as soon as they can get there today? Tell them they shall have half a sovereign apiece."

"Right, I will. Good day."

"Tuesday week," said Mr Bowyer as they drove off; "that was the date of Main's first letter, and the day on which, by his account, Rewse was taken ill. Then if that was the shot that killed Rewse, he must have been lying dead in the place while Main was writing those letters reporting his sickness to his mother. The cold-blooded scoundrel!"

"Yes," Hewitt replied, "I think it probable in any case that Tuesday was the day that Rewse was shot. It wouldn't have been safe for Main to write the mother lying letters about the smallpox before. Rewse might have written home in the meantime, or something might have occurred to postpone Main's plans, and then there would be impossible explanations required."

Over a very bad road they jolted on, and in the end arrived where the road, now become a mere path, passed a tumble-down old farmhouse.

"This is where the woman lives who cooked and cleaned house for Rewse and Main," Mr Bowyer said. "There is the cottage, scarce a hundred yards off, a little to the right of the track."

"Well," replied Hewitt, "suppose we stop here and ask her a few questions? I like to get the evidence of all the witnesses as soon as possible. It simplifies subsequent work wonderfully."

They alighted, and Mr Bowyer roared through the open door and tapped with his stick. In reply to his summons, a decent-looking woman of perhaps fifty, but wrinkled beyond her age, and better dressed than any woman Hewitt had seen since leaving Cullanin, appeared from the hinder buildings and curtsied pleasantly.

"Good morning, Mrs Hurley, good morning," Mr Bowyer said, "this is Mr Martin Hewitt, a gentleman from London, who is going to look into this shocking murder of our young friend, Mr Rewse, and sift it to the bottom. He would like you to tell him something, Mrs Hurley."

The woman curtsied again. "An' it's the jintleman is welcome, sor, sad doin's as ut is." She had a low, pleasing voice, much in contrast with her unattractive appearance, and characterised by the softest and broadest brogue imaginable. "Will ye not come in? Mother av Hiven! An' thim two livin' together, an' fishin' an' readin' an' all, like brothers! An' trut' ut is, he was a foine young jintleman, indade, indade!"

"I suppose, Mrs Hurley," Hewitt said, "you've seen as much of the life of those two gentlemen here as anybody?"

"True ut is, sor; none more—nor as much."

"Did you ever hear of anybody being on bad terms with Mr Rewse—anybody at all, Mr Main or another?"

"Niver a soul in all Mayo. How could ye? Such a foine young jintleman, an' fair-spoken an' all."

"Tell me all that happened on the day that you heard that Mr Rewse was ill—Tuesday week."

"In the mornin', sor, 'twas much as ord'nary. I was over there at half afther sivin, an' 'twas half an hour afther that I cud hear the jintlemen dhressin'. They tuk their breakfast—though Mr Rewse's was a small wan. It was half afther nine that Mr Main wint off walkin' to Cullanin, Mr Rewse stayin' in, havin' letthers to write. Half an hour later I came away mesilf. Later than that (it was nigh elivin) I wint across for a pail from the yard, an' then, through the windy as I passed I saw the dear young jintleman sittin' writin' at the table calm an' peaceful—an' saw him no more in this warrl'."

"And after that?"

"Afther that, sor, I came back wid the pail, an' saw nor heard no more till two o'clock, whin Mr Main came back from Cullanin."

"Did you see him as he came back?"

"That I did, sor, as I stud there nailin' the fence where the pig bruk ut. I'd been there an' had me oi down the road lookin' for him an hour past, expectin' he might be bringin' somethin' for me to cook for their dinner. An' more by token he gave me the toime from his watch, set by the Town Hall clock."

"And was it two o'clock?"

"It was that to the sthroke, an' me own ould clock was right too whin I wint to set ut. An'—"

"One moment; may I see your clock?"

Mrs Hurley turned and shut an open door which had concealed an old hanging clock. Hewitt produced his watch and compared the time. "Still right, I see, Mrs Hurley," he said; "your clock keeps excellent time."

"'MRS HURLEY,' HE SAID, 'YOUR CLOCK KEEPS EXCELLENT TIME.'"

"It does that, sor, an' nivir more than claned twice by Rafferty since me own father (rest his soul!) lift ut here. 'Tis no bad clock, as Mr Rewse himsilf said oft an' again; an' I always kape ut by the Town Hall toime. But as I was sayin', Mr Main came back an' gave me the toime; thin he wint sthraight to his house, an' no more av him I saw till may be half afther three."

"And then?"

"An' thin, sor, he came across in a sad takin', wid a letther. 'Take ut,' sez he, 'an' have ut posted at Cullanin by the first that can get there. Mr Rewse has the sickness on him awful bad,' he sez, 'an' ye must not be near the place or ye'll take ut. I have him to bed, an' his clothes I shall burn behin' the cottage,' sez he, 'so if ye see smoke ye'll know what ut is. There'll be no docthor wanted. I'm wan mesilf, an' I'll do all for 'um. An' sure I knew him for a docthor ivir since he come. 'The cottage ye shall not come near,' he sez, 'till ut's over one way or another, an' yez can lave whativir av food an' dhrink we want midbetwixt the houses an' go back, an' I'll come and fetch ut. But have the letther posted,' he sez, 'at wanst. 'Tis not contagious,' he sez, 'bein' as I've dishinfected it mesilf. But kape yez away from the cottage.' An' I kept."

"And then did he go back to the cottage at once?"

"He did that, sor, an' a sore stew was he in to all seemin' — white as paper, and much need, too, the murtherin' scutt! An' him always so much the jintleman an' all. Well, I saw no more av him that day. Next day he laves another letther wid the dirthy' plates there mid-betwixt the houses, an' shouts for ut to be posted. 'Twas for the poor young jintleman's mother, sure, as was the other wan. An' the day afther there was another letther, an' wan for the undhertaker, too, for he tells me it's all over, an' he's dead. An' they buried him next day followin'."

"'HE LAVES ANOTHER LETTHER WID THE DIRTHY PLATES ... AN' SHOUTS FOR UT TO BE POSTED.'"

"So that from the time you went for the pail and saw Mr Rewse writing, till after the funeral, you were never at the cottage at all?"

"Nivir, sor; an' can ye blame me? Wid children an' Terence himself sick wid bronchitis in this house?"

"Of course, of course, you did quite right—indeed you only obeyed orders. But now think; do you remember on any one of those three days hearing a shot, or any other unusual noise in the cottage?"

"Nivir at all, sor. 'Tis that I've been thryin' to bring to mind these four days. Such may have been, but not that I heard."

"After you went for the pail, and before Mr Main returned to the house, did Mr Rewse leave the cottage at all, or might he have done so?"

"He did not lave at all, to my knowledge. Sure he *might* have gone an' he might have come back widout my knowin'. But see him I did not."

"Thank you, Mrs Hurley. I think we'll go across to the cottage now. If any people come, will you send them after us? I suppose a policeman is there?"

"He is, sor. An' the serjint is not far away. They've been in chyarge since Mr Bowyer wint away last—but shlapin' here."

Hewitt and Mr Bowyer walked towards the cottage. "Did you notice," said Mr Bowyer, "that the woman saw Rewse *writing letters*? Now what were those letters, and where are they? He has no correspondents that I know of but his mother and sister, and they heard nothing from him. Is this something else?— some other plot? There is something very deep here."

"Yes," Hewitt replied thoughtfully, "I think our inquiries may take us deeper than we have expected; and in the matter of those letters—yes, I think they may lie near the kernel of the mystery."

Here they arrived at the cottage—an uncommonly substantial structure for the district. It was square, of plain, solid brick, with a slated roof. On the patch of ground behind it there were still signs of the fires wherein Main had burnt Rewse's clothes and other belongings. And sitting on the windowsill in front was a big member of the R.I.C., soldierly and broad, who rose as they came, and saluted Mr Bowyer.

"Good day, constable," Mr Bowyer said. "I hope nothing has been disturbed?"

"Not a shtick, sor. Nobody's as much as gone in."

"Have any of the windows been opened or shut?" Hewitt asked.

"This wan was, sor," the policeman said, indicating the one behind him, "when they took away the corrpse, an' so was the next round the corrner. 'Tis the bedroom windies they are, an' they opened thim to give ut a bit av air. The other windy behin'—sittin'-room windy—has not been opened."

"Very well," Hewitt answered, "we'll take a look at that unopened window from the inside."

The door was opened and they passed inside. There was a small lobby, and on the left of this was the bedroom with two single beds. The only other room of consequence was the sitting-room, the cottage consisting merely of these, a small scullery and a narrow closet used as a bathroom, wedged between the bedroom and the sitting-room. They made for the single window of the sitting-room at the back. It was an ordinary sash window, and was shut, but the catch was not fastened. Hewitt examined the catch, drawing Mr Bowyer's attention to a bright scratch on the grimy brass. "See," he said, "that nick in the catch exactly corresponds with the narrow space between the two frames of the window. And look"—he lifted the bottom sash a little as he spoke—"there is the mark of a knife on the frame of the top sash. Somebody has come in by that window, forcing the catch with a knife."

"Yes, yes!" cried Mr Bowyer, greatly excited, "and he has gone out that way too, else why is the window shut and the catch not fastened? Why should he do that? What in the world does *this* thing mean?"

Before Hewitt could reply the constable put his head into the room and announced that one Larry Shanahan was at the door, and had been promised half a sovereign.

"One of the men who heard a shot," Hewitt said to Mr Bowyer. "Bring him in, constable."

The constable brought in Larry Shanahan, and Larry Shanahan brought in a strong smell of whisky. He was an extremely ragged person, with only one eye, which caused him to hold his head aside as he regarded Hewitt, much as a parrot does. On his face sun-scorched brown and fiery red struggled for mastery, and his voice was none of the clearest. He held his hat against his stomach with one hand and with the other pulled his forelock.

"An' which is the honourable jintleman," he said, "as do be burrnin' to prisint me wid a bit o' goold?"

"Here I am," said Hewitt, jingling money in his pocket, "and here is the half-sovereign. It's only waiting where it is till you have answered a few questions. They say you heard a shot fired hereabout?"

"Faith, an' that I did, sor. 'Twas a shot in this house, indade, no other."

"And when was it?"

"Sure, 'twas in the afthernoon."

"But on what day?"

"Last Tuesday sivin-noight, sor, as I know by rayson av Ballyshiel fair that I wint to."

"Tell me all about it."

"I will, sor. 'Twas pigs I was dhrivin' that day, sor, to Ballyshiel fair from just beyond Cullanin. At Cullanin, sor, I dhropped in wid Danny Mulcahy, that intintioned thravellin' the same way, an' while we tuk a thrifle av a dhrink in comes Dennis Grady, that was to go to Ballyshiel similarously. An' so we had another thrifle av a dhrink, or maybe a thrifle more, an' we wint togedther, passin' this way, sor, as ye may not know, bein' likely a shtranger. Well, sor, ut was as we were just forninst this place that there came a divil av a bang that makes us shtop simultaneous. 'What's that?' sez Dan. ''Tis a gunshot,' sez I, 'an' 'tis in the brick house too.' 'That is so,' sez Dennis; 'nowhere else.' And we lukt at wan another. 'An' what'll we do?' sez I. 'What would yez?' sez Dan; ' 'tis none av our business.' 'That is so,' sez Dennis again, and we wint on. Ut was quare, maybe, but it might aisily be wan av the jintlemen emptyin' a barr'l out o' windy or what not. An'—an' so—an' so—" Mr Shanahan scratched his ear, "an' so—we wint."

"And do you know at what time this was?"

Larry Shanahan ceased scratching, and seized his ear between thumb and forefinger, gazing severely at the floor with his one eye as he did so, plunged in computation. "Sure," he said, "'twould be—'twould be—let's see—'twould be—" he looked up, "'twould be half-past two maybe, or maybe a thrifle nearer three."

"And Main was in the place all the time after two," Mr Bowyer said, bringing down his fist on his open hand. "That finishes it. We've nailed him to the minute."

"Had you a watch with you?" asked Hewitt.

"Divil of a watch in the company, sor. I made an internal calculation. 'Tis foive mile from Cullanin, and we never lift till near half an hour after the Town Hall clock had struck twelve. 'Twould take us two hours and a thrifle more, considherin' the pigs, an' the rough road, an' the distance, an'—an' the thrifle of dhrink." His eye rolled slyly as he said it. "That was my calculation, sor."

Here the constable appeared with two more men. Each had the usual number of eyes, but in other respects they were very good copies of Mr Shanahan. They were both ragged, and neither bore any violent likeness to a teetotaler. "Dan Mulcahy and Dennis Grady," announced the constable.

Mr Dan Mulcahy's tale was of a piece with Mr Larry Shanahan's, and Mr Dennis Grady's was the same. They had all heard the shot, it was plain. What Dan had said to Dennis and what Dennis had said to Larry mattered little. Also they were all agreed that the day was Tuesday, by token of the fair. But as to the time of day there arose a disagreement.

"'Twas nigh soon afther wan o'clock," said Dan Mulcahy.

"Soon afther wan!" exclaimed Larry Shanahan with scorn. "Soon afther your grandmother's pig! 'Twas half afther two at laste. Ut sthruck twelve nigh half an hour before we lift Cullanin. Why, yez heard ut!"

"That I did not. Ut sthruck eleven, an' we wint in foive minutes."

"What fool-talk ye shpake, Dan Mulcahy. 'Twas twelve sthruck; I counted ut."

"Thin ye counted wrong. I counted ut, an' 'twas elivin."

"Yez nayther av yez right," interposed Dennis Grady. "'Twas not elivin when we lift; 'twas not, be the mother av Moses!"

"I wondher at ye, Dennis Grady; ye must have been dhrunk as a Kerry cow," and both Mulcahy and Shanahan turned upon the obstinate Grady, and the dispute waxed clamorous till Hewitt stopped it.

"Come, come," he said, "never mind the time then. Settle that between you after you've gone. Does either of you remember—not calculate, you know, but *remember*—the time you got to Ballyshiel?—the actual time by a clock—not a guess."

Not one of the three had looked at a clock at Ballyshiel.

"Do you remember anything about coming home again?"

They did not. They looked furtively at one another and presently broke into a grin.

"Ah! I see how *that* was," Hewitt said good-humouredly. "That's all now, I think. Come, it's ten shillings each, I think." And he handed over the money. The men touched their forelocks again, stowed away the money and prepared to depart. As they went Larry Shanahan stepped mysteriously back again and said in a whisper, "Maybe the jintlemen wud like me to kiss the book on ut? An' as to the toime—"

"Oh, no, thank you," Hewitt laughed. "We take your word for it, Mr Shanahan." And Mr Shanahan pulled his forelock again and vanished.

"There's nothing but confusion to be got from them," Mr Bowyer remarked testily. "It's a mere waste of time."

"No, no, not a waste of time," Hewitt replied, "nor a waste of money. One thing is made pretty plain. That is that the shot was fired on Tuesday. Mrs Hurley never noticed the report, but these three men were close by, and there is no doubt that they heard it. It's the only single thing they agree about at all. They contradict one another over everything else, but they agree completely in that. Of course I wish we could have got the exact time; but that can't be helped. As it is it is rather fortunate that they disagreed so entirely. Two of them are certainly wrong, and perhaps all three. In any case it wouldn't have been safe to trust to mere computation of time by three men just beginning to get drunk, who had no particular reason for remembering. But if by any chance they had agreed on the time we might have been led into a wrong track altogether by taking the thing as fact. But a gunshot is not such a doubtful thing. When three independent witnesses hear a gunshot together there can be little doubt that a shot has been fired. Now I think you'd better sit down. Perhaps you can find something to read. I'm about to make a very minute examination of this place, and it will probably bore you if you've nothing else to do."

But Mr Bowyer would think of nothing but the business in hand. "I don't understand that window," he said, shaking his finger towards it as he spoke. "Not at all. Why should Main want to get in and out by a window? He wasn't a stranger."

Hewitt began a most careful inspection of the whole surface of floor, ceiling, walls and furniture of the sitting-room. At the fireplace he stooped and lifted with great care a few sheets of charred paper from the grate. These he put on the window-ledge. "Will you just bring over that little screen," he asked, "to keep the draught from this burnt paper? Thank you. It looks like letter paper, and thick letter paper, since the ashes are very little broken. The weather has been fine, and there has been no fire in that grate for a long time. These papers have been carefully burned with a match or a candle."

"Ah! perhaps the letters poor young Rewse was writing in the morning. But what can they tell us?"

"Perhaps nothing—perhaps a great deal." Hewitt was examining the cinders keenly, holding the surface sideways to the light. "Come," he said, "see if I can guess Rewse's address in London. 17, Mountjoy Gardens, Hampstead. Is that it?"

"Yes. Is it there? Can you read it? Show me." Mr Bowyer hurried across the room, eager and excited.

"You can sometimes read words on charred paper," Hewitt replied, "as you may have noticed. This has curled and crinkled rather too much in the burning, but it is plainly notepaper with an embossed heading, which stands out rather clearly. He has evidently brought some notepaper with him from home in his trunk. Look, you can just see the ink lines crossing out the address; but there's little else. At the beginning of the letter there is 'My d—' then a gap, and then the last stroke of 'M' and the rest of the word 'mother.' 'My dear Mother,' or 'My dearest Mother' evidently. Something follows too in the same line, but that is unreadable. 'My dear Mother and Sister,' perhaps. After that there is nothing recognisable. The first letter looks rather like 'W,' but even that is indistinct. It seems to be a longish letter—several sheets, but they are stuck together in the charring. Perhaps more than one letter."

"The thing is plain," Mr Bowyer said. "The poor lad was writing home, and perhaps to other places, and Main, after his crime, burned the letters, because they would have stultified his own with the lying tale about smallpox."

Hewitt said nothing, but resumed his general search. He passed his hand rapidly over every inch of the surface of everything in the room. Then he entered the bedroom and began an inspection of the same sort there. There were two beds, one at each end of the room, and each inch of each piece of bed-linen passed rapidly under his sharp eye. After the bedroom he betook himself to the little bathroom, and then to the scullery. Finally he went outside and examined every board of a close fence that stood a few feet from the sitting-room window, and the brick-paved path lying between.

When it was all over he returned to Mr Bowyer. "Here is a strange thing," he said. "The shot passed clean through Rewse's body, striking no bones, and meeting no solid resistance. It was a good-sized bullet, as Dr O'Reilly testifies, and therefore must have had a large charge of powder behind it in the cartridge. After emerging from Rewse's back it *must* have struck something else in this confined place. Yet on nowhere—ceiling, floor, wall nor furniture—can I find the mark of a bullet nor the bullet itself."

"The bullet itself Main might easily have got rid of."

"Yes, but not the mark. Indeed, the bullet would scarcely be easy to get at if it had struck anything I have seen about here; it would have buried itself. Just look round now. Where could a bullet strike in this place without leaving its mark?"

Mr Bowyer looked round. "Well, no," he said, "nowhere. Unless the window was open and it went out that way."

"Then it must have hit the fence or the brick paving between, and there is no sign of a bullet there," Hewitt replied. "Push the sash as high as you please, the shot couldn't have passed *over* the fence without hitting the window first. As to the bedroom windows, that's impossible. Mr Shanahan and his friends would not only have heard the shot, they would have seen it—which they didn't."

"Then what's the meaning of it?"

"The meaning of it is simply this: either Rewse was shot somewhere else and his body brought here afterwards, or the article, whatever it was, that the bullet struck must have been taken away."

"Yes, of course. It's just another piece of evidence destroyed by Main, that's all. Every step we go we see the diabolical completeness of his plans. But now every piece of evidence missing only tells the more against him. The body alone condemns him past all redemption."

Hewitt was gazing about the room thoughtfully. "I think we'll have Mrs Hurley over here," he said; "she should tell us if anything is missing. Constable, will you ask Mrs Hurley to step over here?"

Mrs Hurley came at once and was brought into the sitting-room. "Just look about you, Mrs Hurley," Hewitt said, "in this room and everywhere else, and tell me if anything is missing that you can remember was here on the morning of the day you last saw Mr Rewse."

She looked thoughtfully up and down the room. "Sure, sor," she said, "'tis all there as ord'nary." Her eyes rested on the mantelpiece, and she added at once, "Except the clock, indade."

"Except the clock?"

"The clock ut is, sure. Ut stud on that same mantelpiece on that mornin' as ut always did."

"What sort of clock was it?"

"Just a plain round wan wid a metal case—an American clock they said ut was. But ut kept nigh as good time as me own."

"It *did* keep good time, you say?"

"Faith an' ut did, sor. Mine an' this ran together for weeks wid nivir a minute betune thim."

"Thank you, Mrs Hurley, thank you; that will do," Hewitt exclaimed, with something of excitement in his voice. He turned to Mr Bowyer. "We must find that clock," he said. "And there's the pistol; nothing has been seen of that. Come, help me search. Look for a loose board."

"But he'll have taken them away with him, probably."

"The pistol perhaps—although that isn't likely. The clock, no. It's evidence, man, evidence!" Hewitt darted outside and walked hurriedly round the cottage, looking this way and that about the country adjacent.

Presently he returned. "No," he said, "I think it's more likely in the house." He stood for a moment and thought. Then he made for the fireplace and flung the fender across the floor. All round the hearthstone an open crack extended. "See there!" he exclaimed as he pointed to it. He took the tongs, and with one leg levered the stone up till he could seize it in his fingers. Then he dragged it out and pushed it across the linoleum that covered the floor. In the space beneath lay a large revolver and a common American round nickel-plated clock. "See here!" he cried, "see here!" and he rose and placed the articles on the mantelpiece. The glass before the clock-face was smashed to atoms, and there was a gaping rent in the face itself. For a few seconds Hewitt regarded it as it stood, and then he turned to Mr Bowyer. "Mr Bowyer," he said, "we have done Mr Stanley Main a sad injustice. Poor young Rewse committed suicide. There is proof undeniable," and he pointed to the clock.

"HE TOOK THE TONGS, AND WITH ONE LEG LEVERED THE STONE UP."

"Proof? How? Where? Nonsense, man! Pooh! Ridiculous! If Rewse committed suicide, why should Main go to all that trouble and tell all those lies to prove that he died of smallpox? More even than that, what has he run away for?"

"I'll tell you, Mr Bowyer, in a moment. But first as to this clock. Remember, Main set his watch by the Cullanin Town Hall clock, and Mrs Hurley's clock agreed exactly. That we have proved ourselves today by my own watch. Mrs Hurley's clock still agrees. *This* clock was always kept in time with Mrs Hurley's. Main returned at two exactly. Look at the time by that clock—the time when the bullet crashed into and stopped it."

The time was three minutes to one.

Hewitt took the clock, unscrewed the winder and quickly stripped off the back, exposing the works. "See," he said, "the bullet is lodged firmly among the wheels, and has been torn into snags and strips by the impact. The wheels themselves are ruined altogether. The central axle which carries the hands is bent. See there! Neither hand will move in the slightest. That bullet struck the axle and fixed those hands immovably at the moment of time when Algernon Rewse died. Look at the main spring. It is less than half run out. Proof that the clock was going when the shot struck it. Main left Rewse alive and well at half-past nine. He did not return till two—when Rewse had been dead more than an hour."

"But then, hang it all! How about the lies, and the false certificate, and the bolting?"

"Let me tell you the whole tale, Mr Bowyer, as I conjecture it to have been. Poor young Rewse was, as you told me, in a bad state of health—thoroughly run down, I think you said. You said something of his engagement and the death of the lady. This pointed clearly to a nervous—a mental upset. Very well. He broods, and so forth. He must go away and find change of scene and occupation. His intimate friend Main brings him here. The holiday has its good effect perhaps, at first, but after a while it gets monotonous, and brooding sets in again. I do not know whether or not you happen to know it, but it is a fact that four-fifths of all persons suffering from melancholia have suicidal tendencies. This may never have been suspected by Main, who otherwise might not have left him so long alone. At any rate he *is* left alone, and he takes the opportunity. He writes a note to Main, and a long letter to his mother—an awful, heartbreaking letter, with a terrible picture of the mental agony wherein he was to die—perhaps with a tincture of religious mania in it, and prophesying merited hell for himself in the hereafter. This done, he simply stands up from this table, at which he has been writing, and with his back to the fireplace shoots himself. There he lies till Main returns an hour later. Main finds the door shut, and nobody answers his knock. He goes round to the sitting-room window, looks through, and perhaps he sees the body. Anyway he pushes back the catch with his knife, opens the window and gets in, and *then* he sees. He is completely knocked out of time. The thing is terrible. What shall he—what can he do? Poor Rewse's mother and sister dote on him, and his mother is an invalid—heart disease. To let her see that awful letter would be to kill her. He burns the letter, also the note to himself. Then an idea strikes him. Even without the letter the news of her boy's suicide will probably kill the poor old lady. Can she be prevented hearing of it? Of his death she must know—that's inevitable. But as to the manner? Would it not be possible to concoct some kind lie? And then the opportunities of the situation occur to him. Nobody but himself knows of it. He is a medical man, fully qualified, and empowered to give certificates of death. More, there is an epidemic of smallpox in the neighbourhood. What easier, with a little management, than to call the death one by smallpox? Nobody would be anxious to examine too closely the corpse of a small-pox patient. He decides that he will do it. He writes the letter to Mrs Rewse announcing that her son has the disease, and he forbids Mrs Hurley to come near the place for fear of infection. He cleans the floor—it is linoleum here, you see, and the stains were fresh—burns the clothes, cleans and stops the wound. At every turn his medical knowledge is of use. He puts the smashed clock and the pistol out of sight under the hearth. In a word, he carries out the whole thing rather cleverly, and a terrible few days he must have passed. It never strikes him that he has dug a frightful pit for his own feet. You are suspicious, and you come across. In a perhaps rather peremptory manner you tell him how suspicious his conduct has been. And then a sense of his terrible position comes upon him like a thunderclap. He sees it all. He has deliberately of his own motion destroyed every evidence of the suicide. There is no evidence in the world that Rewse did not die a natural death, except the body, and that you are going to dig up. He sees now (you remind him of it, in fact) that *he* is the one man alive who can profit by Rewse's death. And there is the shot body, and there is the false death certificate, and there are the lying letters, and the tales to the neighbours and everything. He has himself destroyed everything that proves suicide. All that remains points to a foul murder, and to him as the murderer. Can you wonder at his complete breakdown and his flight? What else in the world could the poor fellow do?"

"Well, well—yes, yes," Mr Bowyer replied thoughtfully, "it seems very plausible, of course. But still, look at probabilities, my dear sir, look at probabilities."

"No, but look at *possibilities*. There is that clock. Get over it if you can. Was there ever a more insurmountable alibi? Could Main possibly be here shooting Rewse and halfway between here and Cullanin at the same time? Remember, Mrs Hurley saw him come back at two, and she had been watching for an hour, and could see more than half a mile up the road."

"Well, yes, I suppose you're right. And what must we do now?"

"Bring Main back. I think we should advertise to begin with. Say, 'Rewse is proved to have died over an hour before you came. All safe. Your evidence is wanted,' or something of that sort. And we must set the telegraph going. The police already are looking for him, no doubt. Meanwhile I will look here for a clue myself."

The advertisement was successful in two days. Indeed, Main afterwards said that he was at the time, once the first terror was over, in doubt whether or not it would be best to go back and face the thing out, trusting to his innocence. He could not venture home for money, nor to his bank, for fear of the police.

He chanced upon the advertisement as he searched the paper for news of the case, and that decided him. His explanation of the matter was precisely as Hewitt had expected. His only thought till Mr Bowyer first arrived at the cottage had been to smother the real facts and to spare the feelings of Mrs Rewse and her daughter, and it was not till that gentleman put them so plainly before him that he in the least realised the dangers of his position. That his fears for Mrs Rewse were only too well grounded was proved by events, for the poor old lady only survived her son by a month.

These events took place some little while ago, as may be gathered from the fact that Miss Rewse has now been Mrs Stanley Main for nearly three years.

5

THE AFFAIR OF MRS SETON'S CHILD

It has struck me that many of my readers may wonder that, although I have set down in detail a number of interesting cases wherein Hewitt figured with success, I have scarcely as much as alluded to his failures. For failures he had, and of a fair number. More than once he has found his search met, perhaps at the beginning, perhaps after some little while, by an impenetrable wall of darkness through which no clue led. At other times he has lost time on a false trail while his quarry escaped. At others still the stupidity or inaccuracy of some person upon whom he has depended for information has set his plans to naught. The reason why none of these cases have been embodied in the present papers is simply this: that a problem with no answer, a puzzle with no explanation, an incident with no satisfactory end, as a rule lends itself but poorly to purposes of popular narrative, and it is often difficult to make understood and appreciated any degree of skill and acumen unless it produces a clear and intelligible result. That such results attended Hewitt's efforts in an extraordinary degree those who have followed my narratives so far will need no assurance; but withal impossibilities still remain impossibilities, for Hewitt as for the dullest creature alive. On some other occasion I may perhaps set out at length a case in which Martin Hewitt achieved nothing more than unqualified failure; for the present I shall content myself with a case which, although it was completely cleared up in the end, yet for some while baffled Hewitt because of some of the reasons I have alluded to.

On the ground floor of the building wherein Hewitt kept his office, and in which I myself had my chambers, were the offices of Messrs. Streatley & Raikes, an old-fashioned firm of family solicitors. Messrs. Streatley & Raikes's junior clerk appeared in Hewitt's outer office one morning with the query, "Is your guv'nor in?"

Kerrett admitted the fact.

"Will you tell him Mr Raikes sends his compliments and will be obliged if he can step downstairs for a few minutes? It's a client of ours—a lady—and she's in a great state about losing her baby or something. Say Mr Raikes would bring her up, only she seems too ill to get up the stairs."

This was the purport of the message which Kerrett brought into the inner room, and in three minutes Hewitt was in Streatley & Raikes's office.

"I thought the only useful thing possible would be to send for you, Mr Hewitt," Mr Raikes explained; "indeed, if my client had been better acquainted with London, no doubt she would have come to you direct. She is in a bad state in the inner office. Her name is Mrs Seton; her husband is a recent client of ours. Quite young, and rather wealthy people, so far as I know. Made a fortune early, I believe, in South Africa, and came here to live. Their child—their only child, a little toddler of two years or thereabout—disappeared yesterday in a most mysterious way, and all efforts to find it seem to have failed as yet. The police have been set going everywhere, but there is no news as yet. Mrs Seton seems to have passed a dreadful night, and could think of nothing better to do this morning than to come to us. She has her maid with her, and looks to be breaking down entirely. I believe she's lying on the sofa in my private room now. Will you see her? I think you might hear what she has to say, whether you take the case in hand or not; something may strike you, and in any case it will comfort her to get your opinion. I told her all about you, you know, and she clutched at the chance eagerly. Shall I see if we may go in?"

Mr Raikes knocked at the door of his inner sanctum and waited; then he knocked again and set the door ajar. There was a quiet "Come in," and pushing open the door the lawyer motioned Hewitt to follow him.

On the sofa facing the door sat a lady, very pale, and exhibiting plain signs of grief and physical weariness. A heavy veil was thrown back over her bonnet, and her maid stood at her side holding a bottle of salts. As she saw Hewitt she made as if to rise, but he stepped quickly forward and laid his hand on her shoulder. "Pray don't disturb yourself, Mrs Seton," he said; "Mr Raikes has told me something of your trouble, and perhaps when I know a little more I shall be able to offer you some advice. But remember that it will be very important for you to maintain your strength and spirits as much as possible."

"ON THE SOFA FACING THE DOOR SAT A LADY, VERY PALE, AND EXHIBITING PLAIN SIGNS OF GRIEF."

"This is Mr Martin Hewitt, you know," Mr Raikes here put in—"of whom I was speaking."

Mrs Seton inclined her head, and with a very obvious effort began. "It is my child, you know, Mr Hewitt—my little boy Charley; we can't find him."

"Mr Raikes has told me so. When did you see the child last?"

"Yesterday morning. His nurse left him sitting on the floor in a room we call the small morning-room, where we sometimes allowed him to play when nurse was out, because the nursery was out of hearing, except from the bedrooms. I myself was in the large morning-room, and as he seemed to be very quiet I went to look, and found he was not there."

"You looked elsewhere, of course?"

"Yes; but he was nowhere in the house, and none of the servants had seen him. At first I supposed that his nurse had gone back to the small morning-room and taken him with her—I had sent her on an errand—but when she returned I found that was not the case."

"Can he walk?"

"Oh, yes, he can walk quite well. But he could scarcely have come out from the room without my hearing him. The two rooms, the morning-room and the small sitting-room, are on opposite sides of the same passage."

"Do the doors face each other?"

"No; the door of the small room is farther up the passage than the other. But in any case he was nowhere in the house."

"But if he left the room he must have got out somehow. Is there no other door?"

"Yes, there is a French window, with the lower panels of wood, in the room; it gives on to a few steps leading down into the garden; but that was closed and bolted on the inside."

"You found no trace whatever of him, I take it, on the whole premises?"

"Not a trace of any sort, nor had anybody about the place seen him."

"Did you yourself actually see him in this room, or have you merely the nurse's word for it?"

"I saw her put him there. She left him playing with a box of toys. When I went to look for him the toys were there, scattered on the floor, but he had gone." Mrs Seton sank on the arms of her maid and her breast heaved.

"I'm sure," Hewitt said, "You'll keep your nerves as steady as you can, Mrs Seton: much may depend on it. If you have nothing else to tell me now, I think I will come to your house at once, look at it, and question your servants myself. Meantime, what has been done?"

"The police have been notified everywhere, of course," Mr Raikes said, handing Hewitt a printed bill, damp from the press; "and here is a bill containing a description of the child and offering a reward, which is being circulated now."

Hewitt glanced at the bill and nodded. "That is quite right," he said, "so far as I can tell at present. But I must see the place. Do you feel strong enough to come home now, Mrs Seton?"

Hewitt's business-like decision and confidence of manner gave the lady fresh strength. "The brougham is here," she said, "and we can drive home at once. We live at Cricklewood."

A fine pair of horses stood before the brougham, though they still bore signs of hard work; and indeed they had been kept at their best pace all that morning. All the way to Cricklewood Hewitt kept Mrs Seton in conversation, never for a moment leaving her attention disengaged. The missing child, he learned, was the only one, and the family had only been in England for something less than a year. Mr Seton had become possessed of real property in South Africa, had sold it in London, and had determined to settle here.

A little way past Shoot-up Hill the coachman swung his pair off to the left, and presently entering a gate, pulled up before a large, old-fashioned house.

Here Hewitt immediately began a complete examination of the premises. The possible exits from the grounds, he found, were four in number: the two wide front gates giving on to the carriage-drive, the kitchen and stable entrance, and a side gate in a fence—always locked, however. Inside the house, from the central hall, a passage to the right led to another wherein was the door of the small morning-room. This was a very ordinary room, fifteen feet square or so, lighted by the glass in the French window, the bottom panes of which, however, had been filled in with wood. The contents of a box of toys lay scattered on the floor, and the box itself lay near.

"Have these toys been moved," Hewitt asked, "since the child was missed?"

"No, we haven't allowed anything to be disturbed. The disappearance seemed so wholly unaccountable that we thought the police might wish to examine the place exactly as it was. They did not seem to think it necessary, however."

Hewitt knelt and examined the toys without disturbing them. They were of very good quality, and represented a farmyard, with horses, carts, ducks, geese and cows complete. One of the carts had had a string attached so that it might be pulled along the floor.

"Now," Hewitt said, rising, "you think, Mrs Seton, that the child could not have toddled through the passage, and so into some other part of the house, without you hearing him?"

"Well," Mrs Seton answered with indecision, "I thought so at first, but I begin to doubt. Because he *must* have done so, I suppose."

They went into the passage. The door of the large morning-room was four or five yards further toward the passage leading to the hall, and on the opposite side. "The floor in this passage," Hewitt observed, "is rather thickly carpeted. See here, I can walk on it at a good pace without noise."

Mrs Seton assented. "Of course," she said, "if he got past here he might have got anywhere about the house, and so into the grounds. There is a veranda outside the drawing-room, and doors in various places.'

"Of course the grounds have been completely examined?"

"Oh, yes, every inch."

"The weather has been very dry, unfortunately," Hewitt said, "and it would be useless for me to look for footprints on your hard gravel, especially of so small a child. Let us come back to the room. Is the French window fastened as you found it?"

"Yes; nothing has been changed."

The French window was, as is usual, one of two casements joining in the centre and fastened by bolts top and bottom. "It is not your habit, I see," Hewitt observed, "to open both halves of the window."

"No; one side is always fastened, the other we secure by the bottom bolt because the catch of the handle doesn't always act properly."

"And you found that bolt fastened as I see it now?"

"Yes."

Hewitt lifted the bolt and opened the door. Four or five steps led parallel with the face of the wall to a sort of path which ran the whole length of the house on this side, and was only separated from a quiet public lane by a low fence and a thin hedge. Almost opposite a small, light gate stood in the fence, firmly padlocked.

"I see," Hewitt remarked, "your house is placed close against one side of the grounds. Is that the side gate which you always keep locked?"

Mrs Seton replied in the affirmative, and Hewitt laid his hand on the gate in question. "Still," he said, "if security is the object I should recommend hinges a little less rural in pattern; see here," and he gave the gate a jerk upward, lifting the hinge-pins from their sockets and opening the gate from that side, the padlock acting as hinge. "Those hinges," he added, "were meant for a heavier gate than that;" and he replaced the gate.

"'THOSE HINGES WERE MEANT FOR A HEAVIER GATE THAN THAT.'"

"Yes," Mrs Seton replied; "I am obliged to you; but that doesn't concern us now. The French window was bolted on the inside. Would you like to see the servants?"

The servants were produced, and Hewitt questioned each in turn, but not one would admit having seen anything of Master Charles Seton after he had been left in the small morning-room. A rather stupid groom fancied he had seen Master Charles on the side lawn, but then remembered that that must have been the day before. The cook, an uncommonly thin, sharp-featured woman for one of her trade, was especially positive that she had not seen him all that day. "And she would be sure to have remembered if she had seen him leaving the house," she said, "because she was the more particular since he was lost the last time."

This was news to Hewitt. "Lost the last time?" he asked; "why, what is this, Mrs Seton? Was he lost once before?"

"Oh, yes," Mrs Seton answered, "six or seven weeks ago. But that was quite different. He strayed out at the front gate, and was brought back from the police station in the evening."

"But this may be most important," Hewitt said. "You should certainly have told me. Tell me now exactly what happened on this first occasion."

"But it was really quite an ordinary sort of accident. He was left alone and got out through an open gate. Of course we were very anxious; but we had him back the same evening. Need we waste time in talking about that?"

"But it will be no waste of time, I assure you. What was it that happened, exactly?"

"Nurse was about to take him for a short walk just before lunch. On the front lawn he suddenly remembered a whip which had been left in the nursery, and insisted on taking it with him. She left him and went back for it, taking, however, some little time to find it. When she returned he was nowhere to be seen; but one of the gates was a couple of feet or more open — it had caught on a loose stone in swinging to — and no doubt he had wandered off that way. A lady found him some distance away, and, not knowing to whom he belonged, took him that evening to a police station, and as messages had been sent to the police stations, we had him back soon after he was left there."

"Do you know who the lady was?"

"Her name was Mrs Clark. She left her name and address at the police station, and of course I wrote to thank her. But there was some mistake in taking it down, I suppose, for the letter was returned marked 'not known.'"

"Then you never saw this lady yourself?"

"No."

"I think I will make a note of the exact description of the child and then visit the police station to which this lady took him six weeks ago. Fair, curly hair, I think, and blue eyes? Age two years and three months; walks and runs well, and speaks fairly plainly. Dress?"

"Pale blue llama frock with lace, white under-linen, linen overall, pale blue silk socks and tan shoes. Everything good as new except the shoes, which were badly worn at the backs, through a habit he has of kicking back and downward with his heels when sitting. They were rather old shoes, and only used indoors."

"If I remember aright nothing was said of those shoes in the printed bill?"

"Was that so? No, I believe not. I have been so worried."

"Yes, Mrs Seton, of course. It is most creditable in you to have kept up so well while I have been making my inquiries. Go now and take a good rest while I do what is possible. By the way, where was Mr Seton yesterday morning when you missed the boy?"

"In the City. He has some important business in hand just now."

"And today?"

"He has gone to the City again. Of course he is sadly worried; but he saw that everything possible was done, and his business was very important."

"Just so. Mr Seton was not married before, I presume — if I may?"

"No, certainly not; why do you ask?"

"I beg your pardon, but I have a habit of asking almost every question I can think of; I can't know too much of a case, you know, and most unlikely pieces of information sometimes turn out useful. Thank you for your patience; I will try another plan now."

Mrs Seton had kept up remarkably well during Hewitt's examination, but she was plainly by no means a strong woman, and her maid came again to her assistance as Hewitt left. Hewitt himself made for the police station. Few inspectors indeed of the Metropolitan Police force did not know Hewitt by sight, and the one here in charge knew him well. He remembered very well the occasion, six weeks or so before, when Mrs Clark brought Mrs Seton's child to the station. He was on duty himself at the time, and he turned up the book containing an entry on the subject. From this it appeared that the lady gave the address No. 89, Sedgby Road, Belsize Park.

"I suppose you didn't happen to know the lady," Hewitt asked—"by sight or otherwise?"

"No, I didn't, and I'm not sure I could swear to her again," the inspector answered. "She wore a heavy veil, and I didn't see much of her face. One rum thing I noticed, though: she seemed rather taken with the baby, and as she stooped down to kiss him before she went away I could see an old scar on her throat. It was just the sort of scar I've seen on a man that's had his throat cut and got over it. She wore a high collar to hide it, but stooping shifted the collar, and so I saw it."

"Did she seem an educated woman?"

"Oh yes; perfect lady; spoke very nice. I told her a baby had been inquired after by Mrs Seton, and from the description I'd no doubt this was the one. And so it was."

"At what time was this?"

"7.10 p.m., exactly. Here it is, all entered properly."

"Now as to Sedgby Road, Belsize Park. Do you happen to know it?"

"Oh, yes, very well. Very quiet, respectable road indeed. I only know it through walking through."

"I see a suburban directory on the shelf behind you. Do you mind pulling it down? Thanks. Let us find Sedgby Road. Here it is. See, there *is* no No. 89; the highest number is 67."

"No more there is," the inspector answered, running his finger down the column; "and there's no Clark in the road, that's more. False address, that's plain. And so they've lost him again, have they? We had notice yesterday, of course, and I've just got some bills. This last seems a queer sort of affair, don't it? Child sitting inside the house disappeared like a ghost, and all the doors and windows fastened inside."

Hewitt agreed that the affair had very uncommon features, and presently left the station and sought a cab. All the way back to his office he considered the matter deeply. As a matter of fact he was at a loss. Certain evidence he had seen in the house, but it went a very little way, and beyond that there was merely no clue whatever. There were features of the child's first estrayal also that attracted him, though it might very easily be the case that nothing connected the two events. There was an unknown woman—apparently a lady—who had once had her throat cut, bringing the child back after several hours, and giving a false name and address, for since the address was false, the same was probably the case with the name. Why was this? This time the child was still absent, and nothing whatever was there to suggest in what direction he might be followed, neither was there anything to indicate why he should be detained anywhere, if detained he was. Hewitt determined, while awaiting any result that the bills might bring, to cause certain inquiries to be made into the antecedents of the Setons. Moreover, other work was waiting, and the Seton business must be put aside for a few hours at least.

Hewitt sat late in his office that evening, and at about nine o'clock Mrs Seton returned. The poor woman seemed on the verge of serious illness. She had received two anonymous letters, which she brought with her, and with scarcely a word placed before Hewitt's eyes.

The first he opened and read as follows:—

"The writer observes that you are offering a reward for the recovery of your child. There is no necessity for this; Charley is quite safe, happy, and in good hands. Pray do not instruct detectives or take any such steps just yet. The child is well and shall be returned to you. This I swear solemnly. His errand is one of mercy; pray have patience."

Hewitt turned the letter and envelope in his hand. "Good paper, of the same sort as the envelope," he remarked, "but only a half sheet, freshly torn off, probably because the other side bore an address heading; therefore most likely from a respectable sort of house. The writing is a woman's, and good, though the writer was agitated when she did it. Posted this afternoon, at Willesden."

"You see," Mrs Seton said anxiously, "she knows his name. She calls him 'Charley.'"

"Yes," Hewitt answered; "there may be something in that, or there may not. The name Charles Seton is on the bills, isn't it? And they have been visible publicly all day today. So that the name may be more easily explained than some other parts of the letter. For instance, the writer says that the child's 'errand' is one of mercy. The little fellow may be very intelligent—no doubt is—but children of two years old as a rule do not practise errands of mercy—nor indeed errands of any sort. Can you think of anything whatever, Mrs Seton, in connection with your family history, or indeed anything else, that may throw light on that phrase?"

He looked keenly at her as he asked, but her expression was one of blank doubt merely, as she shook her head slowly and answered in the negative. Hewitt turned to the other letter and read this:—

"Madam,—

"If you want your child you had better make an arrangement with me. You fancy he has strayed, but as a matter of fact he has been stolen, and you little know by whom. You will never get him back except through me, you may rest assured of that. Are you prepared to pay me one hundred pounds (£100) if I hand him to you, and no questions asked? Your present reward,

£20, is paltry; and you may finally bid goodbye to your child if you will not accept my terms. If you do, say as much in an advertisement to the *Standard*, addressed to

"Veritas."

"A man's handwriting," Hewitt commented; "fairly well formed, but shaky. The writer is not in first-rate health—each line totters away in a downward slope at the end. I shouldn't be surprised to hear that the gentleman drank. Postmark, Hampstead; posted this afternoon also. But the striking thing is the paper and envelope. They are each of exactly the same kind and size as those of the other letter. The paper also is a half sheet, and torn off on the same side as the other; confirmation of my suspicion that the object is to get rid of the printed address. I shall be surprised if both these were not written in the same house. That looks like a traitor in the enemy's camp; the question is, which is the traitor?" Hewitt regarded the letters intently for a few seconds and then proceeded. "Plainly," he said, "if these letters are written by people who know anything about the matter, one writer is lying. The woman promises that the child shall be returned without reward or search, and talks generally as if the taking away of the child, or the estrayal, or whatever it was, were a very virtuous sort of proceeding. The man says plainly that the child has been stolen, with no attempt to gloss the matter, and asserts that nothing will get the child back but heavy blackmail—a very different story. On the other hand, can there be any concerted design in these two letters? Are they intended, each from its own side, to play up to a certain result?" Hewitt paused and thought. Then he asked suddenly: "Do you recognise anything familiar either in the handwriting or the stationery of these letters?"

"No, nothing."

"Very well," Hewitt said, "we will come to closer quarters with the blackmailer, I think. You needn't commit yourself to paying anything, of course."

"But, Mr Hewitt, I will gladly pay or do anything. The hundred pounds is nothing. I will pay it gladly if I can only get my child."

"Well, well, we shall see. The man may not be able to do what he offers, after all, but that we will test. It is too late now for an advertisement in tomorrow morning's *Standard*, but there is the *Evening Standard*—he may even mean that—and the next morning's. I will have an advertisement inserted in both, inviting this man to make an appointment, and prove the genuineness of his offer; that will fetch him if he wants the money, and can do anything for it. Have you nothing else to tell me?"

"Nothing. But have you ascertained nothing yourself? Don't say I've to pass another night in such dreadful suspense!"

"I'm afraid, Mrs Seton, I must ask you to be patient a little longer. I have ascertained something, but it has not carried me far as yet. Remember that if there is anything at all in these anonymous letters (and I think there is) the child is at any rate safe, and to be found one way or another. Both agree in that." This he said mainly to comfort his client, for in fact he had learned very little. His news from the City as to Mr Seton's early history had been but meagre. He was known as a successful speculator, and that was almost all. There was an indefinite notion that he had been married once before, but nothing more.

All the next day Hewitt did nothing in the case. Another affair, a previous engagement, kept him hard at work in his office all day, and indeed had this not been the case he could have done little. His City inquiries were still in progress, and he awaited, moreover, a reply to the advertisement. But at about half-past seven in the evening this telegram arrived—

Child returned. Come at once.—Seton.

In five minutes Hewitt was making north-west in a hansom, and in half an hour he was ringing the bell at the Setons' house. Within, Mrs Seton was still semi-hysterical, clasping the child—an intelligent-looking little fellow—in her arms, and refusing to release her hold of him for a moment. Mr Seton stood before the fire in the same room. He was a smart-looking, scrupulously dressed man of thirty-five or thereabouts, and he began explaining his telegram as soon as he had wished Hewitt good-evening.

"The child's back," he said, "and of course that's the great thing. But I'm not satisfied, Mr Hewitt. I want to know why it was taken away, and I want to punish somebody. It's really very extraordinary. My poor wife has been driving about all day—she called on you, by the bye, but you were out" (Hewitt credited this to Kerrett, who had been told he must not be disturbed), "and she has been all over the place uselessly, unable to rest, of course. Well, I have been at home since half-past four, and at about six I was smoking in the small morning-room—I often use it as a smoking-room—and looking out at the French window. I came away from there, and half an hour or more later, as it was getting dusk, I remembered I had left the French window open, and sent a servant to shut it. She went straight to the room, and there on the floor, where he was seen last, she found the child playing with his toys as though nothing had happened!"

"And how was he dressed—as he is now?"

"Yes, just as he was when we missed him."

Hewitt stepped up to the child as he sat on his mother's lap, and rubbed his cheek, speaking pleasantly to him. The little fellow looked up and smiled, and Hewitt observed: "One thing is noticeable: this linen overall is almost clean. Little boys like this don't keep one white overall clean for three days, do they? And see—those shoes—aren't they new? Those he had were old, I think you said, and tan-coloured."

The shoes now on the child's feet were of white leather, with a noticeable sewn ornamentation in silk. His mother had not noticed them before, and as she looked he lifted his little foot higher and said. "Look, mummy, more new shoes!"

"Ask him," suggested Hewitt hurriedly, "who gave them to him."

His father asked him, and the little fellow looked puzzled. After a pause, he said, "Mummy."

"No," his mother answered, "*I* didn't."

He thought a moment and then said, "No, no, not *vis* mummy—course not." And for some little while after that the only answer procurable from him was, "Course not," which seemed to be a favourite phrase of his.

"Have you asked him where he has been?"

"Yes," his mother answered, "but he only says 'Ta-ta.'"

"Ask him again."

She did. This time, after a little reflection, he pointed his chubby arm toward the door and said. "Been dere."

"Who took you?" asked Mrs Seton.

Again Charley seemed puzzled. Then, looking doubtfully at his mother, he said "Mummy."

"No, not mummy," she answered; and his reply was "Course not," after which he attempted to climb on her shoulder.

Then, at Hewitt's suggestion, he was asked whom he went to see. This time the reply was prompt.

"Poor daddy," he said.

"What, *this* daddy?"

"No, not *vis* daddy—course not." And that was all that could be got from him.

"He will probably say things in the next day or two which may be useful," Hewitt said, "if you listen pretty sharply. Now I should like to go to the small morning-room."

In time room in question the door was still open. Outside the moon had risen and made the evening almost as clear as day. Hewitt examined the steps and the path at their foot, but all was dry and hard, and showed no footmark. Then, as his eye rested on the small gate, "See here," he exclaimed suddenly, "somebody has been in, lifting the gate, as I showed Mrs Seton when I was last here. The gate has been replaced in a hurry, and only the top hinge has dropped in its place; the bottom one is disjointed." He lifted the gate once more and set it back. The ground just along its foot was softer than in the parts surrounding, and here Hewitt perceived the print of a heel. It was the heel-mark of a woman's boot, small and sharp and of the usual curved D-shape. Nowhere else within or without was there the slightest mark. Hewitt went some distance either way in the outer lane, but without discovering anything more.

"I think I will borrow those new shoes," Hewitt said on his return. "I think I should be disposed to investigate further in any case, for my own satisfaction. The thing interests me. By the way, Mrs Seton, tell me, would these shoes be more likely to have been bought at a regular shoemaker's or at a baby-linen shop?"

"Certainly I should say at a baby-linen shop," Mrs Seton answered; "they are of excellent quality, and for babies' shoes of this fancy description one would never go to an ordinary shoemaker's."

"So much the better, because the baby-linen shops are fewer than the shoemakers'. I may take these, then? Perhaps before I go you had better make quite certain that there is nothing else about the child which is not your own."

There was nothing, and with the shoes in his pocket Hewitt regained his cab and travelled back to his office. The case, from its very bareness and simplicity, puzzled him. Why was the child taken? Plainly not to keep, for it had been returned almost as it went. Plainly also not for the sake of reward or blackmail, for here was the child safely back, before the anonymous blackmailer had had a chance of earning his money. More, the advertised reward had not been claimed. Also it could not be a matter of malice or revenge, for the child was quite unharmed, and indeed seemed to have been quite happy. No conceivable family complication, previous to the marriage of Mr and Mrs Seton, could induce anybody to take away and return the child, which was undoubtedly Mrs Seton's. Then who could be the "poor daddy" and "mummy"—not *"vis* daddy" and not *"vis* mummy"—that the child had been with? The Setons knew nothing of them. It was difficult to see what it could all mean.

Arrived at his office, Hewitt took a map, and, setting the leg of a pair of compasses on the site of the Setons' house, described a circle, including in its radius all Willesden and Hampstead. Then, with the Suburban Directory to help him, he began searching out and noting all the baby-linen shops in the area. After all, there were not many—about a dozen. This done, Hewitt went home.

In the morning he began his hunt. His design was to call at each of the shops until he had found in which a pair of shoes of that particular pattern had been sold on the day of little Charley Seton's disappearance. The first two shops he tried did not keep shoes of the pattern, and had never had them, and the young ladies behind the counter seemed vastly amused at Hewitt's inquiries. Nothing perturbed, he tried the next shop on his list in the Hampstead district. There they kept such shoes as a rule, but were "out of them at present." Hewitt immediately sent his card to the proprietress, requesting a few minutes' interview.

The lady—a very dignified lady indeed—in black silk, gray corkscrew curls and spectacles, came out with Hewitt's card between her fingers. He apologised for troubling her, and, stepping out of hearing from the counter, explained that his business was urgent. "A child has been taken away by some unauthorised person, whom I am endeavouring to trace. This person bought this pair of shoes on Monday. You keep such shoes, I find, though they are not in stock at present, and, as they appear to be of an uncommon sort, possibly they were bought here."

The lady looked at them. "Yes," she said, "this pattern of shoe is made especially for me. I do not think you can buy them at other places."

"'THIS PATTERN OF SHOE IS MADE ESPECIALLY FOR ME.'"

"Then may I ask you to inquire from your assistants if any were sold on Monday, and to whom?"

"Certainly." Then there were consultations behind counters and desks, and examinations of carbon-papered books. In the end the proprietress came to Hewitt, followed by a young lady of rather pert and self-confident aspect. "We find," she said, "that two pairs of these shoes were sold on Monday. But one pair was afterwards brought back and exchanged for others less expensive. This young lady sold both."

"Ah, then possibly she may remember something of the person who bought the pair which was *not* exchanged."

"Yes," the assistant answered at once, addressing herself to the lady, "it was Mrs Butcher's servant."

The proprietress frowned slightly. "Oh, indeed," she said, "Mrs Butcher's servant, was it? There have been inquiries about Mrs Butcher before, I believe, though not *here*. Mrs Butcher is a woman who takes babies to mind, and is said to make a trade of adopting them, or finding people anxious to adopt them. I know nothing of her, nor do I want to. She lives somewhere not far off, and you can get her address, I believe, from the greengrocer's round the corner."

"Does she keep more than one servant?"

"Oh, I think not; but no doubt the greengrocer can say." The lady seemed to feel it an affront that she should be supposed to know anything of Mrs Butcher, and Hewitt consequently started for the greengrocer's. Now this was just one of those cases in which dependence on information given by other people put Hewitt on the wrong scent. He spent that day in a fatiguing pursuit of Mrs Butcher's servant, with adventures rather amusing in themselves, but quite irrelevant to the Seton case. In the end, when he had captured her, and proceeded to open a cunning battery of inquiries, under plea of a bet with a friend that the shoes could not be matched, he soon found that *she* had been the purchaser who, after buying just such a pair of shoes, had returned and exchanged them for something cheaper. And the only outcome of his visit to the baby-linen shop was the waste of a day. It was indeed just one of those checks which, while they may hamper the progress of a narrative for popular reading, are nevertheless inseparable from the matter-of-fact experience of Hewitt's profession.

With a very natural rage in his heart, but with as polite an exterior as possible, Hewitt returned to the baby-linen shop in the evening. The whole case seemed barren of useful evidence, and at each turn as yet he had found himself helpless. At the shop the self-confident young lady calmly admitted that soon after he had left something had caused her to remember that it was the other customer who had kept the white shoes, and not Mrs Butcher's servant.

"And do you know the other customer?" he asked.

"No; she was quite a stranger. She brought in a little boy from a cab and bought a lot of things for him—a suit of outdoor clothes as well as the shoes."

"Ah! now probably this is what I want. Can you remember anything of the child?"

"Yes; he was a pretty little fellow, about two years old or so, with curls. She called him Charley."

"Did she put the things on him in the shop?"

"Not the frock; but she put on the outer coat, the hat and the shoes. I can remember it all now quite well—now I have had time to think."

"Then what shoes did the child wear when he came in?"

"Rather old tan-coloured ones."

"Then I think this is the person I am after. You say you never saw her at any other time before or since. Try to describe her."

"Well, she was a lady well dressed, in black. She had a very high collar to hide a scar on her neck, like the scars people have sometimes after abscesses, I think. I could see it from the side when she stooped down."

"And are you sure she had nothing sent home? Did she take everything with her?"

"Yes; nothing was sent, else we should know her address, you know."

"She didn't happen to pay with a banknote, did she?"

"No; in cash."

Hewitt left with little more ceremony, and made the best of his way to his friend the inspector at the police station. Here was the woman with the scarred neck again—Charley's deliverer once, now his kidnapper. If only something else could be ascertained of her—some small clue that might bring her identity into view—the thing would be done.

At the station, however, there was something new. A man had just come in, very drunk, and had given himself into custody for kidnapping the child Charles Seton, whose description was set forth on the bill which still appeared on the notice-board outside the station. When Hewitt arrived, the man was lolling, wretched and maudlin, against the rail, and, oblivious of most of the questions addressed to him, was ranting and snivelling by turns. His dress was good, though splashed with mud, and his bloated face, bleared eyes and loose, tremulous mouth proclaimed the habitual drunkard.

"I shay I'll gimmeself up," he proclaimed, with a desperate attempt at dignity; "I'll gimmeself up takin' away lil boy; I'll shacrifishe m'self. Solemn duty shacrifishe m'self f'elpless woman, ain't it? Ver' well then; gimmeself up takin' 'way lil boy, buyin' 'm pair shoes. No harm in that, issher? Hope not. Ver' well then." And he subsided into tears.

"What's your name?" asked the inspector.

"WHAT'S YOUR NAME?" ASKED THE INSPECTOR.

"Whash name? Thash my bishnesh. Warrer wan' know name for? Grapertnence ask gellumshname. I'm gellum, thash wha' I am. Besht of shisters too, besht shis'ers"—snivelling again—"an' I'm ungra'ful beasht. But I shacrifishe 'self; she shan' get 'n trouble. D'y'ear? Gimmeself up shtealin' lil boy. Who says I ain' gellum?"

Nothing more intelligible than this could be got out of him, and presently he was taken off to the cells. Then Hewitt asked the inspector, "What will happen to him now?"

The inspector laughed.

"Oh he'll get very sober and sick and sorry by the morning," he said; "and then he'll have to send home for some money, that's all."

"And as to the child?"

"Oh, he'll forget all about that; that's only a drunken freak. The child has been recovered. You know that, I suppose?"

"Yes; but I am still after the person who took it away. It was a woman. Indeed, I've more than a suspicion that it was the woman who brought the child here when he was lost before—the one with the scar on the neck, you know."

"Is that so?" said the inspector. "Well, that's a rum go, ain't it? What did she bring him back here for if she wanted him again?"

"That I want to find out," Hewitt answered. "And now I want you to do me a favour. You say you expect that man below will want to send home in the morning for money. Well, I want to be the messenger."

The inspector opened his eyes.

"Want to be the messenger? Well, that's easily done; if you're here at the time I'll leave word. But why?"

"Well, I've a sort of notion I know something about his family, and I want to make sure. Shall I be here at eight in the morning, or shall we say nine?"

"Which you like; I expect he'll be shouting for bail before eight."

"Very well, we will say eight. Goodnight."

And so Hewitt had to let yet another night go without an explanation of the mystery; but he felt that his hand was on the key at last, though it had only fallen there by chance. Prompt to his time at eight in the morning he was at the police station, where another inspector was now on duty, who, however, had been told of Hewitt's wish.

"Ah," he said, "you're well to time, Mr Hewitt. That prisoner's as limp as rags now; he's begging of us to send to his sister."

"Does he say anything about that child?"

"Says he don't know anything about it; all a drunken freak. His name's Oliver Neale, and he lives at 10, Morton Terrace, Hampstead, with his sister. Her name's Mrs Isitt; and you're to take this note and bring her back with you, or at any rate some money; and you're to say he's truly repentant," the inspector concluded with a grin.

The distance was short, and Hewitt walked it. Morton Terrace was a short row of pleasant, old-fashioned villas, ivy-grown and neat, and No. 10 was as neat as any. To the servant who answered his ring Hewitt announced himself as a gentleman with a message from Mrs Isitt's brother. This did not seem to prepossess the girl in Hewitt's favour, and she backed to the end of the hall and communicated with somebody on the stairs before finally showing Hewitt into a room, where he was quickly followed by Mrs Isitt.

She was a rather tall woman of perhaps thirty-eight, and had probably been attractive, though now her face bore lines of sad grief. Hewitt noticed that she wore a very high black collar.

"Good morning, Mrs Isitt," he said. "I'm afraid my errand is not altogether pleasant. The fact is, your brother, Mr Neale, was not altogether sober last night, and he is now at the police station, where he wrote this note."

Mrs Isitt did not appear surprised, and took the note with no more than a sigh.

"Yes," she said, "it can't be concealed. This is not the first time by many, as you probably know, if you are a friend of his."

She read the note, and as she looked up Hewitt said—

"No, I have not known him long. I happened to be at the station last night, and he rather attracted my attention by insisting, in his intoxicated state, on giving himself up for kidnapping a child, Charles Seton."

Mrs Isitt started as though shot. Pale of cheek, she glanced fearfully in Hewitt's face and there met a keen gaze that seemed to read her brain. She saw that her secret was known, but for a moment she struggled, and her lips worked convulsively—

"Charles Seton—Charles Seton?" she said.

"Yes, Mrs Isitt, that is the name. The child, as a matter of fact, was stolen by the person who bought these shoes for it. Do you recognise them?"

He produced the shoes and held them before her. The woman sank on the sofa behind her, terrified, but unable to take her eyes from Hewitt's.

"Come, Mrs Isitt," he said, "you have been recognised. Here is my card. I am commissioned by the parents of the child to find who removed him, and I think I have succeeded."

She took the card and glanced at it dazedly; then she sank with a groaning sob with her face on the head of the sofa, and as she did so Hewitt could see a scar on the side of her neck peeping above her high collar.

"SHE SANK WITH A GROANING SOB WITH HER FACE ON THE HEAD OF THE SOFA."

"Oh, my God!" the woman moaned. "Then it has come to this. He will die! he will die!"

The woman's anguish was piteous to see. Hewitt had gained his point, and was willing to spare her. He placed his hand on her heaving shoulder and begged her not to distress herself.

"The matter is rather difficult to understand, Mrs Isitt," he said. "If you will compose yourself, perhaps you can explain. I can assure you that there is no desire to be vindictive. I'm afraid my manner upset you. Pray reassure yourself. May I sit down?"

Nobody could by his manner more easily restore confidence and trust than Hewitt when it pleased him. Mrs Isitt lifted her head and gazed at him once more with a troubled though quieter expression.

"I think you wrote Mrs Seton an anonymous letter," Hewitt said, producing the first of those which Mrs Seton had brought him. "It was kind of you to reassure the poor woman."

"Oh, tell me," Mrs Isitt asked, "was she much upset at missing the little boy? Did it make her ill?"

"She was upset, of course; but perhaps the joy of recovering him compensated for all."

"Yes; I took him back as soon as I possibly could, really I did, Mr Hewitt. And, oh! I was so tempted! My life has been so unhappy! If you only knew!" She buried her face in her hands.

"Will you tell me?" Hewitt suggested gently. "You see, whatever happens, an explanation of some sort is the first thing."

"Yes, yes—of course. Oh, I am a wretched woman." She paused for some little while, and then went on: "Mr Hewitt, my husband is a lunatic." She paused again. "There was never a man, Mr Hewitt, so devoted to his wife and children as my husband. He bore even with the continual annoyance of my brother, whom you saw, *because* he was my brother. But a little more than a year ago, as the result of an accident, a tumour formed on his brain. The thing is incurable except, as a remote possibility, by a most dangerous operation, which the doctors fear to attempt except under most favourable conditions. Without that he must die, sooner or later. Meantime he is insane, though with many and sometimes long intervals of perfect lucidity. When the disease attacked him there was little warning, except from pains in the head, till one dreadful night. Then he rose from bed a maniac and killed our child, a little girl of six, whom he was devotedly attached to. He also cut my own throat with his razor, but I recovered. I would rather say nothing more of that—it is too dreadful, though indeed I think about little else. There was another child, a baby boy, about a year old when his sister died, and he—he died of scarlet fever scarcely four months ago.

"My husband was taken to a private asylum at Willesden, where he now is. I visited him frequently, and took the baby, and it was almost terrible to see—a part of his insanity, no doubt—how his fondness for that child grew. When it died, I never dared to tell him. Indeed, the doctors forbade it. In his state he would have died raving. But he asked for it, sometimes earnestly, sometimes angrily, till I almost feared to visit him. Then he began to demand it of the doctors and attendants, and his excitement increased day by day. I was told to prepare for the worst. When I visited him he sometimes failed to recognise me, and at others demanded the child fiercely. I should tell you that it was only just about this time that it was found that the tumour existed, and the idea of the operation was suggested; but of course it was impossible in his disturbed condition. I scarcely dared to go to see him, and yet I did so long to! Dr Bailey did indeed suggest that possibly we might find he would be quieted by being shown another child; but I myself felt that to be very unlikely.

"It was while things were in this state, and about six or seven weeks ago, that, walking toward Cricklewood one morning, I saw a little fellow trotting along all alone, who actually startled me—startled me very much—by his resemblance to our poor little one. The likeness was one of those extraordinary ones that one only finds among young children. This child was a little bigger and stronger than ours was when he died, but then it was older—probably very nearly the age and size our own would have been had it lived. Nobody else was in sight, and I fancied the child looked about to cry, so I went to it and spoke. Plainly it had strayed, and could not tell me where it lived, only that its name was Charley. I took it in my arms and it grew quite friendly. As I talked to it suddenly Dr Bailey's suggestion came in my mind. If any child could deceive my poor husband, surely this was the one. Of course I should have to find its parents—

probably through the police; but why not at any rate take it to Willesden in the meantime for an hour or so? I could not resist the temptation—I took the first available cab.

"The result of the experiment almost frightened me. My poor husband received the child with transports of delight, kissed it, and laughed and wept over it like a mother rather than a father, and refused to give it up for hours. The child of course would not answer to its strange name at first, but he seemed an adaptable little thing, and presently began calling my poor husband 'daddy.' I had not been so happy myself for months as I was as I watched them. I had told Dr Bailey—what I fear was not strictly true—that I had borrowed the child from a friend. At length I felt I must go and take the boy to the police, and with great difficulty I managed to get it away, my poor husband crying like a child. Well, I took the little fellow to the station I judged nearest to where I found him, and gave him up to the care of the inspector. But I was a little frightened at having kept him so long, and gave a false name and address. Still, I learned from the inspector that the child had been inquired after, and by whom.

"DADDY!"

"My husband was quiet for some days after this, but then he began to ask for his boy with more vehemence than ever. He grew worse and worse, and soon his ravings were terrible. Dr Bailey urged me to bring the child again, but what could I do? I formed a desperate idea of going to Mrs Seton, telling her the whole thing, and imploring her to let me take the child again. But then would that be likely? Would she allow her child to be placed in the arms of a lunatic—one indeed who had already killed a child of his own? I felt that the thing was impossible. Still, I went to the house, and walked about it again and again, I scarcely knew why. And my poor husband in his confinement screamed for his child till I dared not go near him. So it was when one morning—last Monday morning—I had passed the front of the Setons' house and turned up the lane at the side. I could see over the low fence and hedge, and as I came to the French window with the steps I saw that the window was open at one side and little Charley was standing on the top step. He recognised me, smiled and called just as my own child would have done; indeed, as I stood there I almost fell into the delusion of my poor mad husband. I took the gate in my hands, shaking it impatiently, and in attempting to open it from the wrong end, found the hinges lift out. I could see that nobody else was in the room behind the French window. There was the temptation—the overwhelming temptation—and I was distracted. I took the little fellow hurriedly in my arms and pulled the window to, so that the bottom bolt fell into the floor socket; then I replaced the gate as I found it, and ran to where I knew there was a cab-stand. Oh! Mr Hewitt, was it so very sinful? And I meant to bring him back that same afternoon, I really did.

"The child was in indoor clothes, and had no hat. I called at a baby-linen shop and bought hat, cloak, frock and a new pair of shoes. Then I hurried to Willesden. Again the effect was magical. My husband was happy once more; but when at last I attempted to take the child away he would not let it go. It was terrible. Oh, I can't describe the scene. Dr Bailey told me that, come what might, I must stay that night in a room his wife would provide for me and keep the child, or perhaps I must sit up with my husband and let the child sleep on my knee. In the end it was the latter that I did.

"By the morning my senses were blunted, and I scarcely cared what happened. I determined that as I had gone so far I would keep the child that day at least; indeed, as I say, whether by the influence of my husband I know not, but I almost felt myself falling into his delusion that the child was ours. I went home for an hour at midday, taking the child, and then my wretched brother saw it and got the whole story from me. He told me that reward bills were out about the child, and then I dimly realised that its mother must be suffering pain, and I wrote the note you spoke of. Perhaps I had some little idea of delaying pursuit— I don't know. At any rate I wrote it, and posted it at Willesden as I went back. My husband had been asleep when I left, but now he was awake again and asking for the child once more. There is little more to say. I stayed that night and the next day, and by that time my husband had become tranquil and rational as he had not been for months. If only the improvement can be sustained, they think of operating tomorrow or the next day.

"I carried Charley back in the dusk, intending to put him inside one of the gates, ring, and watch him safely in from a little way off, but as I passed down the side lane I saw the French window open again and nobody near. I had been that way before and felt bolder there. I took his hat and cloak (I had already changed his frock) and, after kissing him, put him hastily through the window and came away. But I had forgotten the new shoes. I remembered them, however, when I got home, and immediately conceived a fear that the child's parents might trace me by their means. I mentioned this fear to my brother, and it appeared to frighten him. He borrowed some money of me yesterday, and, it seems, got intoxicated. In that state he is always anxious to do some noble action, though he is capable, I am grieved to say, of almost any meanness when sober. He lives here at my expense, indeed, and borrows money from his friends for drink. These may seem hard things for a sister to say, but everybody knows it. He has wearied me, and I have lost all shame of him. I suppose in his muddled state he got the notion that he would accuse himself of what I had done and so shield me. I expect he repented of his self-sacrifice this morning, though."

Hewitt knew that he had, but said nothing. Also he said nothing of the anonymous letter he had in his pocket, wherein Mr Oliver Neale had covertly demanded a hundred pounds for the restoration of Charley Seton. He guessed, however, that that gentleman had feared making the appointment that the advertisement answering his letter had suggested.

To Mr and Mrs Seton Hewitt told the whole story, omitting at first names and addresses. "I saw plainly," he said in course of his talk, "that the child might easily have been taken from the French window. I did not say so, for Mrs Seton was already sufficiently distressed, and the notion that the child was kidnapped, and not simply lost, might have made her worse just then. The toys—the cart with the string on it in particular—had been dragged in the direction of the window, and then nothing would be easier than for the child to open the window itself. There was nothing but a drop bolt, working very easily, which the child must often have seen lifted, and you will remember that the catch did not act. Once the child had opened the window and got outside, the whole thing was simple. The gate could be lifted, the child taken, and the window pulled to, so that the bolt would fall into its place and leave all as before.

"As to the previous occasion, I thought it curious at first that the child should stray before lunch and yet not be heard of again till the evening, and then apparently not be overfatigued. But beyond these little things, and what I inferred from the letter, I had very little to help me indeed. Nothing, in fact, till I got the shoes, and they didn't carry me very far. The drunken rant of the man in the police station attracted me because he spoke not only of taking away the child, but of buying it shoes. Now nobody could know of the buying of the shoes who did not know something more. But I knew it was a woman who had taken Charley, as you know, from the heel-mark and the evidence of the shop people, so that when the bemused fool talked of his sister, and sacrificing himself for her, and keeping her out of trouble, and so on, I ranged the case up in my mind, and, so far as I ventured, I guessed it aright. The police inspector knew nothing of the matter of the shoes, nor of the fact of the person I was after being a woman, so thought the thing no more than a drunken freak.

"And now," Hewitt said, "before I tell you this woman's name, don't you think the poor creature has suffered enough?"

Both Mrs Seton and her husband agreed that she had, and that, so far as they were concerned, no further steps should be taken. And when she was told where to go, Mrs Seton went off at once to offer Mrs Isitt her forgiveness and sympathy. But Mrs Isitt's punishment came in twenty-four hours, when her husband died in the surgeon's hands.

6

THE CASE OF THE WARD LANE TABERNACLE

I

Among the few personal friendships that Martin Hewitt has allowed himself to make there is one for an eccentric but very excellent old lady named Mrs Mallett. She must be more than seventy now, but she is of robust and active, not to say masculine, habit, and her relations with Hewitt are irregular and curious. He may not see her for many weeks, perhaps for months, until one day she will appear in the office, push directly past Kerrett (who knows better than to attempt to stop her) into the inner room, and salute Hewitt with a shake of the hand and a savage glare of the eye which would appall a stranger, but which is quite amiably meant. As for myself, it was long ere I could find any resource but instant retreat before her gaze, though we are on terms of moderate toleration now.

After her first glare she sits in the chair by the window and directs her glance at Hewitt's small gas grill and kettle in the fireplace—a glance which Hewitt, with all expedition, translates into tea. Slightly mollified by the tea, Mrs Mallett condescends to remark, in tones of tragic truculence, on passing matters of conventional interest—the weather, the influenza, her own health, Hewitt's health, and so forth, any reply of Hewitt's being commonly received with either disregard or contempt. In half an hour's time or so she leaves the office with a stern command to Hewitt to attend at her house and drink tea on a day and at a time named—a command which Hewitt obediently fulfils, when he passes through a similarly exhilarating experience in Mrs Mallett's back drawing-room at her little freehold house in Fulham. Altogether Mrs Mallett, to a stranger, is a singularly uninviting personality, and indeed, except Hewitt, who has learnt to appreciate her hidden good qualities, I doubt if she has a friend in the world. Her studiously concealed charities are a matter of as much amusement as gratification to Hewitt, who naturally, in the course of his peculiar profession, comes across many sad examples of poverty and suffering, commonly among the decent sort, who hide their troubles from strangers' eyes, and suffer in secret. When such a case is in his mind it is Hewitt's practice to inform Mrs Mallett of it at one of the tea ceremonies. Mrs Mallett receives the story with snorts of incredulity and scorn, but takes care, while expressing the most callous disregard and contempt of the troubles of the sufferers, to ascertain casually their names and addresses; twenty-four hours after which Hewitt need only make a visit to find their difficulties in some mysterious way alleviated.

"SLIGHTLY MOLLIFIED BY THE TEA."

Mrs Mallett never had any children, and was early left a widow. Her appearance, for some reason or another, commonly leads strangers to believe her an old maid. She lives in her little detached house with its square piece of ground, attended by a housekeeper, older than herself, and one maid-servant. She lost her only sister by death soon after the events I am about to set down, and now has, I believe, no relations in the world. It was also soon after these events that her present housekeeper first came to her, in place of an older and very deaf woman, quite useless, who had been with her before. I believe she is moderately rich, and that one or two charities will benefit considerably at her death; also I should be far from astonished to find Hewitt's own name in her will, though this is no more than idle conjecture. The one possession to which she clings with all her soul—her one pride and treasure—

is her great-uncle Joseph's snuff-box, the lid of which she steadfastly believes to be made of a piece of Noah's original ark, discovered on the top of Mount Ararat by some intrepid explorer of vague identity about a hundred years ago. This is her one weakness, and woe to the unhappy creature who dares hint a suggestion that possibly the wood of the ark rotted away to nothing a few thousand years before her great-uncle Joseph ever took snuff. I believe he would be bodily assaulted. The box is brought out for Hewitt's admiration at every tea ceremony at Fulham, when Hewitt handles it reverently, and expresses as much astonishment and interest as if he had never seen or heard of it before. It is on these occasions only that Mrs Mallett's customary stiffness relaxes. The sides of the box are of cedar of Lebanon, she explains (which very possibly they are), and the gold mountings were worked up from spade guineas (which one can believe without undue strain on the reason). And it is usually these times, when the old lady softens under the combined influence of tea and Uncle Joseph's snuff-box, that Hewitt seizes to lead up to his hint of some starving governess or distressed clerk, with the full confidence that the more savagely the story is received the better will the poor people be treated as soon as he turns his back.

It was her jealous care of Uncle Joseph's snuff-box that first brought Mrs Mallett into contact with Martin Hewitt, and the occasion, though not perhaps testing his acuteness to the extent that some did, was nevertheless one of the most curious and fantastic on which he has ever been engaged. She was then some ten or twelve years younger than she is now, but Hewitt assures me she looked exactly the same; that is to say, she was harsh, angular, and seemed little more than fifty years of age. It was before the time of Kerrett, and another youth occupied the outer office. Hewitt sat late one afternoon with his door ajar when he heard a stranger enter the outer office, and a voice, which he afterwards knew well as Mrs Mallett's, ask "Is Mr Martin Hewitt in?"

"Yes, ma'am, I think so. If you will write your name and—"

"Is he in *there*?" And with three strides Mrs Mallett was at the inner door and stood before Hewitt himself, while the routed office-lad stared helplessly in the rear.

"Mr Hewitt," Mrs Mallet said, "I have come to put an affair into your hands, which I shall require to be attended to at once."

Hewitt was surprised, but he bowed politely, and said, with some suspicion of a hint in his tone, "Yes—I rather supposed you were in a hurry."

She glanced quickly in Hewitt's face and went on: "I am not accustomed to needless ceremony, Mr Hewitt. My name is Mallett—Mrs Mallett—and here is my card. I have come to consult you on a matter of great annoyance and some danger to myself. The fact is I am being watched and followed by a number of persons."

Hewitt's gaze was steadfast, but he reflected that possibly this curious woman was a lunatic, the delusion of being watched and followed by unknown people being perhaps the most common of all; also it was no unusual thing to have a lunatic visit the office with just such a complaint. So he only said soothingly, "Indeed? That must be very annoying."

"Yes, yes; the annoyance is bad enough, perhaps," she answered shortly; "but I am chiefly concerned about my great-uncle Joseph's snuff-box."

This utterance sounded a trifle more insane than the other, so Hewitt answered, a little more soothingly still: "Ah, of course. A very important thing, the snuff-box, no doubt."

"It is, Mr Hewitt—it is important, as I think you will admit when you have seen it. Here it is," and she produced from a small handbag the article that Hewitt was destined so often again to see and affect an interest in. "You may be incredulous,

Mr Hewitt, but it is, nevertheless, a fact that the lid of this snuff-box is made of the wood of the original ark that rested on Mount Ararat."

She handed the box to Hewitt, who murmured, "Indeed! Very interesting—very wonderful, really," and returned it to the lady immediately.

"That, Mr Hewitt, was the property of my great-uncle, Joseph Simpson, who once had the honour of shaking hands with his late Majesty King George the Fourth. The box was presented to my uncle by—," and then Mrs Mallett plunged into the whole history and adventures of the box, in the formula wherewith Hewitt subsequently became so well acquainted, and which need not be here set out in detail. When the box had been properly honoured Mrs Mallett proceeded with her business.

"I am convinced, Mr Hewitt," she said, "that systematic attempts are being made to rob me of this snuff-box. I am not a nervous or weak-minded woman, or perhaps I might have sought your assistance before. The watching and following of myself I might have disregarded, but when it comes to burglary I think it is time to do something."

"Certainly," Hewitt agreed.

"Well, I have been pestered with demands for the box for some time past. I have here some of the letters which I have received, and I am sure I know at whose instigation they were sent." She placed on the table a handful of papers of various sizes, which Hewitt examined one after another. They were mostly in the same handwriting, and all were unsigned. Every one was couched in a fanatically-toned imitation of scriptural diction, and all sorts of threats were expressed with many emphatic underlinings. The spelling was not of the best, the writing was mostly uncouth, and the grammar was in ill shape in many places, the "thous" and "thees" and their accompanying verbs falling over each other disastrously. The purport of the messages was rather vaguely expressed, but all seemed to make a demand for the restoration of some article held in extreme veneration. This was alluded to in many figurative ways as the "token of life," the "seal of the woman," and so forth, and sometimes Mrs Mallett was requested to restore it to the "ark of the covenant." One of the least vague of these singular documents ran thus:—

"Thou of no faith put the bond of the woman clothed with the sun on the stoan sete in thy back garden this night or thy blood beest on your own hed. Give it back to us the five righteous only in this citty, give us that what saves the faithful when the erth is swalloed up."

Hewitt read over these fantastic missives one by one till he began to suspect that his client, mad or not, certainly corresponded with mad Quakers. Then he said, "Yes, Mrs Mallett, these are most extraordinary letters. Are there any more of them?"

"Bless the man, yes, there were a lot that I burnt. All the same crack-brained sort of thing."

"They are mostly in one handwriting," Hewitt said, "though some are in another. But I confess I don't see any very direct reference to the snuff-box."

"Oh, but it's the only thing they *can* mean," Mrs Mallett replied with great positiveness. "Why, he wanted me to sell it him; and last night my house was broken into in my absence and everything ransacked and turned over, but not a thing was taken. Why? Because I had the box with me at my sister's. And this is the only sacred relic in my possession. And what saved the faithful when the world was swallowed up? Why, the ark, of course."

The old lady's manner was odd, but notwithstanding the bizarre and disjointed character of her complaint, Hewitt had now had time to observe that she had none of the unmistakable signs of the lunatic. Her eye was steady and clear, and she had none of the restless habits of the mentally deranged. Even at that time Hewitt had met with curious adventures enough to teach him not to be astonished at a new one, and now he set himself seriously to get at his client's case in full order and completeness.

"Come, Mrs Mallett," he said, "I am a stranger, and I can never understand your case till I have it, not as it presents itself to your mind, in the order of importance of events, but in the exact order in which they happened. You had a great-uncle, I understand, living in the early part of the century, who left you at his death the snuff-box which you value so highly. Now you suspect that somebody is attempting to extort or steal it from you. Tell me as clearly and simply as you can whom you suspect, and the whole story of the attempts."

"That's just what I'm coming to," the old lady answered, rather pettishly. "My uncle Joseph had an old housekeeper, who, of course, knew all about the snuff-box, and it is her son Reuben Penner who is trying to get it from me. The old woman was half crazy with one extraordinary religious superstition and another, and her son seems to be just the same. My great-uncle was a man of strong common sense and a Churchman (though he *did* think he could write plays), and if it hadn't been for his restraint I believe—that is, I have been told—Mrs Penner would have gone clean demented with religious mania. Well, she died in course of time, and my great-uncle died some time after, leaving me the most important thing in his possession (I allude to the snuff-box of course), a good bit of property, and a tin box full of his worthless manuscripts. I became a widow at twenty-six, and since then I have lived very quietly in my present house in Fulham.

"A couple of years ago I received a visit from Reuben Penner. I didn't recognise him, which wasn't wonderful, since I hadn't seen him for thirty years or more. He is well over fifty now, a large, heavy-faced man with uncommonly wild eyes for a greengrocer—which is what he is, though he dresses very well, considering. He was quite respectful at first, and very awkward in his manner. He took a little time to get his courage, and then he began questioning me about my religious feelings. Well, Mr Hewitt, I am not the sort of person to stand a lecture from a junior and an inferior, whatever my religious opinions may be, and I pretty soon made him realise it. But somehow he persevered. He wanted to know if I would go to some place of worship that he called his 'Tabernacle.' I asked him who was the pastor. He said himself. I asked him how many members of the congregation there were, and (the man was as solemn as an owl. I assure you, Mr Hewitt) he actually said five! I kept my countenance and asked why such a small number couldn't attend church, or, at any rate, attach itself to some decent Dissenting chapel. And then the man burst out; mad—mad as a hatter. He was as incoherent as such people usually are, but as far as I could make out he talked, among a lot of other things, of some imaginary woman—a woman standing on the moon and driven into a wilderness on the wings of an eagle. The man was so madly possessed of his fancies that I assure you for a while he almost ceased to look ridiculous. He was so earnest in his rant. But I soon cut him short. It's best to be severe with these people—it's the only chance of bringing them to their senses. 'Reuben Penner,' I said, 'shut up. Your mother was a very decent person in her way, I believe, but she was half a lunatic with her superstitious notions, and you're a bigger fool than she was. Imagine a grown man, and of your age, coming and asking me, of all people in the world, to leave my church and make another fool in a congregation of five, with *you* to rave at me about women in the moon! Go away and look after your greengrocery, and go to church or chapel like a sensible man. Go away and don't play the fool any longer; I won't hear another word!'

"'REUBEN PENNER,' I SAID, 'SHUT UP!'"

"When I talk like this I am usually attended to, and in this case Penner went away with scarcely another word. I saw nothing of him for about a month or six weeks, and then he came and spoke to me as I was cutting roses in my front garden. This time he talked—to begin with, at least—more sensibly. 'Mrs Mallett,' he said, 'you have in your keeping a very sacred relic.'

"'I have,' I said, 'left me by my great-uncle Joseph. And what then?'

"'Well'—he hummed and hawed a little—'I wanted to ask if you might be disposed to part with it.'

"'What?' I said, dropping my scissors—'sell it?'

"'Well, yes,' he answered, putting on as bold a face as he could.

"The notion of selling my uncle Joseph's snuff-box in any possible circumstances almost made me speechless. 'What!' I repeated. 'Sell it?—*sell* it? It would be a sinful sacrilege!'

"His face quite brightened when I said this, and he replied, 'Yes, of course it would; I think so myself, ma'am; but I fancied you thought otherwise. In that case, ma'am, not being a believer yourself, I'm sure you would consider it a graceful and a pious act to present it to my little Tabernacle, where it would be properly valued. And it having been my mother's property—'

"He got no further. I am not a woman to be trifled with, Mr Hewitt, and I believe I beat him out of the garden with my basket. I was so infuriated I can scarcely remember what I did. The suggestion that I should sell my uncle Joseph's snuff-box to a greengrocer was bad enough; the request that I should actually *give* it to his 'Tabernacle' was infinitely worse. But to claim that it had belonged to his mother—well I don't know how it strikes you, Mr Hewitt, but to me it seemed the last insult possible."

"'I AM NOT A WOMAN TO BE TRIFLED WITH.'"

"Shocking! shocking! of course," Hewitt said, since she seemed to expect a reply. "And he called you an unbeliever, too. But what happened after that?"

"After that he took care not to bother me personally again; but these wretched anonymous demands came in, with all sorts of darkly hinted threats as to the sin I was committing in keeping my own property. They didn't trouble me much. I put 'em in the fire as fast as they came, until I began to find I was being watched and followed, and then I kept them."

"Very sensible," Hewitt observed, "very sensible indeed to do that. But tell me as to these papers. Those you have here are nearly all in one handwriting, but some, as I have already said, are in another. Now before all this business did you ever see Reuben Penner's handwriting?"

"No, never."

"Then you are not by any means sure that he has written any of these things?"

"But then who else could?"

"That, of course, is a thing to be found out. At present, at any rate, we know this: that if Penner has anything to do with these letters he is not alone, because of the second handwriting. Also we must not bind ourselves past other conviction that he wrote any one of them. By the way, I am assuming that they all arrived by post?"

"Yes, they did."

"But the envelopes are not here. Have you kept any of them?"

"I hardly know; there may be some at home. Is it important?"

"It may be; but those I can see at another time. Please go on."

"These things continued to arrive, as I have said, and I continued to burn them till I began to find myself watched and followed, and then I kept them. That was two or three months ago. It is a most unpleasant sensation, that of feeling that some unknown person is dogging your footsteps from corner to corner and observing all your movements for a purpose you are doubtful of. Once or twice I turned suddenly back, but I never could catch the creatures, of whom I am sure Penner was one."

"You saw these people, of course?"

"Well, yes, in a way—with the corner of my eye, you know. But it was mostly in the evening. It was a woman once, but several times I feel certain it was Penner. And once I saw a man come into my garden at the back in the night, and I feel quite sure that was Penner."

"Was that after you had this request to put the article demanded on the stone seat in the garden?"

"The same night. I sat up and watched from the bathroom window, expecting someone would come. It was a dark night, and the trees made it darker, but I could plainly see someone come quietly over the wall and go up to the seat."

"Could you distinguish his face?"

"No; it was too dark. But I feel sure it was Penner."

"Has Penner any decided peculiarity of form or gait?"

"No; he's just a big, common sort of man. But I tell you I feel certain it was Penner."

"For any particular reason?"

"No, perhaps not. But who else could it have been? No, I'm very sure it must have been Penner."

Hewitt repressed a smile and went on. "Just so," he said. "And what happened then?"

"He went up to the seat, as I said, and looked at it, passing his hand over the top. Then I called out to him. I said if I found him on my premises again by day or night I'd give him in charge of the police. I assure you he got over the wall the second time a good deal quicker than the first. And then I went to bed, though I got a shocking cold in the head sitting at that open bathroom window. Nobody came about the place after that till last night. A few days ago my only sister was taken ill. I saw her each day, and she got worse. Yesterday she was so bad that I wouldn't leave her. I sent home for some things and stopped in her house for the night. Today I got an urgent message to come home, and when I went I found that an entrance had been made by a kitchen window, and the whole house had been ransacked, but not a thing was missing."

"Were drawers and boxes opened?"

"Everywhere. Most seemed to have been opened with keys, but some were broken. The place was turned upside down, but, as I said before, not a thing was missing. A very old woman, very deaf, who used to be my housekeeper, but who does nothing now, was in the house, and so was my general servant. They slept in rooms at the top, and were not disturbed. Of course the old woman is too deaf to have heard anything, and the maid is a very heavy sleeper. The girl was very frightened, but I pacified her before I came away. As it happened, I took the snuff-box with me. I had got very suspicious of late, of course, and something seemed to suggest that I had better make sure of it, so I took it. It's pretty strong evidence that they have been watching me closely, isn't it, that they should break in the very first night I left the place?"

"And are you quite sure that nothing has been taken?"

"Quite certain. I have spent a long time in a very careful search."

"And you want me, I presume, to find out definitely who these people are, and get such evidence as may ensure their being punished?"

"That is the case. Of course I know Reuben Penner is the moving spirit—I'm quite certain of that. But still I can see plainly enough that as yet there's no legal evidence of it. Mind, I'm not afraid of him—not a bit. That is not my character. I'm not afraid of all the madmen in England; but I'm not going to have them steal my property—this snuff-box especially."

"Precisely. I hope you have left the disturbance in your house exactly as you found it?"

"Oh, of course, and I have given strict orders that nothing is to be touched. Tomorrow morning I should like you to come and look at it."

"I must look at it, certainly," Hewitt said, "but I would rather go at once."

"Pooh—nonsense!" Mrs Mallett answered, with the airy obstinacy that Hewitt afterwards knew so well. "I'm not going home again now to spend an hour or two more. My sister will want to know what has become of me, and she mustn't suspect that anything is wrong, or it may do all sorts of harm. The place will keep till the morning, and I have the snuff-box safe with me. You have my card, Mr Hewitt, haven't you? Very well. Can you be at my house tomorrow morning at half-past ten? I will be there, and you can see all you want by daylight. We'll consider that settled. Good-day."

Hewitt saw her to his office door, and waited till she had half descended the stairs. Then he made for a staircase window which gave a view of the street. The evening was coming on murky and foggy, and the street lights were blotchy and vague. Outside a four-wheeled cab stood, and the driver eagerly watched the front door. When Mrs Mallett emerged he instantly began to descend from the box with the quick invitation, "Cab, mum, cab?" He seemed very eager for his fare, and though Mrs Mallett hesitated a second she eventually entered the cab. He drove off, and Hewitt tried in vain to catch a glimpse of the number of the cab behind. It was always a habit of his to note all such identifying marks throughout a case, whether they seemed important at the time or not, and he has often had occasion to be pleased with the outcome. Now, however, the light was too bad. No sooner had the cab started than a man emerged from a narrow passage opposite, and followed. He was a large, rather awkward, heavy-faced man of middle age, and had the appearance of a respectable artisan or small tradesman in his best clothes. Hewitt hurried downstairs and followed the direction the cab and the man had taken, toward the Strand. But the cab by this time was swallowed up in the Strand traffic, and the heavy-faced man had also disappeared. Hewitt returned to his office a little disappointed, for the man seemed rather closely to answer Mrs Mallett's description of Reuben Penner.

"'CAB, MUM?'"

II

Punctually at half-past ten the next morning Hewitt was at Mrs Mallett's house at Fulham. It was a pretty little house, standing back from the road in a generous patch of garden, and had evidently stood there when Fulham was an outlying village. Hewitt entered the gate, and made his way to the front door, where two young females, evidently servants, stood. They were in a very disturbed state, and when he asked for Mrs Mallett assured him that nobody knew where she was, and that she had not been seen since the previous afternoon.

"But," said Hewitt, "she was to stay at her sister's last night, I believe."

"Yes, sir," answered the more distressed of the two girls—she in a cap—"but she hasn't been seen there. This is her sister's servant, and she's been sent over to know where she is, and why she hasn't been there."

This the other girl—in bonnet and shawl—corroborated. Nothing had been seen of Mrs Mallett at her sister's since she had received the message the day before to the effect that the house had been broken into.

"And I'm so frightened," the other girl said, whimperingly. "They've been in the place again last night."

"Who have?"

"The robbers. When I came in this morning—"

"But didn't you sleep here?"

"I—I ought to ha' done, sir, but—but after Mrs Mallett went yesterday I got so frightened I went home at ten." And the girl showed signs of tears, which she had apparently been already indulging in.

"And what about the old woman—the deaf woman; where was she?"

"She was in the house, sir. There was nowhere else for her to go, and she was deaf and didn't know anything about what happened the night before, and confined to her room, and—and so I didn't tell her."

"I see," Hewitt said with a slight smile. "You left her here. She didn't see or hear anything, did she?"

"No sir; she can't hear, and she didn't see nothing."

"And how do you know thieves have been in the house?"

"Everythink's tumbled about worse than ever, sir, and all different from what it was yesterday; and there's a box o' papers in the attic broke open, and all sorts o' things."

"Have you spoken to the police?"

"No, sir; I'm that frightened I don't know what to do. And missis was going to see a gentleman about it yesterday, and—"

"Very well, I am that gentleman—Mr Martin Hewitt. I have come down now to meet her by appointment. Did she say she was going anywhere else as well as to my office and to her sister's?"

"No, sir. And she—she's got the snuff-box with her and all." This latter circumstance seemed largely to augment the girl's terrors for her mistress's safety.

"Very well," Hewitt said, "I think I'd better just look over the house now, and then consider what has become of Mrs Mallett—if she isn't heard of in the meantime."

The girl found a great relief in Hewitt's presence in the house, the deaf old house-keeper, who seldom spoke and never heard, being, as she said, "worse than nobody."

"Have you been in all the rooms?" Hewitt asked.

"No, sir; I was afraid. When I came in I went straight upstairs to my room, and as I was coming away I see the things upset in the other attic. I went into Mrs Perk's room, next to mine (she's the deaf old woman), and she was there all right, but couldn't hear anything. Then I came down and only just peeped into two of the rooms and saw the state they were in, and then I came out into the garden, and presently this young woman came with the message from Mrs Rudd."

"Very well, we'll look at the rooms now," Hewitt said, and they proceeded to do so. All were in a state of intense confusion. Drawers, taken from chests and bureaux, littered about the floor, with their contents scattered about them. Carpets and rugs had been turned up and flung into corners, even pictures on the walls had been disturbed, and while some hung awry, others rested on the floor and on chairs. The things, however, appeared to have been fairly carefully handled, for nothing was damaged except one or two framed engravings, the brown paper on the backs of which had been cut round with a knife and the wooden slats shifted so as to leave the backs of the engravings bare. This, the girl told Hewitt, had not been done on the night of the first burglary; the other articles also had not on that occasion been so much disturbed as they now were.

Mrs Mallett's bedroom was the first floor front. Here the confusion was, if possible, greater than in the other rooms. The bed had been completely unmade and the clothes thrown separately on the floor, and everything else was displaced. It was here, indeed, that the most noticeable features of the disturbance were observed, for on the side of the looking-glass hung a very long, old-fashioned gold chain untouched, and on the dressing-table lay a purse with the money still in it. And on the looking-glass, stuck into the crack of the frame, was a half sheet of notepaper with this inscription scrawled in pencil:—

To Mr Martin Hewitt.
Mrs Mallett is alright and in frends hands. She will return soon alright, if you keep quiet. But if you folloe her or take any steps the conseqinses will be very serious.

This paper was not only curious in itself, and curious as being addressed to Hewitt, but it was plainly in the same handwriting as were the most of the anonymous letters which Mrs Mallett had produced the day before in Hewitt's office. Hewitt studied it attentively for a few moments, and then thrust it in his pocket and proceeded to inspect the rest of the rooms. All were the same—simply well-furnished rooms turned upside down. The top floor consisted of three comfortable attics, one used as a lumber room and the others used respectively as bedrooms for the servant and the deaf old woman. None of these rooms appeared to have been entered, the girl said, on the first night, but now the lumber-room was almost as confused as the rooms downstairs. Two or three boxes were opened and their contents turned out. One of these was what is called a steel trunk—a small one—which had held old papers; the others were filled chiefly with old clothes.

The servant's room next this was quite undisturbed and untouched; and then Hewitt was admitted to the room of Mrs Mallett's deaf old pensioner. The old woman sat propped up in her bed, and looked with half-blind eyes at the peak in the bedclothes made by her bent knees. The servant screamed in her ear, but she neither moved nor spoke.

Hewitt laid his hand on her shoulder and said, in the slow and distinct tones he had found best for reaching the senses of deaf people, "I hope you are well. Did anything disturb you in the night?"

But she only turned her head half toward him and mumbled peevishly, "I wish you'd bring my tea. You're late enough this morning."

Nothing seemed likely to be got from her, and Hewitt asked the servant, "Is she altogether bedridden?"

"No," the girl answered; "leastways she needn't be. She stops in bed most of the time, but she can get up when she likes— I've seen her. But missis humours her and lets her do as she likes—and she gives plenty of trouble. I don't believe she's as deaf as she makes out."

"Indeed?" Hewitt answered. "Deafness *is* convenient sometimes, I know. Now I want you to stay here while I make some inquiries. Perhaps you'd better keep Mrs Rudd's servant with you if you want company. I don't expect to be very long gone, and in any case it wouldn't do for her to go to her mistress and say that Mrs Mallett is missing, or it might upset her seriously."

Hewitt left the house and walked till he found a public-house where a post-office directory was kept. He took a glass of whisky and water, most of which he left on the counter, and borrowed the directory. He found "Greengrocers" in the "Trade" section and ran his finger down the column till he came on this address:—

"Penner, Reuben, 8, Little Marsh Row, Hammersmith, W."

Then he returned the directory and found the best cab he could to take him to Hammersmith.

Little Marsh Row was not a vastly prosperous sort of place, and the only shops were three—all small. Two were chandlers', and the third was a sort of semi-shed of the greengrocery and coal persuasion, with the name "Penner" on a board over the door.

The shutters were all up, though the door was open, and the only person visible was a very smudgy boy, who was in the act of wheeling out a sack of coals. To the smudgy boy Hewitt applied himself. "I don't see Mr Penner about," he said; "will he be back soon?"

The boy stared hard at Hewitt. "No," he said, "he won't. 'E's guv' up the shop. 'E paid 'is next week's rent this mornin' and retired."

"THE BOY STARED HARD AT HEWITT."

"Oh!" Hewitt answered sharply. "Retired, has he? And what's become of the stock, eh! Where are the cabbages and potatoes?"

"'E told me to give 'em to the pore, an' I did. There's lots o' pore lives round 'ere. My mother's one; an' these 'ere coals is for 'er, an' I'm goin' to 'ave the trolley for myself."

"Dear me!" Hewitt answered, regarding the boy with amused interest. "You're a very business-like almoner. And what will the Tabernacle do without Mr Penner?"

"I dunno," the boy answered, closing the door behind him. "I dunno nothin' about the Tabernacle—only where it is."

"Ah, and where is it? I might find him there, perhaps."

"Ward Lane—fust on left, second on right. It's a shop wot's bin shut up; next door to a stableyard." And the smudgy boy started off with his trolley.

The Tabernacle was soon found. At some very remote period it had been an unlucky small shop, but now it was permanently shuttered, and the interior was lighted by holes cut in the upper panels of the shutters. Hewitt took a good look at the shuttered window and the door beside it, and then entered the stableyard at the side. To the left of the passage giving entrance to the yard there was a door, which plainly was another entrance to the house, and a still damp mud-mark on the step proved it to have been lately used. Hewitt rapped sharply at the door with his knuckles.

Presently a female voice from within could be heard speaking through the key-hole in a very loud whisper. "Who is it?" asked the voice.

Hewitt stooped to the key-hole and whispered back, "Is Mr Penner here now?"

"No."

"Then I must come in and wait for him. Open the door."

A bolt was pulled back and the door cautiously opened a few inches. Hewitt's foot was instantly in the jamb, and he forced the door back and entered. "Come," he said in a loud voice, "I've come to find out where Mr Penner is, and to see whoever is in here."

Immediately there was an assault of fists on the inside of a door at the end of the passage, and a loud voice said, "Do you hear? Whoever you are, I'll give you five pounds if you'll bring Mr Martin Hewitt here. His office is 25, Portsmouth Street, Strand. Or the same if you'll bring the police." And the voice was that of Mrs Mallett.

Hewitt turned to the woman who had opened the door, and who now stood, much frightened, in the corner beside him. "Come," he said, "your keys, quick, and don't offer to stir, or I'll have you brought back and taken to the station."

The woman gave him a bunch of keys, without a word. Hewitt opened the door at the end of the passage, and once more Mrs Mallett stood before him, prim and rigid as ever, except that her bonnet was sadly out of shape and her mantle was torn. "Thank you, Mr Hewitt," she said. "I thought you'd come, though where I am I know no more than Adam. Somebody shall smart severely for this. Why, and that woman—*that* woman," she pointed contemptuously at the woman in the corner, who was about two-thirds her height, "was going to *search* me—*me*! Why—" Mrs Mallett, blazing with suddenly revived indignation, took a step forward, and the woman vanished through the outer door.

"Come," Hewitt said, "no doubt you've been shamefully treated; but we must be quiet for a little. First I will make quite sure that nobody else is here, and then we'll get to your house."

Nobody was there. The rooms were dreary and mostly empty. The front room, which was lighted by the holes in the shutters, had a rough reading-desk and a table, with half a dozen wooden chairs. "This," said Hewitt, "is no doubt the Tabernacle proper, and there is very little to see in it. Come back now, Mrs Mallett, to your house, and we'll see if some explanation of these things is not possible. I hope your snuff-box is quite safe?"

Mrs Mallett drew it from her pocket and exhibited it triumphantly. "I told them they should never get it," she said, "and they saw I meant it, and left off trying."

She had straightened her bonnet and concealed the rent in her mantle as best she could. As they emerged in the street she said, "The first thing, of course, is to bring the police into this place."

"No, I think we won't do that yet," Hewitt said. "In the first place, the case is one of assault and detention, and your remedy is by summons or action; and then there are other things to speak of. We shall get a cab in the High Street, and you shall tell me what has happened to you."

Mrs Mallett's story was simple. The cab in which she left Hewitt's office had travelled west, and was apparently making for the locality of her sister's house; but the evening was dark, the fog increased greatly, and she shut the windows and took no particular notice of the streets through which she was passing. Indeed, with such a fog that would have been impossible. She had a sort of undefined notion that some of the streets were rather narrow and dirty, but she thought nothing of it, since all cabmen are given to selecting unexpected routes. After a time, however, the cab slowed, made a sharp turn, and pulled up. The door was opened, and "Here you are, mum," said the cabby. She did not understand the sharp turn, and had a general feeling that the place could not be her sister's, but as she alighted she found she had stepped directly upon the threshold of a narrow door, into which she was immediately pulled by two persons inside. This, she was sure, must have been the side-door in the stable-yard, through which Hewitt himself had lately obtained entrance to the Tabernacle. Before she had recovered from her surprise the door was shut behind her. She struggled stoutly, and screamed, but the place she was in was absolutely dark; she was taken by surprise, and she found resistance useless. They were men who held her, and the voice of the only one who spoke she did not know. He demanded in firm and distinct tones that the "sacred thing" should be given up, and that Mrs Mallett should sign a paper agreeing to prosecute nobody before she was allowed to go. She, however, as she asserted with her customary emphasis, was not the sort of woman to give in to that. She resolutely declined to do anything of the sort, and promised her captors, whoever they were, a full and legal return for their behaviour. Then she became conscious that a woman was somewhere present, and the man threatened that this woman should search her. This threat Mrs Mallett met as boldly as the others. She should like to meet the woman who would dare attempt to search her, she said. She defied anybody to attempt it. As for her Uncle Joseph's snuff-box, no matter where it was, it was where they would not be able to get it. That they should never have, but sooner or later they should have something very unpleasant for their attempts to steal it. This declaration had an immediate effect. They importuned her no more, and she was left in an inner room and the key was turned on her. There she sat, dozing occasionally, the whole night, her indomitable spirit remaining proof through all those doubtful hours of darkness. Once or twice she heard people enter and move about, and each time she called aloud to offer, as Hewitt had heard, a reward to anybody who should bring the police or communicate her situation to Hewitt. Day broke and still she waited, sleepless and unfed, till Hewitt at last arrived and released her.

On Mrs Mallett's arrival at her house Mrs Rudd's servant was at once despatched with reassuring news, and Hewitt once more addressed himself to the question of the burglary. "First, Mrs Mallett," he said, "did you ever conceal anything—anything at all, mind—in the frame of an engraving?"

"No, never."

"Were any of your engravings framed before you had them?"

"Not one that I can remember. They were mostly Uncle Joseph's, and he kept them with a lot of others in drawers. He was rather a collector, you know."

"Very well. Now come up to the attic. Something has been opened there that was not touched at the first attempt."

Mrs Mallett's indignation at the second burglary was something to see. But there was triumph in her manner; she still had the snuff-box.

"See now," said Hewitt, when the attic was reached, "here is a box full of papers. Do you know everything that was in it?"

"No, I don't," Mrs Mallett replied. "There were a lot of my uncle's manuscript plays. Here, you see, 'The Dead Bridegroom, or the Drum of Fortune,' and so on; and there were a lot of autographs. I took no interest in them, although some were rather valuable, I believe."

"Now bring your recollection to bear as strongly as you can," Hewitt said. "Do you ever remember seeing in this box a paper bearing nothing whatever upon it but a wax seal?"

"Oh yes, I remember that well enough. I've noticed it each time I've turned the box over—which is very seldom. It was a plain slip of vellum paper with a red seal, cracked and rather worn—some celebrated person's seal, I suppose. What about it?"

Hewitt was turning the papers over one at a time. "It doesn't seem to be here now," he said. "Do you see it?"

"No," Mrs Mallett returned, examining the papers herself, "it isn't. It appears to be the only thing missing. But why should they take it?"

"I think we are at the bottom of all this mystery now," Hewitt answered quietly. "It is the Seal of the Woman."

"The *what*? I don't understand."

"The fact is, Mrs Mallett, that these people have never wanted your Uncle Joseph's snuff-box at all, but that seal."

"Not wanted the snuff-box? Nonsense! Why, didn't I tell you Penner asked for it—wanted to buy it?"

"Yes, you did, but so far as I can remember you never spoke of a single instance of Penner mentioning the snuff-box by name. He spoke of a sacred relic, and you, of course, very naturally assumed he spoke of the box. None of the anonymous letters mentioned the box, you know, and once or twice they actually did mention a seal, though usually the thing was spoken of in a roundabout and figurative way, as is the manner of many people of strange beliefs in speaking of anything they particularly venerate. Moreover, remember that when they had entrapped you last night, the moment you mentioned the snuff-box specifically by name they ceased troubling you, and contented themselves with shutting you up. All along, these people—Reuben Penner and the others—have been after the seal, and you have been defending the snuff-box."

"But why the seal?"

"Did you never hear of Joanna Southcott?"

"Oh yes, of course; she was an ignorant visionary who set up as prophetess eighty or ninety years ago or more."

"Joanna Southcott, as you may see by any suitable book of reference, gave herself out as a prophetess in 1790. She was an ignorant woman, and no doubt deceived herself, and really believed in the extravagant claims she put forward. She was to be the mother of the Messiah, she said, and she was the woman driven into the wilderness, as foretold in the twelfth chapter of the Book of Revelation. She died at the end of 1814, when her followers numbered more than 100,000, all fanatic believers, though, of course, mostly ignorant people. She had made rather a good thing in her lifetime by the sale of seals, each of which was to secure the eternal salvation of the holder. At her death, of course, many of the believers fell away, but others held on as faithfully as ever, asserting that 'the holy Joanna' would rise again and fulfil all the prophecies. These poor people dwindled in numbers gradually, and although they attempted to bring up their children in their own faith, the whole belief has been practically extinct for years now. You will remember that you told me of Penner's mother being a superstitious fanatic of some sort, and that your Uncle Joseph had checked her extravagances. The thing seems pretty plain now. Your uncle Joseph possessed himself of Joanna Southcott's seal by way of removing from poor old Mrs Penner an object of a sort of idolatry, and kept it as a curiosity. Reuben Penner grew up strong in his mother's delusions, and to him and the few believers he had gathered round him at his Tabernacle the seal was an object worth risking anything to get. I should think that probably it is the only one remaining in existence at the present moment. You see, he tried every way of getting at it. First, he tried to convert you to his belief. Then he tried to buy it; and you will remember his mentioning that it had been his mother's—a suggestion which you, thinking of the snuff-box, naturally resented. After that he and his friends tried anonymous letters, and at last, grown desperate, they resorted to watching you, burglary, and kidnapping. Their first night's raid was unsuccessful, so last night they tried kidnapping you by the aid of a cabman—possibly one of themselves. When they had got you, and you had at last given them to understand that it was your Uncle Joseph's snuff-box you were defending, they tried the house again, and this time were successful. On the occasion of their first burglary they avoided the top floor, because of the servant sleeping there. This time she went home—they probably saw her go—and they got at the box in the attic. I guessed they had succeeded then, from a simple circumstance. They had begun to cut out the backs of framed engravings for purposes of search, but only some of the engravings were so treated. That meant either that the article wanted was found behind one of them, or that the intruders broke off in their picture-examination to search somewhere else, and were then successful, and so under no necessity of opening the other engravings. You assured me that nothing could have been concealed in any of the engravings, so I at once assumed that they had found what they were after in the only place wherein they had not searched the night before—the attic—and probably among the papers in the trunk."

"But then if they found it there, why didn't they return and let me go?"

"Because you would have found where they had brought you. They probably intended to keep you there till the dark of the next evening, and then take you away in a cab again and leave you some distance off. To prevent my following and possibly finding you they left here on your looking-glass this note" (Hewitt produced it), "threatening all sorts of vague consequences if you were not left to them. They knew you had come to me, of course, having followed you to my office. And now Penner feels himself anything but safe. He has relinquished his greengrocery and dispensed his stock in charity, and probably, having got the seal—the only thing he coveted in the world—he has taken himself off. Not so much perhaps from fear of punishment as for fear the seal may be taken from him, and with it the salvation his odd belief teaches him it will confer." And then Hewitt related the circumstance of the smudgy boy and his sack of coals.

Mrs Mallett sat silently for a little while, and then said in a rather softened voice, "Mr Hewitt, I am not what is called a woman of sentiment, as you may have observed, and I have been most shamefully treated over this wretched seal—if that was really what Penner wanted. But if all you tell me has been actually what has happened, I have a sort of perverse inclination to forgive the man in spite of myself. The thing probably had been his mother's—or, at any rate, he believed so—and his giving up his little all to attain the object of his ridiculous faith, and distributing his goods among the poor people and all that—really it's worthy of an old martyr, if only it were done in the cause of a faith a little less stupid—though, of course, *he* thinks his is the only religion, as others do of theirs.

But then"—Mrs Mallett stiffened again—"there's not much to prove your theories, is there?"

Hewitt smiled. "Perhaps not," he said, "except that, to my mind, at any rate, everything points to my explanation being the only possible one. The thing presented itself to you, from the beginning, as an attempt on the snuff-box you value so highly, and the possibility of the seal being the object aimed at never entered your mind. I saw it whole from the outside, and on thinking the thing over after our first interview, I remembered Joanna Southcott. I think you will find I am right."

"Well, if you are, as I said, I half believe I shall forgive the man. We will advertise, if you like, telling him he has nothing to fear if he can give an explanation of his conduct consistent with what he calls his religious belief, absurd as it may be."

That night fell darker and foggier than the last. The advertisement went into the daily papers, but Reuben Penner never saw it. Late the next day a bargeman passing Old Swan Pier struck some large object with his boat-hook and brought it to the surface. It was the body of a drowned man, and it was afterwards identified as that of Reuben Penner, late greengrocer, of Hammersmith. How he came into the water there was nothing to show. Others have been drowned by accident on those foggy nights; but then there have also been suicides in the river Thames on nights just as foggy. Nobody knew there was no money nor any valuables found on the body, and there was a story of a large, heavy-faced man who had given a poor woman—a perfect stranger—a watch and chain and a handful of money down near Tower Hill on that foggy evening. But this again was only a story, not definitely authenticated. What was certain was that, tied securely round the dead man's neck with a cord, and gripped and crumpled tightly in his right hand, was a soddened piece of vellum paper, blank, but carrying an old red seal, of which the device was almost entirely rubbed and cracked away. Nobody at the inquest quite understood this.

The Red Triangle
Being Some Further Chronicles of
Martin Hewitt, Investigator

CONTENTS

1.	The Affair of Samuel's Diamonds	213
2.	The Case of Mr Jacob Mason	244
3.	The Case of the Lever Key	275
4.	The Case of the Burnt Barn	304
5.	The Case of the Admiralty Code	334
6.	The Adventure of Channel Marsh	364

1

THE AFFAIR OF SAMUEL'S DIAMONDS

I

I have already recorded many of the adventures of my friend Martin Hewitt, but among them there have been more of a certain few which were discovered to be related together in a very extraordinary manner; and it is to these that I am now at liberty to address myself. There may have been others—cases which gave no indication of their connection with these; some of them indeed I may have told without a suspicion of their connection with the Red Triangle; but the first in which that singular accompaniment became apparent was the matter of Samuel's diamonds. The case exhibited many interesting features, and I was very anxious to report it, with perhaps even less delay than I had thought judicious in other cases; but Hewitt restrained me.

"No, Brett," he said, "there is more to come of this. This particular case is over, it is true, but there is much behind. I've an idea that I shall see that Red Triangle again. I may, or, of course, I may not; but there is deep work going on—very deep work, and whether we see more of it or not, I must keep prepared. I can't afford to throw a single card upon the table. So, as many notes as you please, Brett, for future reference; but no publication yet—none of your journalism!"

Hewitt was right. It was not so long before we heard more of the Red Triangle, and after that more, though the true connection of some of the cases with the mysterious symbol and the meaning of the symbol itself remained for a time undiscovered. But at last Hewitt was able to unmask the hideous secret, and for ever put an end to the evil influence that gathered about the sign; and now there remains no reason why the full story should not be told.

I have told elsewhere of my first acquaintance with Martin Hewitt, of his pleasant and companionable nature, his ordinary height, his stoutness, his round, smiling face—those characteristics that aided him so well in his business of investigator, so unlike was his appearance and manner to that of the private detective of the ordinary person's imagination. Therefore I need only remind my readers that my bachelor chambers were, during most of my acquaintance with Hewitt, in the old building near the Strand, in which Hewitt's office stood at the top of the first flight of stairs; where the plain ground-glass of the door bore as inscription the single word "Hewitt," and the sharp lad, Kerrett, first received visitors in the outer office.

Next door to this old house, at the time I am to speak of, a much newer building stood, especially built for letting out in offices. It happened that one day as Hewitt left his office for a late lunch, he became aware of a pallid and agitated Jew who was pervading the front door of this adjoining building. The man exhibited every sign of nervous expectancy, staring this way and that up and down the busy street, and once or twice rushing aimlessly half-way up the inner stairs, and as often returning to the door. Apprehension was plain on his pale face, and he was clearly in a state that blinded his attention to the ordinary matters about him, just as happens when a man is in momentary and nervous expectation of some serious event.

Noting these things as he passed, with no more than the observation that was his professional habit, Hewitt proceeded to his lunch. This done with, he returned to his office, perceiving, as he passed the next-door building, that the distracted Jew was no longer visible. It seemed plain that the person or the event he had awaited with such obvious nervousness had arrived and passed; one more of the problems, anxieties or crises that join and unravel moment by moment in the human ant-hill of London, had perhaps closed for good or ill within the past half-hour; perhaps it had only begun.

A message awaited Hewitt at his office—an urgent message. The housekeeper had come in from next door, Kerrett reported, with an urgent request that Mr Martin Hewitt would go immediately to the offices of Mr Denson, on the third floor. The housekeeper seemed to know little or nothing of the business, except that a Mr Samuel was alone in Mr Denson's office, and had sent the message.

With no delay Hewitt transferred himself to the next-door offices. There the housekeeper, who inhabited a uniform and a glass box opposite the foot of the first flight of stairs, directed Hewitt, with the remark that the gentleman was very impatient and very much upset. "Third floor, sir, second door on the right; name Denson on the door. There's no lift."

"W.F. Denson" was the complete name, followed by the line "Foreign and Commission Agent." This Hewitt read with some little difficulty, for the door was open, and on the threshold stood that same agitated Jew whom Hewitt had seen at the front door.

A little less actively perturbed now, he was nevertheless still nervously pale. "Mr Martin Hewitt?" he cried, while Hewitt was still only at the head of the stairs. "Is it Mr Martin Hewitt?"

Hewitt came quietly along the corridor, using eyes and ears as he came. The Jew was a man of middle height, very obviously Jewish, and with a slight accent that hinted a Continental origin.

"I have just received your message," Hewitt said, "and, as you see, I am here with no delay. Is Mr Denson in?"

"No—good heafens no—I would gif anything if he was, Mr Hewitt. Come in, do! I haf been robbed—robbed by Denson himself, wit'out a wort of doubt. It is terrible—terrible! Fifteen t'ousant pounds! It ruins me, Mr Hewitt, ruins me! Unless you can recover it! If you recover it, I will pay—pay—oh, I will pay fery well indeed!"

There was a characteristically sudden moderation of the client's emphasis when he came to the engagement to pay. Hewitt had observed it in other clients, but it did not disturb him.

"First," he said, "you must tell me your difficulty. You say you have been robbed of fifteen thousand pounds—"

"Tiamonts, Mr Hewitt—tiamonts! All from the case—here is the case, empty—"

"Let us be methodical. We will shut the door and sit down." Hewitt pressed his client into a chair and produced his notebook. "It will be better to begin at the beginning. First, I should like to know your name, and a few such particulars as that."

"Lewis Samuel, Hatton Garden—150, Hatton Garden—tiamont merchant."

"Yes. And what is your connection with Mr Denson?"

"Business—just business," Samuel responded. He pronounced it "pishness," and it seemed his favourite word. "Like this; I will tell you. I haf known him some time, and did at first small pishness. He bought a little tiamont and haf it set in pracelet, and he pay—straightforward pishness. Then he bought some very good paste stones, all set in gold, and he pay—quite straightforward pishness. At the same time he says, 'I am pishness man myself, Mr Samuel,' he says, 'and I like to make a little moneys as well as pay out sometimes. Don't you want any little agencies done? I do all foreign commissions, and I can forwart and receive and clear at dock and custom house. If you send any tiamonts I can consign and insure—very cheapest rates to you, special. If you want brokerage or buy and sell for you, confidential, I can do it with lowest commission. Especially I haf good connection with America. I haf many rich Americans, principals and customers,' he says, 'and often I could do pishness for you when they come over.'"

"By which he meant he might sell them diamonds?" Hewitt queried.

"Just so, Mr Hewitt—reg'lar pishness. And after that two or three little parcels of tiamonts he bought—for American customers, he says. But he says he can do bigger pishness soon. Ay, so he has—goot heavens, he has! But I tell you. I do also one or two small pishnesses with him, and that is all right—he treat me very well and I pay when it suits. Then he says, 'Samuel,' he says, very friendly now inteet, 'Samuel, could you get a nice large lot of tiamonts for an American customer I expect here soon?' And I say, 'Of course I can.' 'Enough,' he says, 'to fit out a rich man's wife—that is, to pegin. He is not long rich, and he will want more soon—ah, she will make him pay! But to pegin—a good fit-out of tiamonts, eh?'

"I tell him yes, and I offer usual commission. But no, says Denson, he wants no commission; he will make his own profit. That I don't mind so long as I get mine; so I agree to put the tiamonts in at a price. The American, he says, is to come over about a big company deal, and when it is through he will pay well. So last week I pring a peautiful collection all cut but unset, and I wait out in that room while Denson shows them to his customer."

"You mean you let them out of your sight?"

"Yes—that is not so uncommon; reg'lar pishness. You see I was out here—this is the only way out. Denson was in the inner office with the stones and the American. Neither could get out without passing here. And I had done pishness with him alretty."

"Well?"

"You see I wait downstairs with my case—this case—till Denson sends down. He doesn't want me to show—fery natural, you see, in pishness. When I sell to make a profit, perhaps for somebody else, I don't want that somebody to know my customer, else he sells direct and I lose my profit—fery natural. See?"

"Of course, I understand. It's a point of business among you gentlemen to keep your own customers to yourselves. And often, no doubt, diamonds pass through several hands before reaching the eventual customer, leaving a profit in each."

"Always, Mr Hewitt—always, you might say. Well, you see, Denson sends down that his customer is in, and I come up. Denson comes out from the inner office, takes my case, and I wait in there."

The case which Samuel showed Hewitt was of black leather, perhaps eighteen inches long by a foot wide. The arrangement of the office was simple. In this, the outer room, a small space was partitioned off by means of a ground glass screen, and it was in there that Samuel meant that he had waited.

"Well, he took the case in, and I could hear some sound of talking—but not much, you see, the door being shut. After a time the door opens and I hear Denson say: 'Very well, think over it; but don't be long or you'll lose the chance. Excuse me while I put them back in the safe.' Then he shuts the door and brings the case to me and goes back. But of course I stay till I haf looked very carefully through all the tiamonts, in the different compartments of the case, in case one might haf dropped on the floor, or got changed, you know. That is pishness."

"Just so. And they were all right?"

"All right and same as the list—I know well a tiamont that I haf seen once. So I go away, and afterwards Denson tells me that the American liked much the stones but wouldn't quite come up to price. That, of course, is fery usual pishness. 'But he will rise, Samuel,' Denson says. 'I know him quite well, and them tiamonts is as good as sold with a good profit for me; and a good one for you, too, I bet,' he says. I was putting the lot to him for fifteen t'ousant pounds, and it would have been a nice profit in that for me. And then Denson he chaffs me and he says, 'Ah! Samuel,' he says, 'wasn't you afraid my customer and me would hook it out o' the window with all your stones?' I don't like that sort o' joke in pishness, you see, but I say, 'All right—I wasn't afraid o' that. The window was a mile too high, and besides I could see it from where I was a-sitting.' And so I could, you see, plain enough to see if it was opened."

The ground-glass partition, in fact, cut off a part of the window of the outer office, which, being at an angle with the inner room, gave a side view of the window that lighted that apartment.

"Denson laughed at that," Samuel went on. "'Ha-ha!' says he, 'I never thought of that. Then you could see the American's hat hanging up just by the window—rum hat, ain't it?' And that was quite true, for I had noticed it—a big, grey wideawake, almost white."

Hewitt nodded approvingly. "You are quite right," he said, "to tell me everything you recollect, even of the most trivial sort; the smallest thing may be very valuable. So you took your diamonds away the first time, last week. What next?"

"Well, I came again, just the same, today, by appointment. Just the same I sat in that place, and just the same Denson took the case into the inner room. 'He's come to buy this time, I can see,' Denson whispers, and winks. 'But he'll fight hard over the price. We'll see!' and off he goes into the other room. Well, I waited. I waited and I waited a long time. I looked out sideways at the window, and there I see the American's big wideawake hat hanging up just inside the other window, same as last time. So I think they are a long time settling the price, and I wait some more. But it is such a very long time, and I begin to feel uneasy. Of course, I know you cannot sell fifteen t'ousant wort' of tiamonts in five minutes—that is not reasonable pishness. But I could hear nothing at all now—not a sound. And the boy—the boy that came down to call me up—he wasn't come back. But there I could see the big wideawake hat still hanging inside the window, and of course I knew there was only one door out of the inner room, right before me, so it seemed foolish to be uneasy. So I waited longer still, but now it was so late, I thought they should have come out to lunch before this, and then I was fery uneasy—fery uneasy inteet. So I thought I would pretend to be a new caller, and I opened the outer office door and banged it, and walked in very loud and knocked on the boy's table. I thought Denson would come when he heard that, but no—there was not a sound. So I got more uneasy, and I opened the window and leaned out as far as I could, to look in at the other window. There I could see nothing but the big hat and the back of a chair and a bit of the room—empty. So I went and banged the outer door again, and called out, 'Hi! Mr Denson, you're wanted! Hi! d'y'ear?' and knocked with my umbrella on the inner door; and, Mr Hewitt—you might have knocked me down with half a feather when I got no answer at all—not a sound! I opened the door, Mr Hewitt, and there was nobody there—nobody! There was my leather case on the table, open—and empty! Fifteen t'ousant pounds in tiamonts, Mr Hewitt—it ruins me!"

Hewitt rose, and flung wide the inner office door. "This is certainly the only door," he said, "and that is the only window—quite well in view from where you sat. There is the wideawake hat still hanging there—see, it is quite new; obviously brought for you to look at, it would seem. The door and the window were not used, and the chimney is impossible—register grate. But there was one other way—there."

The inner wall of each of the rooms was the wall of the corridor into which all the offices opened, and this corridor was lighted—and the offices partly ventilated—by a sort of hinged casement or fanlight close up by the ceiling, oblong, and extending the most of the length of each room. Plainly an active man, not too stout, might mount a chair-back, and climb very quietly through the opening. "That's the only way," said Hewitt, pointing.

"Yes," answered Samuel, nodding and rubbing his knuckles together nervously. "I saw it—saw it when it was too late. But who'd have thought o' such a thing beforehand? And the American—either there wasn't an American at all, or he got out the same way. But, anyway, here I am, and the tiamonts are gone, and there is nothing here but the furniture—not worth twenty pound!"

"Well," Hewitt said, "so far, I think I understand, though I may have questions to ask presently. But go on."

"Go on? But there is no more, Mr Hewitt! Quite enough, don't you think? There is no more—I am robbed!"

"But when you found the empty room, and the case, what did you do? Send for the police?"

The Jew's face clouded slightly. "No, Mr Hewitt," he said, "not for the police, but for you. Reason plain enough. The police make a great fuss, and they want to arrest the criminal. Quite right—I want to arrest him, and punish him too, plenty. But most I want the tiamonts back, because if not it ruins me. If it was to make choice between two things for me, whether to punish Denson or get my tiamonts, then of course I take the tiamonts, and let Denson go—I cannot be ruined. But with the police, if it is their choice, they catch the thief first, and hold him tight, whether it loses the property or not; the property is only second with them—with me it is first and second, and all. So I take no more risks than I can help, Mr Hewitt. I have sent for you to get first the stones—afterwards the thief if you can. But first my property; you can perhaps find Denson and make him give it up rather than go to prison. That would be better than having him taken and imprisoned, and perhaps the stones put away safe all the time ready for him when he came out."

"Still, the police can do things that I can't," Hewitt interposed; "stop people leaving or landing at ports, and the like. I think we should see them."

Samuel was anxiously emphatic. "No, Mr Hewitt," he said, "certainly not the police. There are reasons—no, *not* the police, Mr Hewitt, at any rate, not till you have tried. I cannot haf the police—just yet."

Martin Hewitt shrugged his shoulders. "Very well," he said, "if those are your instructions, I'll do my best. And so you sent for me at once, as soon as you discovered the loss?"

"Yes, at once."

"Without telling anybody else?"

"I haf tolt nobody."

"Did you look about anywhere for Denson—in the street, or what not?"

"No—what was the good? He was gone; there was time for him to go miles."

"Very good. And speaking of time, let me judge how far he may have gone. How long were you kept waiting?"

"Two hours and a quarter, very near—within five minutes."

"By your watch?"

"Yes—I looked often, to see if it was so long waiting as it seemed."

"Very good. Do you happen to have a piece of Denson's writing about you?"

Samuel looked round him. "There's nothing about here," he said, "but perhaps we can find—oh here—here's a post-card." He took the card from his pocket, and gave it to Hewitt.

"There is nothing else to tell me, then?" queried Hewitt. "Are you sure that you have forgotten nothing that has happened since you first arrived—*nothing at all*?" There was meaning in the emphasis, and a sharp look in Hewitt's eyes.

"No, Mr Hewitt," Samuel answered, hastily; "there is nothing else I can tell you."

"Then I will think it over at once. You had better go back quietly to your office, and think it over yourself, *in case* you have forgotten something; and I need hardly warn you to keep quiet as to what has passed between us—unless you tell the police. I think I shall take the liberty of a glance over Mr Denson's office, and since his office boy still stays away, I will lend him my clerk for a little. He will keep his eyes open if any callers come, and his ears too. Wait while I fetch him."

II

It was at this point that my humble part in the case began, for Hewitt hurried first to my rooms.

"Brett," he exclaimed, "are you engaged this afternoon?"

"No—nothing important."

"Will you do me a small favour? I have a rather interesting case. I want a man watched for an hour or so, and I haven't a soul to do it. Kerrett *may* be known, and I *am* known. Besides, there is another job for Kerrett."

Of course, I expressed myself willing to do what I could.

"Capital," replied Hewitt. "Come along—you like these adventures, I know, or I wouldn't have asked you; and you know the dodges in this sort of observation. The man is one Samuel, a Jew, of 150 Hatton Garden, diamond dealer. I'll tell you more afterwards. Kerrett and I are going into the offices next door, and I want you to wait thereabout. Presently I will come downstairs with him and he will go away. An hour or so will be enough, probably."

I followed Hewitt downstairs. He took Kerrett with him and locked his office door. I saw them both disappear within the large new building, and I waited near a convenient postal pillar-box, prepared to seem very busy with a few old letters from my pocket until my man's back was turned.

In a very few minutes Hewitt reappeared, this time with a man—a Jew, obviously—whom I remembered having seen already at the door of that office more than an hour before, as I had passed on the way from the bookseller's at the corner. The man walked briskly up the street, and I, on the opposite side, did the same, a little in the rear.

He turned the corner, and at once slackened his pace and looked about him. He took a peep back along the street he had left, and then hailed a cab.

For a hundred yards or more I was obliged to trot, till I saw another cab drop its fare just ahead, and managed to secure it and give the cabman instructions to follow the cab in front, before it turned a corner. The chase was difficult, for the horse that drew me was a poor one, and half a dozen times I thought I had lost sight of the other cab altogether; but my cabman was better than his animal, and from his high perch he kept the chase in view, turning corners and picking out the cab ahead among a dozen others with surprising certainty. We went across Charing Cross Road by way of Cranborne Street, past Leicester Square, through Coventry Street and up the Quadrant and Regent Street. At Oxford Circus the Jew's cab led us to the left, and along Oxford Street we chased it past Bond Street end. Suddenly my cab pulled up with a jerk, and the driver spoke through the trapdoor. "That fare's getting down, sir," he said, "at the corner o' Duke Street."

I thrust a half-crown up through the hole and sprang out. "'E's crossing the road, sir," the cabman finally reported, and I hurried across the street accordingly.

The man I was watching was strikingly Jewish enough, and easy to distinguish in a crowd. I had almost overtaken him before he had gone a dozen yards up the northern end of Duke Street. He walked on into Manchester Square. There a small, neat brougham, with blinds drawn, was being driven slowly round the central garden. I saw Samuel walk hurriedly up to this brougham, which stopped as he approached. He stepped quickly into the carriage and shut the door behind him. The brougham resumed its slow progress, and I loitered, keeping it in view, though the blinds were drawn so close that it was impossible to guess who might be Samuel's companion, if he had one. I think I have said that when the Jew came to the office door with Hewitt I perceived that he was a man I had seen before that day. I was now convinced that I had also seen that same brougham, at the same time; but of this presently.

The carriage made one slow circuit, and then Samuel got out and shut the door quickly again. I took the precaution of turning my back and letting him overtake and pass me on his way back through Duke Street. At the end of the street he mounted an omnibus going east, and I took another seat in the same vehicle. The rest was uninteresting. He went direct to No. 150 Hatton Garden, and there remained. I read his name on the door-post among a score of others, and after a twenty-minutes' wait I returned to my rooms. I had no doubt that it was the meeting in the brougham that Hewitt wished reported, and I remembered his rule was never to watch a man a moment after the main object was secured.

Hewitt was out, and he did not return till after dusk. Then he came straightway to my rooms.

"Well, Brett," he said, "what's the report? As a matter of fact, Samuel is my client, as I shall explain presently. I don't like spying on a client, as a rule, but I was convinced that he was keeping something back from me, and there was something odd about his whole story. But what did you see?"

I told Hewitt the tale of my pursuit as I have told it here. "I came away," I concluded, "after it seemed that he was settled in his office for a bit. But there is another thing you should know. When he first came out with you I recognised him at once as a man I had seen at that same door a little after two o'clock—say a quarter past."

"Yes?" answered Hewitt. "I saw him there myself a little sooner—something like two, I should say. What was he doing?"

"Well," I replied, "he was doing pretty well what he did in Manchester Square. For as a matter of fact the brougham also was here then—just outside the next-door office. I think I might swear to that same brougham—though of course I didn't notice it so particularly that first time."

Hewitt whistled. "Oh!" he said. "Tell me about this. Did he get into the brougham this time?"

"Yes. He came out of the office door with a black leather case in his hand and a very scared look on his face. And he popped into the brougham, leather case, scared look and all."

"Ho—ho!" said Hewitt, thoughtfully, and whistled again. "A black leather case, eh! Come, come, the plot thickens. And what happened? Did the carriage go off?"

"No; I saw nothing more—shouldn't have noticed so much, in fact, if the whole thing hadn't looked a trifle curious. Nervous, pallid Jew with a black case—as though he thought it was dynamite and might go off at any moment—closed brougham, blinds drawn, Jew skipped in and banged the door, but brougham didn't move; and I fancied—perhaps only fancied—that I saw a woman's black veil inside. But then I turned in here and saw no more."

Hewitt sat thoughtfully silent for a few moments. Then he rose and said, "Come next door, and I'll tell you how we stand. The housekeeper will let us in, and we'll see if you can identify that black case anywhere."

It seemed that Hewitt had by this established a good understanding with the housekeeper next door. "Nobody's been, sir," the man said, as he admitted us and closed the heavy doors. "Office boy not come back, nor nothing."

We went up to Denson's office on the third floor, the door of which the housekeeper opened; and having turned on the electric light, he left us.

"Now, is that anything like the case?" Hewitt asked, when the housekeeper was gone; and he lifted from under the table the very black case I had seen Samuel take into the brougham.

I said that I felt as sure of the case as of the brougham. And then Hewitt told me the whole tale of Samuel and his loss of fifteen thousand pounds' worth of diamonds, just as it appears earlier in this narrative.

"Now, see here," said Hewitt, when he had made me acquainted with his client's tale, "there is something odd about all this. See this postcard which Samuel gave me. It is from Denson, and it makes this morning's appointment. See! 'Be down below at eleven sharp' is the message. He came and he waited just two hours and a quarter, as he tells me, being certain to the time within five minutes. That brings, us to a quarter-past one—the time when he finds he is robbed; and he came downstairs in a very agitated state at a quarter-past one, as I have since ascertained. At two I pass and see him still dancing distractedly on the front steps—certainly very much like a man who has had a serious misfortune, or expects one. At a quarter-past two—that was about it, I think?" (I nodded) "At a quarter-past two you see him, still agitated, diving into the brougham with this black case in his hand; and a little afterward—after all this, mind—he tells me this story of a robbery of diamonds from that very case, and assures me that he sent for me the moment he discovered the loss—that is to say, at a quarter-past one, a positive lie—and has told nobody else. He further assures me that he has told me everything that has happened up to the moment he meets me. Then he goes away—to his office, as he tells me. But you find him posting to Manchester Square in a cab, and there once more plunging into that same mysterious closed brougham. Now why should he do that? He has seen the person in that brougham, presumably, an hour before, and there can be nothing more to communicate, except the result of his interview with me—a thing I warned him to keep to himself. It's odd, isn't it?"

"It is. What can be his motive?"

"I want to know his motive. I object to working for a client who deceives me—indeed, it's unsafe. I may be making myself an accomplice in some criminal scheme. You observe that he never called for the police—a natural impulse in a robbed man. Indeed, he expressly vetoes all communication with the police."

"Of course he gave reasons."

"But the reasons are not good enough. I can't stop a man leaving this country anywhere round the coast except by going to the police."

"Can it be," I suggested, "that Samuel and Denson are working in collusion, and have perhaps insured the stones, and now want your help to make out a case of loss?"

"Scarcely that, I think, for more than one reason. First, it isn't a risk any insurer would take, in the circumstances. Next, the insurer would certainly want to know why the police were not informed at once. But there is more. I have not been idle this while, as you would know. I will tell you some of the things I have ascertained. To begin with, Samuel is known in Hatton Garden only as a dealer on a very small and peddling scale. A dabbler in commissions, in fact, rather than a buyer and seller of diamonds in quantities on his own account. His office is nothing but a desk in a small room he shares with two others—small dealers like himself. When I spoke to the people most likely to know, of his offering fifteen thousand pounds' worth of diamonds on his own account, they laughed. An investment of two or three hundred pounds in stones was about his limit, they said. Now that fact offers fresh suggestions, doesn't it?" Hewitt looked at me significantly.

"You mean," I said after a little consideration, "that Samuel may have been entrusted with the diamonds to sell by the real owner, and has made all these arrangements with Denson to get the gems for themselves and represent them as stolen?"

Hewitt nodded thoughtfully. "There's that possibility," he said. "Though even in that case the owner would certainly want to know why the police had not been told, and I don't know what satisfactory answer Samuel could make. And more, I find that no such robbery has been reported to any of the principal dealers in Hatton Garden today; and, so far as I can ascertain, none of them has entrusted Samuel with anything like so large a quantity of diamonds as he talks of—lately, at any rate."

"Isn't it possible that the diamonds are purely imaginary?" I suggested. "Mightn't there be some trick played on that basis? Perhaps a trick on the American customer—if there was one."

Hewitt was thoughtful. "There are many possibilities," he said, "which I must consider. The diamonds may even be stolen property to begin with; that would account for a great deal, though perhaps not all. But the whole thing is so oddly suspicious, that unless my client is willing to let me a great deal further into his confidence tomorrow morning I shall throw up the case."

"Did you direct any inquiries after Denson?"

"Of course; which brings me to the other things I have ascertained. He has not been here long—a few months. I cannot find that he has been doing any particular business all the time with anybody except Samuel. With him, however, he seems to have been very friendly. The housekeeper speaks of them as being 'very thick together.' The rooms are cheaply furnished, as you see. And here is another thing to consider. The housekeeper vows that he never left his glass box at the foot of the stairs from the time Samuel went upstairs first to the time when he came down again, vastly agitated, at a quarter-past one, and sent a message; and during all that time *Denson never passed the box*! And the main door is the only way out."

"But wasn't he there at all?"

"Yes, he was there, certainly, when Samuel came. But note, now. Observe the sequence of things as we know them now. First, there is Denson in his office; I can find nothing of any American visitor, and I am convinced that he is a total fiction, either of Denson's or Samuel and Denson together. Denson is in his office. To him comes Samuel. Neither leaves the place till Samuel comes down at a quarter-past one o'clock. I told you he sent some sort of message. The housekeeper tells me that he called a passing commissionaire and gave him something, though whether it was a telegram or a note he did not see; nor does he know the commissionaire, nor his number—though he could easily be found if it became necessary, no doubt. Samuel sends the message, and waits on the steps, watching, in an agitated manner (as would be natural, perhaps, in a man engaged in an anxious and ticklish piece of illegality) for an hour, when this mysterious brougham appears. He takes this black case into the brougham, and he obviously brings it out again, for here it is. Whatever has happened, he brings it out empty. Then he sends the housekeeper for me. When at length I arrive, Denson has certainly gone, but there was an opportunity for that while the housekeeper was absent on the message to my office—*after* all Samuel's agitation, and after he had carried his case to and from the brougham."

"The whole thing is odd enough, certainly, and suspicious enough. Have you found anything else?"

"Yes. Denson lives, or lived, in a boarding house in Bloomsbury. He has only been there two months, however, and they know practically nothing of him. Today he came home at an unusual time, letting himself in with his latchkey, and went away at once with a bag, but the accounts of the exact time are contradictory. One servant thought it was before twelve, and another insisted that it was after one. He has not been back."

"And the office boy—can't you get some information out of him?"

"He hasn't been seen since the morning. I expect Denson told him to take a whole holiday. I can't find where he lives, at the moment, but no doubt he will turn up tomorrow. Not that I expect to get much from him. But I shan't bother. Unless

Mr Samuel will answer satisfactorily some very plain questions I shall ask—and I don't expect he will—I shall throw up the commission. He called, by the way, not long ago, but I was out. We shall see him in the morning, I expect."

A look round Denson's office taught me no more than it had taught Hewitt already. There were two small rooms, one inside the other, with ordinary and cheap office furniture. It was quite plain that any man of ordinary activity and size could have got out of the inner room into the corridor by the means which Samuel suggested—through the hinged wall-light, near the ceiling. Hewitt had meddled with nothing—he would do no more till he was satisfied of the *bonâ fides* of his client; certainly he would not commit himself to breaking open desks or cupboards. And so, the time for my attendance at the office approaching—I was working on the *Morning Ph[oe]nix* then, and ten at night saw my work begin—we shut Denson's office, and went away.

III

In the morning I was awakened by an impatient knocking at my bedroom door. Going to bed at two or three I was naturally a late riser, and this was about nine. I scrambled sleepily out of bed, and turned the key. Hewitt was standing in my sitting-room, with a newspaper in his hand.

"Sorry to break your morning sleep, Brett," he said, "but something interesting has happened in regard to that business you helped me with yesterday, and you may like to know. Crawl back into bed if you like."

But I was already in my dressing-gown, and groping for my clothes. "No, no, come in and tell me," I said. "What is it?"

Hewitt sat on the bed. "I'll tell you in due order," he said. "First, I saw Samuel again last night—after you had gone away. You remember I went back to my office; I had a letter or two to write which I had set aside in the afternoon. Well, I wrote the letters, shut up, and went downstairs. I opened the outer door, and there was Samuel, in the act of ringing the housekeeper's bell. He said he was very anxious, and couldn't sleep without coming to hear if I had made any progress; he had called before, but I was out. I half thought of taking him back to my office, but decided that it wasn't worth while. So I walked along to the corner of the Strand, till I got him well under the lights. Then I stopped and talked to him. 'You ask about the progress in your case, Mr Samuel,' I said. 'Now, I have sometimes met people who seem to consider me a sort of prophet, seer, or diviner. As a matter of fact, I am nothing but a professional investigator, and even if I were possessed of such an amazing genius as I lay no claim to, I could never succeed in a case, nor even make progress in it, if my client started me with false information, or only told me half the truth. More, when I find that such is the state of affairs, and that if I am to succeed I must begin by investigating my client before I proceed with his case, I throw that case up on the instant—invariably. Do you understand that? Now I must tell you that I have made no progress with your case, none; for that very reason.'"

"He protested, of course—vowed he had told me the simple truth, and so forth. I replied by asking him certain definite questions. First, I asked him whose the diamonds were. He repeated that they were his own. To that I simply replied, 'Good evening, Mr Samuel,' and turned away. He came after me beseechingly, and prevaricated. He said something about another party having an interest, but the matter being confidential. To that I responded by asking him with whom he had communicated before sending for me, and who was the person in the brougham which he had twice entered. That flabbergasted him. He said that he couldn't answer those questions without bringing other parties into the matter, to which I answered that it was just those other parties that I meant to know about, if I were to move a step in the matter. At this he got into a sad state—imploring, actually imploring, me not to desert him. He said he should do something desperate—something terrible—that night if I didn't relieve his mind, and undertake the case. What he meant he'd do I didn't know, of course, but it didn't move me. I said finally that I would deal only with principals, and that until I had the personal instructions of the actual owner of the diamonds, in addition to a complete explanation of the brougham incident, I should do nothing, and I recommended him to go to the police; and with that I left him."

"And you got nothing more from him than that?"

"Nothing more; but it was something, you see. He admitted, to all intents, that the diamonds were not his own. And now see here. I suppose I left him about ten o'clock. Here is a paragraph in one of this morning's newspapers. It is only in the one paper; the matter seems to have occurred rather late for press."

Hewitt gave me the paper in his hand, pointing to the following paragraph:

"HORRIBLE DISCOVERY.—A shocking discovery was made just before midnight last night, near the York column, where a police-constable found the dead body of a man lying on the stone steps. The body, which was fully clothed in the ordinary dress of a labouring man, bore plain marks of strangulation, and it was evident that a brutal murder had been committed. A singular circumstance was the presence of a curious reddish mark upon the forehead, at first taken for a wound, but soon discovered to be a mark apparently drawn or impressed on the skin. At the time of going to press, no arrest had been made, and so far the affair appears a mystery."

"Well," I said, "this certainly seems curious, especially in the matter of the mark on the forehead. But what has it all to do—"

"To do with Samuel and his diamonds, you mean? I'll tell you. *That dead man is Denson!*"

"Denson?" I exclaimed. "Denson? How?"

"I get it from the housekeeper next door. It seems that when the police came to examine the body they found, among other things—money and a watch, and the like—a piece of an addressed envelope, used to hold a few pins—the pins stuck in and the paper rolled up, you know. There was just enough of it to guess the address by—that of the office next door; and it was the only clue they had. So they came along here at once and knocked up the housekeeper. He went with them and instantly recognised Denson, disguised in labourer's clothes, but Denson, he says, unmistakably."

"And the mark on the forehead?"

"That is very odd. It is an outlined triangle, rather less than an inch along each side. It is quite red, he says, and seems to be done in a greasy, sticky sort of ink or colour."

"Was anything found—the diamonds?"

"No. He says there was money—two or three five-pound notes, I believe, some small change, a watch, keys and so forth; but there's not a word of diamonds."

I paused in my dressing. "Does that mean that the murderer has got them?" I asked. Hewitt pursed his lips and shook his head. "It *may* mean that," he said, "but does it look altogether like it when five-pound notes are left? On the other hand, there is the disguise; the only reason that we know of for that would be that he was bolting with the diamonds. But the really puzzling thing is the mark on the forehead. Why that? Of course, the picturesque and romantic thing to suppose is that it is the mark of some criminal club or society. But criminal associations, such as exist, don't do silly things like that. When criminals rob and murder, they don't go leaving their tracks behind them purposely—they leave nothing that could possibly draw attention to them if they can help it; also, they don't leave five-pound notes. But I'm off to have a look at that mark. Inspector Plummer is in charge of the case—you remember Plummer, don't you, in the Stanway Cameo case, and two or three others?

Well, Plummer is an old friend of mine, and not only am I interested in this matter myself, but now that it becomes a case of murder, I must tell the police all I know, merely as a loyal citizen. I've an idea they will want to ask our friend Mr Samuel some very serious questions."

"Will you go now?"

"Yes, I must waste no more time. You get your breakfast and look out for me, or for a message."

Hewitt was off to Vine Street, and I devoted myself to my toilet and my breakfast, vastly mystified by this tragic turn in a matter already puzzling enough.

It was not a messenger, but Hewitt himself, who came back in less than an hour. "Come," he said, "Plummer is below, and we are going next door, to Denson's office. I've an idea that we may get at something at last. The police are after Samuel hot-foot. They think he should be made sure of in any case without delay; and I must say they have some reason, on the face of it."

We joined Plummer at once—I have already spoken of Plummer in my accounts of several of Hewitt's cases in which I met him—and we all turned into the office next door. There we found a very frightened and bewildered office boy, whom Denson had given a holiday yesterday, after sending him down to Samuel. He had come to his work as usual, only to meet the housekeeper's tale of the murder of his master and the end of his business prospects. He had little or no information to impart. He had only been employed for a month or six weeks, and during that time his work had been practically nothing.

Plummer nodded at this information, and sniffed comprehensively at the office furniture. "I know this sort o' stuff," he said. "This is the way they fit up long firm offices and such. This place was taken for the job, that's plain, by one or both of 'em."

The boy's address was taken, and he was given a final holiday, and asked to send up the housekeeper as he went out. Plummer passed Hewitt a bunch of keys.

The housekeeper entered. "Now, Hutt," said Martin Hewitt, "you were saying yesterday, I think, that the main front door was the only entrance and exit for this building?"

"That's so, sir—the only one as anybody can use, except me."

"Oh! then there *is* another, then?"

"Well, not exactly to say an entrance, sir. There's a small private door at the back into the court behind, but that's only opened to take in coals and such, and I always have the key. This house isn't like yours, sir; you have no back way into the court as we have. It's a convenience, sometimes."

"Ah, I've no doubt. Do you happen to have the key with you?"

"It's on the bunch hanging up in my box, sir. Shall I fetch it?"

"I should like to see it, if you will."

The housekeeper disappeared, and presently returned with a large bunch of keys.

"This is the one, Mr Hewitt," he explained, lifting it from among the rest.

Hewitt examined it closely, and then placed beside it one from the bunch Plummer had given him. "It seems you're not the only person who ever had a key exactly like that, Hutt," he said. "See here—this was found in Mr Denson's pocket."

Plummer nodded sagaciously. "All in the plant," he said. "See—it's brand new; clean as a new pin, and file marks still on it."

"Take us to this back door, Hutt," Hewitt pursued. "We'll try this key. Is there a back staircase?"

There *was* a small back staircase, leading to the coal-cellars, and only used by servants. Down this we all went, and on a lower landing we stopped before a small door. Hewitt slipped the key in the lock and turned it. The door opened easily, and there before us was the little courtyard which I think I have mentioned in one of my other narratives—the courtyard with a narrow passage leading into the next street.

Martin Hewitt seemed singularly excited. "See there," he said, "that is how Denson left the building without passing the housekeeper's box! And now I'm going to make another shot. See here. This key on Denson's bunch attracted my attention because of its noticeable newness compared with most of the others. *Most* of the others, I say, because there is one other just as bright—see! This small one. Now, Hutt, do you happen to have a key like that also?"

Hutt turned the key over in his hand and glanced from it to his own bunch. "Why, yes, sir!" he said presently. "Yes, sir! It's the same as the key of the fire-hose cupboards!"

"Does that key fit them all? How many fire-hose cupboards are there?"

"Two on each floor, sir, one at each end, just against the mains. And one key fits the lot."

"Show us the nearest to this door."

A short, narrow passage led to the main ground-floor corridor, where a cupboard lettered "Fire Hose" stood next the main and its fittings. "We have to keep the hose-cupboards locked," the housekeeper explained apologetically, "'cause o' mischievous boys in the offices."

This key fitted as well as the other. A long coil of brown leather hose hung within, and in a corner lay a piece of chamois leather evidently used for polishing the brass fittings. This Hewitt pulled aside, and there beneath it lay another and cleaner piece of chamois leather, neatly folded and tied round with cord. Hewitt snatched it up. He unfastened the cord; he unrolled the leather, which was sewn into a sort of bag or satchel; and when at last he spread wide the mouth of this satchel, light seemed to spring from out of it, for there lay a glittering heap of brilliants!

"What!" cried Plummer, who first got his speech. "Diamonds! Samuel's diamonds!"

"Diamonds, at any rate," replied Hewitt, "whether Samuel's or somebody else's. But they can't have been there long. How often is this cupboard opened?"

"Every Saturday reg'lar, sir," replied the housekeeper; "just to dust it out and see things is right."

"Now, see here!" said Martin Hewitt, "I've had luck in my conjectures as yet, and I'll try again. Here is what I believe has happened. Every word that Samuel told me about the theft of those diamonds was true, except as to their ownership. Denson has planned all along to rob him of as big a collection of diamonds as he could prompt him to get together, and he has played up to this for months. His smaller dealings one way and another were ground-bait. Very artfully he let Samuel take the diamonds safely away once, in order that he should be less watchful and less suspicious the second time. This second time he does the trick exactly as we see. He hangs up the imaginary American's hat, he escapes by the fanlight, and he goes out by the back way to avoid the housekeeper's observation. He has arranged beforehand for this, too. He has seized an opportunity when the housekeeper has been out of his box to get wax impressions of these two keys, and he has made copies of them. And here we come on a curious thing. It is easy enough to understand why he should foresee and get himself a key for the back door, in order to make his escape. But why the key of the hose-cupboard? Why, indeed, should he leave the diamonds behind him at all? It is plain that he meant to come back for them—probably at night. He would have been wholly free from observation in that quiet courtyard, and he could let himself in, get the diamonds, and leave again without exciting the smallest alarm or suspicion. But why take all the trouble? Why not stick to the plunder from the beginning? The plain inference is that he feared somebody or something. He feared being stopped and searched, or he feared being waylaid *sometime during yesterday*. By whom? There's the puzzle, and I can't see the bottom of it, I confess. If I could, perhaps I might know something of last night's murder.

"As to Samuel's prevarications, there is only one explanation that will fit, now that the rest is made clear. He must have been entrusted with these diamonds by a private owner, for sale—secretly. Some lady of conspicuous position in difficulties, probably—perhaps unknown to her husband. Such things occur every day. A common expedient is to sell the stones and have good paste substituted, in the same settings. Samuel would be just the man to carry through a transaction of that sort. That would account for everything. The jewels are *en suite*, cut, but unset—taken from a set of jewellery, and paste substituted. Samuel arranges it all for the lady, finds a customer—Denson—who treats him exactly as he has told us. When he realises the loss Samuel doesn't know what to do. He mustn't call the police, being bound to secrecy on the lady's behalf. He sends her a hasty message, and remains keeping watch by Denson's office. She hurries to him with all possible secrecy, keeping her carriage blinds down; he dashes into the brougham to describe the disaster, taking his case with him in his frantic desire to explain things fully. The lady fears publicity, and won't hear of the police—she instructs him to consult me: and consequently, of course, when I recommend communicating with the police he won't listen to the suggestion. Samuel has arranged with the lady to hurry off and report progress as soon as he has consulted me, and this he does, the lady having appointed Manchester Square for the interview. Perhaps she hints some suspicion of Samuel's honesty—rather natural, perhaps, in the circumstances. That terrifies him more than ever, and leads to his frantic appeals to me when I throw the case up. Come, there's my guess at the facts of the case, and I'll back it with twopence and a bit more. Eh, Plummer?"

"I don't take your bet," answered Plummer. "The thing's plain enough; except the murder. There's something deeper there."

Hewitt became grave. "That's true," he said, "and something I can see no way into, as yet. But come—you take this parcel of diamonds, as representing the law. And here comes one of your men, I think."

We had been approaching the front door during this talk, and now a police constable appeared, and saluted Plummer. "Samuel's just been brought in, sir," he reported. "He's half dead with fright, and he's sent a message to Lady H—in P—Square; and he says he wants Mr Martin Hewitt to come and speak for him."

"Poor Samuel!" Hewitt commented. "Come, we'll go and make him happy. Here are the diamonds, and, those safely accounted for, there's no evidence to connect him with the murder. We'll get him out of the mess as soon as possible."

And so they did. Hewitt's reading of the case was correct to a tittle, as it turned out, and with very little delay Samuel was released. But with the message from the police station, the fat was in the fire as regarded Lady H—. Her husband necessarily became acquainted with everything, and there was serious domestic trouble.

Samuel was glad enough to get quit of the business with no worse than a bad fright, as may well be supposed. He showed himself most grateful to Hewitt in after times, giving him excellent confidential advice and information more than once in matters connected with the diamond trade. He is still in business, I believe, in a much larger way, and I have no doubt he is the wiser for his experience, and for the lesson which Hewitt did not forget to rub well in: that it is useless and worse to place a confidential matter in the hands of a man of Hewitt's profession, and at the same time withhold particulars of the case, however unessential they may appear to be.

But meantime, on the way to Vine Street I asked Hewitt what led him to suppose that the new key on Denson's bunch fitted a lock in that particular office building.

"Call it a lucky guess, if you like," Hewitt answered; "but as a matter of fact it was prompted by pure common sense. Plummer showed me the things found on the body, and I saw at once that the keys offered the only chance of immediate information. I went through them one by one. There was his latchkey—the key with which he had gone into his lodgings to fetch away the disguise. There was another largish key, equally old—probably the key of his office door. There were other smaller keys, also old—plainly belonging to bags and trunks and drawers and so forth. And then there was the large, perfectly new key. What was that? It was not the key of any bag or drawer, clearly—it was the key of a door—a door with a lever lock. What door? Had Denson some other office? Perhaps he had, but first it was best to begin by trying it on places we were already acquainted with. At once I thought of Denson's disappearance unobserved by the housekeeper. Could this be the key of some private exit from the office building? I resolved to test that conjecture first, and it turned out to be the right one. Being successful so far, of course I turned to the other new key and tried that, as you saw."

"But what of that triangular mark on the man's forehead?"

Martin Hewitt became deeply thoughtful. "That," he said, "is a matter wholly beyond me at present, as indeed is the whole business of the murder. Whether we shall ever know more I can't guess, but the matter is deep—deep and difficult and dark. As to the mark itself, that seems to have been impressed from an engraved stamp of some sort. It is a plain equilateral triangle in red outline, measuring about an inch on each side. It is in a greasy, sticky sort of red ink, which may be smeared, but is very difficult, if not impossible, to rub away. What it means I can't at present conjecture. I have told you my reasons for not thinking it the sign of any gang of criminals.

But whose sign is it? Surely not that of some self-constituted punisher of crime? For such a person, with no risk to himself, could have handed Denson over to the police, if he knew of his offence. Can he have been murdered by an accomplice? But he used no accomplice; if one thing is plain in all that story of the stolen diamonds it is that Denson did the thing wholly by himself. Besides, an accomplice would have taken the keys and have gone and secured the diamonds for himself; else why the murder at all? But no keys were taken—nothing was taken, as far as we can tell. And why was the body placed in that conspicuous position? It is pretty certain that the crime cannot have happened where the body was found—somebody must have heard or seen a struggle in such a place as that. As it is, I should say, the body was probably brought quietly to the spot in a cab, or some such conveyance.

"But mystery envelops this crime everywhere. So far as I can see, there is no clue whatever beyond the Red Triangle, which, as yet, I cannot understand. The strangling points to the murder being committed by a powerful man, certainly, and it is a form of crime that may have been perpetrated silently. But beyond that I can see nothing. The apparent motivelessness of the thing makes the mystery all the darker, and the circumstances we are acquainted with, instead of helping us, seem to complicate the puzzle.

"What was it that Denson feared when he left those diamonds behind him, when he might have carried them away? And why should he fear it in daytime and not at night, since it would seem plain that he meant to have returned for the stones at night? Where did he go to disguise himself yesterday—we know it was not in his lodgings—and where has he left the clothes he discarded?"

All these doubts and mysteries were destined to be cleared up, in more or less degree; but it was not till Hewitt and I had witnessed other singular adventures that the answer came to the problem, the real meaning of the Red Triangle was made apparent, and its connection with the theft of Samuel's diamonds grew clear. For indeed the connection proved in the end to be very intimate indeed. Once, a little later, we were allowed to see a shade farther into the mystery, as I shall tell in the proper place; but even then the real secret remained hidden from us till the appointed end.

So ended the case of Samuel's diamonds, so far as concerned Samuel himself and the owner; but the case of the Red Triangle had only begun.

2

THE CASE OF MR JACOB MASON

I

The mystery of Denson's death remained a mystery, despite all the police could do. The coroner's jury returned a verdict of "Murder by some person or persons unknown"—which, indeed, was all that could be expected of them; for they had no more before them than the bare fact that the body, disguised in the clothes of a labourer, had been found on the steps near the Duke of York's column, just before midnight, by a police constable. But for the housekeeper's identification, even the name of the victim would have been unknown. The jury certainly wasted some time in idle speculation as to the strange triangular mark found on the forehead, without a speck of evidence to help them; but in the end they returned their verdict, and went home.

But the police knew a little more than the jury, though that little rather confused than helped them. They exercised their judgment at the inquest in withholding all evidence of the theft of diamonds on which the victim had been engaged, the curious particulars of which I have already related. In this they followed their usual course in cases where the evidence withheld could give the jury no help in arriving at their verdict, and at the same time might easily hamper further investigations if revealed. For the theft had been frustrated by Martin Hewitt's exertions, as we have seen, and in any case the thief was now dead and beyond the reach of human punishment. The one matter now remaining for the police was inquiry into the murder of this same thief, and the one object of their exertions the apprehension of the murderer or murderers.

The case, as I have already said, was in the hands of Inspector Plummer, an intelligent officer and an old friend of Hewitt's. A few days' work after the inquest yielded Plummer so little result that he called at Hewitt's office to talk matters over.

"I suppose," Plummer began, "it's no use asking if you've heard anything more of that matter of Denson's murder?"

Hewitt shook his head. "I haven't heard a word," he said. "If I had, it would have come on to you at once. But I hope you've had some luck yourself?"

"Not a scrap; time wasted; and the few off-chance clues I tried have led nowhere, so that I'm where I was at the start. The thing is quite the oddest in all my experience. See how we stand. Here's a man, Denson, who has just pulled off one of the cleverest jewel robberies ever attempted. He so arranges it that he walks safely off with fifteen thousand pounds' worth of diamonds, leaving the victim, Samuel, stuck patiently in an office for an hour or two before he even begins to suspect anything is wrong, and *then* unable to set the police after him, for the reasons you discovered. But this Denson doesn't carry the plunder off straightway, as he so easily might have done—he conceals it in the very house where the robbery was committed, taking with him a key by aid of which he may return and get it. Why? As you explained, it was probably because he feared somebody—feared being stopped and searched *on the day of the robbery*—not after, since it was plain he meant to return for his booty at night. Who could this have been, and why did Denson fear him? Mystery number one. Then this Denson is found dead that same night disguised in the clothes of a labourer, in a most conspicuous spot in London—the last place in the world one would expect a murderer to select for depositing his victim's body, for it is evidently *not* the place where the murder was committed. More, on the forehead there is this extraordinary impressed mark of a Red Triangle. Now, what can all that mean? Robbery, perhaps one thinks. But the body isn't robbed! There are three five-pound notes on it, besides a sovereign or two and some small change, a watch and chain, keys and all the rest of it. Then one guesses at the diamonds. Perhaps it was an accomplice in the robbery, who finds that Denson is about to bolt with the whole lot. But if there's one thing plain in this amazing business it is that Denson *had* no accomplice; he did the whole thing alone, as you discovered, and he needed no help. More than that, if this were the work of an accomplice why didn't he get the jewels? There were the keys to his hand and he left them! And would such a person actually go out of his way to put the body where it must be discovered at once, instead of concealing it till he could himself get away with the diamonds? Of course not. But there was no accomplice, and it's useless to labour that farther. All these arguments apply equally against the theory that it was the work of some criminal gang. They would have taken all they could get, notes, keys, diamonds and all, and they wouldn't have been so foolish as to exhibit the body with that extraordinary mark; criminal gangs are not such fools as to take unnecessary chances and gratuitously leave tracks behind them, as you know well enough. Well then, there we stand. So far, do you see any more in it than I do?"

Hewitt shook his head. "No," he said, "I can't say I do. All the considerations you have mentioned have already occurred to me. I talked them over, in fact, with my friend Brett. My connection with the case ceased, of course, with the discovery of the jewels, and about the murder I know no more than has been told me. I never saw the body, and so had no opportunity of picking up any overlooked clue; though doubtless you have seen to that. I know not a tittle more than you have just summarised, and on that alone the thing seems mystery pure and unadulterated."

"All there is beyond that was ascertained by the divisional surgeon on examination of the body. The man died from strangulation, as you know, and the natural presumption from that was that the murderer must have been a powerful man. But the surgeon is of the positive opinion—he is certain, in fact—that Denson was strangled with an instrument—a tourniquet."

"A tourniquet?"

"Yes, a surgeon's tourniquet, such as is used to compress a leg or arm and so stop a flow of blood. He considers the marks unmistakable. Now that might point to the murderer being a medical man."

"Conjecturally, yes; though, of course, it justifies nothing more than conjecture."

"Precisely. Well, that was something, but precious little. A tourniquet is a common thing enough—no more than a band with screw fittings, and there was nothing to show that the tourniquet used was any different from a thousand others; and I can see no particular reason why a doctor should commit a murder like this any more than any other man; in which the divisional surgeon agreed with me. And doctor or none, that Red Triangle was altogether unaccounted for. About that, too, by the way, the divisional surgeon told me a little, but a very useless little. The mark was not properly dried, owing to its slightly greasy nature, and although it was almost impossible to remove it wholly, it *was* possible to scrape off a little of the ink, or colour. Here is a little of it on a paper—quite dried now, of course."

Plummer carefully took from his pocket a small folded paper, unfolded it, and revealed a smaller paper within. On this were two little smears of a bright red colour. "There—that's the stuff," he said. "The surgeon examined it, and he reports it to be rather oddly constituted—so as to bear some affinity of meaning, possibly, to the triangle. For the stuff is a compound of three substances—animal, vegetable and mineral; there is a fine vegetable oil, he says, some waxy preparation, certainly of animal origin, and a mineral—cinnabar: vermilion, in fact. But though there *may* be some connection between the triangle and the substances representing the three natural kingdoms, it gives nothing practical—nothing to go on."

Martin Hewitt had been closely examining the marks on the paper, and now he answered, "I'm not so sure of that, though, Plummer. I think at least that it gives us another conjecture. I should guess that the man you want, as well as being acquainted with the use of the tourniquet, has at some time travelled in, or to, China."

"Why?"

"Unless I am wider of the mark than usual, this is the pigment used on Chinese seals. A Chinaman's seal acts for his signature on all sorts of documents; it is impressed or printed by hand pressure from a little engraved stone die, precisely as this triangle seems to have been, and the ink or colour is almost always red, compounded of vermilion, wax, and oil of sesamum."

Plummer sat up with a whistle. "Phew! Then it may have been done by a Chinaman!"

Hewitt shrugged his shoulders. "It's possible," he said; "of course, though, the sign, the triangle, is not a Chinese character. As a character, of course it is the Greek *Delta*. But it may be no character at all. In the signs of the ancient Cabala, the triangle, apex upward as it was in this case, was the symbol of fire; apex downward, it signified water."

Plummer patted the side of his head distractedly. "Heavens!" he said, "don't tell me I'm to search all China, and Greece, and—wherever the cabalistic pundits come from!"

"Well, no," Hewitt answered with a smile. "I think I should, at any rate, begin in this country. I rather think you might make a beginning at Denson. That is what I should do if the case were mine. See if anything can be ascertained of his previous life—probably under another name or names. *He* may have been in China. Yes, certainly, as we stand at present, I should begin at Denson."

"I think I will," the inspector replied, "though there's precious little to begin on there. I'd like to have you with me on this job, but, of course, that's impossible, since it's purely a police matter. But something, some information, may come your way, and in that case you'll let me know at once, of course."

"Of course I shall—it's a serious matter, as well as a strange one. I wish you all luck!"

Plummer departed to grapple with his difficulties, but in fact it was Hewitt who first heard fresh news of the Red Triangle, and that from a wholly unexpected quarter.

It was, indeed, only two days after Plummer's visit that Kerrett brought into Hewitt's private room the card of the Rev. James Potswood, with a request for a consultation. Mr Potswood's name was known to Hewitt, as, indeed, it was to many people, as that of a most devoted clergyman, rector of a large parish in north-west London, who devoted not only all his time and personal strength to his work, but also spent every penny of his private income on his parish. It was not a small income that Mr Potswood spent in this unselfish way, for he came of a wealthy family, and though a good part of his parish was inhabited by well-to-do people, there was quite enough poverty and distress in the poorer quarters to cause this excellent man often to regret that his resources were not even larger. He was a spare active grey-whiskered man of nearly sixty, with prominent and not very handsome features, though his face was full of frank and simple kindliness.

"My errand, Mr Hewitt," he said, "is of a rather vague, not to say visionary, character, and I doubt if you can help me. But at any rate I will explain the trouble as well as I can. In the first place, am I right in supposing that you were in some way professionally engaged in connection with that extraordinary case of murder a week or so ago—the case in which a man named Denson was found dead on the steps by the Duke of York's column?"

"Yes—and no," Hewitt answered. "I was professionally engaged on a certain matter about which you will not wish me to particularise—since it is the business of a client—and in course of it I came upon the other affair."

"Then before I ask what you know of that mysterious event, Mr Hewitt, I will tell you my story, so that you may judge whether you are able to reveal anything, or to do anything. Of course, what I say is in the strictest confidence."

"Of course."

"I have a parishioner, a Mr Jacob Mason, of whom I have seen very little of late years—scarcely anything at all, in fact, till a few days ago. He is fairly well to do, I believe, living a somewhat retired life in a house not far from my rectory. For many years he has laboured at natural science—chemistry in particular— and he has a very excellently fitted laboratory attached to his house. He is a widower, with no children of his own, but his orphan niece, a Miss Creswick, lives under his guardianship. Mr Mason was never a very regular churchgoer, but years ago I saw much more of him than I have of late. I must be perfectly frank with you, Mr Hewitt, if you are to help me, and therefore I must tell you that we disagreed on points of religion, in such a way that I found it difficult to maintain my former regard for Mr Mason. He had a curiously fantastic mind, and he was constantly being led to tamper with things that I think are best left alone—what is called spiritualism, for instance, and that horrible form of modern superstition which we hear whispers of at times from the Continent—the alleged devil-propitiation or worship. It was not that he did anything I thought morally wrong, you understand—except that he dabbled. And he was always running after some new thing—animal magnetism, or telepathy, or crystal-gazing, or theosophy, or someone of the score of such things that have an attraction for a mind of that sort. And it was a characteristic of each new enthusiasm with him that it prompted him to try to convert *me*; and that in such terms—terms often applied to the doctrines of that religion of which I am a humble minister—as I could in nowise permit in my presence. So that our friendly intercourse, though not interrupted by any definite breaking off, fell away to almost nothing. For which reason I was a little surprised to receive a visit from Mr Mason on the afternoon of the day on which the newspapers printed the report of the finding of the body of Denson. You may remember that only one morning paper mentioned the matter, and that very briefly; but there were full reports in all the evening papers."

"Yes, the discovery was made very late the previous night."

"So I gathered. Well, I was told that Mr Mason had been shown into my study, and there I found him. He was in an extremely nervous and agitated state, and he had an evening paper in his hand. With scarcely a preliminary word he burst out, 'Have you seen this in the paper? This—this murder? There—there's the report.' And he thrust the paper into my hands.

"I had not seen or heard anything of the matter, in fact, till that moment, and now he gave me little leisure to read the report. He walked up and down the room, nervously clasping his hands, sometimes together, sometimes at his sides, sometimes before him, shaking his head in a shuddering sort of way, and bursting out once or twice as though the words were uncontrollable, 'What ought I to do? What *can* I do?'

"I looked up from the paper, and he went on, 'Have you read it? It's a murder—a horrid murder. The poor wretched fellow was trying to escape, but he couldn't. It's a murder!'

"'It certainly seems so,' I said. 'But what—did you know this man, Denson?'

"'No, of course not,' Mason replied, 'but there it is, plain enough, and here's another paper with just the same report, but a little shorter.' He pulled the second paper from his pocket. 'I got what different papers I could, but these are the two fullest. It's plain enough it's a brutal murder, isn't it? And the man was a merchant, or an agent, or something, in Portsmouth Street, but he was found in labourer's clothes—proof that he feared it and was trying to escape it; but he couldn't—he couldn't—no! nor anybody. It's awful, awful!'

"'But I don't understand,' I said. 'Won't you sit down?' For Mason continued to pace distractedly about the room. 'What is it you think this unfortunate man was trying to escape? And what am I to do in the matter?'

"He stopped, pressed both hands to his head, and seemed to control himself by a great effort. 'You must excuse me,' he said. 'I'm a bit run down lately, and my nerves are all wrong. I'm talking rather wildly, I'm afraid. I really hardly know why I came to you, except that I haven't a soul I can talk to about—well, about anything, scarcely.'

"He took a chair, and sat for a little while with his head forward on his hand and his eyes directed towards the floor. Then he said, in a musing way, rather as though he was thinking aloud than talking to me, 'You were right, after all, Potswood, and I was a fool to disregard your warnings. I oughtn't to have dabbled—I should have left those things alone.'

"I said nothing, thinking it best not to disturb him, but to leave him free to say what he wanted to say in his own way. He remained quiet for a minute or two more, and then sat up with an appearance of much greater composure. 'You mustn't mind me, Potswood,' he said. 'As I've told you, I'm in a bad state of nerves, and at best I'm an impulsive sort of person, as you know. I needn't have bothered you like this—I came rushing round here without thinking, and if the house had been a bit farther off I should have come to my senses before I reached you. After all, there's nothing so much to disturb one's-self about, and this man—this Denson—may very well have deserved his fate. Don't you think that likely?'

"He added this last question with an involuntary eagerness that scarcely accorded with the indifferent tone with which he had begun. I answered guardedly. I said of course nobody could say what the unhappy man's sins might have been, but that whatever they were they could never justify the fearful sin of murder. 'And,' I added, 'if you know anything of the matter, Mason, or have the smallest suspicion as to who is the guilty person, I'm sure you won't hesitate in your duty.'

"'My duty?' he said. 'Oh yes, of course; my duty. You mean, of course, that any law-abiding citizen who knows of evidence should bring it out. Just so. Of course *I* haven't any evidence—that paper gave me the first news of the thing.'

"'I think,' I rejoined, 'that anybody who was possessed of even less than evidence—of any suspicion which might lead to evidence—should go at once and place the authorities in possession of all he knows or suspects.'

"'Yes,' he said—very calmly now, though it seemed at cost of a great effort—'so he should; so he should, no doubt, in any ordinary case. But sometimes there are difficulties, you know—great difficulties.' He stopped and looked at me furtively and uneasily. 'A man might fear for his own safety—he might even know that to say what he knew would be to condemn himself to sudden death; and more, perhaps, more. Suppose—it might be, you know—suppose, for instance, a man was placed between the alternatives of neglecting this duty and of breaking a—well an oath, a binding oath of a very serious—terrible—character? An oath, we will say, made previously, without any foreknowledge of the crime?'

"I said that any such oath taken without foreknowledge of the crime could not have contemplated such an event, and that however wrong the taking of such an oath might have been in itself, to assist in concealing such a crime as this murder was infinitely worse—infinitely worse than taking the oath, and infinitely worse than breaking it. Though as to the latter, I repeated that any such engagement made without contemplation or foreknowledge of such a crime would seem to be void in that respect. I went further—much further. I conjured him to make no secret of anything he might know, and not to burden his conscience with complicity—for that was what concealment would amount to—in such a terrible crime. I added some further exhortations which I need not repeat now, and presently his assumed calmness departed utterly, and he became even more agitated than when first he came. He would say nothing further, however, and in the end he went away, saying he would 'think over the matter very seriously.'

"It was quite plain to me that my poor friend was suffering acutely from the burden of some terrible secret, and that in his impulsive way he had rushed to confide in me at the first shock of the news of this murder, and that afterwards his courage had failed him. But I conceived it my duty not to allow such a matter to stand thus. Therefore, giving Mason a few hours for calm consideration, I called on him in the evening. I was told that he was not very well and had gone to bed; he had, however, left a message, in case I should call, to the effect that he would come and see me in the morning. I waited the whole of that next morning and the whole of the afternoon, and saw nothing of him. In the evening urgent parish work took me away, but next morning I called again at Mason's house and saw him. This time he avoided the subject—tried to dodge it, in fact. But I was not to be denied, and the result was another scene of alternate agitation and forced calmness. I will not weary you, Mr Hewitt, with useless repetition, but I may say that I have seen Mason twice since then without bringing him to any definite resolve. As a matter of fact, I believe that he is restrained from saying anything further by fear—sheer terror. He has even gone so far as to deny absolutely that he knows anything of the matter—and then has contradicted himself a minute afterwards. At last, this morning, I have brought him a degree further. In the last few days I made it my business to acquaint myself, as far as possible, with the exact circumstances of the tragedy, so far as they are known, and in course of my inquiries I saw the housekeeper of the offices next door—the man who identified the body as Denson's. He either could not, or would not, tell me very much, but he *did* say that you had been working in some way in connection with the case, and that you knew as much of it as anybody. That gave me an idea. This morning I told Mason that not only he, but I also had a duty in respect to this matter, and my duty was to see that nothing in connection with such a crime as this should be hushed up on any consideration or for anybody's fancies. I said that if he liked he need tell me no more, but might take *you* into consultation professionally, as your client, allowing me first to see you and to assure you that, consistently with his own safety, he was anxious to further the ends of justice. I said that, as your client, your first duty would be to protect him, that your professional practice would keep your mouth absolutely sealed, and that you already knew a good deal about the crime—perhaps more than he suspected. I protested that this seemed to me the very least he could do, and I warned him that if he refused to do even this, I should have to consider whether it was consistent with my character, as a clergyman and a loyal citizen, any longer to conceal the fact that he was keeping back information that might lead to the apprehension of the murderer. This frightened him, and between the fear of the threat and the fear that you might already know more than he suspected, he authorised me—he was even eager about it—

to come and see you; always, of course, under a pledge of strict professional secrecy."

"So far your account is quite clear, Mr Potswood," Hewitt said. "You have done your best, now I must do mine. You wish me to see Mason at once, no doubt?"

"I arranged to bring you to his house, if you were willing and your engagements permitted, at three this afternoon. Will that do? I have been keeping you, I see—it is past one already. Will you lunch with me at my club?"

"With great pleasure—more especially as I have a few questions to ask as we go along. Is it far?"

"Just at this end of Pall Mall—we will walk, if you like."

"Tell me now," said Hewitt as they went, "anything you know about Mr Mason's habits, family connections, and so forth, as fully and as minutely as you please. Has he any friends connected with China, for instance?"

"China? Why, no, I think not; except—but I'll tell you all I know. Mr Mason has no family connections, so far as I am aware—at any rate, in London—except his niece, Miss Creswick. She is within a few months of twenty-one, a charming girl, but horribly shut in, for Mason has almost no visitors. Miss Creswick was his sister's daughter; she lost her mother first and then her father, and was left to the guardianship of her uncle. He was also trustee under the will, and he has, I believe, discretion to keep charge of her property, if he thinks fit, till she reaches the age of twenty-five; though in case of his death she is to inherit in the ordinary way, on coming of age. She is a very dutiful and, indeed, an affectionate niece; though I must say he is scarcely fair to her, keeping her, as he does, so completely secluded from the society of young people of her own age. Mere thoughtlessness, I think; he has had no children of his own, his mind is wholly occupied with his science and his fads, and he makes himself a recluse without a thought of the girl. And that brings me to what I was about to say at first, when you asked me if Mr Mason had any friends connected with China. There is a young doctor—Lawson is his name—some very distant connection of the family, I think, who had a professional appointment of some sort in Shanghai for a year or two, but who is now in London trying to work up a small practice of his own. If you hadn't mentioned China I shouldn't have thought of him, since he never goes to the house now—or, at any rate, is supposed not to go."

"Doesn't go to the house? And why is that?"

"Well, there was a disagreement. What it was I don't quite know, but in the first place it had some connection with some of Mason's experiments—something which Lawson declined to help him with for professional reasons, or else something he declined to do for Lawson, I don't know which. But the thing went further, for, as a matter of fact, there was something between the young people—Lawson is only twenty-eight—and Mason put an end to that. It had been something like a formal engagement, I think, but in the quarrel—Mason was always quarrelling with somebody when he *had* friends, and that's why he has so few now—in the quarrel things were said that ended in a rupture. Whether young Lawson was fortune-hunting or not I cannot say, but Mason certainly accused him of it, and promised to keep back the girl's money as long as he could. In the meantime Mason declared an end to the engagement, and poor Helen was brokenhearted; for as I have said, she is an affectionate girl, and she hadn't a friend to confide in. But I'm boring you—you don't want to know all these things, surely?"

"On the contrary, I can't possibly know too much, and the particulars can't possibly be too minute. Nine cases out of ten I bring to an issue by means of a triviality. You were saying a little while back that there were almost *no* visitors at Mr Mason's house; but you said 'almost,' and that means there are some. Who are they?"

"Very occasionally—rarely, in fact—there are one or two members of learned societies with whom he had been in correspondence, or who are old friends. There is a Professor Hutton and a Dr Burge, I believe; but they don't appear once in six months; and there is Mr Everard Myatt, who is more frequent. He does not profess to be a great man of science, but he is interested in chemistry as an amateur, and is, I fancy, a sort of disciple of Mason's. He has noticed a sad difference in Mason just lately, and he even called on me yesterday, though I hardly knew him by sight, in the hope that I would back up his urgent suggestion that Mason should go off for a change and a rest. Beyond these I don't think I know of a single visitor. But here we are at the Megatherium."

II

Mr Jacob Mason's house stood in its own grounds in a quiet suburban road. It was not a very large house, but it straggled about comfortably in the manner of detached houses built in the suburbs at a time when space was less valuable than now, and it consisted of two floors only. The front door was not far from the road, and was clearly visible to passengers who might chance to look through either of the two iron gates that opened one on each end of the semicircular drive.

All these things Martin Hewitt noticed as the Rev. Mr Potswood pushed open one of these gates, and the two walked up the drive. The front door stood in a portico, and a French window gave access to the roof of this portico from a bedroom or dressing-room. As Hewitt and his companion approached the house the French window was pushed open, and a man appeared—a middle-aged, slightly stoutish man with a short, grey beard; commonplace enough in himself, but now convulsed with noisy anger, shaking his fists and stamping on the portico-roof.

"Get out!" he shouted. "Don't come near my house again, or I'll have you flung out! Go away and take your friends with you! D'you hear? Go away, sir, and don't come here annoying me! Go! Go at once!"

Mr Potswood absolutely staggered with amazement. "Why," he gasped, "it's Mason! He's mad—clean mad! Why, Mason, my poor friend, don't you know me?"

"Get out, I say!" cried Mason. "Give me no more of your talk! I won't have you here!" And now Hewitt caught a glimpse of a girl's face at the window behind the man—a pale and handsome face, drawn with anxiety and fear.

Hewitt seized the clergyman quickly by the arm. "Come," he whispered hurriedly, "come away at once. There is a reason for this. Get away at once. If you can answer back angrily, do so, but at any rate, come away."

He hurried back to the gate, half dragging the astounded rector, who was all too honest a soul to be able to counterfeit an anger he did not feel, even if his amazement had not made him speechless. Hewitt closed the gate behind him and said as he walked, "Where is the rectory? We will go there. He may have sent a message while you were out."

Mechanically the rector took the first turning. "But he's mad!" he protested. "Mad, poor fellow! Merciful heavens, Mr Hewitt, his whole tale must have been a delusion! A mere madman's fancy! Poor fellow! We must go back, Mr Hewitt—we really must! We can't leave that poor girl there alone with a raving maniac!"

"No," Hewitt insisted, "come to the rectory. That is no madness, Mr Potswood. Couldn't you see the colour of the man under the eyes, and the shaking of his beard? That was not anger and it was not madness. It was terror, Mr Potswood—sheer, sick terror! Terror, or some emotion very much like it."

"But, if terror, why that outburst? What does it mean? If it were terror, why not rather welcome our company and help?"

"Don't you see, Mr Potswood?" answered Hewitt. "Don't you guess? *Mason is watched, and he knows it!* He was acting his anger before unseen eyes—and he knew they were on him!"

"God be merciful to us all," ejaculated the clergyman. "Poor man—poor sinner! What is this unspeakable thing which has him in its clutches? What had he done to give himself over to such a power?"

"We can tell nothing, and guess nothing, as yet," Hewitt answered. "Let us see if he has sent you a message. It seems likely. If he has it may help us. If not—then I think we must do something decisive at once. But don't hurry so! It is hard to restrain one's self, I know, but there may be eyes on us, Mr Potswood, and we must not seem to be persisting in our errand."

So they went through the quiet streets for the two or three furlongs that seemed so many miles to the good parson. Arrived at the rectory, Mr Potswood pushed impatiently through the gate, and was hurrying toward the house, when he perceived a bent little old man standing among some shrubs with his own gardener, who was digging.

"There's Mason's gardener!" the rector exclaimed, and went to meet him.

The old man touched his hat, looked sharply towards Hewitt, who was waiting near the rectory door, and then disappeared round a corner of the house, the rector following. In a few seconds Mr Potswood reappeared, with a slip of paper in his hand. "Here," he said, "see this! The old man was told to give it to nobody but me, and in nobody else's presence. He's been waiting since one o'clock."

Scrawled on the paper, in trembling and straggling letters, were these words:—

"You must not bring Mr Martin Hewitt to my house this afternoon. I am watched. It is hopeless. Do not desert me. Bring him tonight after dark at eight. I shall want his best skill, and you shall know all. After dark. Come to the back gate in the lane, which will be ajar, and through the conservatory at the side, where my niece will be waiting at eight, after dark. Burn this and do not let it out of your sight first. Send a line by this man to say you will do as I ask, but do not say what it is, for fear of accidents. Send at once. Do come at eight, with Mr Hewitt."

"We must do as he says," remarked Hewitt. "We know nothing of this matter, and we must be guided till we do. Just write an unsigned note—'All shall be as you request,' or words to that effect, and be sure the man gives it to him. Let him out behind through the churchyard, if possible, and tell him not to go straight from one house to the other. Is he an intelligent man?"

"Yes—uncommonly shrewd, I believe. He says he can't have been followed. He knows several gardeners hereabout, and he seems to have called on each of them on his way—in at the front of the garden and out at the back each time, after a few minutes' conversation. Gipps is rather a cunning old fellow."

"Ah," said Hewitt admiringly, "that's the sort of messenger I often want. I'll give him half a crown for himself and the money to pay for a telegram on his way. He knows nothing essential, of course?"

"No—only that his master is in some sort of trouble, and warned him that he might be followed."

"That is good. I shall telegraph to Detective-Inspector Plummer, of Scotland Yard. All right—I quite understand that all I have heard is confidential. I shall tell Plummer nothing till I may—indeed, as yet I have very little to tell that would help him. But I think it will be well to have the police within call— we may want them at a moment's notice; I have no police powers, you see, and Plummer has the Denson case in hand. I will ask him to be here, at this house, before a quarter to eight, if you will allow me."

And so the telegram went to Plummer, and Hewitt, accepting the rector's invitation to an early dinner before starting on their visit, resigned himself to wait. He did not like the waste of time, as he frankly told Mr Potswood. He would have preferred to see Mason at once, at any risk, and to take what means he thought necessary without delay. But as it seemed that the risk was to be chiefly Mason's, and as Mason knew all of which both he and the rector were ignorant, Mason must be allowed to choose his own time.

The excellent Mr Potswood endured agonies of suspense, though he also insisted that Mason's wishes must be observed exactly. "What is it all—what can it be?" he ejaculated again and again. "What dreadful influence can thus compass a man about, here in London, in these times?"

It was autumn, and night fell early. Dinner was over at last, and they had scarcely left the table when Plummer arrived, anxious and eager.

"You'll have to trust me a little, Plummer," Hewitt said, when he had made him known to the rector. "I can tell you nothing now—know nothing, in fact, or very little more than nothing. The fact is, I'm going to see a man who promises information to me alone, in confidence, as his client, and I don't know how long I may have to keep you in the dark. But this is where the trail lies hot, and I know that's where you want to be. More, if you're wanted suddenly you'll be at hand. You have a man or two with you, I suppose, as I suggested?"

"Three of the best of them. They will follow us up. Is it far?"

"No, close enough. It is a house in a walled garden—not a high wall. We go in at a gate from the lane behind, and I think you should wait at that gate, and put your men at hand. We mustn't go in as a crowd. The rector had better go first, and you and I will follow on the opposite side of the road."

So the procession was formed, and it was still some three minutes short of eight o'clock when Hewitt and Plummer joined the clergyman at the door in the garden wall behind Mason's house. The door was ajar as had been promised in Mason's note. Leaving Plummer on guard without, Martin Hewitt and the rector stepped as silently as possible through the little kitchen garden and across a strip of lawn toward where a dull light illuminated the conservatory, at the right-hand end of the house. The door of the conservatory was ajar also, and this the rector pushed open.

"Miss Creswick!" the rector called, in a loud whisper. "Miss Creswick!" And with that a girl appeared within.

"Oh, Mr Potswood," she said, "I'm so glad you've come! I can't think what's wrong with poor uncle! I'm afraid he must be going mad! He is terrified at something, and he has been getting worse, till he could hardly speak or walk. Dr Lawson has been—about an hour ago, and since then uncle has been much quieter, in his study."

They were entering the dimly-lighted drawing-room now. "Dr Lawson?" queried the rector. "Rather an unusual visitor, isn't he? How long has he been gone?"

Miss Creswick flushed slightly through all her paleness and grief. "I don't know," she said. "He let himself out, I fancy. He said he could not stay long when he came, but I didn't hear him go; I have been upstairs, and the servants are in the kitchen—they say uncle's mad, and I'm really afraid he is!"

They left the drawing-room, and walked along the corridor and the hall to the opposite side of the house, where the study lay. Miss Creswick tapped gently at the door, but there was no answer. She tapped again, louder, and then came the faint sound of a quick step on the carpet, and then a slight scraping noise, as when a door is closed over a carpet it will scarcely pass. "That's the window into the garden," said Miss Creswick. "Why is he going out? Uncle! Uncle Jacob!"

But now the silence was wholly unbroken. Hewitt snatched quickly at the door-handle. "Locked!" he said. "Come—the quickest way into the garden!"

They ran out at the front door, and round toward the study window. It was a French window, exactly at the opposite end of the house to the conservatory, and now the gaslight streamed out through one half of it, which stood curtainless and ajar, while the curtain was drawn across the other half. Hewitt was the least familiar with the place, but he was quickest on his legs, and more seriously alarmed than the others. He reached the window first—and instantly turned and thrust the rector back against Miss Creswick. "Quick! take her away," he said; "we are too late!" and in the same moment, even as Hewitt dashed over the threshold, he snatched a whistle from his pocket, and blew his hardest.

There on the floor lay Mason, his face dreadful and staring and black; tight in his neck was the band of a tourniquet, and fresh and wet on his forehead was the Red Triangle.

Hewitt snatched at the screw of the tourniquet behind the neck, and loosened it as quickly as hands could turn. But it was too late. Too late, the examining surgeon afterwards said, by a quarter of an hour.

Plummer was at the window with his men at his heels even before the tourniquet was half unscrewed.

"Round the wall of the garden," shouted Hewitt, "and whistle up the police! He's only this moment out!"

The house was alive with shouts and screams. The rector came running back, and Hewitt, busy with his useless attempt at restoration, called now for a doctor. People were scampering in the street, and Hewitt left the victim to the care of the rector, and himself joined Plummer, all in fewer seconds than it may be told in.

But Plummer and his men were beaten, for nothing—not so much as a moving shadow—was seen in the garden or about the walls. Worse, the general trampling would obliterate possible tracks. Plummer set a guard of police about the wall, and came in for consultation with Hewitt.

The body was carried into another room, and Hewitt and Plummer began an examination of the study.

"No signs of a struggle," commented Plummer, "and there was no noise, they say. That's very odd."

"From what I have seen and heard today," said Hewitt, "it is as I should have expected. I believe the man was almost killed by terror before he was strangled—dazed, stricken dumb, paralysed, deafened by it—everything but blinded, poor wretch. And to have been blinded would have been a mercy."

And then, as they made their examination systematically, calmly and without flurry, Hewitt told the whole tale of his day's adventures, together with all he had heard from the rector. "The man's dead," he said, "and his confidence is at an end. Indeed, I never had it—the case, so far as I am concerned, is over before I have even touched it. I haven't had a chance, Plummer; and the thing is deep and dark, deep and dark. Oh, if only the man had let me come to him in the daylight, spite of all! This might all have been averted.... There has been a close search here, too. See how everything is turned over. But, stay!"

A low fire smouldered in the grate, and on it lay ashes of many burnt papers. Hewitt passed the shovel carefully under these ashes, lifted them out and placed them gently on the table under the light of the gas-pendant.

"I must leave you," said Plummer. "There'll be an inspector here from the station in a moment—he won't interfere with you, and if anybody can get information out of this room it's you. The next thing for me is plain. I must make sure of Dr Lawson, if he can be found."

"That is quite right, without a doubt," Hewitt responded. "I may find anything or nothing in this room, and, meanwhile, he was the last person known to have been here, and the only visitor, and he was not heard to go out, unless we heard him go when we were outside the study door. More, it was plainly someone familiar with the place who was able to get away so quickly by the window and the garden."

"And his interest in getting rid of Mason, too—the girl of age in a few months, and all obstacles to getting hold of her, and her money, removed. And—and the surgical tourniquet, the Chinese colour and everything!"

"Quite right, you must make sure of him, as you say. You will get his address from the rector. Meanwhile I'll try to begin my little contribution to the case—to begin it as best I can, after all the chances have made it useless."

III

It was after nine when Plummer returned. The rector had just rejoined Hewitt in the study, having left poor Miss Creswick, utterly broken down, in her room, in charge of a scarcely less terrified servant. Plummer tapped, and pushed the study door open.

"That's done clean and sure enough," he said, with professional calmness. "And he's a cool hand, is that Dr Lawson. But have you found anything more? We shall want all we can get."

"We shall," Hewitt assented, "and we shall find more than we've got now, or I'm grievously mistaken. But tell me first what you've done."

He removed the blotting pad, on which the paper ashes still lay, and very carefully shut it away in a wide drawer where no draught could disturb it; he also shut another drawer which stood open.

"We had no difficulty in finding Dr Lawson," Plummer began. "We met him, in fact, leaving his surgery. I went back with him into the gaslight, and there put it to him plump. Well, he was staggered, badly. Any man would be, of course. But he pulled himself together wonderfully soon, and the first thing he said was that he was just on his way to Mason's house. I thought at first, of course, that he meant to deny that he had been there already, and I gave him the usual warning about what he said being used in evidence. But he went on, and I've got it all safely noted. He admitted that he had been here, at about seven o'clock or just before, and he said he came because Mr Mason sent for him. That doesn't seem likely, does it, on the facts as we know them?"

"Why, no," said the rector. "The last time he was here he was ordered out, and I know of no reason why he should have been asked to come today. We must ask if anybody was sent."

"I have asked," replied Plummer, "just now, and none of the servants was sent. But Lawson's story is that he *was* sent for and came, though he said he shouldn't say what Mason wanted to see him about till he knew more of the case. Looks as though he hadn't quite got his story ready yet, doesn't it? He had thought over the point about not being seen to go away, though; he said he had let himself out at about half-past seven, being familiar with the ways of the house. And he said that Mason was rather unwell—nervously upset—when he left him, but that was all."

"It's terrible," said the rector, "terrible. It seems impossible to believe it of young Lawson; and yet—and yet!" And then after a pause—"Good heavens!" he burst out again. "Why, I only realise it now! There is the other crime, too! Denson! Two murders! Two—and most certainly by the same hand! Mr Plummer, I *can't* believe it! Oh, there's more behind, more behind, Mr Hewitt."

"There *is* more," said Hewitt, "as you will see when I tell you the little I have been able to ascertain. There *is* more behind, though I see little of it yet. First—"

There was a sharp knock at the front door, followed by a ring, muffled in the distant kitchen. Hewitt started up. "Who is this late visitor at this unvisited house?" he said. "If it is the police, well enough. But if anybody else—*anybody*—you may call me Doctor, or anything you please, except Martin Hewitt. Don't forget that!"

There were hurried steps in the hall, a question or two, and the study door was pushed open. Two servants—they would not venture from the kitchen singly this dreadful night—made a confused announcement of "Mr Myatt," and were instantly pushed aside by Mr Myatt himself, anxious and agitated.

The late Mr Mason's closest scientific friend was a palish, black-bearded man, of above middle height, with stooping shoulders and a very quick pair of eyes. There was something about his face that somehow reminded Hewitt of portraits he had seen of John Knox, and yet it was not such a face as his; it seemed oddly unlike in its very likeness.

"What is this dreadful news, Mr Potswood?" he cried. "I heard people talking in the next street on my way home. Is it true? But the servants have told me so. They say our poor friend—but there has been an arrest, hasn't there?"

The rector nodded gravely.

"And who? Tell me about it, Mr Potswood—tell me!"

"I think I must see how Miss Creswick is doing," said Hewitt, speaking across to Plummer and making for the door.

"Certainly, doctor, certainly!" answered Plummer with a nod.

Hewitt closed the door behind him, leaving the rector in the full tide of his account of the day's events; but Hewitt's way took him to the kitchen, where the servants were cowering and whispering together, frightened and bewildered.

"Is there any paint or varnish of any sort in the place?" he asked sharply. "Give me anything there is—black, if possible—and a brush, quickly."

"There's—there's Brunswick black, sir, for the stove," said the cook.

"That will do; be quick. Oh, there's Gipps, the gardener! You're just the man I want, Gipps. Come and find me a board or a plank, quick as you please!" And Hewitt pushed the old gardener before him into the garden by the kitchen door.

A quarter of an hour later, Mr Everard Myatt, having heard all that was to be told of his friend's terrible death and the arrest of Mr Lawson, turned to go, meeting Hewitt at the study door on his way.

"And how is poor Miss Creswick by now, doctor?" he asked anxiously.

Hewitt shook his head. "No better than you could expect," he said, "but, on the whole, no worse. She mustn't be seen tonight, of course, but, perhaps, if you could call round in the morning with the rector—"

"Of course—of course! Poor girl—and Dr Lawson suspected, too—what a terrible blow for her! Anything I can do, doctor, of course, as I said to Mr Potswood—anything I can do I will do as gladly as such sad circumstances permit."

The rector had been coming to the door with Mr Myatt, but Plummer, catching a sign from Hewitt, restrained him unseen, and Hewitt and the visitor walked into the hall together.

"They have put out the light, it seems," Hewitt said. "I wonder why—unless people from the crowd have been coming into the garden and staring in through the glass panels. I wonder if we can find the door-handle. Yes, here it is. Dark outside, too! Goodnight—mind how you go on the steps!"

Mr Myatt checked and stumbled in the dark porch, and reached quickly downward.

"There's a board standing across the porch," he said.

"A board?" replied Hewitt. "So there is. Let me move it, or it'll upset somebody. Goodnight!"

Mr Myatt strode off into the dark night, and Hewitt, noiselessly lifting the board he had himself placed in position, hastened back to the study.

He swung up the board, all sticky and shiny with Brunswick black, and laid it across a spread newspaper, on the table. There on the top, in the midst of the black varnish, were the prints of all five finger-tips of a hand, where Mr Myatt had felt for the obstruction in the porch.

Hewitt opened the drawer he had shut a little while back, and took therefrom a sheet of writing-paper. And when, with the lens from his pocket, he began to examine that paper in comparison with the finger-marks on the board, Plummer and the rector could see that there were also two distinct finger-marks on the paper and one faint one—all red. Plummer came to look.

"What's this?" he said. "Was this what you were going to tell us about?"

Hewitt did not reply for a few moments, but continued his examination. Then he rose and turned to Plummer.

"You've still got that piece of paper in your pocket, I suppose," he said, "with the little red smudges of colour put there by the police surgeon?"

"Yes—here it is," and the detective took it from his waistcoat pocket.

"Thanks," said Hewitt. "Now, see here. That is a little of the red stuff taken from the mark on Denson's forehead a week ago, and found to consist of vermilion, oil and wax. You have seen the second impression of that awful mark on the forehead of your poor friend Mason, Mr Potswood, tonight. This room has been searched for papers before we began, and papers have been burnt. In the search this drawer was opened—containing, as you see, nothing but a supply of new headed note-paper. The note-paper was hastily lifted to see if anything else lay beneath, and here, on the bottom sheet, these finger-marks were left in that same adhesive, freely marking red—a sort of stuff that sticks to and marks whatever it touches. The hand that lifted that paper was the hand that impressed that ghastly mark; and the hand that left its print on this black varnish was Mr Everard Myatt's! Now compare the two!"

Plummer had snatched the lens, and was narrowly comparing the marks ere Hewitt had well finished speaking.

"They are!" he cried, as the rector bent excitedly over him. "They are the same! See—forefinger and middle finger—the same, every line!"

"I needn't tell you," pursued Hewitt, "certainly I needn't tell Plummer, that that is the most certain and scientific method of identification known. The police know that—and use it. But now there is some more. You saw me take that charred paper from the fire. Sometimes words may be read on charred paper — it depends on the paper and the ink. Most of the cinders were too much broken to yield any information, though we may try again by daylight. But one was suggestive. See it!" Hewitt very carefully pulled out the flat drawer that held the cinders.

"You see," he went on, "that one — this — is different from the rest. It has retained its original form better, and has been less broken, because of being of thicker paper. It is a crumpled envelope. Look at the flap — it has never been closed down. Moreover, on that same flap you may read in embossed letters, still visible, part of the name of this house. Plain inference — this was an envelope intended for a letter never sent, and so crumpled up and dropped into the waste-paper basket. But why should such an apparently unimportant thing as that be carefully brought from the wastepaper basket and burnt? Somebody was anxious that the smallest scrap of paper evidencing a certain correspondence should be destroyed. But look closely at the front of the envelope — the ink shows a rather lighter grey than the paper. The address is incomplete — at any rate, no more than some of the first line and a little of the second is at all visible now; but it is plain that the first line begins with an E. The letters immediately following are not distinct, but next there is a capital M beginning a name which is clearly Myatt or Myall. Now, *that* is why, when Myatt came here, I took the first steps to hand to get an impression of his fingertips, in order to compare them with the marks on that paper."

"But why," asked the astonished rector, "why did he come back?"

"Nothing but a bold measure to see how things were going — he came as his own spy, that's all. He's a keen and dangerous man. Don't you remember telling me how he called on you yesterday, though you hardly knew him by sight, merely to ask you to persuade Mason to take a holiday? It struck me as a little odd at the time. He was pumping you, Mr Potswood—he wanted to find what Mason had been saying! And he is not alone—plainly he is not alone, for poor Mason knew they were watching everywhere. But come—this is no time for speculation. Plummer—you must hold him safely—we'll pick up evidence enough when you've got him. I wouldn't leave it, Plummer—I'd take him tonight!"

"You're right—right, as usual, Mr Hewitt," Plummer agreed. "More especially as the rector was—well, a little incautious in talking to him just now."

"I? What did I say?" Mr Potswood asked, astonished. "I had no suspicions—how could I have—"

"No, Mr Potswood," the detective replied, "you had no suspicions, and for that very reason, in the excitement of the narrative, you called Mr Martin Hewitt by his right name at least twice! And after I had called him 'doctor,' too!" he added regretfully.

"Is that so?" asked Hewitt.

The poor rector was sadly abashed. "But I really wasn't aware of it, Mr Hewitt!" he protested. "I hardly think I could—but, there, perhaps I did! Of course, if Inspector Plummer remembers it—"

"He'll be off!" exclaimed Hewitt. "With that hint, and finding the black stuff on his hands, he'll smell a rat instantly! Come, Mr Potswood—you can show us the nearest way to his house, at any rate! Come—we may get him yet!"

But the good rector's slip of the tongue was fatal, and Myatt was not yet to meet the fate that fitted him. The house was not far—less than a mile away. It was a detached house, but quite a small one—smaller than Mason's. Plummer blocked every exit with a man, but his caution was wasted. Myatt was gone.

There was the house and the furniture and two servants, just as it might have been any day in the year when Myatt was out for an hour. But now he was out for good. The police watched and waited all night, and all the next day; they waited and watched for a week, and the house was under observation after that, but Myatt never returned. He had made his plans, it was plain, for just such a flight, whenever the necessity might arise; and when he was assured that danger threatened, he simply vanished in the dark of a London night. Search brought no information — not a scrap of telltale paper lay in Calton Lodge — not a letter, not a line. Though, indeed, the police were to see more of Myatt's work yet — and so was Hewitt.

Dr Lawson's detention did not last the night out. The unhappy Mason had indeed sent to him, by a chance messenger, having grown desperate in long waiting for the return of Gipps from the rectory. Mason was ready to call in any aid, to recall any of the friendships he had sacrificed in the past. But Lawson was long in coming, having received the note after a long professional round, and when at last he arrived, Mason was a little reassured by the promise of Hewitt's visit. Therefore, he did not tell the doctor so much as he might have done. Nevertheless, he talked wildly and vaguely, so that Dr Lawson feared some disturbance of his reason. The doctor quieted and soothed him, however, and when he left he promised to return after his consultation hour at the surgery was over. He must have been watched away from the house, and then the blow fell that sealed for ever the lips of Jacob Mason.

Poor Miss Creswick was taken from the old house in which she could no longer remain, and for a few months she stayed at the rectory, tended lovingly by the rector's excellent wife — stayed there, in fact, till her wedding-day, which took place early the next year; so that for her and Dr Lawson the tragedy ended in happiness, after all.

"God forgive me," cried the rector in the grey of the morning, when it became clear that Myatt had escaped — "God forgive me! Through my stupidity a horrible creature has been set loose in the world to work his diabolical will afresh!"

"Never mind," said Hewitt. "It was not stupidity, Mr Potswood—nothing but your openness of character. You were not trained to the cunning that we must use in my profession. And there will be more than Myatt to take—he was not alone! It is plain that Mason was found to be wavering in whatever horrible allegiance he had bound himself, and he was watched. No, Myatt was not alone!"

"No, I fear not," replied the clergyman. "I fear not: there is horrible mystery still. The watching and besetting that terrified him so much; the fact that he seems to have yielded up his life without a struggle—and that with help so near; and the connection—what could it have been?—between Mason and the other victim—Denson. That is a deep mystery indeed! And that horrible sign! Mr Hewitt, you have done much—but not all!"

"No," replied Martin Hewitt, "not nearly all. It is even doubtful whether or not it will be my lot to come across the thing again; but it will be in the hands of the police. And, after all, we have achieved something. For we know that if Myatt can be captured we shall be at the heart of the mystery."

3

THE CASE OF THE LEVER KEY

I

In some of the cases which we now know to have been connected with the Red Triangle, there was nothing, in the first place, to show any such association. In some of these cases the connection has become apparent only since the final clearing up of the whole mystery, and with these cases we have no present concern; but in others it revealed itself during the investigation of the case. It was to this second category that the next case belonged—the next at all connectible, that is, after that of the mysterious death of Mr Jacob Mason and the flight of Everard Myatt.

The case was remarkable in other respects also; first, because in one of its features it had a resemblance to the case of Samuel's diamonds, which first brought the Red Triangle to Hewitt's notice; next, because in its course Hewitt encountered what he declared to be the most ingenious and baffling cryptogram that he had ever seen in the length of his strange experience; and thirdly, because I was the means of placing that cryptogram in his hands, owing to one of those odd chances that arise again and again in real life—are, indeed, so common as to pass almost unregarded—and yet might be thought improbable if offered in the guise of a mere story. Hewitt has often alluded to the curious persistence of such chances in his experience. I think I have elsewhere mentioned a certain police officer's prolonged search after a criminal for whose arrest he held a warrant, ending in the discovery—because of a misdirected call—that the man had been living all the time next door to himself; and I have also told of the other detective inspector, who, being sent in search of a criminal of whom he had but the meagrest and most unsatisfactory particulars, and whom he scarcely hoped ever to run down, actually *fell over* the man as he was leaving the office where he had received his information, in the doorway of which the fellow had stooped to tie his shoelace! But, as Hewitt would say, nothing but the exceptional nature of the surrounding circumstances makes these things seem extraordinary. What more ordinary experience, for example, than to meet a friend in some London street—perhaps one friend of the only dozen or so you have among the four millions of people about you? The odds against you two, of all the millions, choosing the one street of the thousands in London to walk down at the same minute of time, would seem incalculable; and yet the chance comes off so often as to be a matter of the most ordinary experience.

On this occasion I was expecting orders from my editor to produce certain articles on the subject of the London hospitals. It will be remembered that the matter was very much in the air a few years ago, and as nothing is professionally more uncomfortable than to be called on suddenly for an accurate and reasonable leading article on a subject one knows nothing about, I wrote to my friend, Barton McCarthy, who is house-surgeon at St. Augustine's, and he replied by an offer to tell me anything I cared to ask if I would call at the hospital.

I set out accordingly some little time after a breakfast even later than ordinary, and called in at Hewitt's office on my way downstairs, to say that I should not be lunching at our usual place that day.

"No," Hewitt answered, "nor shall I, I expect. I'm off to the City, at once. I have an urgent message to go immediately to Kingsley, Bell and Dalton's, in Broad Street, where a big bond robbery has just been discovered. Perhaps I can give you a lift in my cab?"

We hurried off together accordingly. Hewitt knew nothing of the case he had to examine, and so could tell me nothing, beyond the short urgent request that he would come at once, and that the matter involved the loss of bonds to a very large amount; and he dropped me at a convenient spot, whence my walk to the hospital was but a short one.

I saw my friend McCarthy, and bothered him very successfully for nearly an hour, getting all the information I had expected, and more, during a very interesting walk through the great hospital.

"You get some idea in a place like this," said McCarthy, as we came at last into the receiving room for accident cases, "you get some idea, Brett, of the size of this great London machine working about us. You might walk about the streets for a week and never see a serious accident, or even an accident at all, and yet, you see, here they come all day long—a stream of people damaged or killed in the machine."

A decent workman was having a gashed hand dressed and strapped, and a navvy with bandages about his head was being led away by a friend. Nurses and dressers were waiting ready to take their orderly turns at the incoming casualties, and as we looked a more serious case was brought in on an ambulance by two policemen. The patient was a ragged, disreputable-looking fellow of middle age, in grimy and tattered clothes, whose head had been roughly bandaged by the policemen who brought him. He had been knocked down and kicked on the head by a butcher's cart-horse, it seemed, in Moorgate Street, and he was quite insensible. A very short examination showed that the case was nothing trivial, and McCarthy sent me to sit in his private room to wait lunch, while he gave the matter his personal attention.

When he returned he brought a small crumpled envelope in his hand. "That case is put to bed," he said, "still insensible."

"Is it very bad?" I asked.

"Slight fracture of the occipital, and, of course, concussion of the brain—probably contusion, too, I expect we shall find presently. Not so over serious for a healthy man, but I'm afraid he's an old soaker—the sort that crumple up at a touch. Nobody knows him, and there's nothing to identify him in the pockets—a few coppers, an old knife, and so on. So we can't send to tell his friends—unless we bring in your friend Martin Hewitt to trace 'em out, which would come too expensive. Besides," McCarthy added, dropping into a seat before his desk, "if he's got any friends they'll come, sooner or later, when they miss him. This is the only thing he'd got beside what's in the pockets—he'd been sent on a message, probably."

My friend held up the crumpled envelope and took from it a small key. "He'd got this envelope gripped tightly in his hand," he said, "but there was no address on it, so we tore it open in the hope of finding one inside. But there was nothing there but the key. If you were a very promising pupil of your friend Hewitt, I should expect you to take a glance at it and tell us the man's address at once, together with his age, birthplace, when vaccinated, and the residence of his maternal grandmother. But you're not, so I'll let you off."

McCarthy turned the key idly about in his hand and tried it on a lock in his desk. "Stopped up," he remarked, withdrawing it, and peeping into the barrel; "not dirt, either—stopped up with paper! What's that for?"

He took a pin to clear the barrel, and the paper came away quite readily. It was a tight little roll, which the surgeon pulled out into a small strip rather less than three inches long and about half-an-inch broad.

THE RED TRIANGLE

"Hullo!" he exclaimed. "Look here! Here's a job for Martin Hewitt, after all! Figures! What does that mean? And what an amazing place to put them in! A key barrel! By Jove, Brett, this looks like one of your favourite adventures. Somebody sends a key in an envelope, and a row of incomprehensible figures rolled up inside the key. Look at it!"

I took the key and the paper. The key was of a good sort; small, inscribed "Tripp's Patent" on the bow, and it evidently belonged to a superior lever lock. The paper which had come from the barrel was very thin and tough—a kind I have seen used in typewriters. It had been very carefully and closely rolled, and then pushed into the key so that its natural tendency to open out held it tightly within. Written upon it with a fine pen appeared a series of very minute figures, thus:—

```
9, 8, 14, 4, 20, 18, 5, 9; 15, 19, 20,
0, 3, 9, 8, 5; 3, 23, 0, 0, 5, 13, 14,
19; 19, 20, 0, 0, 0, 0, 6, 1; 5, 20, 0,
0, 0, 0, 3, 22; 1, 15, 0, 0, 0, 0, 18,
5; 1, 8, 20, 11, 18, 9, 5, 20; 12, 5,
23, 14, 14, 1, 1, 20.
```

"Well," inquired McCarthy, "what do you make of it?"

"Not much as yet," I admitted. "But it's pretty certain it must be a cryptogram or code-writing of some sort; and if that's the case, I *think* I might back myself to read it—with a little time." For I well remembered the case of the "Flitterbat Lancers," and the lesson in cypher-reading which Hewitt then gave me.

"Come," my friend replied, much interested, "let's see how you do it. Meantime we'll get on with our lunch."

I took a pencil and a spare sheet of paper, and I studied those figures all through lunch and for some little time after. It soon became plain that the problem was much more difficult than it looked, and I said so. "At the first glance," I said, "it looked a fairly easy cypher; but as a matter of fact, I don't think it's easy at all. One assumes, of course, that the figures stand for letters, and on that assumption two or three peculiarities are noticeable. First, the highest number written here is 23, so that all the letters indicated, in whatever order they may come, are within the compass of the twenty-six letters of the alphabet. Next, the numbers most frequently repeated, if we except the noughts, are 5 and 20, which occur seven times each. Now, the vowel most frequently occurring in average English writing is e, and you will at once perceive that e is number five in the alphabet, counting from the beginning. More, if we go on counting so, we shall find that 20 is *t*, which is one of the most frequently occurring consonants. This would seem to hint that the cypher is of the very simplest description, consisting of the mere substitution of figures for letters in the exact order of the alphabet. But what, then, of the noughts? What can they mean? More especially when we consider that in three places there are actually four noughts in succession; for, of course, no letter is repeated four times successively in any English word, nor in any foreign word that I can imagine. But let us put down the letters in substitution for the figures, on the supposition that the figures stand for letters in their alphabetical order, leaving the noughts as they are. Then we get this."

I rapidly pencilled the letters on the spare paper, thus:—*i, h, n, d, t, r, e, i; o, s, t, 0, c, i, h, e; c, w, 0, 0, e, m, n, s; s, t, 0, 0, 0, 0, f, a; e, t, 0, 0, 0, 0, 0, c, v; a, o, 0, 0, 0, 0, r, e; a, h, t, k, r, i, e, t; l, e, w, n, n, a, a, t*.

"See there," I said. "Now, I can make nothing of that. When I come to examine the comparative frequency of the different letters, I find them much as they might be expected to be in a sentence of normal English, and any change would destroy the proportion. *E* and *t* are the most frequent, and then come *a, n, i, r, s,* and *c*. But as they stand they all mean nothing. It is possible that this may be one of the difficult variable letter cyphers, which Hewitt might read, but I can't. But even then, if the values of the letters change as they would do, they would get out of their normal proportions of frequency; so that a variable letter cypher seems unlikely. And there is another oddity. Look, and you will see that, counting the noughts in, the letters go in groups of eight, with a semi-colon at the end of each group. Now, it is impossible that the message can be a sentence in which every word has exactly eight letters—or, at least, I should think so. It can scarcely be that the semi-colon itself means a letter—it would be singular for one letter to occur with such curious regularity as that. There is no other visible division between the words, nor any single one of the usual aids by which the reader of secret cypher is able to take a hold of his work. No, I'm afraid I must give it up; for the present, at any rate. But I really think it is a thing that would vastly interest Hewitt, if I might show it to him. I suppose I mustn't?"

"Well," McCarthy answered, "perhaps it isn't strictly according to rule, but I think I might venture to lend it to you till tomorrow, if that will do. Indeed, I think, on second thoughts, that I may consider myself quite justified, since it may lead to the man's identification, and it will be a sufficient answer to any inquiry to say that I have shown it to Mr Martin Hewitt for that purpose. But you'll be careful of it, won't you? Do you want the key, too?"

"I think, if I may, I will take the key and the envelope all together. You can never tell what may or what may not help him, and the three things may hang together, and perhaps explain each other in some mysterious way."

"Very good—here's the whole bag of tricks. It's a queer business altogether, and I must say I feel inquisitive; certainly, if Hewitt can get anything out of those figures I shall be mighty curious to know how he does it. You'll come in again tomorrow, then?"

I promised I would, and walked off with the crumpled envelope, the little key, and the puzzling strip of figures. Since the lesson from Hewitt which I have alluded to, I had often amused myself with cryptogram reading, and I had never found a cypher message in a newspaper "agony-column" the meaning of which I could not get at with a little trouble. But this was something altogether beyond me; and if I have any reader who prides himself on his ability to read secret cypher, I recommend him to try his skill on this one before he reads further.

The circumstances, too, seemed as puzzling as the writing itself. Why, if any person wished to send a note and a key in a closed envelope, should he take the trouble to pack the note inside the key? Why, especially when the note was already written in so baffling a cypher? Whither had this ragged messenger been going with the mysterious package, and who had sent him, and why?

Guessing and musing, I reached home, and found that Hewitt had returned before me. I made my way into his office, and came on him sitting at his desk with a large lens, attentively examining a broken brass padlock.

"Am I bothering you?" I asked. "Are you on the bond robbery, now?"

Martin Hewitt nodded, with a jerk of the hand toward the padlock. "It's a tough job," he said, "and I shall shut myself up presently and think hard over it; just now I can't see my way into it at all. But what have you got there?"

"Never mind," I said, "you're too busy now. I came across something very odd at the hospital, which I thought would interest you—that's all."

"Very well, let me see it. I haven't begun my bout of cogitation yet. Show me."

I put the envelope, the key and the paper on the table before him. Hewitt, with a glance of surprise, picked up the key and examined it. "That's curious," he said, and straightway began fitting the key to the broken padlock on the desk.

"Why, man alive!" he cried, with a sudden burst of excitement, "where did you get this? This—this is the article—the key—the very thing I want!" He sprang to his feet and stared in my face in sheer amazement. "Heavens, Brett, the thing's almost supernatural! I've a broken lever padlock here, and of all things in the world I wanted to find the one key that fitted it; and you calmly walk in and clap down the very thing under my nose! Where did you get it?"

I told him the tale of the man who had been knocked down in Moorgate Street, and I explained exactly how the paper, the key and the envelope were found in relation to each other, and why I had brought them.

"And when was the man knocked over?" Hewitt asked.

"Some time between one and two o'clock, I should say," I replied. "They brought him in well before two, at any rate."

Hewitt stared into vacancy for a moment, thinking hard. Then he said, "Brett, I believe you've saved my reputation—not that it could have suffered much, perhaps, in such a desperate case. But as a fact I had already advised the calling in of the police, and should, perhaps, even have given up the part of the case still left me. But this ought to put me on the proper track. You see, every one of these patent lever locks differs in some slight degree from all the rest, and only its own key will fit it; and here, by this amazing piece of good luck, is the one key for this very lock, and the man who had it is detained in hospital. Come, I'm off to see him. Insensible, you say, when you left?"

"Yes," I answered, "and likely to be so for some time, McCarthy thinks; so you probably won't get much information out of him just yet. But the cypher—"

"I'll examine the cypher as I go along, I think. But I should like to take a look at the man, at any rate, even if he can't tell me anything. Will you give me a note to your friend McCarthy?"

"Of course," I answered, readily, and sat down to scribble the few lines necessary to introduce Hewitt.

When I had finished, Hewitt, who had been examining the cryptogram meanwhile, remarked: "This cypher is something out of the common, Brett. I certainly don't expect to be able to read it in the cab-journey—perhaps not in a week of study. The man who devised this is a man of abilities altogether beyond the average."

"I have had my best try at it," I said, "but it beats me wholly. I brought it purely as a matter of curiosity, to show you; it was the merest chance that I brought the key as well."

"And if you hadn't I should probably have put the cypher aside until the case was over, and so have missed the whole thing. Another lesson never to despise what seem like trifles. If you have studied the cypher you have no doubt observed—but there, we'll talk that over afterwards, and the whole case if you like. I'll go now, and I'll tell you all about the business when time permits."

II

Here is the case of the bond robbery as it had been presented to Martin Hewitt that morning, while I was at St. Augustine's Hospital, and as I learned it from him later. I had been a little puzzled to hear Hewitt say that the case had seemed so desperately hopeless that he advised the calling in of the police, because my experience had rather been that it was Hewitt who was commonly called in—often too late—when the police were beaten, and I had never before heard of a case in which this order of things was reversed. It turned out, however, as will be seen, that in the state of the matter as it first presented itself the only measures that seemed possible were such as it was in the power of the police alone to adopt.

Messrs. Kingsley, Bell, and Dalton were an old-established firm of brokers whose operations were not enormous nor much in the eye of the public, but who carried on a steady and reputable business in a set of offices high up in a great building in Broad Street—a building so large that the notice "Offices to let" was a permanent fixture in the front porch. The firm's clients were chiefly steady-going investors of the old-fashioned sort, who wished to avoid all speculative fireworks, and to deal through a firm whose habits were conformable to their own. The last Kingsley had left the firm and soon afterward died, some few years back, and now the head of the firm was Mr Robert Stanstead Bell, a gentleman of some sixty years of age. There were a couple of sleeping partners—relations—but the one other active partner was Mr Clarence Dalton, a young man but recently advanced to partnership, and, it was said, likely to become Mr Bell's son-in-law whenever the old gentleman's daughter Lilian should be married.

The steady, even round of business to which Kingsley, Bell, and Dalton, and their clerks were accustomed was suddenly interrupted by an appalling loss. It was discovered that bonds were missing from the safe, bonds to the amount of some £25,000; and whence, how, or when they were taken was an utter mystery. It was this loss which had occasioned the urgent message to Hewitt.

When Hewitt reached the spot he was shown at once into an inner office, where Mr Bell sat waiting. The old gentleman was in a sad state of agitation, and it was with some difficulty that Hewitt got from him a reasonably connected account of the trouble.

"The loss comes at such a time, Mr Hewitt," the senior partner explained, "that I don't know but it may ruin us utterly, unless my clients' property can be recovered. We have had to pay out heavy sums of late to the representatives of dead or retiring partners, and other circumstances combine with these to make the matter in this way even more terribly serious than the very large amount of the loss would seem to suggest. So I beg you will do what you can."

"That of course," responded Hewitt. "But please tell me, as clearly as you can, the precise circumstances of the case. Where were the bonds taken from?"

"This safe," Mr Bell answered, turning toward a very large and heavy one, which might almost have been called a small strong room. "They were kept, together with others, in this box, one of several, as you see. The box was fastened, like the rest, with a Tripp's patent lever padlock, the only key of which I kept, together with the key of the safe."

The box indicated was one of ordinary thin sheet iron, japanned black—something like what is called a deed box.

"The padlock has been broken open, I see," Hewitt observed.

"Yes, but I did that myself this morning. It had been blocked up in some way, so that the key wouldn't turn—doubtless in order to cause delay when next the box should come to be opened. As it was I might have desisted and put off opening it till later, but I had a reason for wishing to refer at once to a list which was in the box, and so I decided to break the padlock. It was more difficult than one might expect, with such a small padlock."

"And then you discovered your loss?"

"Then I discovered the loss, Mr Hewitt, though it was a mere chance even then. For see! All the bonds have not been taken, and those left are placed on the top, while the space below is filled with dummies. I hardly know why I turned them over—for the list was at the top—but I did, and then—" Mr Bell finished with a despairing gesture.

"And this was some time this morning?"

"At about half-past eleven."

"And when did you last open the box before that?"

"Ten days ago at least, I should think—and even then the bonds may have been gone, for I only opened it to refer to the same list, and I examined nothing else."

"You say that some bonds are left and others are gone. I presume those taken are such as would be easy to negotiate, and those left are such as would be difficult. Is that the fact?"

"Precisely."

"Then the thief evidently knows the ropes, and altogether the matter would seem awkward. For anything short of ten days, you see, and quite possibly for even a longer time than that, these bonds have been in the undisturbed possession of some person who could easily dispose of them, and would certainly do so without a moment's delay."

Mr Bell nodded sadly. "Quite true," he said.

"But now tell me a little more. You say you yourself keep the only key of the padlock, as well as the key of the safe. So that you open the safe every morning yourself and close it at night?"

"Just so."

"And do you never entrust the keys to anybody else?"

"The key of the safe is on a separate bunch from the key of the box. This second bunch, with the key of the box, is *always* in my pocket, and not a soul else ever touches it. The other bunch, with the outer key of the safe, I sometimes hand to my partner, or to the head clerk, Mr Foster, if something is wanted from the safe when I am busy. Though, as a rule, the safe door is open so long as I am about the place. Nothing but the books can be taken out without the use of other keys for the drawers and boxes, which I keep on the private bunch."

"And would it be possible for anybody—anybody at all, mind—to get at that private bunch of keys in such a way, for instance, as to be able to take a wax impression of the key of that bond-box?"

"No, certainly not," Mr Bell answered with decision. "Certainly not. At any rate, not in this office," he added.

"Ah, not in this office. Anywhere else?"

"No, nor anywhere else, I should think," the other replied, though this time a little more thoughtfully. "There's only my own family at home and the servants and—"

"Anybody who has access to this room of the office?" Hewitt asked keenly.

Mr Bell seemed a little startled.

"Why, no," he said, "nobody at home comes to the office—not even a visitor, except, of course, my junior partner, who visits the room pretty frequently."

"Very well. You don't remember ever mislaying the keys temporarily, I suppose, either here or at home?"

"No-o," Mr Bell replied slowly. "I can't say that I do remember anything of the sort. No—and I believe I should be sure to remember if I had."

"Ah! And when you realised your loss what did you do? Told your partner first, I suppose?"

"No—he doesn't know of the discovery. He went out just before I made it, and I don't expect him in again today." But as Mr Bell spoke there grew plain in his face the pallor of a new fear.

Martin Hewitt observed it, but kept his thoughts to himself. "Well," he said, "you didn't tell your partner. Nor the police?"

"No, Mr Hewitt. You see, of course, the first thing the police attempt is to catch and punish the thief, and they make the recovery of the property a subsidiary object. But for me, Mr Hewitt, the recovery of the property, as I have explained, is the one great consideration. Punish the thief by all means, but first save me from ruin, Mr Hewitt! That is why I sent for you; for that, and because I thought it might be advisable to keep the matter quiet, till you had taken some steps."

"There is something in that consideration, certainly. So you have told nobody of the loss, except me?"

"Nobody but Foster, my head clerk—an old and faithful servant. It was he, in fact, who suggested sending for you. As he put it very forcibly, you can act for *me* and my interests, while the police act for themselves, and—very properly, of course, as police—in the interest of the community."

"Very well. I see you have several clerks in the outer office. Do they ever come into this room?"

"Never, unless they are sent for."

"If you and your partner were out, and one of the clerks came in *without* being sent for, the rest would know it, of course?"

"Certainly."

"I observe three private rooms opening out of this. What are they?"

"This is a sort of extra inner room where I have private interviews with clients—I was in there with a client for half an hour this morning before I discovered the loss. The next is a mere little box of a room where the correspondence clerk sits and works. The other is a larger place—it is shared between my partner, Mr Clarence Dalton, and the head clerk, Mr Foster."

"Now let me have your broken padlock—and the key. I see you have forced up the front plate with a screwdriver. I will borrow that screw-driver, if you please, and force it off completely."

Hewitt's client produced a screwdriver from a drawer, and in a very few moments the interior of the little padlock lay uncovered. Hewitt examined the lock attentively for some few minutes, trying the key several times against the levers. Then he stood up and said—

"Mr Bell, you have made a mistake. This is not your lock at all!"

"Not my lock!" exclaimed the broker. "What do you mean? I tell you it is the lock of that box, and I broke it open myself!"

"Yes," answered Hewitt calmly, "it was on that box, and you broke it open yourself; but all the same it is not your lock. Let me explain. These are very good little padlocks, with an excellent lever action, 'dogged against detent,' as the technical phrase goes; so that only the key properly made for each lock will open it. They are so good, indeed, as locks, that it would be a waste of time to try picking them, when, because of their small size, it is so very easy to break them apart, just as you have done yourself, and just as I could probably have done in half the time, having had rather more experience. Now that is what has been done with *your* lock by the person who has your bonds. But of course a broken lock has one disadvantage as compared with a skilfully picked lock—it shows at the first glance what has happened. In this case, Mr Bell, *your* lock has been broken and taken away, and the thief, having first provided himself with another padlock of precisely the same make and size, has substituted *that*, locked it with its proper key and so left it!"

"What! Then that was why—"

"That, of course, was why you supposed it to be out of order when you attempted to open it with *your* key. As a matter of fact, it is even now in perfectly good order, except for the damage we have jointly committed with the screw-driver. And now, observe! That lock was shut by another key; if the man that did that is as sharp as I suppose he is, he will have got rid of that key at once. But perhaps he hasn't; and if not, then the man who has that key is the thief. At any rate, the key is the clue we must hunt for. Let us have your clerks in one by one, and look at their keys. Some are out at lunch by this time, probably?"

"No—I said they might be wanted, so kept them. I thought you might prefer to see them before they went out."

"Very well thought of, but perhaps scarcely judicious, on the whole. Because if there *is* a guilty person among them it may give him a hint; and the odds are rather against its being very useful, considering the possibility—even probability—that the bonds and the collateral evidence left here days ago. But we'll look at their keys, by all means, and then they may go to lunch as soon as you please. Let me do the talking, or perhaps you'll start a scare. Send for the nearest clerks first, then the others. As each comes in, mention his name, so that I can hear it. Say, 'Oh, Mr Brown'—or Jones, or what not—'have you some keys about you?' Don't mention my name, and I will do the rest. Push to the door of the safe, and lock this drawer in the table."

Mr Bell did as Hewitt directed, and then called the head clerk, Mr Foster, from his room, with the prescribed inquiry about keys.

"Yes, Mr Foster," Hewitt added pleasantly, "I'm not sure that the lock is quite in order, but I promised to open it for Mr Bell, so we'll try."

Mr Foster, a slim, active old gentleman, grown grey in the firm's service, pulled a bunch of keys from his pocket, and Hewitt scrutinised each narrowly. "No," he said, "I'm afraid none of these will do. Stay," he added suddenly, and turning his back, carried the bunch to the window. "No," he concluded, as he came back to the table and tried one of the keys fruitlessly. "No, I'm afraid none of those will do. Thank you, Mr Foster. You don't happen to have any more, do you?"

No, Mr Foster hadn't any more, and he retired to his room. Then Mr Bell called the correspondence clerk, Mr Henning. Mr Henning was a much younger man than the head clerk—twenty-six or so—pale and blue-eyed, with weak whiskers and a straggling moustache. His keys were just as readily produced as Mr Foster's, but again Hewitt's examination was unsuccessful. The only other key he had belonged to the typewriter, and *that* did not fit.

Then came Mr Potter, the bookkeeper, round, and tubby, and puffy, and his keys went under inspection in the same way, taking a little longer this time, with two separate dashes to the light of the window. Then there was Mr Robson, young and spruce, Mr Clancy, older and less tidy, and four or five more. All the keys were examined, all with the same lack of success, and all the clerks were sent away to take their turns at lunch.

"No," Hewitt reported, as soon as he and Mr Bell were alone again, "it was certainly none of those keys. Though indeed, my little attempt was desperate at best. A man would be a fool to keep *that* key longer than he needed it, and especially to string it with his others. Still, of course, it is by just such blunders as that that nine criminals out of ten are discovered. And now let me take a good look at that box and its contents."

He lifted the box from the safe to the table, and narrowly scrutinised its exterior, especially about the hasp, where the padlock had been. "Either the thief was an experienced hand," he said, "or he took some steady practice with a few such padlocks as this before setting to work. There are no signs of banging about or slipping of tools anywhere."

"But, of course, banging or anything violent would have been noticed in a place like this," Mr Bell remarked.

"In office hours, yes," responded Hewitt. "But we mustn't forget that office hours are only seven or eight out of the twenty-four."

"But you don't suspect burglary, do you?"

"I'm afraid, as yet, I've precious little ground for suspecting anything definite," Hewitt answered; "but we must keep awake to every possibility. Now let us see the dummies." He turned them over, and loosened them wherever they were tied. "Yes," he remarked, "quite neatly done. Filled in with ordinary blank foolscap, such as, no doubt, you have in your office—but, then, it is in every other office, too; every stationer has it by the ream. No marks anywhere—no old newspapers, nothing that could give the shadow of a clue." He dropped the last of the papers, and turned to his client. "Mr Bell," he said, "this thing has been thought out to the last inch. There is something like genius in this robbery—if genius is the capacity for taking pains. My advice to you is to call in the Scotland Yard people at once."

"Do you mean you can do nothing?" asked Mr Bell despairingly. "Don't tell me that, Mr Hewitt!"

"No, I don't mean that," Hewitt answered. "I mean that until I have had time to think the thing over very thoroughly I can't tell what I can or ought to do. Meantime, I think the police should know; not because I think they can see farther into the thing than I can—for, indeed, I don't think they can; but simply because the thief is getting a longer start every moment, and the police are armed with powers that are not at my disposal. They can get search warrants, stop people at ports and railway stations, arrest suspects—do a score of things that will be necessary. Send to Scotland Yard and get Detective Inspector Plummer, if he's available—he's as good a man as they have. Tell him that you've engaged me, or, better still, write a note to the Scotland Yard authorities, and let me have it, to send or not as I think best, after I have turned the thing over in my mind. I shall take one good look round this office, and then run back to my rooms for an hour or two's hard consideration of whatever I may see. One or two small things I *have* seen already—though I'd rather not mention them till I've made up my mind how they bear. Matters seem likely to have gone so far that perhaps the regular police course of catching the thief first will be the best plan, if it can be done. Meantime, it will be my business to keep my eye first on the recovery of the bonds. But I think we must have the police, Mr Bell. Now, I'll take my general look round."

III

After Martin Hewitt had rushed off to St. Augustine's Hospital with the key, the envelope, and the cypher I had brought him, I heard nothing of him till dusk fell—about six. Then I received this telegram:—

> "Cypher read. Most interesting case. If you can spare an hour be outside 120 Broad Street at six thirty.—
> HEWITT."

I had to be at my office between eight and nine, and to keep Hewitt's appointment I should probably have to sacrifice my dinner. But I was particularly curious to know the meaning of that cypher, and just as curious to know how it could be read; and, moreover, I knew that any case that Hewitt called interesting would probably be interesting above the common. So I took my hat and sought a cab.

I was first at the meeting-place—indeed, a little before my time. No. 120 Broad Street was a great new building of offices, most, if not all, closed at this time—a fact indicated by the shutting of one of the halves of the big front door, where a charwoman was sweeping the steps under the board which announced that offices were to be let. I waited nearly a quarter of an hour, and then at last a hansom stopped and deposited Hewitt and another older gentleman before me.

"Hope we haven't kept you waiting, Brett," Hewitt said. "This is Mr Bell, of Kingsley, Bell and Dalton; it took me a little longer than I expected to reach him. His offices are shut, and the clerks all gone, but we are going to turn up the lights for a bit. The lift man is gone too, I expect, so we shall have a good long stair-climb."

As to the lift man Hewitt was right, and during our long climb I received, briefly, an account of the loss Mr Bell's firm had suffered. "I have told Mr Bell," Hewitt said, "that it was you who happened across the key in such an odd fashion, and when I wired I was sure he would be glad to let you see the upshot of your strange bit of luck. I was also pretty sure that you would like to see it, too. For I really believe that this case—which I confess seemed pretty near hopeless a few hours ago—is coming to an issue now, and here."

"Did you get any information out of the man in the hospital?" I asked.

"Not a scrap," Hewitt replied. "He was still insensible, and though I saw his clothes, and they told me a good deal about the gentleman's personal habits—which are not dazzlingly noble, to put it mildly—they told me nothing else whatever, except that he had recently been knocked down in the mud, which I knew already. But the cypher has told me something, as I will explain presently."

By this time we had reached the high floor in which the offices stood, and Mr Bell, all wonder and pale agitation, unlocked the outer door, and turned on the electric light.

"Now," cried Hewitt, "show me your ventilators!"

There were some, it seemed, in the top panes of the windows, but these were not what Hewitt wanted. There were others in the form of upright chambers or flues, made of metal, and painted the same colour as the walls about them. They rose from the floor in corners and wall angles, and could be shut or opened by means of lids over their upper ends. These were more to Hewitt's mind, and he went about from one to another, groping under the lids, and poking down into the flues with a walking-stick. There was a wire-grating, or diaphragm, it seemed, in each of them, two or three feet down, and we could hear the end of the stick raking on this at each investigation. One after another of these ventilators Hewitt examined, till he had examined them all, in outer and inner rooms, without result; and I could see that he was disappointed.

"There must be another somewhere," he said, and hunted afresh.

But plainly he had tried them all, and now he could do no more than try them all again, with as little result.

"It *is* a ventilator," he said, positively. "Unless—" he broke off thoughtfully and stood silent for a few moments. "Ah! of course!" he resumed presently. "We'll send for the housekeeper and a candle. Which is the nearest empty office—the nearest office to let? Is there one on this floor?"

"I think not," Mr Bell answered. "But there's one on the floor below, just opposite the lift—I see the bill on the door every day as I come up."

"We'll try that, then. I'll rake out every ventilator in this palatial edifice before I'll call myself beaten. Come, call the housekeeper. Is there a speaking tube? Tell him to bring a light."

The housekeeper came, wonderingly, with a watchman's oil-lantern, and we all went to the floor below. Opposite the lift was a glass door from which a bill had recently been torn.

"Why, it's let!" said Mr Bell.

"Yes, sir," assented the housekeeper. "Let a day or two ago to a Mr Catherton Hunt. Or, at least, a deposit was paid."

"But see — the door's not locked," Hewitt observed, pushing it open. "I think we'll trespass on Mr Catherton Hunt's new offices, since they seem quite empty, and he hasn't taken possession. Come — ventilators!"

It was a small office — an outer room of moderate size, and one smaller inner room. Hewitt at once attacked the ventilators in the larger apartment — there were two of them — but retired disappointed from each. There was one ventilator only in the small room. Hewitt tilted the lid, which was at about the level of his eyes, thrust in his hand, and drew forth a bundle of folded papers; thrust in his hand again and drew forth another bundle; did it again, and drew forth more!

Mr Bell fell upon the first bundle almost as a dog falls upon a bone; and now he snatched eagerly at each successive paper or bundle, till Hewitt raked the grating with his stick, and declared that there were no more. "Is that all?" he asked.

Mr Bell went tremblingly from paper to paper, and, at last, said that he believed it really was. "I can verify it by the list upstairs," he added, "if you are sure there are no more."

"No more," repeated Hewitt, rattling his stick in the ventilator again. "Let us go and verify, by all means."

We sent the puzzled housekeeper away, and returned to the office above, and presently Mr Bell, now beginning so far to recover from his amazement as to express incoherent gratitude, reported that the bonds were correct and complete to the last and least.

"Very well," said Hewitt, "then my part of the business is done, though I must say I've had luck, or rather, Brett has had it for me. But the police must come on now. I think, Mr Bell, we'll go along to Scotland Yard when we leave here. They'll be wanting to see Mr Catherton Hunt, I expect, whoever he is — and somebody in your office, too, if I'm not sadly mistaken."

"Who?" gasped Mr Bell.

"That, perhaps, you can help to point out. See here — do you know whose figures they are?" and Hewitt produced the small slip of paper containing the cypher.

"They're very small," remarked Mr Bell, putting on his glasses; "very small indeed; but I think — why they're Henning's, I do believe!"

"Ah! one or two other little things seemed to point that way. Henning is your correspondence clerk, I believe, and I expect this thin little slip is a specimen of your typewriter paper. Have you any of his written figures for comparison?"

"Well no — I hardly think — you see he typewrites his letters, and although I know his writing very well I can't at the moment put my hand on any figures of his."

"Never mind — it's mere matter of curiosity; the police will ask him questions in the morning. What *I* believe has happened is this. Our friend Henning — if he's the man — has a friend outside a great deal cleverer than himself — though he would seem to have his share of cunning, too. Between them they resolved to rob you in the way they have done — temporarily. Henning was to take advantage of his position in that little inner room to get at the safe some day when it was open and when you were engaged in your own private inner room with a client, so leaving the safe unwatched. He was provided with a spare patent padlock and key, of the sort you used on that black box, and his confederate had drilled him in the trick of breaking that particular sort of padlock open, with other spare specimens. He got his opportunity this morning."

"Only this morning?"

"This morning, I think, else we should never have got these bonds back, nor even have heard of them again. I think you said you were engaged with a client for half an hour?"

"Yes, from about half-past ten to eleven."

"That was his chance, and he took it. He broke the padlock, took out the bonds, substituted the dummies he had already prepared in his own desk, and locked the box again with the new padlock. Meantime Hunt had paid a deposit, pending references, on the office below—the nearest empty room. Of course, he wouldn't get the key until the tenancy was finally accepted—which he never intended it should be. But he easily arranged to have the door left unlocked for a day or two, on some convenient excuse—arranging decorations, or what not. And the bill was taken down, so that prospective and prospecting tenants were kept away. The bonds being stolen, Henning took the first opportunity of carrying them to the empty office— probably piecemeal—a thing he could easily manage almost under your nose, before you were aware of your loss. There he was to conceal them, either in the chimney, under the boards, or in the ventilator, as he might find convenient—and he found the ventilator most convenient. Then he was to apprise his confederate of the fact that the robbery had been effected in order that Hunt might come and quietly fetch the plunder away. The message was to take an ingenious form. Hunt was to have a fellow waiting about in the street, and as soon as Henning could get out—say to lunch—he was just to *send the key* by this messenger—the key with which he had locked the new padlock on the black box. You see the advantages of that simple arrangement. First, the key, which is evidence, is got rid of in a safe and effectual way—a thing that couldn't be done as well by merely flinging it away on or near the premises, where it might be found. Next, the message is perfectly secret—the messenger could never guess what the key meant, nor could any other person not in the confederate's confidence. And, at the same time, the key tells all that is necessary; the robbery has been effected—come and remove the plunder.

"But something unforeseen happens. No sooner are the bonds stolen and safely hidden than you go to the box, find something wrong with the lock, break it open and discover the loss. This was a thing that they trusted would not happen till after the bonds were safely got away. More, I am sent for, the clerks are kept in from lunch, and so on. Henning gets into a funk, and resolves to send a message of special urgency to his confederate. For that purpose he uses a cypher which the two have agreed upon—the most ingenious cypher I have ever seen used for the purpose. He doesn't wish to make his message any more conspicuous than he need, so he writes his cypher on this scrap of paper and rolls it inside the key—probably another expedient agreed upon in case of necessity. Then the key goes into an envelope, for greater security of the cypher message, and the messenger gets it when Henning is at last released for lunch. What happened to the message we know; and here it is.

"Now I will not weary you with a detailed account of the different ways in which I attacked this cypher, but I will take the shortest possible cut to the true interpretation. A very short examination of the cryptogram shows that while no number is included above 23, the numbers, in their relative frequency, roughly agree with the relative frequency of the corresponding letters of the alphabet, *a* for 1, *b* for 2, and so on."

Here I handed Hewitt the pencilled note I had made at the hospital, with letters substituted for the figures, thus:—*i, h, n, d, t, r, e, i; o, s, t, 0, c, i, h, e; c, w, 0, 0, e, m, n, s; s, t, 0, 0, 0, 0, f, a; e, t, 0, 0, 0, 0, c, v; a, o, 0, 0, 0, 0, r, e; a, h, t, k, r, i, e, t; l, e, w, n, n, a, a, t.*

Hewitt took the paper and went on. "If that were all the thing would be childishly simple. But you will see that we seem as far from the solution as ever; for the letters as they stand mean nothing, though in fact they are in normal relative frequency;

so that if they mean other letters, all the rules are upset, and we are at a standstill. I admit that for a long time the thing bothered me. But a peculiarity struck me. Not only were the figures, or letters, disposed in groups of *eight*, but there were also *eight* such groups—sixty-four altogether. What did that suggest? What but a chessboard?"

"A chessboard?" I queried.

"Just so—a chessboard. Eight squares each way—sixty-four altogether. So I drew a rough representation of a chessboard, and set out the letters on it, in their order, like this:—

```
i   h   n   d   t   r   e   i
o   s   t   0   c   i   h   e
c   w   0   0   e   m   n   s
s   t   0   o   o   0   f   a
e   t   0   o   o   0   c   v
a   o   0.  o   o   0   r   e
a   h   t   k   r   i   e   t
l   e   w   n   n   a   a   t
```

"Now, there was my chessboard with my letters on it. I tried reading them downward, across, upward and diagonally, in the direction of the moves of different chess pieces—king, queen, rook and bishop. Nothing came of that, whatever I did; the thing was as unreadable as ever. But there remained one chess-move to try—the eccentric move of the knight; the move of one square forward, backward or sideways, and then one square diagonally, or, as it has sometimes been more concisely expressed, the move to the next square but one of a different colour from that on which it rests. I tried the knight's move, and I read the cypher.

"I began at the top left-hand corner, just as one does in reading a book. I read the moves downward—*i* to *w*, *e* and *h*, and found that led to nothing. So I took the one alternative move, and, with a little consideration, skipped along from *i* to *t* in the second line of squares, *t* in the top line, *h* in the second line, *e* in the third, *r* in the top and *e* in the second. That gave me an idea. There were the letters *i*, *t*, *t*, followed by the word *here*. I tried back from the *i* again, and taking in the reverse order the *w*, *e* and *h* which I had first given up, I read my own name, as you can see it, from the *h* on the bottom line but one, moving upward. So I had the words *Hewitt here*. I need not carry you through all the steps, which will now be plain enough to you. But I found that the message actually began in the *right*-hand corner, and read thus, the noughts counting for nothing—

"'*Invent loss disc take at once Martin Hewitt here fear watch.*'

"The noughts were plainly merely inserted to fill in unneeded squares, and keep the rest of the figures in their proper relative places when the cypher was written in line. At first I was a little puzzled to understand what seemed to be the first word *invent*. But it was quite clear that *loss disc* meant 'loss discovered,' so I concluded that here in the beginning was a contraction also, and that *in* was a separate word. In that case *vent* could be a contraction for no other word but 'ventilator,' in accordance with the sense of the words. So I concluded that the meaning of the whole sentence was simply this: 'The plunder is in the ventilator, the loss is discovered, take away the booty at once; Martin Hewitt is here, and I fear I may be watched.' There is the reading, and our little adventure this evening is what it has led to.

"Of course, the confederate wouldn't go groping about the squares so painfully as I have had to do. To him the reading would be simple enough, for the order of the moves would be preconcerted. Each of the conspirators would have, as a guide, both to reading and writing the cypher, a drawn set of squares, numbered in the order of the moves—1 where we have the *i*, 2 where we have the *n*, 3 where we have the *v*, and so on. With that before him, either reading or writing in this extraordinary cryptogram would be easy and quick enough. And now for Scotland Yard!"

IV

We learned late on the following day that Henning had not appeared at the office. From that we assumed that he must have met his confederate in the evening, and, finding that he had not received the message sent, conceived that something was wrong, and made himself safe. The confederate, Hunt, however, made his appearance early next morning, but escaped.

What happened is best told in Plummer's words when he called on Hewitt in the afternoon.

"I went round this morning," he said, "as I said I would last night. I took a good man with me, and we got the dummy bonds that had been put in Bell's box and popped 'em in the ventilator, where the real ones had been hidden. You see, we'd got nothing *legal* against Catherton Hunt as yet, but if we could only grab him with those dummy bonds on him it might help, with the other evidence we could scrape up (and especially if we could take Henning), to sustain a charge of conspiracy to steal. Well, he came so quick he was on us before we were quite ready. We'd got the dummies in their place, and I was in front of the door telling my man the likeliest corner to wait in, when suddenly up pops the lift right in front of me, with a gentleman in it—clean-shaven. I looked at him and he looked at me. I had a sort of distant notion that I might have seen him before, and it's pretty certain he had something more than a distant notion about me. 'Down again,' he says to the lift man, before the gate was swung, 'I've forgotten something!' And down the lift went. You'll understand I had no idea he was the man we wanted; but as the lift went down and my eyes were on the man's face, I saw who he was! When he stood straight before me I had no more than a vague notion that I'd seen him somewhere before. But down the lift went, and in the flash of time when he'd nearly disappeared, and the bottom part of his face was hidden by the sill of the lift opening—the part of his face where his beard had been when we met him last—I saw it was Myatt!"

"Myatt? Good heavens!"

"Everard Myatt, Mr Hewitt, the man that murdered Mr Jacob Mason! Everard Myatt, for a thousand, with his beard shaved! And we've lost him again! What could we do? We shouted and ran downstairs, and that was all. He'd gone, of course. And when we asked the hall porter he told us that Mr Catherton Hunt had just come down the lift and hurried out!"

4

THE CASE OF THE BURNT BARN

I

Everard Myatt—or Catherton Hunt—was lost again. Martin Hewitt had been wholly successful, for he had recovered Mr Bell's missing bonds; but the police caught neither of the conspirators. Investigation at Henning's lodgings showed that careful preparations must have been made for an immediate flight if it should become necessary, and the flight had taken place. The man in the hospital, who had been knocked down in carrying from one to the other the extraordinary message that Hewitt deciphered, remained insensible for a few days, and could not be questioned till some time later still. Then he professed to have forgotten all about the message on which he was going when he met his accident, and the medical men in attendance informed the police that it was quite possible that the fellow's statement was true. He said that he *did* carry messages sometimes, when he could get a job, but he could remember nothing of the message of the key, nor of who had sent him, nor where he was to go. Nevertheless, the police, although they professed to accept his statement, kept a wary eye on him after his discharge from the hospital, for they had a very great suspicion that he knew more than he chose to tell. But nothing more was heard of the accomplices till another case of Martin Hewitt's brought the news, and that in a manner strange enough.

The matter began, as so many matters of Hewitt's did, with the receipt of a telegram, followed immediately by another. For the first having been handed in at a country office not very long before eight the previous evening, it was not delivered at Hewitt's office till the morning, in accordance with the ancient manners and customs observed in the telegraphic system of this country. It had been despatched from Throckham, in Middlesex, and it was simply a very urgently worded request to Hewitt to come at once, signed "Claire Peytral." The second telegram, which came even as Hewitt was reading the first, on his arrival at his office, ran thus:—

> "Did you receive telegram? See newspapers. Matter life or death. Would come personally but cannot leave mother. Pray answer.—PEYTRAL."

The answer went instantly that Hewitt would come by the next train, for he had seen the morning paper and from that knew the urgency of the case. But a consultation of the railway guide showed that trains to Throckham were fewer than one might suppose, considering the proximity of the village to London, and that the next would leave in about an hour and a quarter; so that I saw Hewitt before he started. He came up to my rooms, in fact, as I was beginning to breakfast.

"See here," he said, "I am sent for in the Throckham case. Have you seen the report?"

As a leader writer, I had little business with the news side of my paper, and indeed I had no more than a vague recollection of some such heading as: "Tragedy in a barn," in one evening paper of the day before, and "Murder at Throckham" in another. So I could claim no very exact knowledge of the affair.

"Here you have a paper, I see," Hewitt said, reaching for it. "Perhaps their report is fuller than that in mine." He gave me his own newspaper and began searching in the other. "No," he said presently, "much the same. News agency report to both papers, no doubt."

The report which I read ran as follows:—

"SINGULAR TRAGEDY.—An extraordinary occurrence is reported from Throckham, a small village within fifteen miles of London, involving a tragic fatality that has led to a charge of murder. On Thursday evening an old barn, for some time disused, was discovered to be on fire, and it was only by extraordinary exertions on the part of the villagers that the fire was extinguished. Upon an examination of the place yesterday morning the body of Mr Victor Peytral, a gentleman who had lived in the neighbourhood for some time, and who had been missing since shortly before the discovery of the fire, was found in the ruins. The body was burnt almost beyond recognition, but not so much as to conceal the fact that the unfortunate gentleman had not perished in the fire, but had been the victim of foul play. The throat was very deeply cut, and there can be no doubt that the murderer must have fired the barn with the object of destroying all traces of the crime. The police have arrested Mr Percy Bowmore, a frequent visitor at the house of the deceased."

"My telegram," said Hewitt, "is plainly from a relative of this Mr Peytral who is dead—perhaps a daughter, since she speaks of being unable to leave her mother. In that case, probably an only child, since there is no other to leave."

"Unless the others are too young," I suggested.

"Just so," Hewitt replied. "Well, Brett," he added, "today is Saturday."

Saturday was, of course, my "off" day, and I understood Hewitt to hint that if I pleased I might accompany him to Throckham.

"Saturday it is," I said, "and I have no engagements. Would you care for me to come?"

"As you please, of course. I can guess very little of the case as yet, naturally, beyond what I have read in the paper; but the subtle sense of my experience tells me that there is all the chance of an interesting case in this. That's *your* temptation. As for myself, I don't mind admitting that—especially in these country cases, where the resources of civilisation are not always close at hand—I'm never loth to have a friend with me who isn't too proud to be made use of. That's *my* temptation!"

No persuasion was needed, and in due time we set out together.

II

It is my experience that places are to be found within twenty miles of London far more rural, far sleepier, far less influenced by the great city that lies so near, than places thrice and four times as far away. They are just too far out to be disturbed by suburban traffic, and too near to feel the influence of the great railway lines. These main lines go by, carrying their goods and their passengers to places far beyond, and it is only by awkward little branch lines, with slow and rare trains, that any part of this mid-lying belt is reached, and even then it is odds but that one must drive a good way to his destination.

Throckham was just such a place as I speak of, and that was the reason why we had such ample time to catch the first of the half-dozen leisurely trains by which one might reach the neighbourhood during the day. The station was Redfield, and Throckham was three miles beyond it.

At Redfield a coachman with a dogcart awaited Hewitt—only one gentleman having been expected, as the man explained, in offering to give either of us the reins. But Hewitt wished to talk to the coachman, and I willingly took the back seat, understanding very well that my friend would get better to work if he first had as many of the facts as possible from a calm informant before discussing them with the dead man's relations, probably confused and distracted with their natural emotions.

The coachman was a civil and intelligent fellow, and he gave Hewitt all he knew of the case with perfect clearness, as I could very well hear.

"It isn't much I can tell you, sir," he said, "beyond what I expect you know. I suppose you didn't know Mr Peytral, my master, that's dead?"

"No. But he was a foreigner, I suppose—French, from the name."

"Well, no, sir," the coachman replied, thoughtfully; "not French exactly, I think, though sometimes he talked French to the mistress. They came from somewhere in the West Indies, I believe, and there's a trifle of—well, of dark blood in 'em, sir, I should think; though, of course, it ain't for me to say."

"Yes—there are many such families in the French West Indies. Did you ever hear of Alexandre Dumas?"

"No, sir, can't say I did."

"Well, he was a very great Frenchman indeed, but he had as much 'dark blood' as your master had—probably more; and it came from the West Indies, too. But go on."

"Mr Peytral, you must understand, sir, has lived here a year or two—I've only been with him nine months. He talked English always—as good as you or me; and he was always called *Mr* Peytral—not Monsieur, or Signor, or any o' them foreign titles. I think he was naturalised. Mrs Peytral, she's an invalid—came here an invalid, I'm told. She never comes out of her bedroom 'cept on an invalid couch, which is carried. Miss Claire, she's the daughter, an' the only one, and she was hoping you'd ha' been down last night, sir, by the last train. She's in an awful state, as you may expect, sir."

"Naturally, to lose her father in such a terrible way."

"Yes, sir, but it's wuss than that even, for her. You see, this Mr Bowmore, that they've took up, he's been sort of keepin' company with Miss Claire for some time, an' there's no doubt she was very fond of him. That makes it pretty bad for her, takin' it both ways, you see."

"Of course—terrible. But tell me how the thing happened, and why they took this Mr Bowmore."

"Well, sir, it ain't exactly for me to say, and, of course, I don't know the rights of it, bein' only a servant, but they say there was a sudden quarrel last night between Mr Peytral and Mr Bowmore. I think myself that Mr Peytral was getting a bit excitable lately, whatever it was. On Thursday night, just after dinner, he went strolling off in the dusk, alone, and presently Mr Bowmore— he came down in the afternoon—went strolling off after him. It seems they went down toward the Penn's Meadow barn, Mr Peytral first, and Mr Bowmore catching him up from behind. A man saw them—a gamekeeper. He was lyin' quiet in a little wood just the other side of Penn's Meadow, an' they didn't see him as they came along together. They were quarrelling, it seems, though Grant—that's the gamekeeper—couldn't hear exactly what about; but he heard Mr Peytral tell Mr Bowmore to go away. He 'preferred to be alone' and he'd 'had enough' of Mr Bowmore, from what Grant could make out. 'Get out o' my sight, sir, I tell you!' the old gentleman said at last, stamping his foot, and shaking his fist in the young gentleman's face. And then Bowmore turned and walked away."

"One moment," Hewitt interposed. "You are telling me what Grant saw and heard. How did it come to your knowledge?"

"Told me hisself, sir—told me every word yesterday. Told me twice, in fact. First thing in the morning when they found the body, and then again after he'd been to Redfield and had it took down by the police. It was because of that they arrested Mr Bowmore, of course."

"Just so. And is this gamekeeper Grant in the same employ as yourself?"

"Oh, no, sir! Mr Peytral's is only just an acre or two of garden and a paddock. Grant's master is Colonel White, up at the Hall."

"Very good. You were saying that Mr Peytral told Mr Bowmore to get out of his sight, and that Mr Bowmore walked away. What then?"

"Well, Grant saw Mr Bowmore walk away, but it was only a feint—a dodge, you see, sir. He walked away to the corner of the little wood where Grant was, and then he took a turn into the wood and began following Mr Peytral up, watching him from among the trees. Came close by where Grant was sitting, following up Mr Peytral and watching him; and so Grant lost sight of 'em."

"Did Grant say what he was doing in the wood?"

"He said he'd found marks of rabbit-snares there, and he was watching to see if anybody came to set any more."

"Yes—quite an ordinary part of his duty, of course. What next?"

"Well, Grant didn't see any more. He waited a bit, and then moved off to another part of the wood, and he didn't notice anything else particular till the barn was on fire. It was dark, then, of course."

"Yes—you must tell me about the fire. Who discovered it?"

"Oh, a man going home along the lane. He ran and called some people, and they fetched the fire-engine from the village and pumped out of the horse-pond just close by. It was pretty much of a wreck by the time they got the fire out, but it wasn't all gone, as you might have expected. You see, it had been out of use for some time, sir, and there was mostly nothing but old broken ploughs and lumber there; and what's more, there was a deal of rain early in the week, as you may remember, sir, so the thatch was pretty sodden, being out o' repair and all—and so was the timber, for the matter o' that, for there's no telling when it was last painted. So the fire didn't go quite so fierce as it might, you see; else I should expect it had been all over before they got to work on it."

"Not at all a likely sort of place to catch fire, it would seem, either," Hewitt commented. "Old ploughs and such lumber are not very combustible."

"Quite so, sir; that's what makes 'em think it so odd, I suppose. But there *was* a bundle or two of old pea-straw there, shied in last summer, they say, being over bundles from the last load, and there left."

"And when was Mr Bowmore seen next?"

"He came strolling back, sir, and told the young lady he'd left her father outside, or something of that sort, I think; said nothing of the quarrel, I believe. But he said the barn was on fire—which he must have known pretty early, sir, for 'tis a mile from the house off that way;" and the coachman pointed with his whip.

"Nothing was suspected of the murder, it seems, till yesterday morning?"

"No, sir. Miss Claire got frightful worried when her father didn't come home, as you would expect, and specially at him not coming home all night. But when the fire was quite put out, o' course the people went away home to bed, and it wasn't till the morning that anybody went in to turn the place over. Then they found the body."

"Badly burnt, I believe?"

"Horrid burnt, sir. If it wasn't for Mr Peytral's being missing, I doubt if they'd have known it was him at all. It took a doctor's examination to see clear that the throat had been cut. But cut it had been, and deep, so the doctor said. And now the body's gone over to Redfield mortuary."

Hewitt asked a few questions more, and got equally direct answers, except where the coachman had to confess ignorance.

But presently we were at the house to which Hewitt had been summoned.

It was a pleasant house enough, standing alone, apart from the village, a little way back from a loop of road that skirted a patch of open green. As we came in at the front gate, I caught an instant's glimpse of a pale face at an upper window, and before we could reach the drawing-room door Miss Claire Peytral had met us.

She was a young lady of singular beauty, which the plain signs of violent grief and anxiety very little obscured. Her complexion, of a very delicate ivory tinge, was scarcely marred by the traces of sleeplessness and tears that were nevertheless clear to see. Her eyes were large and black, and her jetty hair had a slight waviness that was the only distinct sign about her of the remote blend of blood from an inferior race.

"Oh, Mr Hewitt," she cried, "I am so glad you have come at last! I have been waiting—waiting so long! And my poor mother is beginning to suspect!"

"You have not told her, then?"

"No, it will kill her when she knows, I'm sure—kill her on the spot. I have only said that father is ill at—at Redfield. Oh, what shall I do?"

The poor girl seemed on the point of breakdown, and Hewitt spoke sharply and distinctly.

"What you must do is this," he said. "You must attend to me, and tell me all I want to know as accurately and as tersely as you can. In that case I will do whatever I can, but if you give way you will cripple me. It all depends on you, remember. This is my intimate friend, Mr Brett, who is good enough to offer to help us. Now, first, I think I know the heads of the case, from the newspapers, and, more especially, from your coachman. But when you sent for me, no doubt you had some definite idea or intention in your mind. What was it?"

"Oh, he is innocent, Mr Hewitt—he is, really! The only friend I have in the world—the only friend we all have!"

"Steady—steady," Hewitt said, pressing her kindly and firmly into a seat. "You *must* keep steady, you know, if I am to do anything. I expected that would be your belief. Now tell me why you are so sure."

"Mr Hewitt, if you knew him you wouldn't ask. He would never injure my poor father—he went out after him purely out of kindness, because I was uneasy. He would never hurt him, Mr Hewitt, never, never! I can't say it strongly enough—he never would! Oh! my poor father, and now—"

"Steady again!" cried Hewitt, more sharply still. I could see that he feared the hysterical breakdown that might come at any moment after the lengthened suspense Miss Peytral had suffered. "Listen, now—you mustn't frighten yourself too much. If Mr Bowmore is innocent—and you say you are so certain of it—then I've no doubt of finding a way to prove it if only you'll make your best effort to help me, and keep your wits about you. As far as I can see at present there's nothing against him that we need be afraid of if we tackle it properly, and, of course, the police make arrests of this sort by way of precaution in a case like this, on the merest hint. Come now, you say you were uneasy when your father went out after dinner on Thursday night. Why?"

"I don't know, quite, Mr Hewitt. It was my mother that was uneasy, really, about something she never explained to me. My father had taken to going out in the evening after dinner, just in the way he did on Thursday night. I don't know why, but I think it had something to do with my mother's anxiety."

"Did he dress for dinner?"

"No, not lately. He used to dress always, but he has dropped it of late."

Hewitt paused for a moment, thoughtfully. Then he said, "Mrs Peytral is an invalid, I know, and no doubt none the better for her anxiety. But if it could be managed I should like to ask her a few questions. What do you think?"

But this Miss Peytral was altogether against. Her mother was suffering from spinal complaint, it appeared, with very serious nervous complications, and there was no answering for the result of the smallest excitement. She never saw strangers, and, if it could possibly be avoided, it must be avoided now.

"Very well, Miss Peytral, I will first go and look at some things I must see, and I will do without your mother's help as long as I possibly can. But now you must answer a few more questions yourself, please."

Hewitt's questions produced little more substantial information, it seemed to me, than he had already received. Mr Peytral had taken the house in which we were sitting — it was called "The Lodge" simply — two years ago. Before that the family had lived in Surrey, but they had not moved direct from there; there was a journey to America between, on some business of Mr Peytral's, and it was on the return voyage that they had met Mr Percy Bowmore. Mr Bowmore had no friends nearer than Canada, and he was reading for the Bar — in a very desultory way, as I gathered. Miss Peytral's childhood had been passed in the West Indies, at the town of San Domingo, in fact, where her father had been a merchant. Her mother had been a helpless invalid ever since Miss Peytral could remember. As to the engagement with Bowmore, it would seem to have had the full approval of both parents all along. But a rather curious change had come over her father, she thought, a few months ago. What it was that had caused it she could not say, but he grew nervous and moody, often absent-minded, and sometimes even short-tempered and snappish, a thing she had never known before. Also he read the daily papers with much care and eagerness. It was plain that Miss Peytral had no idea of any cause which might have led to a quarrel between Bowmore and her father, and Hewitt's most cunning questions failed to elicit the smallest suggestion of reason for such an occurrence.

Ten days or so ago, Mr Peytral had returned from a short walk after dinner, very much agitated; and from that day he had made a practice of going out immediately after dinner every evening regularly, walking off across the paddock, and so away in the direction of Penn's Meadow. The first visit of Percy Bowmore after this practice had begun was on Thursday, but the presence of the visitor made no difference, as Miss Peytral had expected it would. Her father rose abruptly after dinner and went off as before; and this time Mrs Peytral, who had been brought down to dinner, displayed a singular uneasiness about him. She had experienced the same feeling, curiously enough, on other occasions, Miss Peytral remarked, when her husband had been unwell or in difficulties, even at some considerable distance. This time the feeling was so strong that she begged Bowmore to hurry after Mr Peytral and accompany him in his walk. This the young man had done; but he returned alone after a while, saying simply that he had lost sight of Mr Peytral, whom he had supposed might have come home by some other way; and mentioning also that he had been told that Penn's Meadow barn was on fire.

When it grew late, and Mr Peytral failed to return, Bowmore went out again and made inquiry in all directions. It grew necessary to concoct a story to appease Mrs Peytral, who had been taken back to her bedroom. Bowmore spent the whole night in fruitless search and inquiry, and then, with the morning, came the terrible news of the discovery in the burnt barn; and late in the afternoon Bowmore was arrested.

The poor girl had a great struggle to restrain her feelings during the conversation, and, at its close, Hewitt had to use all his tact to keep her going. Physical exhaustion, as well as mental trouble, were against her, and stimulus was needed. So Hewitt said, "Now you must try your best, and if you will keep up as well as you have done a little longer, perhaps I may have good news for you soon. I must go at once and examine things. First, I should like to have brought to me every single pair of boots or shoes belonging to your father. Send them, and then go and look after your mother. Remember, you are helping all the time."

III

Hewitt examined the boots and shoes with great rapidity, but with a singularly quick eye for peculiarities.

"He liked a light shoe," he said, "and he preferred to wear shoes rather than boots. There are few boots, and those not much worn, although he was living in the country. Trod square on the right foot, inward on the left, and wore the left heel more than the right. It's plain he hated nails, for these are all hand-sewn, with scarcely as much as a peg visible in the lot; and they are all laced, boots and shoes alike. Come, this is the best-worn pair; it is also a pair of the same sort the maid tells me he must have been wearing, since they are missing; low shoes, laced; we'll take them with us."

We left the house and sought our friend the coachman. He pointed out quite clearly the path by which his master had gone on his last walk; showed us the gate, still fastened, over which he had climbed to gain the adjoining meadow, and put us in the way of finding the small wood and the barn.

Both within and without the gate there was a small patch bare of grass, worn by feet; and here Martin Hewitt picked up his trail at once.

"The ground has hardened since Thursday night," he said; "and so much the better—it keeps the marks for us. Do you see what is here?"

There were footmarks, certainly, but so beaten and confused that I could make nothing of them. Hewitt's practised eye, however, read them as I might have read a rather illegibly written letter.

"Here is the right foot, plain enough," he said, carefully fitting the shoe he had brought in the mark. "He alighted on that as he came over the gate. Half over it is another footmark—Bowmore's, I expect, for I can see signs of others, in both directions—going and coming. But we shall know better presently."

He rose, and we followed the irregular track across the meadow. Like most such field-tracks, its direction was plainly indicated by the thin and beaten grass, with a bare spot here and there. Hewitt troubled to take no more than a glance at each of these spots as we passed, but that was all he needed. The meadow was bounded by a hedge, with a stile; and at the farther side of this stile my friend knelt again, with every sign of attention.

"A little piece of luck," he reported. "The left shoe has picked up a tiny piece of broken thorn-twig just here. See the mark? The shoe was a little soddened in the sole by this time, and the thorn stuck. I hope it stuck altogether. If it did it may help us wonderfully when we get to the barn, for the trouble there will be the trampling all round of the people at the fire."

So we went on till we reached the edge of the little wood. The field-path skirted this, and here Hewitt dropped on his knees and set to work with great minuteness.

"Keep away from the track, Brett," he warned me, "or you may make it worse. The police have been here, I see, and quite recently, coming from the direction of Redfield. Here are two pairs of unmistakable police boots and another heavy pair with them; no doubt they brought the gamekeeper along with them, to have things fully explained."

From the corner of the wood to a point forty yards along the path; back to the corner again, and then into the wood Hewitt went, carefully examining every inch of the ground as he did so. Then at last he rejoined me.

"I think the gamekeeper has told the truth," he said. "It's pretty plain, thanks to the soft ground hereabout, notwithstanding the policemen's boots. Here they came together—the thorn-twig sticks to the shoe still, you see—and here they stopped. The marks face about, and Bowmore's steps are retraced to the corner of the wood. Peytral's turn again and go on, and Bowmore's turn into the edge of the wood and come along among the trees. You don't see them in the grassy parts quite as well as I do, I expect, but there they are. We'll keep after Peytral's prints. Bowmore's come back in the same track, I see."

The next stile led to Penn's Meadow. This meadow—a large one—stretched over a rather steep hump of land, at the other side of which the barn stood. From the stile two paths could be discerned—one rising straight over the meadow in the direction of the barn, and the other skirting it to the left, parallel with the hedge.

"Here the footprints part," Hewitt observed, musingly; "and what does that mean? Manoeuvring—or what?"

He thought a moment, and then went on: "We'll leave the tracks for the present and see the barn. That is straight ahead, I take it."

When we reached the top of the rise the barn came in view, a blackened and sinister wreck. The greater part of the main structure was still standing, and even part of the thatched roof still held its place, scorched and broken. Off to the right from where we stood the village roofs were visible, giving indication of the position of the road to Redfield. A single human figure was in sight—that of a policeman on guard before the barn.

"Now we must get rid of that excellent fellow," said Hewitt, "or he'll be offering objections to the examination I want to make. I wonder if he knows my name?"

We walked down to the barn, and Hewitt, assuming the largest possible air, addressed the policeman.

"Constable," he said, "I am here officially—here is my card. Of course you will know the name if you have had any wide experience—London experience especially. I am looking into this case on behalf of Miss Peytral—co-operating with the police, of course. Where is your inspector?"

He was a rather stupid countryman, this policeman, but he was visibly impressed—even flurried—by Hewitt's elaborate bumptiousness. He saluted, tried to look unnaturally sagacious, and confessed that he couldn't exactly say where the inspector was, things being put about so just now. He might be in Throckham village, but more likely he was at Redfield.

"Ah!" Hewitt replied, with condescension. "Now, if he is in the village, you will oblige me, constable, by telling him that I am here. If he is not there, you will return at once. I will be responsible here till you come back. Don't be very long, now."

The man was taken by surprise, and possibly a trifle doubtful. But Hewitt was so extremely lofty and so very peremptory and official, that the inferior intelligence capitulated feebly, and presently, after another uneasy salute, the village policeman had vanished in the direction of the road. The moment he had disappeared Hewitt turned to the ruined barn. The door was gone, and the scorched and charred lumber that littered the place had a look of absolute ghostliness—perhaps chiefly the effect of my imagination in the knowledge of the ghastly tragedy that the place had witnessed. Well in from the doorway was a great scatter of light ashes—plainly the pea-straw that the coachman had spoken of. And by these ashes and partly among them, marked in some odd manner on the floor, was a horrible black shape that I shuddered to see, as Hewitt pointed it out with a moving forefinger, which he made to trace the figure of a prostrate human form.

"Did you never see that before in a burnt house?" Hewitt asked in a hushed voice. "I have, more than once. That sort of thing always leaves a strange stain under it, like a shadow."

But business claimed Martin Hewitt, and he stepped carefully within. Scarcely had he done so, when he stood suddenly still, with a low whistle, pointing toward something lying among the dirt and ashes by the foot of that terrible shape.

"See?" he said. "Don't disturb anything, but look!"

I crept in with all the care I could command, and stooped. The place was filled with such a vast confusion of lumber and cinder and ash that at first I failed to see at all what had so startled Hewitt's attention. And even when I understood his direction, all I saw was about a dozen little wire loops, each a quarter of an inch long or less, lying among a little grey ash that clung about the ends of some of the loops in clots. Even as I looked another thing caught Hewitt's eye. Among the straw-ashes there lay some cinders of paper and card, and near them another cinder, smaller, and plainly of some other substance. Hewitt took my walking-stick, and turned this cinder over. It broke apart as he did so, and from within it two or three little charred sticks escaped. Hewitt snatched one up and scrutinised it closely.

"Do you see the tin ferrule?" he said. "It has been a brush; and that was a box of colours!" He pointed to the cinder at his feet. "That being so," he went on, "that paper and card was probably a sketchbook. Brett! come outside a bit. There's something amazing here!"

We went outside, and Hewitt faced me with a curious expression that for the life of me I could not understand.

"Suppose," he said, "*that Mr Victor Peytral is not dead after all?*"

"Not dead?" I gasped; "but—but he is! We know—"

"It seems to me," Hewitt pursued, with his eyes still fixed on mine, "that we know very little indeed of this affair, as yet. The body was unrecognisable, or very near it. You remember what the coachman said? 'If it wasn't for Mr Peytral's being missing,' he said, 'I doubt if they'd have known it was him at all.' I think those were his exact words. More, you must remember that the body has not been seen by either of Peytral's relatives."

"But then," I protested, "if it isn't his body whose is it?"

"Ah, indeed," Hewitt responded, "whose is it? Don't you see the possibilities of the thing? There's a colour-box and a sketch-book burned. Who carried a colour-box and a sketchbook? Not Peytral, or we should have heard of it from his daughter; she made a particular point of her father's evening strolls being quite aimless, so far as her knowledge or conjecture went; she knew nothing of any sketching. And another thing—don't you see what *those* things mean?" He pointed toward the place of the little wire loops.

"Not at all."

"Man, don't you see they've been boot-buttons? When the boots shrivelled, the threads were burnt and the buttons dropped off. Boot-buttons are made of a sort of composition that burns to a grey ash, once the fire really gets hold of them — as you may try yourself, any time you please. You can see the ash still clinging to some of the shanks; and there the shanks are, lying in two groups, six and six, as they fell! Now Peytral came out in laced shoes."

"But if Peytral isn't dead, where is he?"

"Precisely," rejoined Hewitt, with the curious expression still in his eyes. "As you say, where is he? And as you said before, who is the dead man? Who is the dead man, and where is Peytral, and why has he gone? Don't you see the possibilities of the case *now*?"

Light broke upon me suddenly. I saw what Hewitt meant. Here was a possible explanation of the whole thing—Peytral's recent change of temper, his evening prowlings, his driving away of Bowmore, and lastly, of his disappearance—his flight, as it now seemed probable it was. The case had taken a strange turn, and we looked at one another with meaning eyes. It might be that Hewitt, begged by the unhappy girl we had but just left to prove the innocence of her lover, would by that very act bring her father to the gallows.

"Poor girl!" Hewitt murmured, as we stood staring at one another. "Better she continued to believe him dead, as she does! Brett, there's many a good man would be disposed to fling these proofs away for the girl's sake and her mother's, seeing how little there can be to hurt Bowmore. But justice must be done, though the blow fall—as it commonly does—on innocent and guilty together. See, now, I've another idea. Stay on guard while I try."

He hurried out toward the farther side of the broad band of trampled ground which surrounded the burnt barn, and began questing to and fro, this way and that, receding farther from me as he went, and nearing the horse-pond and the road. At last he vanished altogether, and left me alone with the burnt barn, my thoughts, and—that dim shape on the barn floor. It was broad day, but I felt none too happy; and I should not have been at all anxious to keep the police watch at night.

Perhaps Hewitt had been gone a quarter of an hour, perhaps a little more, when I saw him again, hurrying back and beckoning to me. I went to meet him.

"It's right enough," he cried. "I've come on his trail again! There it is, thorn-mark and all, by the roadside, and at a stile—going to Redfield—probably to the station. Come, we'll follow it up! Where's that fool of a policeman? Oh, the muddle they *can* make when they really try!"

"Need we wait for him?" I asked.

"Yes, better now, with those proofs lying there; and we must tell him not to be bounced off again as I bounced him off. There he comes!"

The heavy figure of the local policeman was visible in the distance, and we shouted and beckoned to hurry him. Agility was no part of that policeman's nature, however, and beyond a sudden agitation of his head and his shoulders, which we guessed to be caused by a dignified spasm of leisurely haste, we saw no apparent acceleration of his pace.

As we stood and waited we were aware of a sound of wheels from the direction of Redfield, and as the policeman neared us from the right, so the sound of wheels approached us from the left. Presently a fly hove in sight—the sort of dusty vehicle that plies at every rural railway station in this country; and as he caught sight of us in the road the driver began waving his whip in a very singular and excited manner. As he drew nearer still he shouted, though at first we could not distinguish his words. By this time the policeman, trotting ponderously, was within a few yards. The passenger in the fly, a thin, dark, elderly man, leaned over the side to look ahead at us, and with that the policeman pulled up with a great gasp and staggered into the ditch.

"'Ere 'e is!" cried the fly-driver, regardless of the angry remonstrances of his fare. "'Ere 'e is! 'E's all right! It ain't 'im! 'Ere he is!"

"Shut your mouth, you fool!" cried the angry fare. "*Will* you stop making a show of me?"

"Not me!" cried the eccentric cabman. "I don't want no fare, sir! I'm drivin' you 'ome for honour an' glory, an' honour an' glory I'll make it! 'Ere 'e is!"

Hewitt took in the case in a flash—the flabbergasted policeman, the excited cabman and the angry passenger. He sprang into the road and cried to the cabman, who pulled up suddenly before us.

"Mr Victor Peytral, I believe?" said Martin Hewitt.

"Yes, sir," answered the dark gentleman snappishly, "but I don't know you!"

"There has been a deal of trouble here, Mr Peytral, over your absence from home, as no doubt you have become aware; and I was telegraphed for by your daughter. My name is Hewitt—Martin Hewitt."

Peytral's face changed instantly. "I know your name well, Mr Hewitt," he said. "There's a matter—but who is this?"

"My friend, Mr Brett, who is good enough to help me today. If I may detain you a moment, I should like a word with you aside."

"Certainly."

Mr Peytral alighted, and the two walked a little apart.

I saw Hewitt talking and pointing toward the burnt barn, and I well guessed what he was saying. He was giving Peytral warning of what he had discovered in the barn, explaining that he must give the information to the police, and asking if, in those circumstances, Peytral wished to go home, or to make other arrangements. Often Hewitt's duty to his clients and his duty as a law-upholding citizen between them put him in some such delicate position.

But there was no hesitation in Mr Victor Peytral. Plainly he feared nothing, and he was going home.

"Very well, then," I heard Hewitt say as they turned towards us, "perhaps we had better go on slowly and let my friend cut across the fields first to break the news. Brett—I knew you would be useful, sooner or later."

And so I hurried off, with the happy though delicate mission to restore both father and lover to Miss Claire Peytral.

IV

Miss Peytral had to be put to bed under care of a nurse, for the revulsion was very great, and so was her physical prostration. Bowmore, now set free, and in himself a very pleasant young fellow, came with hurried inquiries and congratulations, and then rushed off to London to cable to his friends in Canada, for fear of the effect of newspaper telegrams.

When at last Hewitt and I sat with Mr Peytral in his study, "Mr Hewitt," said Peytral, "I am not sure how far explanations may go between us. There is more in that death in the barn than the police will ever guess."

Peytral was haggard and drawn, for, as he had let slip already, he had scarce slept an hour since leaving home on Thursday.

"I am tired," he said, "and worn out, but that is not a novelty with me; and I'm not sure but we may be of use to each other. Did my daughter tell you why she sent Mr Bowmore after me on Thursday night?"

Hewitt explained the thing as briefly as possible, just as he had heard it from Miss Peytral.

"Ah," said Peytral, thoughtfully. "So she thought my manner became moody a few months back. It did, no doubt, for I had memories; and more, I had apprehensions. Mr Hewitt, I think I read in the papers that you were in some way engaged in the extraordinary case of the murder of Mr Jacob Mason?"

"That is quite correct. I was."

"There was another case, a little while before, which possibly you may not have heard of. A man was found strangled near the York column, by Pall Mall, with just such a mark on his forehead as was found on Mr Mason's."

"I know that case, too, as well as the other."

"Do you know the name of the murderer?"

"I think I do. We speak in confidence, of course, as client and professional man?"

"Of course. What was his name?"

"I have heard two—Everard Myatt and Catherton Hunt."

"Neither is his real name, and I doubt if anybody but himself knows it. Twenty years ago and more I knew him as Mayes. He was a Jamaican. Mr Hewitt, that man's foul life has been justly forfeit a thousand times, but if it belongs to anybody it belongs to me!"

It was terrible to see the sudden fiery change in the old man. His lassitude was gone in a flash, his eyes blazed and his nostrils dilated.

For a little while he sat so, his mouth awork with passion; then he sank back in his chair with a sigh.

"I am getting old," he said, more quietly, "and perhaps I am not strong enough to lose my temper.... Well, as I said, Mayes was a Jamaican, a renegade white. Do you remember that in the black rebellion of 1865, there was a traitorous white man among the blacks? Eyre hanged a few rebels, and rightly, but the worst creature on all that island escaped — probably escaped by the aid of that very white skin that should have ensured him a greater punishment than the rest. He escaped to Hayti. Now you have probably heard something of Hayti, and of the common state of affairs there?"

We both had heard, and, indeed, the matter had been particularly brought to Hewitt's notice by the case which I have told elsewhere as "The Affair of the Tortoise." As for me, I had read Sir Spenser St. John's book on the black republic, and I had been greatly impressed by the graphic picture it gives of the horrible, blood-stained travesty of regular government there prevailing. Nothing in the worst of the South American Republics is to be remotely compared to it. In the worst periods there was not a crime imaginable that could not be, and was not, committed openly and with impunity by anybody on the right side of the so-called "government"; and the "government" was nothing but an organised crime in itself.

"Well," Peytral pursued, "then I need not expatiate on it, and you will understand the sort of place that Mayes fled to, and how it suited him. He was a man of far greater ability than any of the coarse scoundrels in power, and he was worse than all of them. He was not such a fool as to aim at ostensible political power — that way generally led to assassination. He was the jackal, the contriver, the power behind the throne, the instigator of half the devilry set going in that unhappy place, and he profited by it with little risk; he was the confidential adviser of that horrible creature Domingue. If you know anything of Hayti you will know what that means.

"At this time I was comparatively a young man, and a merchant at Port-au-Prince. It was a bad place, of course, and business was risky enough, but, for that very reason, profits were large, and that was an attraction to a sanguine young man like myself. I did very well, and I had thoughts of getting out of it with what I had made. But it was a fatal thing to be supposed wealthy in Port-au-Prince, unless you were a villain in power, or partner with one. I was neither, and I was judged a suitable victim by Mayes. Not I alone, either—no, nor even only I and my fortune. Gentlemen, gentlemen, my poor wife, who now lies—"

Peytral's utterance failed him. He rose as if choking, and Hewitt rose to quiet him. "Never mind," he said, "sit quiet now. We understand. Rest a moment."

The old man sank back in his chair, and for a little while buried his face in his hands. Then he went on.

"I needn't go into details," he said, huskily. "It is enough to say that every devilish engine of force and cunning was put in operation against me. So it came that at last, on a hint from a hanger-on of the police-office, who had enough humanity in him to remember a kindness he had experienced at my hands, that we took flight in the middle of the night—my poor wife, myself, and our three children, with nothing in the world but our bare lives and the clothes we wore. I might have tried to get aboard a foreign ship in the harbour, but I knew that would be useless. I should have been given up on whatever criminal charge Mayes chose to present, and my wife and children with me. I had hope of somehow getting to San Cristobel, where I had a friend—over the border in the other Government of the island, the Dominican Republic. That was eighty miles away and more, across swamps, and forests and mountains. Well, we did it—we did it. We did it, Mr Hewitt, and I dream of it still. They hunted us, sir—hunted us with dogs. We hid from them a whole day among the rank weeds—up to our shoulders in the water of a pestilential fever-swamp; Claire, the baby, on her mother's back, and both the boys on mine. They died—they died next day. My two beautiful boys, gentlemen, died in my arms, and I was too weak even to bury them!"

There was another long pause, and the man's head was bowed in his hands once more. Presently he went on again, but at first without lifting his head.

"We did it, gentlemen," he said—"we did it. We crawled into San Cristobel at the end of five days; and from that moment my dear wife has never once stood upright on her feet. So we came out of it, and the baby, Claire, was the one that suffered least. She was too young to understand, and her mother—her mother saved her, when I could not save the boys!"

He paused again, and presently sat up, pale, but in full command of himself. "You will excuse me, gentlemen, I am sure, and make allowances for my feelings," he said. "There is not a great deal more to tell. Mayes did not last long in Hayti. Domingue was overthrown, and Mayes left the island, I was told, and made for another part of the world. Years afterward I heard of his being in China, though what truth there may have been in the rumour I cannot say.

"My friend in San Cristobel—he was a cousin, in fact—put me on my legs again, and after a while he helped me to begin business at San Domingo, under my present name, Peytral, which, in fact, was my mother's maiden name. There came a sudden push in trade with the United States about this time, and I went into my affairs with the more energy to distract my thoughts. In fifteen years—to cut a long story short—I had made the small competency which I have brought to England with me, with the idea of a peaceful end to my life and my wife's; though I doubt if I am to have that now. I doubt it, and I will tell you why. Mr Hewitt, when I went away without warning on Thursday night I was dogging Mayes!"

Hewitt nodded, with no sign of surprise. "And the man killed in the barn?"

"That is one more of his thousand crimes, without a doubt. Though it differs. Do you know what drew my attention to the murders of the men Denson and Mason, and so set me thinking? In each case the murder was by strangulation, and the medical evidence at the inquests showed that it was effected by means of a tourniquet. In fact, in the second case, the tourniquet itself was left behind."

"Yes," Hewitt replied, "I loosened it myself—but, unfortunately, I was too late."

"Well, now," Peytral went on, "in Hayti, in my time, Mayes's enemies had a habit of dying suddenly in the night, by strangulation, and a tourniquet was always the instrument. And just as murder was quite a popular procedure in that accursed place, so strangulation by tourniquet became for a while the most common form of the crime. It was rapid, effective, and silent, you see. So that a murder by tourniquet, quite an unknown thing in this country, took my attention at once, and when another followed it so soon, I felt something like certainty. And the triangle was suggestive, too."

"Were Mayes's victims marked in that way in Hayti?"

"No, there was no mark. But"—here Mr Peytral's features assumed a curious expression—"there are things which are not believed in this country—which are laughed at, in fact, and called superstition. You know something of Hayti, and therefore you must have heard of Voodoo—the witchcraft and devil-worship of the West Indies. Well, Mayes was as deep in that as he was in every other species of wickedness. It sounds foolish, perhaps, here in civilised England, and you may laugh, but I tell you that Mayes could make men do as he wished, with their consent or against it! And he used a thing—it was generally known that he used a thing marked with a triangle—a Red Triangle—by the use of which he could bend men to his will!"

Hewitt was listening intently, with no sign of laughter at all, notwithstanding his client's apprehension. And I remembered the case of Mr Jacob Mason, and how that victim had so fervently expressed his wish to the excellent clergyman,

Mr Potswood, that he had never dabbled in the strange devilries of Myatt—or Mayes, as we were now learning to call him.

"At any rate," Peytral resumed, "you will understand that the conjunction of the tourniquet with the Red Triangle in the two cases you know of caused me some excitement. My daughter, as you have said, noticed a change in my habits from that time; my wife did more—she knew the reason. Mr Hewitt, I am an older man, but there is hotter blood in my veins than in yours. My father was English—though you might scarcely suppose it—but my mother, to whose name I have reverted, was a French Creole. So perhaps my natural instincts come nearer to those of our savage ancestry than do yours. Whether or not you will understand me I do not know, but I can tell you that even now, in cold blood—for my paroxysm has exhausted itself and me—it seems to me that it would be my duty, not to say my sacred duty, to tear that man to pieces with my hands whenever and wherever I could put them on him! My old passions may have slept, I find, but they are alive still, and I found them waking when I realised that Mayes was alive and in England. The words 'sane' and 'insane' are elastic in their application, but I doubt if you would have called me strictly sane of late. I evolved mad schemes for the destruction of this wretch, and I was ready to devote myself and everything I possessed to the purpose. More than once I contemplated coming to you—seeing that you had met the man in one of his villainies—with the idea of enlisting your aid. But I reflected that you would probably make yourself no party to a plan of private revenge, and I hesitated. And then—then, a little more than a week ago, I saw the man himself! Changed, without doubt, but not half as much changed as I am myself. Nevertheless, sure as I am of him now, I hesitated then. For it was here in the meadow that you know, near the barn, and the thing seemed so likely to be illusion that I almost suspected my senses. It was dusk, and he was walking and talking with another man, a good deal younger. And presently, while I was still confounded with surprise, and as they passed behind a clump of trees, Mayes was gone, and I saw his companion alone. He was a young man — an artist, it would seem, with sketchbook and colours."

I started, and Hewitt and I glanced at each other. Peytral saw it and paused. "Never mind," said Hewitt. "Please go on."

"After that I came out every night, in the hope of seeing my enemy again. On several evenings I saw the young artist waiting by the barn expectantly, but nobody joined him. I found that this young man was lodging at a cottage in the village, and I resolved not to lose sight of him.

"At last, on Thursday night, I saw Mayes again. Mr Bowmore was here, and when I left the house he troubled me much by coming after me. I was obliged to tell him that I wished to be alone, and I was in a nervously explosive state when I did it. He seemed reluctant to go; my anger blazed out, and I violently ordered him off. From what he has told me it seems that he followed me still, but lost sight of me near Penn's Meadow. Well, be that as it may, I saw Mayes and the young artist again. I watched from a rather awkward spot, and dusk was falling, so that I could not see all that passed; but presently I was aware that Mayes was making off by the road alone, and I followed him.

"From that moment I think I really was mad, though my madness did not drive me to attack him at once. I had a feeling of curiosity to see where he would go, and a curious cruel idea of letting him run for a little first — as a cat feels, I suppose, with a mouse. You may judge that I was not in my normal state of mind from the fact that all through yesterday and part of today I never as much as thought of telegraphing home to say that I had gone to London. For it was to London I followed him. I took no ticket at the station — I got on the platform by stealth, and entered the train unobserved, for he and one boy were the only passengers, and I feared attracting attention. It was easy enough, in such a station as Redfield, and I paid my fare at London. And after all I lost him! Lost him in London!"

"How?"

"Like a fool. I saw him enter a house, and waited. Followed him again, and waited at another. I might have flung him into the river from the Embankment, and I refrained. And then—whether it began at a dark corner or in a group of people I cannot tell, but I suddenly discovered that I was following a stranger—a stranger of about Mayes's form and stature. It was what I should have expected, and provided for, in London streets at night!

"If I have been mad, it was then I was worst. I suppose by that time it must have been too late to get back home, but I never thought of that. I ran the streets the whole night, like a fool, hunting for Mayes. I kept on all day yesterday. I waited and watched hours at the two houses he had visited; and it was not till early this morning that I flung myself on a bed in a private hotel in Euston Road. I slept a little, and my paroxysm was over. Perhaps I am more fortunate than I am disposed to think, since I am as yet in no danger of trial for murder."

This passionate, wayward, stricken man was plainly the object of fascinated interest to Hewitt. My friend waited a moment, and then said—"The houses he called at—I should like to know them. And where you lost sight of him."

Peytral sat back, and gazed thoughtfully for fully half a minute in Hewitt's face. "Do you know," he said at length, "I don't think I'll answer that question now. I'd like to leave it for a day or two. Yesterday I wouldn't have told you, even on the rack—no, not a word! I should have said, 'Take your own chances, and get him if you can. As for me, I consider him *my* prey, and what scent I have picked up I shall use myself!' A mad fancy, you will think, perhaps. For me the question is, was I sanest then or now? I will take a day or two to think."

V

In less than a day or two the identity of the victim of the burnt barn was established. For Hewitt had his idea, and he communicated with Plummer, of Scotland Yard. The man with the buttoned boots and the sketchbook was the artist who had been staying at the cottage in the village, but who, singularly enough, had never been seen to draw, and had left no drawings behind him. He had warned the people of the cottage that he might be away for a night or two, and he had stayed away for two nights before; so that his disappearance did not disturb them, and when they heard that Mr Peytral's body had been found in the barn they accepted the news as fact. They recognised at once a photograph produced by Plummer as that of their late lodger. And the photograph had been procured from Messrs. Kingsley, Bell and Dalton, the intended victims in the bond case, and it was one of Henning, their vanished correspondence clerk!

That his death would be convenient to Mayes, the greater scoundrel, was plain enough. The bond robbery had been brought to naught, thanks to Martin Hewitt, and Henning was now useless. Worse, he might be caught, or give himself up, and was thus a perpetual danger. And probably he wanted money. This being so, it was a singular fact that at the inquest the surgeon who had examined the wound gave it as his most positive opinion that it had been self-inflicted. And it was inflicted with a razor, Henning's own, as was very clearly proved after inquiry. For the razor was found in the barn by the police, entangled with the blackened frame of an old lantern. Here was still another puzzle; one to which the final revelation of the mystery of the Red Triangle gave an answer, as will be seen in due place.

5

THE CASE OF THE ADMIRALTY CODE

I

Quick on the heels of the case of the Burnt Barn followed the next of the Red Triangle affairs. Indeed, the interval was barely two days. Mr Victor Peytral, it will be remembered, had declined to reveal to Hewitt the addresses of the two houses in London which he had seen Mayes visit, desiring to think the matter over for a few days first; but before anymore could be heard from him, news of another sort was brought by Inspector Plummer.

It may give some clue to the period whereabout the whole mystery of the Red Triangle began to be cleared up if I say that at the time of Plummer's visit this country was on the very verge of war with a great European State. It is a State with which the present relations of England are of the friendliest description, and, since the dreaded collision was happily averted, there is no need to particularise in the matter now, especially as the name of the country with which we were at variance matters nothing as regards the course of events I am to relate. Though most readers will recognise it at once when I say that the war, had it come to that, would have been a naval war of great magnitude; and that during the time of tension swift but quiet preparations were going forward at all naval depôts, and movements and dispositions of our fleet were arranged that extended to the remotest parts of the ocean.

It was at the height of the excitement, and, as I have said, two days after the return of Hewitt and myself from Throckham, when the case of the Burnt Barn had been disposed of, that Detective-Inspector Plummer called. I was in Hewitt's office at the time, having, in fact, called in on my way to learn if he had heard more from Mr Victor Peytral, for, as may be imagined, I was as eager to penetrate the mystery of the Triangle as Hewitt himself—perhaps more so, since Hewitt was a man inured to mysteries. I had hardly had time to learn that Peytral had not yet made up his mind so far as to write, when Plummer pushed hurriedly into the room.

"Excuse my rushing in like this," he said, "but your lad told me that it was Mr Brett who was with you, and the matter needs hurry. You've heard no more of that fellow—Myatt, Hunt, Mayes, whatever his name is last—since the barn murder, of course? Has Peytral given you the tip he half promised?"

Hewitt shook his head again. "Brett has this moment come to ask the same question," he said. "I have heard nothing."

"I must have it," said Plummer, emphatically. "Do you think he will tell me?"

Hewitt shook his head again. "Scarcely likely," he said. "He's an odd fellow, this Mr Peytral—a foreigner, with revenge in his blood. I have done him and his daughter some little service, and he told me all his private history; but he seemed even then disposed to keep Mayes to himself and let nobody interfere with his own vengeance. But I will wire if you like. What is it?"

"I'll tell you," said Plummer, pushing the door close behind him. "I'll tell you—in confidence, of course—because you've seen more of this mysterious rascal than I have, and—equally in confidence, of course—Mr Brett may hear, too, since he's been in several of the cases already. Well, of course, we all know well enough that we want this creature—Mayes, we may as well call him, I suppose, now—for three murders, at least, to say nothing of other things. That's all very well, and we might have got him with time. But now we want him for something else; and it's such a thing that *we must have him at once*, or else"—and Plummer pursed his lips and snapped his fingers significantly. "We can't wait over this, Mr Hewitt; *we've got to have that man today*, if it can be done. And there's more than ordinary depending on it. It's the country this time. The Admiralty telegraphic code has been stolen!"

"By Mayes?"

Plummer shrugged his shoulders. "That's to be proved," he said; "but he was seen leaving the office at about the time the loss occurred, and that's enough to set me after him; and there's not another clue of any sort. Mr Hewitt, I wish you were in the official service!"

Hewitt smiled. "You flatter me," he said, "as you have done before. But why in this case particularly?"

"It's a case altogether out of the ordinary, and one of a string of such, all of which you have at your fingers' ends. And I don't mind confessing that this man Mayes is a little too big a handful for one—for me, at any rate. I wish you could work with me over this; in fact, in the special circumstances I've a good mind to ask to have you retained, as an exceptional measure. But the thing's urgent, and there's red-tape!"

Hewitt had taken a glance at his desk tablet, which he now flung down.

"I'll do it for love," he said, "if necessary. My appointment list is uncommonly slack just now, and even if it weren't, I'd make a considerable sacrifice rather than be out of this. This fellow Mayes is a dangerous man; and I feel it a point of honour that he shall not continue to escape. Moreover, I have begun to form a certain theory as to the Red Triangle, and all there is at the back of it—a theory I would rather keep to myself till I see a little more, since as it stands it may only strike you as fantastic, and if it is wrong it may lead some of us off the track; but it is a theory I wish to test to the end. So I'm with you, Plummer, if you'll allow it; and you can make your official application for a special retainer or not, just as you please."

Plummer was plainly delighted.

"Most certainly I will," he said. "Shall I give you the heads of the case, or will you come to the Admiralty and see for yourself?"

"Both, I think," said Hewitt. "But first I will send a telegram to Peytral. Then you can give me the heads of the case as we go along, and I will look at the place for myself. I am in this case heart and soul, pay or no pay—and I expect my friend Brett would like to be in it, too. Is there any objection?"

"Well," Plummer answered, a little doubtfully, "we're glad of outside help, of course, but I'm not sure, officially—"

"Of course you are always glad of outside help," Hewitt interrupted, "and in this case we may possibly find Brett more useful than you think. Consider now. He has seen a good deal of these cases—quite as much as you, in fact—but he is the only one of the three of us whom Mayes does not know by sight. Remember, Mayes saw us both in the affair of Mr Jacob Mason, and he saw you again in the case of the Lever Key—escaped, in fact, because he instantly recognised you. I'll answer for Brett's discretion, and I'm sure he'll be glad to help, even if, for official reasons, you may not find it possible to admit him wholly into your counsels."

Of course I willingly assented, and the conditions understood, Plummer offered no further objection. Hewitt despatched his telegram, and in a very few minutes we were in a cab on the way to the Admiralty.

"This is the way of it," Plummer said. "You will remember that when we lost Mayes at the end of the Lever Key case, I was waiting for him in that city office, with an assistant, and that we only saw him for an instant in the lift. Well, that assistant was a very intelligent man of mine, named Corder—a fellow with a wonderful memory for a face. Now Corder is on another case just now, and we'd put him on, dressed like a loafer, to hang about Whitehall and the neighbourhood, watching for someone we want. Well, this morning there came an urgent message to the Yard from the Admiralty, to ask for a responsible official at once, and I was sent. As I came along I saw Corder lounging about, and of course I took no notice—it would not do for us people from the Yard to recognise each other too readily in the street. But Corder came up, and made pretence to ask me for a match to light his pipe; and under cover of that he told me that he had seen Mayes not an hour before, coming out of the Admiralty. At this, of course, I pricked up my ears. I didn't know what they wanted me for, but if there was mischief, and that fellow had been there, it was likely at least that he might have been in it. Corder was quite positive that it was the man, although he had only seen him for a moment in the lift. He hadn't seen him go into the Admiralty office, but he was passing as he came out, and noted the time exactly, so that he might report to me at the first opportunity. The time was 11.32, and Mayes jumped into a hansom and drove off. He walked right out into the middle of the road to stop the hansom—you know how wide the road is there—so that Corder couldn't hear his direction to the cabman, but he took the number as the cab went off. Corder ought to have collared him then and there, I think, but he was in a difficult position. It would have endangered the case he was on, which is very important; and besides, he didn't realise how much we wanted him for, having only been brought in as an assistant at the tail of our bond case. Still less did he guess—any more than myself—what I was going to hear at the Admiralty office."

"At any rate," interrupted Hewitt, "you've got the number of the cab?"

"Here it is," Plummer answered, "and I've already set a man to get hold of the cabman. You'd better note the number—92,873."

Hewitt duly noted the number, and advised me to do the same, in case I should chance to meet the cab during the afternoon; and as we neared our destination Plummer gave us the rest of the case in outline.

"In the office," he said, "I found them in a great state. A copy of the code, or cypher, in which confidential orders and other messages are sent to the fleet all over the world, and in which reports and messages are sent back, had disappeared during the morning. It was in charge of a Mr Robert Telfer, a clerk of responsibility and undoubted integrity. He kept it in a small iron safe, which is let into the wall of his private room. It was safe when he arrived in the morning, and he immediately used it in order to code a telegram, and locked it in the safe again at 10.20. Two hours later, at 12.20, he went to the safe for it again, in order to de-code a message just received, and it was gone! And the lock of the safe is one that would take hours to pick, I should judge. There isn't a shade of a clue, so far as I can see, except this circumstance of Mayes being seen leaving by Corder—just between Telfer's two visits to the safe, you perceive. And of course there may be nothing in that, except for the character of the man. And that's all there is to go on, as far as I can see. I needn't tell you how important the thing is at a time like this, and how much would be paid for that secret code by a certain foreign Government. We have made hurried arrangements to have certain places watched, and as soon as I have taken you to the office I must rush off and make a few more arrangements still. But here we are."

Mr Robert Telfer's room was at the side of a long and gloomy corridor on the upper floor, and the door was distinguished merely by a number and the word "Private" painted thereon. We found Mr Telfer sitting alone, and plainly in a state of great nervous tension. He was a man of forty or thereabout, thin, alert, and using a single eye-glass. Plummer introduced us by name, and rapidly explained our business.

"I told you the name of the party I am after, Mr Telfer," Plummer said, "and I went straight to Mr Martin Hewitt, as being most likely to have information of him. Mr Hewitt, whose name you know already, of course, is kind enough, seeing we're in a bad pinch, and pushed for time, to come in and give us all the help he can. Both he and his friend, Mr Brett, know a good deal of the doings of the person we're after, and their assistance is likely to be of the very greatest value. Do you mind giving Mr Hewitt any information he may ask? I must rush over to the Yard to put some other inquiries on foot, and to set an observation or two, but I'll be back presently."

"Certainly," Mr Telfer answered, "I'm only too anxious to give any information whatever—so long as it is nothing departmentally forbidden—which will help to put this horrible matter right. Please ask me anything, and be patient if my answers are not very clear. I have been much overworked lately, as you may imagine, and have had very little sleep; and now this terrible misfortune has upset me completely; for, of course, I am held responsible for that copy of the code, and if it isn't recovered, and quickly, I am ruined—to say nothing, of course, of the far more serious consequences in other directions."

"That is the safe in which it was kept, I presume?" Hewitt said, indicating a small one let into the wall. "May I examine it?"

"Certainly." Mr Telfer turned and produced the keys from his pocket. "The code was here, lying on this shelf when I needed it this morning at ten. I took it out, used it, returned it to the same place exactly, and locked the safe door. Then I took the draft of the telegram, together with the copy in cypher, into the Controller's room, gave it into safe hands, and returned here."

Hewitt narrowly examined the lock of the safe with his pocket lens. "There are no signs of the lock having been picked," he said, "even if that were possible. As a matter of fact, this is a lock that would take half a day to pick, even with a heavy bag of tools. No, I don't think that was the way of it. You have no doubt about locking the safe door at 10.20, I suppose, before you went to the Controller's room?"

"No possible doubt whatever. You see, I left the whole bunch of keys hanging in the lock while I coded the telegram. It was a short one, and was soon done. Then I returned the code to its place, locked the safe, and then used another key on the bunch to lock a drawer in this desk. I had no occasion to go to the safe again till about 12.20, when the Controller's secretary came here with a telegram to be de-coded. The safe was still locked then, but when it was opened the code was gone."

"You had had no occasion to go to the safe in the meantime?"

"None at all. I locked it at 10.20, and I unlocked it two hours later, and that was all."

"You were not in the room the whole of the time, of course?"

"Oh, no. I have told you that at 10.20 I went to the Controller's room, and after that I went out two or three times on one occasion or another. But each time I locked the door of the room."

"Oh, you did? That is important. And you took all your keys with you, I presume?"

"Yes, all. The keys on the bunch I took in my pocket, of course, and the room door key I also took. There are one or two rather important papers on my desk, you see, and anybody from the corridor might come in if the door were left unlocked."

"The lock of the door would be a good deal easier to pick than that of the safe," Hewitt observed, after examining it. "But that would be of no great use with the safe locked. Shortly, then, the facts are these. You locked the code safely away at 10.20, you left the room two or three times, but each time the door, as well as the safe, was locked, and the keys in your pocket; and then, at 12.20, or two hours exactly after the code had been put safely away, you opened the safe again in presence of the Controller's secretary, and the code had vanished. That is the whole matter in brief, I take it?"

"Precisely." Mr Telfer was pallid and bewildered. "It seems a total impossibility," he said; "a total, absolute, physical impossibility; but there it is."

"But as no such thing as a physical impossibility ever happens," Hewitt replied calmly, "we must look further. Now, are there any other ways into this room than by that door into the corridor? I see another door here. What is that?"

"That door has been locked for ages. The room on the other side is one like this, with a door in the corridor; it is used chiefly to store old documents of no great importance, and I believe that whole stacks of them, in bundles, are piled against the other side of that same door. We will send for the key and see, if you like."

The key was sent for, and the door from the corridor opened. As Telfer had led us to expect, the place was full of old papers in bundles and parcels, thick with ancient dust, and these things were piled high against the door next his room, and plainly had not been disturbed for months, or even years.

"There remains the skylight," said Hewitt, "for I perceive, Mr Telfer, that your room is lighted from above, and has no window; while the grate is a register. There seems to be no opening in that skylight but the revolving ventilator. Am I right?"

"Quite so. There is no getting in by the skylight without breaking it, and, as you see, it has not been broken. Certainly there are men on the roof repairing the leads, but it is plain enough that nobody has come that way. The thing is wholly inexplicable."

"At present, yes," Hewitt said, musingly. He stood for a few moments in deep thought.

"Plummer is longer away than I expected," he said presently. "By the way, what was the external appearance of the missing code?"

"It was nothing but a sort of thin manuscript book, made of a few sheets of foolscap size, sewn in a cover of thickish grey paper. I left it in the safe doubled lengthwise, and tied with tape in the middle."

"Its loss is a very serious thing, of course?"

"Oh, terribly, terribly serious, Mr Hewitt," Telfer replied, despairingly. "I am responsible, and it will put an end to my career, of course. But the consequences to the country are more important, and they may be disastrous—enormously so. A great sum would be paid for that code on the Continent, I need hardly say."

"But now that you know it is taken, surely the code can be changed?"

"It's not so easy as it seems, Mr Hewitt," Telfer answered, shaking his head. "It means time, and I needn't tell you that with affairs in their present state we can't afford one moment of time. Some expedients are being attempted, of course, but you will understand that any new code would have to be arranged with scattered items of the fleet in all parts of the world, and that probably with the present code in the hands of the enemy. Moreover, all our messages already sent will be accessible with very little trouble, and they contain all our strategical coaling and storing dispositions for a great war, Mr Hewitt; and they can't, they *can't* be altered at a moment's notice! Oh, it is terrible!... But here is Inspector Plummer. No news, I suppose, Mr Plummer?"

"Well, no," Plummer answered deliberately. "I can't say I've any news for *you*, Mr Telfer, just yet. But I want to talk about a few things to Mr Hewitt. Hadn't we better go and see if your telegram is answered, Mr Hewitt? Unless you've heard."

"No, I haven't," Hewitt replied. "We'll go on at once. Good day for the present, Mr Telfer. I hope to bring good news when next I see you."

"I hope so, too, Mr Hewitt, most fervently," Telfer answered; and his looks confirmed his words.

We walked in silence through the corridor, down the stairs, and out by the gates into the street. Then Plummer turned on his heel and faced Hewitt.

"That man's a wrong 'un," he said, abruptly, jerking his thumb in the direction of the office we had just left. "I'll tell you about it in the cab."

As soon as our cab was started on its way back to Hewitt's office Plummer explained himself.

"He's been watched," he said, "has Mr Telfer, when he didn't know it; and he'll be watched again for the rest of today, as I've arranged. What's more, he won't be allowed to leave the office this evening till I have seen him again, or sent a message. No need to frighten him too soon—it mightn't suit us. But he's in it, alone or in company!"

"How do you know?"

"I'll tell you. It seems the lead roofs are being repaired at the Admiralty, and the plumbers are walking about where they like. Now I needn't tell you I've had a man or two fishing about among the doorkeepers and so on at the Admiralty, and one of them found a plumber he knew slightly, working on the roof. That plumber happens to be no fool—a bit smarter than the detective-constable, it seems to me, in fact. Anyhow, he seems to have got more out of my man than my man got out of him; and soon after I reached the Yard he turned up, asking to see me. He said he'd heard that a valuable paper was missing (he didn't know what) from the room with the skylight in the top floor, where the gentleman with the single eye-glass was, and where the safe was let in the wall; and he wanted to know what would be the reward for anybody giving information about it. Of course I couldn't make any promise, and I gave him to understand that he would have to leave the amount of the reward to the authorities, if his information was worth anything; also, that we were getting to work fast, and that if he wished to be first to give information he'd better be quick about it; but I promised to make a special report of his name and what he had to say if it were useful. And it will be, or I'm vastly mistaken! For just you see here. Our friend, Mr Telfer, says he put that code safely away at 10.20 in the safe, and that he never went to the safe again till 12.20, when the Controller's secretary was with him; never went to it for anything whatever, observe. Well, the plumber happened to be near the skylight at half-past eleven, and he is prepared to swear that he saw Mr Telfer—'the gent with the eye-glass,' as he calls him—go to the safe, unlock it, take out a grey paper, folded lengthwise, with red tape round it, re-lock the safe, and carry that paper out into the corridor! The plumber was kneeling by a brazier, it seems, which was close by the skylight, and he is so certain of the time because he was regulating his watch by Westminster Hall clock, and compared it when the half-hour struck, which was just while Telfer was absent in the corridor with the paper. He was only gone a second or two, and you will remember that Corder saw Mayes leaving the premises within two minutes of that time!"

"Yes!"

"Well, Telfer was back in a second or two, *without the paper*, and went on with his affairs as before. That's pretty striking, eh?"

"Yes," Hewitt answered thoughtfully, "it is."

"It was a sort of shot in the dark on the part of the plumber, for he knew nothing else—nothing about Telfer legitimately having the keys of the safe, nor any of the particulars we have been told. He merely knew that a paper was missing, and having seen a paper taken out of the safe he got it into his head that he had possibly witnessed the theft; and he kept his knowledge to himself till he could see somebody in authority. Mighty keen, too, about a reward!"

"And now you are having Telfer supervised?"

"I am. Not that we're likely to get the code from him; that's passed out, sure enough, in Mayes's hands—or else his pockets."

To this confident expression of opinion Hewitt offered no reply, and presently we alighted at his office, eager to learn if Peytral had given the information Hewitt so much desired. Sure enough a telegram was there, and it ran thus:

"On the night you know of, Mayes went first to 37 Raven Street, Blackfriars, then to 8 Norbury Row, Barbican. Message follows."

"Now we're at work," Hewitt said, briskly, "and for a while we part. I shall make a few changes of dress, and go to take a look at 37 Raven Street, Blackfriars. Will you two go on to Norbury Row? You'll have to be careful, Plummer, and not show yourself. That is where Brett will be useful, since he isn't known; if anybody is to be seen let it be him. I shall be very careful myself—though I shall have some little disguise; and I fancy I shall not be so likely to be seen as you."

"What are we to do?" I asked.

"Well, of course, if you see Mayes in the open, grab him instantly. I needn't tell Plummer *that*. I think Plummer would naturally seize him on the spot, rush him off to the nearest station and go back with enough men to clear out No. 8 Norbury Row. If you don't see him you'll keep an observation, according to Plummer's discretion. But, unless some exceptional chance occurs, I hope you won't go rushing in till we communicate with each other—we must work together, and I may have news. My instinct seems to tell me that yours is the right end of the stick, at Barbican. But we must neglect nothing, and that is why I want you to hold on there while I make the necessary examination at the other end. Do you know this Norbury Row, Plummer?"

"I think I know every street and alley in the City," Plummer answered. "There is a very good publican at the corner of Norbury Row, who's been useful to the police a score of times. He keeps his eyes open, and I shall be surprised if he can't give us *some* information about No. 8, anyhow. Moon's his name, and the house is 'The Compasses.' I shall go there first. And if you've any message to send, send it through him. I'll tell him."

On the stairs Plummer and I encountered another of his assistants. "I've got the cab, sir," he reported. "Waiting outside now. Took up a fare in Whitehall, opposite the Admiralty, and drove him to Charterhouse Street; got down just by the Meat Market. That's all the man seems to know."

Plummer questioned the cabman, and found that as a matter of fact that was all he did know. So, telling him to wait to take us our little journey, we returned and reported his information to Hewitt.

"Just as I expected," he said, quietly. "He stopped the cab a bit short of his destination, of course,—just as you will, no doubt. There's not a great deal in the evidence, but it confirms my idea."

II

We followed Mayes's example by stopping the cab in Charterhouse Street, and walking the short remaining distance to Barbican. Norbury Row was an obscure street behind it, at the corner of which stood "The Compasses," the public-house which Plummer had mentioned. We did not venture to show ourselves in Norbury Row, but hastened into the nearest door of "The Compasses," which chanced to be that of the private bar.

A stout, red-faced, slow-moving man with one eye and a black patch, stood behind the bar. Plummer lifted his finger and pointed quickly toward the bar-parlour; and at the signal the one-eyed man turned with great deliberation and pulled a catch which released the door of that apartment, close at our elbows. We stepped quickly within, and presently the one-eyed man came rolling in by the other door.

"Well, good art'noon, Mr Plummer, sir," he said, with a long intonation and a wheeze. "Good art'noon, sir. You've bin a stranger lately."

"Good afternoon, Mr Moon," Plummer answered, briskly. "We've come for a little information, my friend and I, which I'm sure you'll give us if you can."

"All the years I've been knowed to the police," answered Mr Moon, slower and wheezier as he went on, "I've allus give 'em all the information I could, an' that's a fact. Ain't it, Mr Plummer?"

"Yes, of course, and we don't forget it. What we want now—"

"Allus tell 'em what—ever I knows," rumbled Mr Moon, turning to me, "allus; an' glad to do it, too. 'Cause why? Ain't they the police? Very well then, I tells 'em. Allus tells 'em!"

Plummer waited patiently while Mr Moon stared solemnly at me after this speech. Then, when the patch slowly turned in my direction and the eye in his, he resumed, "We want to know if you know anything about No. 8 Norbury Row?"

"Number eight," Mr Moon mused, gazing abstractedly out of the window; "num—ber eight. Ground-floor, Stevens, packing-case maker; first-floor, Hutt, agent in fancy-goods; second-floor, dunno. Name o' Richardson, bookbinder, on the door, but that's bin there five or six year now, and it ain't the same tenant. Richardson's dead, an' this one don't bind no books as I can see. I don't even remember seein' him *very* often. Tallish, darkish sort o' gent he is, and don't seem to have many visitors. Well, then there's the top-floor—but I s'pose it's the same tenant. Richardson used to have it for his workshop. That's all."

"Have you got a window we can watch it from?"

Mr Moon turned ponderously round and without a word led the way to the first floor, puffing enormously on the stairs.

"You *can* see it from the club-room," he said at length, "but this 'ere little place is better."

He pushed open a door, and we entered a small sitting-room. "That's the place," he said, pointing. "There's a new packing-case a-standing outside now."

Norbury Row presented an appearance common enough in parts of the city a little way removed from the centre. A street of houses that once had sheltered well-to-do residents had gradually sunk in the world to the condition of tenement-houses, and now was on the upward grade again, being let in floors to the smaller sort of manufacturers, and to such agents and small commercial men as required cheap offices. No. 8 was much like the rest. A packing-case maker had the ground-floor, as Moon had said, and a token of his trade, in the shape of a new packing-case, stood on the pavement. The rest of the building showed nothing distinctive.

"There y'are, gents," said Mr Moon, "if you want to watch, you're welcome, bein' the p'lice, which I allus does my best for, allus. But you'll have to excuse me now, 'cos o' the bar."

Mr Moon stumped off downstairs, leaving Plummer and myself watching at the window.

"Your friend the publican seems very proud of helping the police," I remarked.

Plummer laughed. "Yes," he said, "or at any rate, he is anxious we shan't forget it. You see, it's in some way a matter of mutual accommodation. We make things as easy as possible for him on licensing days, and as he has a pretty extensive acquaintance among the sort of people we often want to get hold of, he has been able to show his gratitude very handsomely once or twice."

The house on which our eyes were fixed was a little too far up the street for us to see perfectly through the window of the second-floor, though we could see enough to indicate that it was furnished as an office. We agreed that the unknown second-floor tenant was more likely to be our customer, or connected with him, than either of the others. Still, we much desired a nearer view, and presently, since the coast seemed clear, Plummer announced his intention of taking one.

He left me at the post of observation, and presently I saw him lounging along on the other side of the way, keeping close to the houses, so as to escape observation from the upper windows. He took a good look at the names on the door-post of No. 8, and presently stepped within.

I waited five or six minutes, and then saw him returning as he had come.

"It's the top floors we want," he said, when he rejoined me in Mr Moon's sitting-room. "The packing-case maker is genuine enough, and very busy. So is the fancy-goods agent. I went in, seeing the door wide open, and found the agent, a little, shop-walkery sort of chap, hard at work with his clerk among piles of cardboard boxes. I wouldn't go further, in case I were spotted. Do you think you'd be cool enough to do it without arousing suspicion? Mayes doesn't know you, you see. What do you think? We don't want to precipitate matters till we hear from Hewitt, but on the other hand I don't want to sit still as long as anything can be ascertained. You might ask a question about book-binding."

"Of course," I said. "If you will let me I'll go at once—glad of the chance to get a peep. I'll bespeak a quotation for binding and lettering a thousand octavos in paste grain, on behalf of some convenient firm of publishers. That would be technical enough, I think?"

I took my hat and walked out as Plummer had done, though, of course, I approached the door of No. 8 with less caution. The packing-case maker's men were hammering away merrily, and as I mounted the stairs I saw the little fancy-goods agent among his cardboard boxes, just as Plummer had said. The upper part of the house was a silent contrast to the busy lower floors, and as I arrived at the next landing I was surprised to see the door ajar.

I pushed boldly in, and found myself alone in a good-sized room plainly fitted as an office. There were two windows looking on the street, and one at the back, more than half concealed behind a ground glass partition or screen. I stepped across and looked out of this window. It looked on a narrow space, or well, of plain brick wall, containing nothing but a ladder, standing in one corner. And the only other window giving on this narrow square space was in the opposite wall, but much lower, on the ground level.

I saw these things in a single glance, and then I turned—to find myself face to face with a tallish, thin, active man, with a pale, shaven, ascetic face, dark hair, and astonishingly quick glittering black eyes. He stood just within the office door, to which he must have come without a sound, looking at me with a mechanical smile of inquiry, while his eyes searched me with a portentous keenness.

"Oh," I said, with the best assumption of carelessness I could command, "I was looking for you, Mr Richardson. Do you care to give a quotation for binding at per thousand crown octavo volumes in paste grain, plain, with lettering on back?"

"No," answered the man with the eyes, "I don't; I'm afraid my carelessness has led you into a mistake. I am not Richardson the bookbinder. He was my predecessor in this office, and I have neglected to paint out his name on the door-post."

I hastened to apologise. "I am sorry to have intruded," I said. "I found the door ajar and so came in. You see the publishing season is beginning, and our regular binders are full of work, so that we have to look elsewhere. Good day!"

"Good-day," the keen man responded, turning to allow me to pass through the door. "I'm sorry I cannot be of service to you—on this occasion."

From first to last his eyes had never ceased to search me, and now as I descended the stairs I could *feel* that they were fixed on me still.

I took a turn about the houses, in order not to be observed going direct to "The Compasses," and entered that house by way of the private bar, as before.

"That is Mayes, and no other," said Plummer, when I had made my report and described the man with the eyes. "I've seen him twice, once with his beard and once without. The question now is, whether we hadn't best sail in straight away and collar him. But there's the window at the back, and a ladder, I think you said. Can he reach it?"

"I think he might—easily."

"And perhaps there's the roof, since he's got the top floor too. Not good enough without some men to surround the house. We must go gingerly over this. One thing to find out is, what is the building behind? Ah, how I wish Mr Hewitt were here now! If we don't hear from him soon we must send a message. But we mustn't lose sight of No. 8 for a moment."

There was a thump at the sitting-room door, and Mr Moon came puffing in and shouldered himself confidentially against Plummer. "Bloke downstairs wants to see you," he said, in a hoarse grunt that was meant for a low whisper. "Twigged you outside, I think, an' says he's got somethink partickler to tell yer. I believe 'e's a 'nark'; I see him with one o' your chaps the other day."

"I'll go," Plummer said to me hurriedly. "Plainly somebody's spotted me in the street, and I may as well hear him."

I knew very well, of course, what Moon meant by a 'nark.' A 'nark' is an informer, a spy among criminals who sells the police whatever information he can scrape up. Could it be possible that this man had anything to tell about Mayes? It was scarcely likely, and I made up my mind that Plummer was merely being detained by some tale of a petty local crime.

But in a few minutes he returned with news of import. "This fellow is most valuable," he said. "He knows a lot about Mayes, whom, of course, he calls by another name; but the identity's certain. He saw me looking in at No. 8, he says, and guessed I must be after him. He seems to have wondered at Mayes's mysterious movements for a long time, and so kept his eye on him and made inquiries. It seems that Mayes sometimes uses a back way, through the window you saw on the opposite side of the little area, by way of that ladder you mentioned. It's quite plain this fellow knows something, from the particulars about that ladder. He wants half a sovereign to show me the way through a stable passage behind and point out where our man can be trapped to a certainty. It'll be a cheap ten shillingsworth, and we mustn't waste time. If Hewitt comes, tell him not to move till I come back or send a message, which I can easily do by this chap I'm going with. And be sure to keep your eye on the front door of No. 8 while I'm gone."

The thing had begun to grow exciting, and the fascination of the pursuit took full possession of my imagination. I saw Plummer pass across the end of the street in company with a shuffling, out-at-elbows-looking man with dirty brown whiskers, and I set myself to watch the door of the staircase by the packing-case maker's with redoubled attention, hoping fervently that Mayes might emerge, and so give me the opportunity of capping the extraordinary series of occurrences connected with the Red Triangle by myself seizing and handing him over to the police.

So I waited and watched for something near another quarter of an hour. Then there came another thump at the door, and once more I beheld Mr Moon.

"Man askin' for you in the bar, sir," he said.

"Asking for me?" I asked, a little astonished. "By name?"

"Mr Brett, 'e said, sir. He's the same chap, you know. He's got a message from Inspector Plummer, 'e says."

"May he come up here?" I asked, mindful of maintaining my watch.

"Certainly, sir, if you like. I'll bring him."

Presently the shuffling man with the dirty whiskers presented himself. He was a shifty, villainous-looking fellow of middle height, looking a "nark" all over. He pulled off his cap and delivered his message in a rum-scented whisper. "Inspector Plummer says the front way don't matter now," he said. "'E can cop 'im fair the other way if you'll go round to him at once. If Mr Martin Hewitt's here 'e'd rather 'ave 'im, but on'y one's to come now."

Naturally, I thought, Plummer would prefer Hewitt; but in this case I should for once be ahead of my friend, and have the pleasure of relating the circumstances of the capture to him, instead of listening, as usual, to his own quiet explanations of the manner in which the case had been brought to a successful issue. So I took my hat and went.

"Best let me go in front," whispered the "nark." "You bein' a toff might be noticed." It was a reasonable precaution, and I followed him accordingly.

We went a little way down Barbican, and presently, taking a very narrow turning, plunged into a cluster of alleys, through which, however, I could plainly perceive that our way lay in the direction of the back of the house in Norbury Row. At length my guide stopped at what seemed a stable yard, pushed open a wicket gate, and went in, keeping the gate open for me to follow.

It was, indeed, a stable yard, littered with much straw, which the "nark" carefully picked to walk on as noiselessly as possible, motioning me to do the same. It was a small enough yard, and dark, and when my guide very carefully opened the door of a stable I saw that that was darker still.

He pushed the door wide so as to let a little light fall on another door which I now perceived in the brick wall which formed the side of the stable. After listening intently for a moment at this door, the guide stepped back and favoured me with another puff of rum and a whisper. "There's no light in that there passage," he said, "an' we'd better not strike one. I'll catch hold of your hand."

He pulled the stable door to, and took me by the hand. I heard the inner door open quietly, and we stepped cautiously forward. We had gone some five or six yards in the darkness when I felt something cold touch the wrist of the hand by which I was being led. There was a loud click, my hand was dropped, and I felt my wrist held fast, while I could hear my late guide shuffling away in the darkness.

I could not guess whether to cry out or remain quiet. I called after the man in a loud whisper, but got no answer. I used my other hand to feel at my right wrist, and found that it was clipped in one of a pair of handcuffs, the other being locked in a staple in the wall. I tugged my hardest to loosen this staple, but it held firm. The thing had been so sudden and stealthy that I scarce had time to realise that I was in serious danger, and that, doubtless, Plummer had preceded me, when a light appeared at an angle ahead. It turned the corner, and I perceived, coming toward me, carrying a lamp, the pale man of the eyes, whom I had encountered not an hour before—in a word, Mayes.

His eyes searched me still, but he approached me with a curiously polite smile.

"No, Mr Brett," he said, "my name is not Richardson, and I am not a bookbinder. Not that I am particular about such a thing as a name, for you have heard of me under more than one already, and you are quite at liberty to call me Richardson if you like. I am sorry to have to talk to you in this uncomfortable place, but the circumstances are exceptional. But, at least, I should give you a chair."

He stepped back a little way and pressed a bell-button. Presently the fellow who had decoyed me there appeared, and Mayes ordered him to bring me a chair at once, which he did, with stolid obedience. I sat in it, so that my wrist rested at somewhere near the level of my shoulder.

"Mr Brett," Mayes pursued, when his man was gone, "I am not so implacable a person as you perhaps believe me; in fact, I can assure you that my disposition is most friendly."

"Then unfasten this handcuff," I said.

"I am sorry that that is a little precaution I find it necessary to take till we understand each other better. I am glad to see you, Mr Brett, though I am sure you will not think me rude if I say that I should have preferred Mr Martin Hewitt in your place. But perhaps his turn will come later. I have a proposition to make, Mr Brett. I should like you to join me."

"To join you?"

"Exactly." He nodded pleasantly. "You needn't shrink; I shan't ask you to do anything vulgar, or even anything that, with your present prejudices, you might consider actively criminal. You can help me, you see, in your own profession as a journalist; and in other ways. And my enterprise is greater than you may imagine. Join me, and you shall be a great man in an entirely new sphere. A small matter of initiation is necessary, and that is all. You have only to consent to that."

I said nothing.

"You seem reluctant. Well, perhaps it is natural, in your present ignorance. This is no vulgar criminal organisation that I have, understand. I have taken certain measures to provide myself with the necessary tools in the shape of money, and so forth, but my aims are larger than you suspect—perhaps larger than you can understand. And I work with a means more wonderful than you have experience of. For instance, here is today's work. You know about the lost Naval Code, of course— it is what you came about. That document is now lying in the desk you stood by in the room where we spoke of paste grain book covers and the like. It was there then at your elbow. It will be sold for many thousands of pounds by tomorrow, and all the puny watchings and dodgings that have been devised cannot prevent it. The money will go to aid me in the attainment of the power of which you may have a part, if you wish. The means of attaining this I scruple no more about than you did today about the story of the bookbindings." He bowed with a slight smile and went on.

"Come now, Mr Brett, put aside your bourgeois prejudices and join me. Your friend Plummer is coming gladly, I feel sure, and he will be useful, too. And from what I have seen from Mr Martin Hewitt, I have no doubt I can make it right with him. If I can't it will be very bad for him, I can assure you; you have heard and seen something of my powers, and I need say no more. But Hewitt is a man of sense, and will come in, of course, and you had better come with your friends. I want one or two superior men. Mason—you know about Jacob Mason, of course—Mason was a fool, and he was lost—inevitably. The others"—he made a gesture of contempt—"they are mere vulgar tools. They will have their rewards if they are faithful, of course; if not—well, you remember Denson in the Samuel diamond business? He was *not* faithful, and there was an end of him. I may tell you that Denson was made an example, for one was needed. I assigned him a certain operation, and, having brought it to success, he endeavoured to embezzle— did embezzle—the proceeds. He was made a conspicuous example, in a most conspicuous public place, to impress the others. They didn't know *him*, but they knew well enough what the Red Triangle meant! Ah, my excellent recruit—for so I count you already—there is more in that little sign than you can imagine! It is more than a sign—it is an implement of very potent power; and you shall learn its whole secret in that little form of initiation I spoke of. See now, a present example. Telfer, the Admiralty clerk, gave up that document at my mere spoken word. He will deny it to his dying day, and he will be ruined for the act; but he gave me the paper himself, at my mere order. If he were one of my own—if he had passed through the initiation I offer you, I would have protected him;

as it is, he must take his punishment, and though it is only I who will benefit, he will still deny the fact! Ha! Mr Brett, do you begin to perceive that I do not boast when I tell of powers beyond your understanding?"

Truly I was amazed, though I could not half understand. The circumstances of the loss of the Admiralty code had been so inexplicable, and now these incredible suggestions of the prime actor in the matter were more mysterious still.

"Ha! you are amazed," he went on, "but if you will come further into my counsels I will amaze you more. What are you now? A drudge of a journalist, and if ever you make a thousand a year to feed yourself with you will be lucky. Come to me and you shall be a man of power. There is a place beyond the sea where I may be king, and you a viceroy. Don't think I am raving! It is true enough that I am an enthusiast, but I have power, power to do anything I please, I tell you! What are the greatest powers among men on this earth? Some will say the pen, or the sword, or love, or what not. Men of the world will say, money and lies; and they will be very nearly right. Money and lies will move continents, but I have one greater power still—the very apex of the triangle! That power I revealed to Jacob Mason. He thought to betray it, and it killed him. That power I will reveal to you, if you will accept the alternative I offer."

"The alternative?"

"Yes, the alternative, for an alternative it is, of course. If you will go through the form of initiation, I shall keep you here a little till I can trust you—which will be very soon. But if not—well, Mr Brett, I wish to be as friendly as you please, but having been at the trouble of catching you, and having got you here safely, you who know so much now, you who could be so dangerous if you ever got away—eh? Well, you know my methods, and you have seen them exemplified, and you will understand."

There was no anger in his voice as he uttered this threat, nor even, I thought, in his eyes. But what there was was worse.

"But I'm sure you will not make things unpleasant," he concluded. "You will go through the little form I have arranged, if only for curiosity. Just think over it for a moment, while I go to close my little office."

He took the lamp and turned away, but as he reached the angle of the passage, there came a sound that checked his steps. I could hear a noise of feet and hurried voices, and then suddenly arose a shout in a voice which seemed to be Plummer's. "Here!" it cried. "Help! This way, Hewitt! Brett!"

I shouted back at the top of my voice, wondering where Plummer was, and what it might all mean. And with that Mayes turned, and I saw that he was about to make for the door I had entered by. I resolved he should not pass me if I could prevent it, and I sprang up and seized my chair in my left hand, shouting aloud for help as I did so.

Mayes came with a bound, and flung his lighted lamp full at my head. It struck the chair and smashed to a thousand pieces, and in that instant of time Mayes was on me. Plainly he had no weapon, or he would have used it; but I was at disadvantage enough, with my right wrist chained to the wall. I clung with all my might, and endeavoured to swing my enemy round against the wall in order that I might clasp my hands about him, and I shouted my loudest as I did it. But the chair and the broken glass hampered me, and Mayes was desperate. The agony in my right wrist was unbearable, and just as I was conscious of a rush of approaching feet a heavy blow took me full in the face, and I felt Mayes rush over me while I fell and hung from the wrist.

I had a stunned sense of lights and voices and general confusion, and then I remembered nothing.

III

I came to myself on the floor of a lighted room, with Hewitt's face over mine. My wrist seemed broken, though it was free, there was oil and blood on my clothes, and in my left hand I still gripped a piece of Mayes's coat.

"Stop him!" I cried. "He's gone by the stable! Have they got him?"

"No good, Brett," Hewitt answered soberly. "You did your best, but he's gone, and Peytral after him!"

"Peytral?"

"Yes. He brought his own message to town. But see if you can stand up."

I was well enough able to do that, and, indeed, I had only fainted from the pain of the strain on my wrist. Several policemen were in the room, beside Hewitt and Plummer. Mayes's stronghold was in the hands of his enemies.

Then I suddenly remembered.

"The Admiralty code!" I cried. "It was in the office desk. Have you got it?"

"No," Hewitt answered. "Come, Plummer, up the ladder!"

Little time was lost in forcing Mayes's desk, and there the document was found, grey cover, red tape and all intact. The police were left to make a vigorous search for any possible copy, and the original was handed to Plummer, as chief representative of the law present. He had been trapped precisely as I had been, except that he had been led further, and shut in a cellar as well as fastened by the wrist. Mayes, it seemed, had wasted very little time in attempting to pervert him, and I have no doubt that, whatever fate might have been reserved for me, Plummer would never have left the place alive had it not been for the timely irruption of Hewitt, with Peytral and the police.

In half an hour Peytral returned. He had dashed out in chase of the fugitive, but failed even to see him—lost him wholly in the courts, in fact. For some little while he persevered, but found it useless.

The dirty-whiskered man made no attempt to escape, though there was talk of another man having got away in the confusion by way of the stable roof. The police were left in charge of the place, and we deferred a complete exploration till the next day.

Hewitt's tale was simple enough. He had endued himself in somewhat seedy clothes, and had visited 37 Raven Street, Blackfriars, which he found to be merely a tenement house. It took some time to make inquiries there, with the necessary caution, because of the number of lodgers; and then the inquiries led to nothing. It was an experience common enough in his practice, but none the less an annoying delay, and when he returned to his office he found Mr Peytral already awaiting him. Peytral described his following of Mayes at much greater length and detail than before, and he and Hewitt had come on to Norbury Row at once and asked news of Mr Moon.

Mr Moon's description of the successive disappearances of Plummer and myself, and of our continued absence, so aroused Hewitt's suspicions that he instantly procured help from the nearest station, and approached the door of Mayes's office. A knock being unanswered, the door was instantly broken in. The room was found to be unoccupied, but the ladder was still standing at the open window, by which Mayes had descended to the back premises. Down this ladder Hewitt went, with the police after him. The rest I had seen myself.

"But what," I said, "what is this mystery? Why did Telfer give up the code, and what is the power that Mayes talks of?"

"It is a power," replied Hewitt, "that I have suspected for some time, and now I am quite sure of it. A secret, dangerous and terrible power which I have encountered before, though never before have I known its possibilities carried so far. It is hypnotism!"

"Hypnotism!" I exclaimed. "But can a person be hypnotised against his will?"

"In a sense, in most cases, he cannot. That is the explanation of Mayes's proposals to you to go through a 'form of initiation.' If you had consented, the 'form' would have been a process of hypnotism. Once or twice repeated, and you would have been wholly under his control, so that if he willed it and forbade you, you could tell nothing of what he wished kept secret, and you would have committed any crime he might suggest. Consider poor Jacob Mason! Remember how he struggled to tell what he knew, oppressed by the horror of it, and how it all ended! And remember Henning the clerk, Mayes's tool in that case of bond robbery! What has happened to him? He committed suicide, as you know, immediately after Mayes had left him at the barn. Brett, this power of hypnotism, a power for healing in the hands of a good man, may become a terrible power for evil in the hands of a villain!"

"But Telfer, today? He seems to have known nothing of Mayes, and he was not one of his regular creatures—Mayes himself told me so."

"About that I don't know. But I expect we shall find that he has been willingly hypnotised at some time or another, perhaps more than once, by this same scoundrel Mayes. Possibly in one of Mayes's appearances in respectable society, at an evening party, or the like. In a case of that sort the hypnotist may impress a certain formula—a word, a name, or a number—on the subject's mind, by the repetition of which, at any future time, that same subject may be instantly hypnotised. So that, once having become hypnotised, on any innocent occasion, the subject is in the power of the hypnotist, more or less, ever after. The hypnotist says: 'When I repeat such and such a sentence or number to you in future, you will be hypnotised,' and hypnotised the subject duly is, instantly. Supposing such a case in this matter of Mr Telfer, it would only be necessary for Mayes to meet him in the corridor, repeat his formula and command the victim to bring out the paper he specified.

This done he could similarly order him to *forget the whole transaction*, and this the victim would do, infallibly."

It is only necessary to say here, parenthetically, that later inquiry proved the truth of Hewitt's supposition. Twice or three times Mr Telfer had been hypnotised in a friend's chambers, by a plausible tall man whose acquaintance his host had made at some public scientific gathering. And in the end it became possible to identify this man with Mayes.

Mr Moon, of "'The Compasses," was of great comfort to me that evening. My cuts and bruises were washed in his house, and my inner man revived with his food and drink.

"Allus glad to oblige the p'lice," said Mr Moon; "allus. 'Cos why? Ain't they the p'lice? Very well then!"

6

THE ADVENTURE OF CHANNEL MARSH

I

Mayes's stronghold was taken, but Mayes had escaped us once again; the cage was in our hands, but the bird had flown.

Martin Hewitt, however, had his plans, as he was soon to show. The recovery of the Admiralty code was a good stroke, and was a satisfactory ending to an important case; but that, and even the capture of the curious premises behind the Barbican, made but a halting-place in his pursuit of Mayes, and as soon as I was in some degree recovered from my struggle, and the captured place had been hastily searched, the chase was resumed without a moment's delay; and that adventure was entered upon which saw the end of the Red Triangle and its unholy doings—which came terribly near to seeing the end of Hewitt himself, in fact.

I have not described the den near the Barbican with any great particularity, but I have said that the office, accessible from the open street, was only connected with the hidden premises behind—premises, as was afterwards discovered, held under a separate tenancy—by an easily-shifted ladder. It was in these hidden premises, approached by the maze of courts and the stable-yard, that the main evidences of Mayes's way of life were observable. The passage where my wrist had been locked to the wall, and the room or cellar in which Plummer had been confined, were the only parts of the lower premises fitted for the detention of prisoners, with the exception of one very low and wholly unlighted cellar, entered by a trapdoor and a very steep flight of brick steps. This place smelt horribly faint and stagnant; but it produced on my mind, both then and when I examined it later, an effect of horror and repulsion more than could be accounted for by the smell alone. Of its history nothing was discovered, and perhaps the feeling (though others experienced it as well as myself) was the effect of mere fancy; but I have never got rid of a conviction that that black cellar, or rather pit—for it was very narrow—had been the instrument of crimes never to be told.

There were one or two rooms sparely furnished—one as a bedroom, a larger room, with a long table, a sofa, and several chairs; and in one of the smaller rooms was found a stove, ladles and crucibles for the melting down of metals—gold or silver. It was in this same room also that the table stood, in the drawers of which were found papers, letters and formulæ— things giving more than a hint of the use to which Mayes had put his friendship with Mr Jacob Mason, for of every possible manner and detail in which science—more particularly the science of chemistry—could aid in the commission of crime, there were notes in these same drawers.

But most of these things were observed in detail later. The thing that set us once more on the trail of Mayes, that very night and that very hour, was found in the isolated office facing the street. It was a cheque-book, quite full of unused cheques.

"This cheque-book," said Hewitt to Inspector Plummer and myself, "was in the drawer below that in which we discovered the Admiralty code. The Eastern Consolidated is the bank, as you see—Upper Holloway branch. Now we must follow this at once, before waiting to search any further. There may be something more important as a clue, or there may not, but at any rate, while we are looking for it we are losing time. This may bring us to him at once."

"You mean that he may have some address in Holloway," suggested Plummer, "and we may get it from the bank?"

"There's that possibility, and another," Hewitt answered. "He has had to bolt without warning or preparation, with nothing but the clothes he ran in—probably very little money. Money he will want at once, and he would rather not wait till the morning to get it; if he can get it at once it will mean thirteen or fourteen hours' start at least. More, he will know very well that this place will be searched, that this cheque-book will be discovered soon enough, and that consequently the bank will be watched. This is what he will do—what he is doing now, very likely. He will knock up the resident manager of that bank and try to get a cheque cashed tonight. I don't think that can be done; in which case he will probably try to make some arrangement to have money sent him. Either way, we must be at the Upper Holloway branch of the Eastern Consolidated Bank as soon as a hansom can get us there."

Thus it was settled, and Hewitt and Plummer went off at once, leaving Plummer's men, with the City police, in charge of the raided premises; leaving some of them also to make inquiries in the neighbourhood. Mr Victor Peytral had shown himself anxious to accompany Hewitt and Plummer, but had been dissuaded by Hewitt. I guessed that Hewitt feared that some hasty indiscretion on the part of this terribly wronged man might endanger his plans. Peytral, however, seemed tractable enough, and left immediately after them; he had business, he said, which he expected would occupy him for a day or two, and when it was completed he would see us again.

As for myself I only remained long enough to ascertain that the police could find no trace of the direction of Mayes's flight in the immediate neighbourhood. They had little to aid them. He had gone without a hat, and his dress was in some degree disordered by his struggle with me; but the latter defect he might easily have remedied in the courts as he ran, and they could gather no tidings of a hatless man. So I took my way to my office, my wrist growing stiffer and more painful as I went, so that I was not sorry to arrange for another member of the staff to take my duty for the night, and to get to bed a few hours earlier than usual, after the day's fatigue and excitement.

II

Going to bed uncommonly soon I woke correspondingly early in the morning; but I was no earlier than Hewitt, who was at my door, in fact, ere my breakfast was well begun.

"Well," I asked eagerly, almost before my friend had entered, "have you got him at last?"

"Not yet," Hewitt answered. "But he did exactly as I had expected. Plummer and I knocked up the bank manager, who lives over the premises at the Upper Holloway branch. He was a very decent fellow—rather young for the post—but he was naturally a bit surprised, possibly irritated, at being bothered by one and another after office hours. I showed him the chequebook, and asked him if it belonged to any customer of his.

"'Why, yes,' he said, examining the numbers, 'I remember this because it is the first of a new series, and we issued it the day before yesterday to a new customer. Where did you get it?'

"'We are very anxious to see that customer,' I said. 'Has he been here this evening?'

"The manager seemed a trifle surprised, but answered readily enough. 'Yes,' he said, 'he was here not an hour ago.'

"'Wanting to draw money?' I asked. But that the manager wouldn't tell me, of course. So that it was necessary for Plummer to step in and reveal the facts that this was a police matter, and that he was a detective-inspector. That made some difference. The manager told us that our man had opened an account at the bank only two days before; and I'd like you to guess what name he had opened it under."

"Not Myatt?" I said. "After the chase—"

"No, not Myatt."

"Catherton Hunt?"

"No, nor Catherton Hunt. He had opened it in the name of Mayes!"

"What! his actual name?"

"His actual original name, according to Peytral. The account was transferred, it would seem, from another bank; and I have an idea we may find that he has been shifting his money about from one bank to another as safety suggested, using his real name with it. You remember we could find no trace of a banking account when the police raided and ransacked Calton Lodge after Mason was killed? Quite probably he has had small current accounts in other names at various times to aid in his schemes, but his main account has always stood in his real name; and by that, you see, we get some confirmation of Peytral's story. Well, as I say, the account was opened in the name of Mayes, and the cheque-book was issued which we discovered last night. The Upper Holloway branch saw no more of its customer till yesterday evening, long after hours, when he drove up in a hansom."

"Oh," I said, "in a hansom, was it? The men left behind could get no news of him."

"Yes, we ascertained that last night; we called back, of course, the last thing. I expect he got the first cab visible and drove off to a hatter's a fair distance away, and then on to the bank. At any rate, he knocked up the manager and told him that he had a sudden need for money that very night; could he have some?

"The manager told him it would be impossible. Even if he had been willing to do it, against all regulations, it would still be impossible. For the strongroom and every cash receptacle in it was locked with two separate locks with different keys, and though he had one of these keys himself, it was useless without the other, which was in the possession of his second in command, who lived some distance out of London. This course is the usual precaution adopted in branch banks of this sort; opening and closing, morning and evening, have to be done by chief and assistant together. And I tell you, Brett, I believe that it was only the being informed of this fact that prevented Mayes from trying some of his hypnotic tricks on the bank manager; in which case there would have been a big bank robbery—perhaps something worse in addition."

"Murder?"

"Murder with a tourniquet, perhaps—perhaps with some other weapon; but, at any rate, probably with the Red Triangle. You know, of course—indeed I told you, I think—that in most cases—not all—it is necessary to get the subject's consent to the *first* exercise of hypnotism on him. I told you also it is possible for the practised hypnotist, while the subject is under the influence of the *first* experiment, to suggest to him a certain word or formula, or even a silent sign, which shall bring him under the influence at any other time, whenever the hypnotist chooses to repeat it—just as must have been done with Mr Telfer, in the case of the Admiralty code. The first suggestion would not be the difficult thing it might seem— it would only require a little time and persuasion. Nothing would be said about hypnotism, of course; perhaps something about a little physical experiment, or the like, and then in a moment or two the subject would be in this creature's power for ever. Remember the little 'ceremony of initiation' that the scoundrel attempted to persuade you to submit to! That meant hypnotism—perhaps death.

"But this is mere speculation. Mayes found that the keys on the premises were not enough to release his money, even if the strict rules of the bank had permitted the cashing of a cheque out of hours. But the manager suggested that perhaps some neighbouring tradesman would exchange cash for a cheque, and, with the view of obliging the new customer, went with him as far as the shop of Mr Isaac Trenaman, a grocer and cheesemonger with a rather large shop at the corner of the road. Mr Trenaman, introduced and assured by the manager, was willing to give as much cash as he could find in the till against Mr Mayes's cheque, and did so to the extent of twenty-seven pounds, a cheque for which sum was duly drawn on one of the tradesman's own cheque forms, and left with him. This done, the bank's new customer took himself off, with thanks and apologies; carrying with him, however, two blank cheque forms from Mr Trenaman's book, the pennies for which he punctiliously paid over the counter. Having no cheque forms with him, he explained, he might find them useful if he could come across some friend who could provide the cash he wished to use that night. And having completed this business so far, this charming new customer of the bank made off into the night."

"And is that all you know of his movements?"

"Yes, as yet. He seems to have made no very definite excuse to the manager for wanting the money in such a hurry—just said something had occurred which made cash necessary, and was very polite and apologetic, generally. The manager formed a notion that it must be for some gambling purpose—he fancied that Mayes said something distantly alluding to that, but wasn't sure."

"Did you ask about the address given to the bank?"

"Of course; but there we gained nothing. The manager couldn't remember it exactly, and the books, of course, were locked up. But we know it already—for what the manager *could* remember was that it was an office address, and somewhere near Barbican! So that we are back at the Barbican den again, where I am going now, with Plummer, to give a day to a minute investigation of the whole place. Meanwhile a watch is being set at the bank in Holloway."

"Do you expect him back there, then?"

"Hardly. You see he knows that by this time we must have found his cheque-book, and will be on the watch. But there is just a chance—a very remote one—that he may send a message; perhaps send somebody to cash a cheque. Though I don't expect it, for he is no fool—he is, indeed, a sort of genius—and that would be a mistake, I think. Still, he is bold, and that is where his money is, and he may make a dash at it. So a couple of Plummer's men are to be waiting there, this morning, in the manager's office, and if anybody comes from Mayes he will be detained. Perhaps you would like to be with them? You can't be of much use with me, and the job will be dull. But there you *may* have a chance of excitement, and you will be useful to come and report if anything does happen. Why, you may even bag Mayes himself!"

"Of course—I'll go anywhere you please. They told you last night, I suppose, that Peytral had business, and had gone off?"

"Yes, and I'm not sorry. He is too dangerous a man to have about us, with his hot blood and the terrible injuries he keeps in memory. As likely as not, if we get Mayes, we should next have to collar Peytral for shooting him, or something. So I'm not sorry he is out of it for a bit. But can you start now? Plummer is in my office and the two men are in a cab outside. The bank opens at nine, and that is in Upper Holloway."

I seized my hat and made ready.

"You should keep your eyes open," Hewitt hinted, "before you get to the bank and when you leave, as well as while you're there. Do you remember how poor Mason was watched? Well, there is probably some watching going on now. Last night, on our way to the bank and back, I believe Plummer and I were watched pretty closely."

III

Plummer's two plain-clothes men and I reached the neighbourhood of the bank with a quarter of an hour to spare, or rather more. We dismissed the cab at some little distance from the spot, and approached singly, so that it was not difficult for us to slip in separately among the dozen or fifteen clerks as they arrived. We passed directly into the manager's room, the door of which opened into the space left for the public before the counter. From this room the whole of the outer office was visible through the glass of the partition. The manager, Mr Blockley, a quick, intelligent man of thirty-six or so, gave us chairs and pointed out how best we could watch the counter without ourselves being observed.

"If a letter is sent," he said, "it will be brought here to me, of course, and I will bring the messenger in. If a cheque is presented from Mayes, I have told the cashier to slide that big ledger off his desk accidentally with his elbow. That will be your signal, and then you can do whatever you think proper. I don't think I can do any more than that."

We took our positions and waited. I felt pretty sure that if Mayes sent at all it would be early, for obvious reasons. And I was right, for the very first customer was our man.

He stepped in briskly scarcely a minute after the manager had ceased speaking, and I remembered having seen him waiting at the street corner as I came along. He was a well-dressed, smart enough looking man, in frock coat and tall hat. He took a letter-case from his pocket, picked out a cheque from the rest of the papers in it, and passed it under the wire grille of the counter.

The cashier took it, turned it over, and shifted mechanically to post the amount in the book on his desk. As he did so his elbow touched the heavy ledger which the manager had pointed out to us, and it fell with a crash. The cashier calmly put his pen behind his ear, and stooped to pick up the book, but even as he did it the two Scotland Yard men were out before the counter, and had sidled up to the stranger, one on each side.

"May we see that cheque, if you please?" asked one, and the cashier turned its face toward him. "Ah, just so; a hundred pounds—Mayes. We must just trouble you to come with us, if you please. There is some explanation wanted about that cheque."

I had followed the two men from the manager's room, and now I saw that while one had laid his hand on the stranger's shoulder the other had taken him by the opposite arm. "Why," said the former, looking into his face, "it's Broady Sims!"

"All right," the man growled resignedly. "It's a cop. I'll go quiet."

But as he spoke I saw the free hand steal out behind him and pitch away a crumpled fragment of paper. One of the policemen saw it too, followed it with his eyes, and saw me snatch it up.

"That's right, sir," he said, "take care of that; and we'll have a cab, in case anything else drops accidentally. It's just a turning over, Broady, that's what it is."

I spread out the piece of paper, and was astonished to find inscribed on it just such another series of figures, in groups of eight, as was found in the cypher message in the Case of the Lever Key.

Here was a great find—a secret message as clear to me as to Mayes himself, and as likely as not the scrap of paper that would hang him! I took one of the plain-clothes men aside while the other kept his hold of Broady Sims.

"This is very important," I said. "It is a cypher message which Mr Hewitt can read—or I, myself, in fact, with a little time. Must you take it with you? If so, I'll make a copy now."

"Well, sir, we're responsible, you see," the man said, "so I think we must take it; so perhaps you'd better make a copy, as you suggest."

"Very well," I said, "that is done in a few seconds. You can take your man off, and I will go direct to Mr Hewitt and Inspector Plummer with the copy." And with that I made the copy, which read thus:—

23, 19, 15, 1, 9, 14, 9, 2; 20, 8, 1,
20, 14, 14, 20, 8; 14, 5, 12, 4, 9, 7,
5, 14; 3, 8, 18, 23, 0, 14, 1, 8; 22,
9, 6, 1, 18, 3, 5, 1; 19, 14, 15, 21,
9, 0, 20, 12; 18, 12, 21, 1, 6, 23, 20,
12; 9, 18, 15, 5, 18, 13, 12, 20.

It struck me to ask the manager if the cheque just presented were one of those procured from Mr Trenaman the night before, and I found that it was. Then I left the policemen with their prisoner and made for the nearest cab-rank. This cypher message, no doubt conveying Mayes's instructions to the man just captured, was probably of the utmost importance, and Hewitt must see it at once; and as the cab ambled along towards Barbican I busied myself in deciphering the figures according to the plan of the knight's move in chess, as Hewitt had explained to me. I could only see two noughts among the numbers, so plainly it was a longer message than the one then deciphered—one of sixty-two letters, in fact. I turned the figures into the letters corresponding in the alphabet, *a* for 1, *b* for 2, and so on, as Hewitt had done, and I arranged these letters in the squares of a roughly drawn chessboard, so that they stood thus:—

w	s	o	a	i	n	i	b
t	h	a	t	n	n	t	h
n	e	l	d	i	g	e	n
c	h	r	w	0	n	a	h
v	i	f	a	r	c	e	a
s	n	o	u	i	0	t	l
r	l	u	a	f	w	t	l
i	r	o	e	r	m	l	t

The letters thus set out, to read off the message was a simple task enough, in view of the key Hewitt had given me. I began, as in the case of the Lever Key message, at the right-hand top corner, and taking the knight's move from *b* to *e* in the last square but one of the third line, thence to *a* at the end of the fifth line, and so to *t* in the seventh line, and from that to *r* (fifth square in bottom line), *u* in seventh line and so on, in the order shown by the Lever Key message, a copy of which I kept as a curiosity in my pocketbook. So I read the message through, and I set it down thus:—

Be at ruin Channel Marsh tonight twelve; wait in hall for instruc. Word final.

The general meaning of this seemed clear enough. The man whom the policeman had recognised as Broady Sims was to be at some spot—a ruined building, it would seem—in a place called Channel Marsh, at midnight, there to wait in the hall for instructions; no doubt for instructions where to take the hundred pounds he was to have got from the bank. "Word final" was not so clear, though I judged—and I think rightly— that it meant that the word "final" was to be used as a password by which the two messengers should know each other.

I was almost at my destination, and was cogitating the message and its meaning, when the cab checked at some traffic in Barbican, just by the "Compasses" public-house, and Mr Victor Peytral hailed me and climbed on the step of the cab.

"I was just going to see if Mr Hewitt was at the place," he said, "and if so to ask him for news. But I am rather in a hurry, and perhaps you can tell me?"

"We are on the track, I think," I answered, "and I have just come across this, which I am taking to Hewitt," and with that I showed him my translation of the cypher, and gave him its history in half a dozen sentences.

"That's good," Peytral answered. "I don't know Channel Marsh, do you? But probably Mr Hewitt does. I won't keep you any longer—I see you're hurrying. But I hope to see you again before long."

He dropped off the step and disappeared, and the cab went on round the corner by the "Compasses."

I found Hewitt and Plummer in the office where, on pretence of bookbindery, I had first seen Mayes face to face the day before. They were near the completion of their examination of this office and all its contents, and soon would begin as systematically on the premises behind. I gave Hewitt my copy of the cypher message, and my translation, with an exact account of how it had come into my possession.

Martin Hewitt studied the message for a minute or two, and then relapsed into grave thought. So he sat for some little time, while Plummer left the room by the window and descended the ladder to speak with his men on guard below.

Presently Hewitt looked up and said: "Brett, this message is most important—probably as important as you suppose it to be. But at the same time I believe you have made a great mistake about it."

"But I haven't misread it, have I? Is there any other way—"

"No, you haven't misread it; you've read every word as it was intended to be read. But it is a very different thing from what you suppose it to be."

"What is it, then?"

Martin Hewitt put the paper on the table and looked keenly in my face. "It is a trap," he said. "It is a trap to catch *me*—unless I flatter myself unduly."

I could not understand. "A trap?" I repeated. "But how?"

"Why should Mayes need to send his confederate instructions by written note? We know the nature of his hold over his subordinates, and we know that it means personal communication. Also, the cheque was in Mayes's own hands last night. More, Mayes knows very well that I have read that cypher—has known it for some time; otherwise how could we have discovered the bonds in the case of the Lever Key? Also, Mayes knows that we have his cheque-book and know his bank.

Didn't I assure you we were watched last night? I believe he knows all we have done. In such circumstances he might risk his jackal's liberty by sending him on the desperate chance of cashing a cheque, but, knowing the risk, he would never have let him come with information on him. And least of all would he have let him come carrying a vital secret written in that very cypher which he knows I read many weeks ago. And then see how that message, instead of being concealed, was positively brought to your notice! That man Broady Sims is a cunning rascal, and the police know him of old as a skilful swindler and bill-forger. A man like that doesn't get rid of a compromising scrap of paper by trundling it out under your nose just at the moment he is arrested, when the attention of everybody is directed to him; no, he would wait his opportunity, and then he would probably slip it into his mouth and swallow it. As it is, he would seem to have succeeded in dropping this paper full in your sight, with an elaborate pretence of secrecy. Now this is what has been done, Brett. That man has been sent to cash a cheque, with very little hope of success, or none, because the first move that Mayes would anticipate on our part would be the watching for him and his cheques at the bank in Upper Holloway. If by any chance the cheques had been cashed, well and good, no harm would have been done, and then Mayes could have gone on to arrange for drawing the rest of his balance—could probably have quite safely come himself to draw it. But if on the other hand, as he fully anticipated, Sims was arrested, what then? Nothing was lost but a penny cheque-form, and even Sims—though Mayes would care nothing about that—could only be searched and then released, for the cheque was perfectly genuine, and there was no charge against him. But since he would certainly be searched, that cypher note was given him, with instructions to make a conspicuous show of attempting to get rid of it. Now that note was written in a cypher which Mayes knew was as plain as print—to whom?

To *me*. I am on his trail, and this note is deliberately flung in my way, open as the day, but with every appearance of secrecy. I am his dangerous enemy, and he knows it—as he told you, in fact, yesterday. If he can clear me away, he can take breath and make himself safe. The purpose of this note is to induce me to go, alone, to this place on Channel Marsh tonight at twelve, in the hope of learning where to find Mayes. There I am to be got rid of—murdered in some way, for which preparation will be made. Mayes judges my character pretty well. He knows that, in such circumstances as he represents, Sims being kept away from his appointment, I should certainly go and take his place, and use his password, to learn what I could. And, Brett, *that is precisely what I shall do!*"

"What? You will go?" I exclaimed. "But you mustn't—the danger! We'd better both go together."

Hewitt smiled. "Why not forty of us?" he said. "No. Here is a chance of bagging our man, for, however I am to be arranged for—whether by shot, steel, or the tourniquet, I make no doubt it is Mayes himself who is to do it. You shall come, however, you and Plummer at least. But we will not go in a bunch—you shall follow me and watch, ready to help when needful. This Channel Marsh is an empty, dark space between two channels of the Lea. It is among the Hackney Marshes, lying between Stratford and Homerton, and I fancy there is a deserted house there, though I can't remember ever having seen it. Do you know it?"

"No; not in the least."

"Well, I must reconnoitre today, and that with a lot of care. I think I told you I was convinced of being watched, and that is a thing you can't prevent in a place like London, if it is skilfully done. Now, Brett, you have done very well this morning. If you want to be on the scene of action tonight at twelve, you must get leave from your editor, mustn't you? How's your wrist?"

It was still extremely stiff, and I told Hewitt that I doubted my ability to hold a pen for two or three days.

"Very well, then; get off and convey your excuses as soon as you please. I shall have a talk with Plummer, and then I shall take a few hours to myself, by myself, in somebody else's clothes. Be in your rooms all the evening, for you may expect a message."

IV

It was at a little past nine in the evening that I next saw Hewitt. He came into my rooms in an incongruous get-up. He wore corduroy trousers, a very dirty striped jersey, a particularly greasy old jacket, and a twisted neckcloth; but over all was an excellent overcoat, and on his head a tall hat of high polish.

"Brought to me by Kerrett," he said, in explanation of the hat and overcoat. "He's been waiting with them for a long time in a court by Milford Lane. A good hat and overcoat will cover anything, and I preferred to enter this building in my own character. I've been wearing that this afternoon," and he pulled out of his pocket an old peaked cap with earpieces tied over the top.

"You mustn't bring your best clothes," he went on, "or you'll spoil them scrambling about boats and groping in ditches. I have done my ditch-groping for the day, and I'm going to change. You had best be putting on older things while I get into newer."

"What sort of place is this Channel Marsh?" I asked.

"Well, I should think there must be a great many better places to spend a night in. It must be the dreariest, wettest flat within many miles of London, and I should like to see the portrait of the man who had the idea of building a house there. For a house there is, or rather the ruins of it—deserted for years, and half carried away by rats and people who wanted slates and firewood and water pipes."

"Is that the place where you intend waiting tonight?"

"It is. I haven't examined it nearly so closely as I should like, for fear of raising a scare. Channel Marsh is almost an island, with a narrow neck of an entrance at each end. A foot-track runs the whole length, and a person in the ruined house can easily see anybody entering the Marsh from either end. For that reason I reconnoitred from a boat—the boat you will go in tonight. I think it is the very dirtiest old tub I ever saw, so that it suited my rig out. I discovered it at a wharf some little way down the river, and I paid a shilling for the hire of it. Channel Marsh is banked a bit on one side, and I crept up under cover of the bank. I learned very little, beyond the general lie of the land, because I was so mighty cautious. I judged it better to be content with half an examination, rather than drive away the game. And even as it is I've an idea I have been seen. I lay up among some reeds till dark, but after that I am *sure* there was somebody on the Marsh—and skulking, too, like me. So after waiting and scouting for a little I gave it up and paddled quietly back."

"But look here, Hewitt," I said, "this seems a bit mad. Why go and risk yourself as you talk of doing? You believe Mayes will be there, at the ruin, or will come there at twelve. Very well, then, why can't the police send enough men to surround the place and capture him for certain?"

Hewitt smiled and shook his head. "My dear Brett," he said, "you haven't seen the place, and I have. It will be hard enough job for you and Plummer to get near the spot unobserved, guided by a man who knows every inch. A trampling crowd of policemen would have as much chance as a herd of elephants, and on such light nights as we are having now they would be seen a mile off. And who knows what scouts he may have out? No, as I say, it will be a great piece of luck if you get through unobserved as it is, and even now I'm not perfectly certain that I couldn't do best alone. However, arrangements are made now, and you are coming, three of you."

"Then what are the arrangements?" I asked.

"Just these. You are to leave here first. Make the best of your way to Mile End Gate, where an old inn stands in the middle of the road. Go to the corner of the turning opposite this, at the south side of the road. At eleven o'clock a four-wheeler will drive up, with Plummer and one of his men in it. The man is one who knows all the geography of Channel Marsh, and he also knows exactly where to find the boat I used today. You will drive to a little way beyond Bow Bridge, and then Plummer's man will lead you to the boat. You had better scull and leave the others to look out. They will know what to do. You will pull along to a place where you can watch till you see me coming on to the Marsh by the path. As soon as you see me you will slip quietly along to a place the policeman will show you, close to the ruin, and watch again. That's all. I don't know whether or not you think it worth while to take a pistol. I certainly shall; but then I'm most likely to want it. Plummer will have one."

I thought it well worth while, and I took my regulation "Webley"—a relic of my old Volunteer captaincy. Then, by way of the underground railway, I gained the neighbourhood of Mile End, and interested myself about its back streets till the time approached to look for Plummer's cab.

Plummer was more than punctual—indeed, he was two or three minutes before his time. The cab drew near the kerb and scarcely stopped, so quickly did I scramble in.

"Good," said Plummer; "we're well ahead of time. Mr Hewitt quite right?"

"Yes," I said. "I left him so an hour and a half ago at his office." And we sat silent while the cab rattled and rumbled over the stony road to Bow Bridge, and the shopkeepers on the way put up their shutters and extinguished their lights.

Bow Bridge was reached and passed, and presently we stopped the cab and alighted. Here Styles, Plummer's man, took the lead, and a little way farther along the road we turned into a dark and muddy lane on the left. We floundered through this for some hundred and fifty yards or so, and then suddenly drew in at an opening on the right. Here we stood for a few moments while our guide groped his way down toward the muddy water we could smell, rather than see, a little way before us.

There were a few broken steps and a broad black thing which was the boat. We got into it as silently as we could manage, and cast off. It was a clumsy, broad-beamed, leaky old conveyance, and that it was as dirty as Hewitt had described it I could feel as I groped for the sculls and got them out. The night was light and dark by turns—changing with the clouds. We shipped the rudder, and Styles steered, or I should probably have run ashore more than once, for the banks were not always distinct, and the channel was narrow and dark. We passed the black forms of several factories with tall chimneys, and then drew out among the Marshes, flat and grey, with wisps of mist lying here and there. So we went in silence for a while, till at last we drew in against the bank on the left and laid hold by a post at a landing-place.

"This is the Channel Marsh," whispered Styles, as we climbed cautiously ashore. "We can't see the house very well from here, but there's where Mr Hewitt will come through."

Looking over the top of the low bank, we could discern a path which traversed the length of the marsh, entering it by a broken gate at a neck of land which we must have passed on our way. Here we crouched and waited. We had heard the half-hour struck on some distant clock soon after entering the boat, and now we waited anxiously for the three-quarters. So long did the time seem to my excited perceptions that I had quite decided that the clock must have stopped, or, at any rate, did not chime quarters, when at last the strokes came, distant and plaintive, over the misty flats.

"A quarter of an hour," Plummer remarked. "He won't be a minute late, nor a minute too early, from what I know of him. How long will it take him from that gate to the ruin?"

"Eight or nine minutes, good," Styles answered.

"Then we shall see him in seven minutes or six minutes, as the case may be," Plummer rejoined in the same low tones.

Slowly the minutes dragged, with not a sound about us save the sucking and lapping of the muddy river and the occasional flop of a water-rat. The dark clouds were now fewer, and the moon was high and only partially obscured by the thinner clouds that traversed its face. More than once I fancied a sound from the direction of the ruin, and then I doubted my fancy; when at last there was a sound indeed, but from the opposite direction, and in a moment we saw Hewitt, muffled close about the neck, walking briskly up the path.

We regained the boat with all possible speed and silence, and I pulled my best, regardless of my stiff wrist. During our watch I had had time to perceive the wisdom of the arrangements which had been made. We had been watching from a place fairly out of sight from the ruin, yet sufficiently near it to be able to reach its neighbourhood before Hewitt; and certainly it was better to approach the actual spot at the same time as Hewitt himself, for then, if he were being watched for, the attention of the watcher would be diverted from us.

Presently we reached the reed-bed that Hewitt had spoken of, and I could see a sort of little creek or inlet. Here I ceased to pull, and Styles cautiously punted us into the creek with one of the sculls. The boat grounded noiselessly in the mud, and we crept ashore one at a time through mud and sedge.

The creek was edged with a bank of rough, broken ground, grown with coarse grass and bramble, and as we peeped over this bank the ruined house stood before us—so near as to startle me by its proximity. It must have been a large house originally—if, indeed, it was ever completed. Now it stood roofless, dismantled, and windowless, and in many places whole rods of brickwork had fallen and now littered the ground about. The black gap of the front door stood plain to see, with a short flight of broken steps before it, and by the side of these a thick timber shore supported the front wall. It struck me then that the ruin was perhaps largely due to a failure of the marshy foundation.

The place seemed silent and empty. Hewitt's footsteps were now plain to hear, and presently he appeared, walking briskly as before. He could not see us, and did not look for us, but made directly for the broken steps. He mounted these, paused on the topmost, and struck a match. It seemed a rather large hall, and I caught a momentary glimpse of bare rafters and plasterless wall. Then the match went out and Hewitt stepped within.

Almost on the instant there came a loud jar, and a noise of falling bricks; and then, in the same instant of time I heard a terrific crash, and saw Hewitt leap out at the front door—leap out, as it seemed, from a cloud of dust and splinters.

I sprang to my feet, but Plummer pulled me down again. "Steady!" he said, "lie low! He isn't hurt. Wait and see before we show ourselves."

It seemed that the floor above had fallen on the spot where Hewitt had been standing. He had alighted from his leap on hands and knees, but now stood facing the house, revolver in hand, watching.

There was a moment's pause, a sound of movement from the upper part of the ruin, another quiet moment, and then a bang and a flash from high on the wall to the right. Hewitt sprang to shelter behind the heavy shore, and another shot followed him, scoring a white line across the thick timber.

Plummer was up, and Styles and I were after him.

"There he is!" cried Plummer, "up on the coping!" I pulled out my own pistol.

"Don't shoot!" cried Hewitt. "We'll take him alive!"

Far to the right, on the topmost coping of the front wall, I could see a crouching figure. I saw it rise to its knees, and once more raise an arm to take aim at Hewitt; and then, with a sudden cry, another human figure appeared from behind the coping and sprang upon the first. There was a moment of struggle, and then the rotten coping crumbled, and down, down, came bricks and men together.

I sickened. I can only explain my feeling by saying that never before had I seen anything that seemed so long in falling as those two men. And then with a horrid crash they struck the broken ground, and the pistol fired again with the shock.

We reached them in a dozen strides, and turned them over, limp, oozing, and lifeless. And then we saw that one was Mayes, and the other—Victor Peytral!

We kept no silence now, but Plummer blew his whistle loud and long, and I fired my revolver into the air, chamber after chamber. Styles started off at a run along the path towards the town lights, to fetch what aid he might.

But even then we had doubt if any aid would avail Mayes. He was the under man in the fall, and he had dropped across a little heap of bricks. He now lay unconscious, breathing heavily, with a terrible wound at the back of the head, and Hewitt foretold—and rightly—that when the doctor did come he would find a broken spine. Peytral, on the other hand, though unconscious, showed no sign of injury, and just before the doctor came sighed heavily and turned on his side.

First there came policemen, and then in a little time a hastily dressed surgeon, and after him an ambulance. Mayes was carried off to hospital, but with a good deal of rubbing and a little brandy, Peytral came round well enough to be helped over the Marshes to a cab.

The trap which had been laid for Hewitt was simple, but terribly effective. The floor above the hall—loose and broken everywhere—was supported on rafters, and the rafters were crossed underneath and supported at the centre by a stout beam. The rafters had been sawn through at both ends, and the rotten floor had been piled high with broken brick and stone to a weight of a ton or more. The end of a loose beam had been wedged obliquely under the end of the one timber now supporting the whole weight, so that a pull on the opposite end of this long lever would force away the bricks on which the beam rested and let the whole weight fall. It was the jar of the beam and the fall of the first few loose bricks that had so far warned Hewitt as to enable him to leap from under the floor almost as it fell.

Peytral's sudden appearance, when we had time to reflect on it, gave us a suspicion as to some at least of the espionage to which Hewitt had been subjected—a suspicion confirmed, later, by Peytral himself after his recovery from the shock of the fall. For fresh news of his enemy had re-awakened all his passion, and since he alone could not find him, he was willing enough to let Hewitt do the tracking down, if only he himself might clutch Mayes's throat in the end. This explained the "business" that had called him away after the Barbican stronghold had been captured; finding both Hewitt and Plummer somewhat uncommunicative, and himself somewhat "out of it," he had drawn off, and had followed Hewitt's every movement, confident that he would be led to his old enemy at last. What I had told him of the cypher message had led him to hunt out Channel Marsh in the afternoon, and to return at midnight. He, of course, regarded the message, as I did myself at the time, as a perfectly genuine instruction from Mayes to Sims, and he came to the rendezvous wholly in ignorance as to what Hewitt was doing, and with no better hope than that he might hear something that would lead him in the direction of Mayes. He had entered the marsh after dark from the upper end, and had lain concealed by the other channel till near midnight; then he had crept to the rear of the ruin and climbed to where an opening seemed to offer a good chance of hearing what might pass in the hall. He had heard Hewitt approach from the front, and the crash that followed. The rest we had seen.

V

Mayes never recovered consciousness, and was dead when we visited the hospital the day after; both skull and spine were badly fractured. And the very last we saw of the Red Triangle was the implement with which it had been impressed, which was found in his pocket.

It was a small triangular prism of what I believe is called soapstone. It was perhaps four inches long, and the face at the end corresponded with the mark that Hewitt had seen on the forehead of Mr Jacob Mason. It fitted closely in a leather case, in the end of which was a small, square metal box full of the red, greasy pigment with which the mark had been impressed.

It was from Broady Sims that we learnt the exact use and meaning of this implement: though he would not say a word till he had seen with his own eyes Mayes lying dead in the mortuary. Then he gasped his relief and said, "That's the end of something worse than slavery for me! I'll turn straight after this."

Sims's story was long, and it went over ground that concerns none of Hewitt's adventures. But what we learned from it was briefly this. It had been Mayes's way to meet clever criminals as they left gaol after a term of imprisonment. In this manner he had met Sims. He had made great promises, had spoken of great ideas which they could put into execution together, had lent him money, and then at last had "initiated" him, as he called it. He had put him to lie back in a chair and had directed his gaze on the Red Triangle held in the air before him: and then the Triangle had descended gently, and he felt sleepy, till at the cold touch of the thing on his forehead his senses had gone. This was done more than once, and in the end the victim found that Mayes had only to raise the Triangle before him to send him to sleep instantly. Then he found that he must do certain things, whether he wanted or not. And it ended in complete subservience; so that Mayes could set him to perpetrate a robbery and then appropriate the proceeds for himself, for by post-hypnotic suggestion he could force him to bring and hand over every penny. More, the poor wretch was held in constant terror, for he knew that his very life depended on the lift of his master's hand. He could be sent into lethargy by a gesture and killed in that state. That very thing was done, in fact, as we have seen, in two cases.

Sims was but one of a gang of such criminals, brought to heel and made victims. Their minds and souls, such as they were, had passed into the miscreant's keeping, and terror reinforced the power of hypnotism. They committed crimes, and when they failed they took the punishment; when they succeeded Mayes took the gains, or at any rate the greater part of them. He went, also, among people who were not yet criminals, and by degrees made them so, to his own profit. The case of Henning, the correspondence clerk, was one that had come under Hewitt's eyes. He used his faculty also with great cunning in other ways—as we had seen in the matter of the Admiralty code. And it was even said among the gang that a man he had once hypnotised he could force by suggestion to commit suicide when he became useless or inconvenient.

Sims and the ragged fellow who had decoyed me into Mayes's den were the only members of the gang whom we could identify after his death, but many others must have shared their relief; and I sincerely hope—though I hardly expect—that they all availed themselves of their liberty to abandon their evil courses. As in fact the two I speak of did, and took to honest work.

All that had remained mysterious in the earlier cases now became clear. In the first, the case of Samuel's diamonds,

Denson had been put into the office where Samuel had found him, by Mayes, with the express design of effecting a diamond robbery. The robbery was effected, and the unhappy Denson formed a plan of making a bolt of it himself with the diamonds. He was, perhaps, what is called a difficult subject in hypnotism—amenable enough to direct influence, but not sufficiently retentive of post-hypnotic suggestion. He hid the jewels and adopted a disguise, but Mayes was watching him better than he supposed. The diamonds were lost, but Denson was found and done to death—probably not in that retreat near Barbican, but at night in some empty street. The diamonds were not found on him, and the body, with the mark of the Triangle still on it, was taken by night to a central spot in London and there left. Mayes probably thought that a notable example like this, so boldly displayed and so conspicuously reported in the Press, would impress his auxiliaries throughout London with the terror that was one of his weapons; for they would well understand the meaning of the Red Triangle, and they would receive a striking illustration of the consequences of rebellion or bad faith. The money and the watch were left in the pockets because they were trifles after the loss of fifteen thousand pounds' worth of diamonds, and their presence in the pockets made the murder the less easy to understand—which was a point gained. And as to the keys—Mayes knew nothing of where the diamonds were hidden, and so had no use for them. For where could he use them? Denson had left his lodgings, and as to the office, that, he would guess, would be in the hands of the police, on Samuel's complaint. The immediate result of this affair on the only honest member of Mayes's circle I have told in the case of Mr Jacob Mason. He was not yet thoroughly in Mayes's hands, but he had "dabbled," as he remorsefully confessed, and Mayes had already found him useful. He was dangerous, and his end came quickly. Another victim who had probably begun innocently enough was Henning, the clerk to

Kingsley, Bell and Dalton, and his death in the Penn's Meadow barn leaves a mystery that never can be positively cleared up. Was it murder or was it suicide by post-hypnotic suggestion? It will be remembered that the fire burst out in the barn after Mayes had left it.

The case of Mr Telfer was explained clearly enough by Hewitt at the time; but it is an example of the snares that lie open for the most innocent person who allows himself to be made the subject of hypnotic experiments at the hands of persons with whom, and with whose objects, he is not thoroughly acquainted. And it must be remembered that at this time there are persons advertising to teach the practice of hypnotism to anybody who will pay; to anybody who may use the terrible power as he pleases. More, the danger is so great that it has led two eminent men of science to issue a public protest and warning, with an urgent plea that the practice of hypnotism be restricted by law at least as closely as that of vivisection.

As to what would have happened if Plummer and I had yielded to Mayes's threats so far as to undergo the "initiation" he proposed, at the time we were helpless in his hands—of that I have little doubt. I cannot suppose that he would have wasted much time over me, once I had fallen lethargic. When Hewitt burst in he would have found me lying dead, with the Red Triangle on my forehead. It would have saved Mayes a lot of noise and struggle, at least.

But I often wonder whether or not there was anything in his reference to the place beyond the sea, where he would make me a great man if I did as he wished. Was it his design, having accumulated sufficient wealth, to return and take his natural place among the enlightened rulers of Hayti? He would not have been so much worse than some of the others.

A fan of Sherlock Holmes?
Then meet Solar Pons

The original fan fiction from the great August Derleth—the Sherlock Holmes of Praed Street.

"the best substitutes for Sherlock Holmes known."
– Vincent Starrett

"an excellent series of adventures in detection in their own right." – *The Chicago Tribune*

For more details and a full list of titles:
visit https://www.hachetteindia.com/home/yellowbacks